Terra

Nova

Copyright © 2025 by MtG
First Edition — 2020

All rights reserved.

Edited by T. Guzowski

No part of this publication may be reproduced in any form, or by any means, electronic or mechanical, including photocopying, recording, or any information browsing, storage, or retrieval system, without permission in writing from M.Guzowski.

ISBN
978-1-7770002-6-4 (Hardcover)
978-1-7770002-4-0 (Paperback)
978-1-7770002-5-7 (eBook)

1. Young Adult Fiction, Vampire

Terra Nova

MtG

To my husband, who always believes in the stories,
even before they are written.

Prologue

I shouldn't even feel betrayed, Cynthia thought, staring at the cage bars she was holding and feeling completely betrayed.

The expression "gilded cage" came to her as she looked around the bedroom: marble floors and dark polished wooden furniture with symmetrically perfect carvings and gold edgings, surrounded them. And in the spot between two wooden and gold bedside tables, where a bed should have been, stood a "king sized" cage instead, which now housed her and Evangeline.

Evangeline. Cynthia looked down and watched Evangeline sleeping beside her.

It was always Evangeline. Evangeline and her best friend Val. Val was the rich and athletic one. Evangeline was the quirky and sweetly innocent one. And she, Cynthia, was the average one. She was of average intelligence, average talents, and even her looks were barely beyond average without makeup and tight clothing. So, why should she have been told anything? Evangeline was full of crap when she said that she hadn't known any of this. She had probably known for a long time, and so had Val.

But of course, she, Cynthia, was the unimportant extra who wasn't even supposed to be part of this story. So, of course, she didn't need to be in the know. She didn't need to be told that she was going to risk her life. It didn't matter that she might get thrown into an animal cage where she was now fed scraps of food through the bars.

God, we're like Hansel and Gretel, she suddenly thought, looking at the large bowl of fruit and chicken laying beside their cage. *We're being fattened up for dinner…and I'm the first course because I'm not the one they need.*

If she had just one final wish, it would be to know when and how all this really started. To understand. And for one second, one final second, if she could just feel like the one that was meant to be somewhere.

Chapter 1

EVANGELINE

Evangeline pedaled as fast as she could. Her parents refused to lend her the car for school. Their city had, after all, "such an accessible public transit system". Only a father who was a dorky librarian and a mother who was an even dorkier professor could think that trolling the public transit system was a great way to learn self-reliance.

Thank God, her brother Raffael had given her a top-of-the-line bike for her last birthday. Though that came with a "mental price". He had smirked and said that it was the only way she would ever graduate from high school, since she had the talent for oversleeping every, single bus.

Last night she mostly hadn't slept. Her stomach had ached non-stop in dull pangs until the early hours of the morning. That was when she passed out and overslept the alarm, the grey faces staring at her in her dreams again.

Undiagnosed stomach pain had been her companion since childhood, but around the time she started high school, what used to be vague, occasional aches turned into ripping pains which came out of nowhere once or twice a year. Every time the pain came, the faces in her dreams became clearer. They had stopped terrifying her years ago. Initially there was a grey man with a sword. After some time though he mostly disappeared and was replaced by a decrepit woman with incredibly long, ragged hair. Sometimes, she was accompanied by another man, spent and shriveled like the first, yet clearly different. This man seemed taller, more square-featured, and had a distinct ring on his pinkie finger with a red jewel embedded in it.

The dreams that they chose to visit were always a recollection of the previous day's events and the man and woman sat somewhere in the distance. Just sat and stared. Evangeline was like their reality show, her mind pushed and prodded to act out her life.

Sometimes the woman tried to say something to her, but Evangeline could never hear. It was like a pantomime mouthing words at her.

With the new and improved stomach pains came new doctors' visits but they never found anything except the occasional blood platelet lows and anemia. One night, a couple of months ago, the pain hit so hard she couldn't stop convulsing on the floor. Her parents rushed her to the ER, where the doctors repeatedly asked if she might be pregnant, to the horror-stricken face of her father.

When they finally decided to believe her that pregnancy wasn't even a possibility at this moment, but still couldn't find any clear answers, Evangeline heard the terms *anxiety, irritable bowel* and *psychosomatic* whispered. So, after seven hours of humiliation in the ER she went home with some laxatives.

She was pissed off and drained when she got home, and it didn't help that the pain had somehow miraculously disappeared. She had sat on her bed and wondered if maybe she was a psychosomatic, gassy lunatic.

Raffael was a physician, specializing in Cardiology, and had moved away from their suburby town of Kitchener to Toronto. He had instructed their parents to call him immediately if Evangeline's pain re-occurred. But, Evangeline had decided to die in misery rather than admit that she was in pain ever again and repeat her hospital experience. So, with her stomach still slightly thudding, she reached the grounds of Resurrection Catholic Secondary, jumped off her bike while it was still moving and almost crashed face first to the ground.

Only a couple of the less desirable members of her high school's population were still outside. One of the girls, a tall and lanky female with long, jet black hair, chortled. The girl, Bambi, was also a senior and in some of Evangeline's classes, though they had never had a real conversation.

At the sound of Bambi's witch-like chortling, Evangeline straightened out, spun around to face her, and did an exaggerated bow. Some random, wanna-be vampires laughed at the display, but Bambi just looked at Evangeline through the mesh that was over her face. The mesh was attached to the black funeral hat she wore. Always. No part of Bambi's body even twitched as her eyes poked at Evangeline. Evangeline raised her eyebrows momentarily and went into the school.

"Woman, I was ready to leave your sorry ass to fend for itself in about thirty seconds" Val's voice pulled Evangeline out of her reverie as she rushed up to her locker to grab her uniform.

"You are an amazingly wonderful friend who would never ditch me because you know I couldn't make it through English without your linguistic genius," Evangeline said with a smirk, now half-running down the hallway.

They were doing a presentation together that day for English and as outgoing as Val was, she was secretly terrified of public speaking, not to mention that she stank at English.

"You are a bastard, you know that?" Val grinned, entering the bathroom behind Evangeline. Evangeline threw her head back and laughed. She chucked off her biking clothes and pulled on her uniform. When she was done, she fixed her explosion of blond as best as she could with a quick finger run-through. She kept her hair just below her ears, letting it go wild in a huge, curly mess, simply because her imagination failed her when she tried to figure out what else she could possibly do with it that wouldn't entail waking up an hour early every morning.

Evangeline looked over at Val and threw a colorless lip gloss at her. Val was almost as tall as Evangeline, hovering around 5'9, with wavy, long, dark brown hair, dark caramel skin, alert, green eyes and the figure of a lean, Olympic swimmer. Evangeline knew Val was the reason for her own miniscule amount of popularity. Still, popularity hadn't changed the fact that the couple of times Val had attempted real makeup she had put The Joker to shame.

They had met at the beginning of grade nine during a partnered, English poetry project. Val later told Evangeline that she had seen Evangeline across the room with her gangly frame, huge black eyes and even more huge hair and decided she was definitely some poetry and arts nerd. Quickly breaking off from her group she had pummeled across the room to snatch up the surprised Evangeline as a partner. Unfortunately for Val, Evangeline hated poetry. Their English project was a flop, but their friendship had been solid since.

When they reached the classroom, Cynthia was leaning on the wall outside the door. Today's heels made her look as tall as Evangeline even though she was about a foot shorter. Twirling her long, platinum hair, she wore a look of absolute enthrallment while she stared at her phone screen.

"I was just about to go in. I had to answer this first though," Cynthia said. Evangeline put her head down to try and hold the snort of laughter in, but was unsuccessful. Cynthia hated going into any room by herself just in case someone might get the insane idea that she didn't have enough friends.

In response to Evangeline's snort, Cynthia threw her hair back, and smacked Evangeline in the face with it while opening the door of the classroom. Val almost choked on her gum and Evangeline stifled more laughter.

After three years Evangeline still wasn't sure why Cynthia insisted on being friends with them, if that's what you could even call it. There were definitely more popular and better-looking people in the school that Cynthia, with her blanket of makeup and perfectly chosen outfits, most definitely had more in common with. However, at some point she and Val had just accepted that Cynthia had attached herself to them and was there to stay.

As soon as they entered the room, Cynthia stalked over to her project partner while Evangeline and Val sat down together. The present book interpretations were to be done in partners, and Cynthia had been the odd one out.

~

"Okay, so I did shitty on that presentation. Why? Because I was literally thrown to the wolves by both of you when we had to choose partners." Cynthia said on their way out at the end of class.

The truth was that Cynthia was their academic weak link and Evangeline didn't enjoy pulling the weight of two whenever she was partnered with her for projects. Lying wasn't Evangeline's strong suit, so she chose to remain silent. Val wasn't even listening.

Cynthia gave them both brief, dirty looks and switched tactics "So, even though you ditched me, I got both of you invited to a party tonight."

"You know, I don't really feel that hot today," Evangeline said.

"Are you shitting me?" Cynthia said, "this is barely the second month of school and you are locking yourself up in your freaky, portrait convent already?"

Evangeline shrugged. She liked drawing, specifically portraits. It let her get the faces from her dreams, out of her head.

"I don't mind going. I heard about it. It's at Eric Gallo's house. Right? Kind of a small, private thing?" Val said.

"Uhm...no. We all go. I have no clue why Eric has been literally stalking you since the first day of school," Cynthia looked at Evangeline, "but he has the ins and outs of every social event for the year so you are not blowing off the first party he invites you to, especially since you haven't been on a single date in a year. It's making all of us look like forest recluses." Cynthia said.

"So? Val hasn't dated any guys either."

"Yeah. Ok," Cynthia snorted, "You are lucky you somehow mastered that mysteriously adorable thing or else your weird hobbies would scare off even the emo guys."

Evangeline's eyes narrowed. She was now irritated on both her and Val's accounts, whose eyes were equally narrowed. Val was insecure enough about being "old-school tomboy" as she had termed it. She didn't need Cynthia rolling her eyes or snorting at the concept of a guy being attracted to her.

But, neither Evangeline nor Val had time to respond. Cynthia's attention span had already jumped to the next topic.

"Isn't this like the fourth Emo wave? Does it ever end? I mean, Twilight was a hundred years ago," she spun her head towards Evangeline "And on the note of pulling the mysterious beauty card, I need some pointers. Ian Horvath is looking great after the summer. He's like suddenly manned up and he's got that gorgeous olive complexion with the super dark eyes. I can see him being into the mysterious, hard to get thing. So, I'm trying to figure out how you pull this thing off... I'm totally not donning a huge, curly mop like you...I can maybe do some dark makeup around my eyes though...get the deep eyed look going like you..."

Evangeline was thrilled they had reached the next classroom at this point and almost ran inside. Cynthia looking at her like some designer purse she was hoping to mimic was more freaky than complimentary. She almost preferred Cynthia's pokes at her dateless life.

~

Evangeline didn't know Eric, but he wasn't bad looking and seemed smart for a jock guy, she thought as she pulled her bike over at a pharmacy on her way home. It was kind of flattering that he wanted her to come...if he really did want her to come and it wasn't just Cynthia scamming her into going...But then again, who cared?

She did like to dress up and it would be a fun way to get Val all "girly" – something Val secretly loved, but was terrified to try and pull off on her own.

She sighed, shrugged her shoulders at herself and picked up some more over-the-counter painkillers

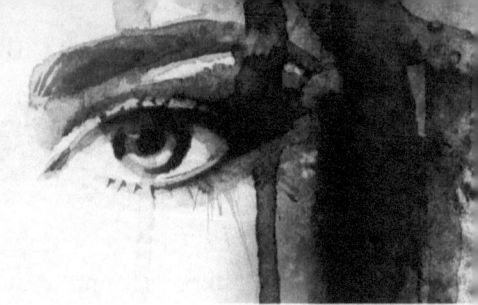

Chapter 2

BAMBI

Bambi was six years old when she arrived in Kitchener.

There's no birth certificate or family history to say where she came from, and no one believed what she remembered.

There was a constant feeling of confusion in her at that time and the details of her days kept disappearing; similar to how the daylight had disappeared from her life at some point before.

What she does remember is that on the day that she would arrive in Kitchener, her entire, skinny frame was being pulled by her mother's unbelievably slim yet powerful hand, somewhere through the darkness of night.

Her mother's face was obstructed almost completely from view by a black hat with a long veil of decorative, black netting hanging off its front rim. She looked up at her mother's face, trying to figure out what was happening, but all she could see was the outline that the veil provided as it moved along the face with gusts of wind.

Bambi's skinny legs were doing their running motions under her long, disheveled dress mostly in the air. Her mother pulled her along so fast that the barren ground around them was a blur.

There was dust. So much dust. She was choking and coughing, trying to understand why there was nothing but dust. No roads, trees or grass. Where were they? She heard voices, commotion and

a roaring sound. A burst of thunderous light exploded in front of her face
and she screamed, pulling back, but her mother grabbed her tighter and with one hand forced her right into the bolt of lightning.

Bambi shut her eyes tight and screamed at the top of her lungs, but she didn't feel pain. Instead, she felt wet mud under her knees and she smelled air filled with the sweet smell of nature. Her tiny, malnourished body shook and her jet-black hair was plastered in long tangles around her face as she opened her eyes. She had no time to get acquainted with her surroundings though because her mother immediately pulled her upright and shakily began to pull them away from the tremendous bolt of lightning, which still hung, suspended in mid-air.

Bambi's knees rattled against each other and she raised her arms towards her mother, asking to be lifted. Her mother looked down at Bambi, breathed in deeply and let out something between a sigh and a cry. Then she pushed Bambi's skinny body away with one hand while pulling her forwards with the other.

They didn't run this time though. Her mother pulled her along at a walking gait, distancing both of them from the lightning bolt, which had somehow been a doorway to this place. Her mother's head was darting from side to side, following every noise and flash of light that reached them through the trees, apparently as fascinated as Bambi was by their new surroundings.

Around them was still the same darkness that Bambi had gotten so accustomed to and yet there were smells and sounds everywhere that she had almost forgotten existed: the wetness of the dissipating rain on her face, leaves rustling, the wings of birds flapping, faraway sounds of insects and the pure smell of life. Mingled with all these were strange things Bambi could not identify: rumbling noises of some sorts of machines which seemed to be tumbling down some distance away, and flickering lights in unnatural shades, visible through the spaces between the trees.

Suddenly they pushed through into a clearing and Bambi saw that the lights were coming out of houses, standing separately, spaced out, with clear-cut grass surrounding them. The manicured grass ended at the forest from which they exited. Her mother was pulling them to the right of one of these houses and Bambi stared at it in wonder.

As she looked at the house a large glass window opened, and a child climbed out of it. It was a girl who looked around the same age as Bambi. Bambi gasped and stopped in her tracks. She had never had much contact with other children and for so long now she had not seen any other human being besides her mother.

The girl had huge locks of blond hair flying wildly all around her big-eyed face and she wore no dress but some strange peasant pants and shirt. Her socked, shoeless feet and outfit would have suggested she were from the lower classes, but she was perfectly clean, with her strange outfit dyed in colorful designs, rather than the drabness that suggested the poor. And she had that wild, golden hair.

The color and shininess of the girl's wild, curly hair was just like the golden strands that Bambi had seen on a beautiful woman, a long time ago. She had visited that woman with her mother in some faraway place just before things went all dark. She would never forget that breathtaking hair, tumbling all the way down to the woman's knees in a shower of pure gold, as the woman spoke strange words to her mother, in hushed tones.

Bambi remained frozen in her spot, staring. The girl stumbled while walking and her hands landed in the wet mud. Standing herself up, she wiped her sopping hands against themselves. Bambi instinctively lowered herself to her knees and placed her own hands in the mud around her feet, feeling its squishiness between her fingers. She looked down at her hands, in awe at the wonderful and almost forgotten feeling of mud, dirt and earth and raised her eyes to her mother, smiling up at her in wonder.

Her mother's hands were at her sides and Bambi now realized that her mother had stopped pulling her, let loose her grip, and was frozen in her spot just as Bambi was, staring at the wild-haired girl. But she wasn't smiling. Her hands were shaking. They were opening and closing in a harsh grip and a sound was coming out of her mother that was frightening, like that of a low growl of a wolf.

"Mamma?" Bambi took hold of one of her mother's hands, and patted it gently, her eyes wide. Her mother, as if hearing her from a distance, began to breathe deeply in and out. Suddenly they heard a slashing sound and turning towards it saw through the trees the gleam of steel pushing through the same bolt of lightning that they had come through, forcing it wider apart. There was the flicker of a gleaming red jewel in the steel of the sword at which her mother's hand grasped Bambi's tightly and Bambi flew through the night again, everything in front and behind them a blur.

~

When she woke up Bambi was in a dark room. She didn't know how or when they got there. Why did everything seem to go in and out of her memory like wisps of clouds? She sighed sadly, convinced that all those smells, sights and sounds had been a dream, but then her nose told her otherwise. There were smells here too and she became suddenly, desperately hopeful.

As her eyes adjusted to the darkness she was certain that she wasn't in the same, dark, cold room she had become used to. There were small windows near the ceiling here, suggesting that this room, although a basement, was not fully underground and although dark curtains covered the windows, evening light entered ever so slightly through them.

She also realized that she felt warm, as she had not felt in a long time, and there were strange, puffy sitting spaces around the walls, and a bizarrely low table in the middle of the room. There were shadowy pictures on the dark walls and strange shelves with indiscernible things on them.

Bambi looked down at her own body and realized that she was lying on one of those puffy sitting spaces, covered in blankets. She felt the softness of one of the blankets between her fingers. She was scared it would disappear like all her memories, and gripped it tighter.

Slowly turning her head, she saw her mother in a sitting position on a leathery looking chair, in a corner of the room. Her dark silhouette was barely visible. Bambi got up shakily, and still gripping the blanket dragged it along the floor as she quietly approached her mother. When she reached her she had the sudden urge to pull up the netted veil off the hat and see her mother's beautiful, deep, dark eyes again. Maybe in this safe, warm room her mother would let her?

Bambi's fingers slowly reached out to the tip of the netted covering and just as they brushed it, her mother gripped Bambi's arm tightly and with hard control moved it away from herself.

"Mamma, where are we?" Bambi whispered. "Can I go outside here?"

"Not today, but maybe soon. Wait here, my *amore*. I will bring you food."

"Mamma, why are you shaking? Did we escape the war, mamma?"

"There is no war here, amore. I am hungry, just like you must be Bambi. I will return and you must wait here quietly like a good girl. Just like I taught you."

"Can I kiss you?" Bambi asked desperately and came even closer to her mother, her arms outstretched in front of her in an embrace. Her mother had been caught off guard and Bambi's little face managed to move right up against the dark veil of the hat before she saw the flash of red from within and heard the loud groan. Then everything was black again.

~

When Bambi awoke this time, she was lying on another puffy sitting spot and a plate of cold chicken and fruits lay on the low table. She smelled it immediately and without thinking stumbled to it, grabbed the food with both hands and began shoving it in her mouth in a way that her mother had once told her was absolutely unacceptable for a young lady of decent breeding. But her mother only sat now in the leathery looking chair in the corner, watching silently through the darkness of her veil.

Chapter 3

VIPS AND SUCH

"You look good," Evangeline lifted a mirror up to Val's face. The three of them were up in her room, getting ready for Eric's party. Cynthia looked at the miniscule amount of facial products that Evangeline had been allowed to apply to Val's face and rolled her eyes. Val noticed but said nothing, putting the mirror down tight lipped.

"I guess natural beauty eludes some people." Evangeline said, annoyed at Cynthia's insensitivity. She turned her face and pointedly stared at the massive makeup bag Cynthia had brought with her.

"Well, I'm sorry some of us can't put on makeup," Cynthia said while smoothing another layer of foundation over her skin, "It looks like you went color blind when picking out foundation. You look like the walking dead."

"Ugh. I'm not wearing foundation," Evangeline groaned. "My stomach is killing me. I took some pain killers but they're just making me feel dopey."

"Pregnant again?" Val said, her smile back.

"Har har. Good one. Here, let's see what you brought in your makeup luggage." Evangeline started to poke through Cynthia's collection of cosmetics, "I need to look a bit more lively or my parents will start asking questions."

"Yeah, you're almost as deathly looking as your creepy friends," Cynthia said, looking around. Evangeline's room was full of paintings and drawings, mostly of faces. A couple in the back were of the disturbing man, standing in a thunderstorm and holding a jeweled sword. More prominent though were the two other faces — the man with the ring and the woman with the insanely long mass of grey hair.

"Alright, let me fix you up," Cynthia said and grabbed the bag out of Evangeline's hands. "The sooner we are good to go, the sooner these faces will stop staring at me."

~

Val, with her perpetual appetite, was finishing off the majority of the snacks Evangeline's parents had laid out for them on the kitchen table. Meanwhile Evangeline's mom was doing her usual, embarrassing oohing and awing over the three of them, made even more so by the fact that, being a linguistics professor meant she oohed and awed much more eloquently than most parents could ever hope to.

Val seemed to love the affectionate geekiness of Evangeline's parents and always veered get-togethers towards Evangeline's house. This was to the disappointment of Cynthia, who preferred flirting with Val's older brothers in Val's much more affluent house, which was generally devoid of both parents and weird paintings.

They finally managed to get out of the house with Evangeline's mom calling after them,

"We know it's Friday night and have fun girls but don't forget that tomorrow is the language open house at 10:00 a.m. Evangeline."

"Oh…oh yeah. Of course. I remember," Evangeline lied, badly as usual, and her father smiled.

"Language open house? What kind of torture is that for a Saturday morning?" Cynthia asked while she was driving the three of them to Eric's house.

"It's language level testing for the Italian courses she's starting," Val answered from the passenger side seat while stuffing her face with snacks she had snuck out of Evangeline's house. Cynthia's lip curled in disgust at the sight.

"You know my mom's a linguistics fanatic. She keeps torturing me with language lessons. We had a blow out and I told them I'm not wasting my time after school learning a bunch of languages unless I can actually use them. So, they agreed to fund a study-abroad year in university if I reach a high enough level in one foreign language," Evangeline said.

"Yeah, so she's been cramming Italian on her own during the summer, trying to skip the beginner level." Val turned her head back to Evangeline.

"Well…have fun with that then…" Cynthia said quietly while staring at the road over the steering wheel, exceedingly intently. Val turned back and raised her eyebrows at Evangeline. It was unlike Cynthia to be either quiet or intent on anything.

"What's wrong?" Evangeline asked in Cynthia's direction.

"What? Nothing." Cynthia didn't move her eyes, "I'm just hoping Val doesn't have an entire side dish stuck in between her teeth," she added as she pulled the car over near Eric's house and jumped out. She immediately returned to her normal self as she rang the doorbell and shoved her way in front of both Evangeline and Val, flipping her hair around and rubbing her lips together while they waited.

Val rolled her eyes, reached over and pushed the door open, "Hey! Eric! Is your ass still sore from me kicking it in rugby?!"

Eric Gallo came out from around a corner using, what he self-labeled, his Latino saunter. He flipped his dark hair back and laughed, then stopped and looked at Val surprised,

"You are looking very femme fatale today. Damn."

Val grabbed him by the neck in a hook and side-kicked his butt with her leg.

"Aren't you going to compliment anyone else?" Cynthia sounded like she was cooing and Evangeline mentally blushed.

"You look like your impeccable self, Cynthia," Eric smiled at her and then shifting his gaze to Evangeline added in something gargly that she was guessing was supposed to resemble a smoldering tone "but Evangeline, well, I'm speechless."

Evangeline looked at him and wondered if he called that voice his Latino smolder. He was good looking and popular, but she couldn't feel any reality behind the show. She had not had a conversation, nor even had a passing thought about him for the last three years of high school, and now she immediately disliked him after just one sentence.

Evangeline smiled directly at him as she walked past him to the rest of the party, "Well, I heard what you just said, so apparently you haven't quite lost your voice."

She heard laughter and looked ahead to see Ian Horvath looking at them from around the corner. He waved at them to join with his beer hand while his black eyes kept grinning. Eric just clicked his tongue as they all entered the already full living room.

~

An hour into the party and Evangeline was not enjoying herself. Eric's idea of a VIP event was to invite the best-looking females he could find — regardless of how lacking in personality they might be. She supposed she could look at it as a compliment to her own appearance, if it wasn't for the fact that the whole concept of the party was offensive. Plus, she couldn't handle yet another conversation with yet another person who had a social media account dedicated to self-care and inspirational quotes. The impulse to fake cry, while saying "my greatest wish is world peace", like in the movie Miss Congeniality, was beginning to overwhelm her.

To top it off, Eric's attempts at sultriness annoyed her almost as much as his half-ass compliments. Seriously, what idiot actually said,

"You know, with flatter shoes you would be the perfect height for me,"?

Unfortunately, her responses of "With high heels you might actually be the right height for me," didn't seem to deter him. Instead, he became competitively determined to get his way.

She got a miniscule amount of amusement from Cynthia's horrified face when she overheard Evangeline introduce herself as Gracie Lou Freebush to some of the queens of internet pre-famous. *That movie has some good lines*, Evangeline smirked at the memory that it was actually Cynthia who had made them all watch Miss Congeniality just a week before, stating that it was an absolute classic.

This amusement couldn't make up for the rest of the night's misery though, which included the fact that her stomach clenched at unexpected moments and gripped her in pain. She mentally calculated that she had taken probably more than the maximum allowable limit of painkillers for one day, so finally managing to get away from Eric she hid in the bathroom.

Evangeline locked the door and sat on the closed toilet. She put her head between her legs and breathed in and out loudly. Cynthia was smoldering Ian with her mystery and Val was all over the place, most likely talking sports or politics. She decided to just sneak out and grab an Uber. She would text Val later and let her know that she went home. She just needed to relax a little and she would be fine...

Evangeline lifted her head and looked up at the ceiling. Taking a deep breath, she straightened herself out and tried to rise, but her whole body began to shake. Her hands felt as if the blood wasn't quite reaching them. Her body quivered and her stomach spasmed and she dropped back down onto the seat. What the hell was wrong with her? Her breaths were coming in faster and shallower and she looked down at her hands to find them blue.

It felt like some horrible food poisoning in which a person's stomach is wrung out and they don't know what end everything will come out of. Except nothing was coming out either end. She wanted it to. She wanted this to stop.

Suddenly the thought of just vomiting whatever in there was killing her seemed like the only option. She held shakily onto the sides of the toilet while sliding down, off it and onto the floor. She was now on her knees and began to slowly turn her body to face the bowl, but her grip wavered and she crashed down. Her forehead hit the bowl, and she started crying. Everything was blurry and she was cold. She needed Val. She needed help.

She couldn't make a sound beyond the hyperventilating gulps she was making, trying to grasp at the air that seemed to be missing. She was beginning to see two of everything as the room spun around her. She needed to somehow gain enough control to open the lock on the bathroom door. Her body felt like a swinging bag of bricks as she lifted herself to a hunched position and crawled to the door. When she finally reached it, she put one hand on it and started sliding it up the frame, trying to reach the lock, while her other arm, wavering and unsteady, tried to support her.

Her vision was so blurry she had no idea how she actually managed to unlock the door, but she felt it sliding open as she pushed her body weight against it. Barely dragging her head above the floor, she crawled out a couple of steps. Then she lay down, closed her eyes, rocking her body spasmodically in the fetal position while her blue face breathed in loud, mini-breaths. Her mind started pulling in and out of some sort of delirium and the woman with the long, scraggly hair was suddenly staring at her curiously.

She heard voices somewhere back in her own world.

"Did she take some fucking drugs? What happened?"

"Call the ambulance."

"She's dead! She's blue! She's fucking blue!"

"She's moving idiot. I can hear her breathing."

"I don't think she does drugs. She likes mountain biking and shit."

"I called the ambulance."

The thought of trying to open her eyes flashed through Evangeline's mind, but it was so much less pain to just drift and let that grey woman stare at her.

The woman was trying to mouth something again with her grey, broken lips. Evangeline focused on that ratty-haired woman and her moving lips and felt no pain.

"Repeat it. Say it," Evangeline heard the words coming out of the woman. It was the first time she had ever heard her. The woman's voice sounded like gentle bells and her words were in a strange accent. The sound was such a contradiction to the woman's haggard appearance that Evangeline tilted her head and looked curiously at the woman.

The woman gasped and reached out a hand towards Evangeline. Evangeline looked at the hand and then around herself. She was still partially in the fetal position, but looking up, towards the woman who was sitting in a large chair in a dark room. Only some parts of the room were visible: a window behind the woman, rising right from the floor and going far up to somewhere indistinguishable, the moon light entering from the outside and placing a sheen on the marble floor under the legs of the chair.

The woman continued mouthing words but Evangeline now heard a different sound. A long, low, tired breath to the right of the woman. She followed the sound with her eyes and the man with the ring came into focus. Their eyes met and for a second his head moved back in surprise. Then his intent, burning eyes focused on her and they stared into each other's faces as if both trying to figure out if the other were real.

Evangeline heard noises from her own world again and felt hands on her. Perhaps someone was lifting her?

The man was disappearing behind a fog. No. She had to focus. It had been so many years of them just staring at her from some misty distance. Today she was with them. Finally with them. She had to hear them.

The marble floors became clear again, but the man was slowly walking away, no longer looking at her. She had to hear the woman before the woman gave up also. She turned her face towards the woman and focused completely on her, tuning everything else out.

"Evangeline," the woman said her name and Evangeline tried to rise, to let the woman know she had heard. She raised one hand. It was easy and smooth and yet almost impossible, like one of those dreams where you feel frozen in place. It was enough though. The woman looked at the hand and suddenly started crying. In between sobs she shouted,

"Say it Evangeline! Say it. Lola. L.O.L.A.H!"

Evangeline couldn't move her mouth. She mentally tried to push her lips. To push the breath through.

"Llll"

It was all that came out, but it was enough. The man stopped and spun around with wavy, ear length hair spinning along with him. She could see the shade of it clearly now. It was grey but not the grey of an older person, rather as if he had had black hair that had been stripped of its color. She looked intently at him. Focused on all the details that were coming to her and pushed again

"L... O... LLL"

"Yes! Lolah and Bambi" the woman said, and Evangeline suddenly lost her concentration, her mind thinking *Bambi? What? Bambi at school? That Bambi?*

She tried to refocus, but it was too late. The connection was gone. Everything was black.

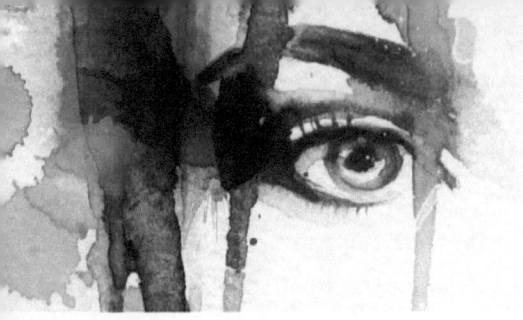

Chapter 4

WAKING UP

Reality flowed back over Evangeline, along with the pain. The deathly grips had subsided into dull aches that pulsated in a rhythmic fashion though, giving her the strength to open her eyes. They landed on her brother's face.

"Hey" Raffael whispered and leaned over, closer to her face.

"Hey, am I pregnant again?" Her voice was slightly croaky and she cleared her throat and grinned at him through the aches.

Raffael smiled, the dark circles under his eyes crinkling a little and his messy, dark brown curls flopping over his eyes. *How long have I been out?* Evangeline thought.

"I need to tell the doctor in charge that you're awake." Raffael said, standing up.

"What's the bad news, Raffael? I know you. Are parents Okay? Tell me…"

Raffael sat back down, put his elbows on his knees and rested his chin in his cupped hands. Locking his black eyes intently on hers he spoke slowly.

"Mom and dad are fine. I forced them to go and take a walk. I'm sure they'll be back soon though. You've been out…around eight hours," he said, looking at the time on his phone, "your blood work has been sent to a center in Toronto to check for a couple of…things. There are some abnormalities…but I guess you already knew that. We'll know more tomorrow. Everything is Okay though." He sat up, looked at the ceiling and rubbed his chin and Evangeline knew he was lying.

"I've been out for eight hours? Raffael?"

Raffael stared at her as if trying to decide what to say, then finally sighed and spoke, "We aren't sure Evangeline. Really. But...it seems that you had a mini stroke...maybe. It's hard to tell. They will do an MRI after twenty-four hours to check if the brain tissue looks different. However, for a mini stroke there may be no difference. In someone your age and with the quick treatment and recovery there may be no signs left."

Evangeline's eyes opened wider than usual. Her brain felt like mush, like the mini stroke had really eaten up all the tissue and she could only think in broken sentences and individual words. She tried to put the fragmented thoughts together into a comprehensible sentence.

"Mini stroke? That's...what...eighty-year-olds have? I don't...I mean...I don't even know what a mini stroke is exactly...as compared to what? A maxi-stroke?"

"It's a blood clot in the brain" Raffael said in a calm, collected tone. *Is this the doctor tone he uses on his patients?* She randomly thought, "The blood clot causes blockage of blood flow to the brain. There's blood in your urine suggesting high blood cell deterioration. It's not certain why, but if your blood cells are deteriorating abnormally fast then the dead blood cells may be clotting in your veins...plus your other signs: the weakness, passing out. But, this is just one theory. Maybe the clot was in your lungs, causing you to lose air and pass out."

Evangeline looked at her brother silently. What was she supposed to say?

"Are you Okay?" Raffael's eyes were moving across her face like a scanner.

"No."

Raffael leaned over and put a hand on her hair, kissing her on the top of her head. She knew he was just trying to comfort her, but it was having the opposite effect. His unnaturally gentle, fatherly manner was making her terrified.

Perhaps he noticed because he straightened his tall frame out and grinned over his mess of hair, which matched hers in everything but the color, "Look, there's a couple of simple blood disorders that they're checking for. They are manageable. Nothing your crazy mop-head can't handle. But there's no point guessing. Let's just wait till tomorrow to get the results. How are you feeling right now? Do you have stomach pain like before?"

Evangeline breathed in through her mouth and then breathed out.

"Just a bit. Not as bad as before. It's a dull ache but I'm not sure if it's coming or going."

He was about to respond when the door opened and her parents entered.

"Oh my God! You're up!" Their mother's straight, brown hair was disheveled and her usually preppy outfit was wrinkled on her tall frame. Raffael stood up, approached his mother and rubbed her shoulder "She just came to, mom. Let me tell the staff in charge, and let me see what I can do about the pain," he directed the last part at Evangeline as he left the room.

~

Evangeline felt as if she were six years old again. Everyone watched over her that Saturday. Her mom chattered continuously in a way that was much too peppy while her dad connected himself to the internet, reverted to his librarian ways and read. With his mad, blond hair flying in every direction and those gangly limbs, characteristic of pretty much everyone in their family, tapping or rocking nervously all over the place, he researched every blood disorder known to mankind in the span of a day. Then he tortured Raffael and any other medical staff that would listen with his regurgitation of new-found, dr.google knowledge.

Val and Cynthia also came and hung out by her bedside. After getting the run-down on her health they caught her up on the drama that followed her passing out.

There had been police looking for drugs, lots of parents involved, and gossip on every social media channel as to what had happened to Evangeline. Friday night, after the abrupt end of the party, it started out with Evangeline being a secret junky. By Saturday late morning it had swung to her having a tragic illness and only six months to live. Evangeline was convinced that Cynthia was involved in the development of the final rumor.

While her friends chatted, Evangeline wondered why she wasn't more upset. After the initial blow she just felt slightly spaced out and dull headed. Maybe she was still in shock? Her mind kept wandering to the half human creatures that chose to visit her in her short coma. They weren't just dreams. Not for this many years. And there was only one Bambi she had ever heard of. And who was Lola? Was it possible that there were two wanna-be vampires with ridiculous names at her school?

Meanwhile, the abdominal pain refused to leave and finally, after a couple of hours of Raffael's persistence, a medical resident came in and hooked her up to an IV with painkillers just as her friends were leaving.

It felt good to be alone with her thoughts at last. She looked at the band aids on her arms and her mind slowly began to turn fuzzy. It was probably the work of the pain killers, she figured and yawned, laying back on the pillow and staring up at the ceiling. It was a stark white. Like those old townhome-style residences in the old Italian towns she saw on the pictures inside her language books. Hundred-year-old bricks cleaned to perfection and then painted and repainted and repainted...

She was suddenly on a street composed of sand, gravel and unusually large, flat cobblestone slabs. Evangeline looked up at an ancient looking residence, painted a flawless white. There were flowers in a rainbow of colors placed inside impeccable clay pots which stood around the front door and on each level of a number of balconies. The layer upon layer of flowers should have been kitschy but the look felt so authentically ancient that kitschiness was impossible.

Evangeline looked up and counted the levels of balconies absentmindedly...one...two...three. She turned her head and the world spun. Now she was facing a building of immense proportions, its facade a combination of marble and granite. Tall, slim Gothic windows encircled it, giving the impression of a cathedral, except that they lacked the customary stained glass, with the windows being filled with regular, though immensely large, glass panes. On the roof, balconies stretched out and hung beyond the many pinnacles and spires. The overall effect was something between a church and a castle.

The building stood against a jagged mountain edge and as she looked at it, it zoomed in, as if through a camera lens, coming towards her until she was looking straight into one of its extensive upstairs windows.

It was dark in the room, except for the light of the moon which shone straight through the window and illuminated the face of a man inside. She saw the wavy, ragged hair, the square features and the shine of the ring on his finger. Her gaze went over his face and the pale, greyish skin on it. His gaze shifted from something in the distance and his eyes stared directly into hers. They both screamed silent screams as they looked at each other. Evangeline's eyes flew open and she was back in her hospital room.

She was still lying on her back. She hadn't moved a muscle through the whole thing. She stretched. Strangely, she wasn't tired anymore and instead felt a surge of energy. She suddenly wanted to dance. She didn't know why and she didn't care. She giggled and reached for her phone by the bedside.

Skimming through her music she smiled. She found it. Pulling out her IV, Evangeline jumped off the bed and, completely oblivious to any pain raised the volume as high as it would go and ran to the middle of the room.

~

Raffael ran into the room. The volume on Evangeline's cell phone was not earth-shattering, but coupled with her top-of-the-lungs shrieking along to the music it was loud enough to get quite a number of nurses and medical residents to run in with him.

They found Evangeline in the middle of the room, dancing like a maniac to Metallica's "Enter Sandman". Evangeline had taken numerous dance lessons but with her hospital gown flailing around and her eyes closed she looked like a bizarre cross between a backup dancer in a music video and a manic, tribal person. One of the residents, half laughing, voiced "what the fuck" to another while a nurse tried to figure out how to approach Evangeline and get her back to bed. Advance from any direction seemed a danger as Evangeline's each new dance move was as unpredictable as the one before it.

Raffael pushed his way past the nurse and with gentle force took Evangeline by the shoulders. He lowered his head to meet her face and prodded her back to bed.

"Hey...hey...Come on. This way."

Evangeline kept singing, but as she focused on his eyes she lowered her voice to a sung whisper and began to follow him like a happy child.

When Evangeline settled down under the covers Raffael looked up at the IV and then at the medical resident who had administered it, "What the fuck did you give her?"

The resident took a step back at Raffael's tone, "It was just Demerol. I know it makes some people a little loopy but you said the pain was quite bad and it seemed like the quickest option."

"Asshole," Raffael knew he was going overboard but couldn't stop himself. Demerol wasn't a wholly wrong choice but it was ridiculously strong and delirium inducing and this was his sister.

"Get her off it and put her on a painkiller from this century," he said to the resident without bothering to look at him.

"You don't work here."

"And neither will you if you piss me off more and I check what kind of dosage you gave her." His words made the resident and the IV bag disappear, making Raffael sure the dosage had been high.

The rest of the medical crowd dispersed and only one nurse remained to help Raffael try to take Evangeline's cell phone from her, but she held it tight in her grip.

"Alright, alright. Just let me lower the volume a little. Okay?" Raffael said.

Evangeline looked at him with narrowed eyes and instead of giving him the cellphone slightly opened her fist and lowered the volume herself. She cocked her head and took his hand, pulling him down towards herself. Then she mouthed the words of the song in a hushed whisper.

"Now I lay me down to sleep, I pray the Lord my soul to keep. If I die before I wake, I pray the Lord my soul to take…Do you remember this song?" She smiled at him so innocently it creeped him out even more than the words of the song. Of course he remembered the song and he remembered the night that went with it, which he instinctively knew she meant. He tucked the covers in around her, avoiding the question but she stared at him more intently and continued to mouth,

"Hush little baby, don't say a word, and never mind that noise you heard. It's just the beasts under your bed, in your closet, in your head...Do you want to see the beast under my bed Raffael? Look behind the painting."

"Wha-"

"The painting. You know which one."

Raffael stared at her, a cold drift moving up his spine and along his arms, making his hair rise. She just smiled again and fell asleep.

Chapter 5

THE NIGHT THEY MET

Evangeline was six years old that night.

Raffael sat beside her on the large, cushioned sill of the living room window, and they both stared out, engrossed in the massive thunderstorm, watching the lightning rip into the forest grounds beyond the yard of their house.

Evangeline's face pressed right into the glass, her amazement at the slashing brightness pushing most of her fear aside.

"Look! That one. It looked like it split up into two bolts when it hit the ground!" She said, pointing to a bolt of lighting right before it disappeared. Raffael twisted his lengthy frame, which he had barely managed to squeeze onto the sill with her and followed her line of vision, but was a second too late. He groaned. The left side of his butt was numb, and he stretched out his long, slightly bony legs from beneath his chin and jumped off the sill. He grabbed the remote control and turned the music up, with his favourite tracks, consisting of anything heavy from any decade imaginable, deafening out the thunder.

He had just finished university and was home for the summer to party it up with his friends before he started medical school and became what he termed *a responsible human being*. His parents, tripping over themselves with pride (and frankly he thought he saw some shock there as well) that he had been accepted to medical school, had been letting him off the hook all summer and his only real responsibility remained babysitting Evangeline on occasion. He didn't mind. Evangeline was his gangly, almost double, that appeared in their lives long after he had stopped pestering his parents for siblings. He mentally called her a "mini accident" since he seriously doubted his parents had planned a second kid fifteen years after their first. Anyways, she was a cool, strange creature with those intense, black eyes that stared out into some imaginary world most of the day.

Evangeline turned away from the window and looked up at him. He grabbed her head in a noogie and planted a loud, sloppy kiss right in the bush of her wild, curly hair. He got a "bleehhhh" in return and laughed.

"How are you feeling?" Raffael said, lifting up her left arm and looking at the band-aid that covered the spot from where her blood had been taken earlier that day.

"Good." She shrugged and smiled, squishing her face back onto the pane of glass. Raffael shook out her arm and let go. It had been over a year now, but the doctors couldn't pinpoint any particular problem with Evangeline. She was seemingly healthy but overly sleepy with sporadic stomach pains. The bloodwork was inconsistent, with results ranging from regular to low iron and blood platelet levels, depending on the day. Nothing else seemed to be wrong and for the majority of the time Evangeline seemed perfectly fine, so her parents had agreed with the doctors to do regular blood work and monitor.

"Hey, you know what?" He said, "You're right. Some of the bolts kind of do look like they're trying to slide open into two, like sliding doors, if you sort of squint your eyes a bit." They both squinted now and tried to catch incoming bolts in their line of vision.

"What's inside the doors? Can we go there?" Evangeline opened her eyes wide and pressed both palms against the glass, splaying out her legs so that she could glue herself even more to the window. She stared out with mouth open.

Raffael laughed. She looked like one of those newborn animals that you see on nature shows; the one that just came out of its mother and is trying to walk but can't because its legs are too long and skinny to hold up its massive head. Totally cute but comical. Then again he wasn't much better, he thought. He had only started to fill in the stretched-out-elastic frame characteristic of their family line in the last year.

"Can we go there? What's through the door?" Evangeline repeated, her face turned towards his now.

"It's not really a door. It just looks like one." Raffael said and saw her features turn utterly disappointed. He scratched his chin, "...although...you know what I was reading about the other day? I was reading about the beginning of the world. Before there was Earth. When there was just totally nothing." He sat back down on the sill and rested his hands on his knees, "And then suddenly there was this huge BANG and out of this Bang came matter."

Evangeline's mouth scrunched up "What's matter?"

"Oh. Stuff. Things. Everything. Matter is everything." This wasn't quite accurate but the best he could do for a six-year-old.

"Oh. Okay." She said, looking confused, but he continued anyways.

"Okay. So, there was nothing. Then this huge thunder bang. Just like now. And suddenly things appeared. But..." Raffael lowered his voice and brought his face close to hers, "every time the thunder banged and matter popped out, something else popped out too. The antimatter. The antimatter is exactly the same as the matter but opposite."

"That doesn't make sense. Opposite isn't same," Evangeline said and put her hands on her hips, "you're weird."

"Exactly," he grinned, "So, imagine if there was another Raffael that popped out. The same as me. But perfectly normal."

She burst out laughing and he continued, "But, then the weirdest thing of all happened. Normal Raffael disappeared. All the antimatter twins disappeared, and no one knows where they went."

"Oh." She was quiet for a while, looking like she was pondering her own existence, then suddenly lifted her chin up "can we have chips?"

Raffael burst out laughing and got up "Sure. You can't tell mom and dad though. I've already fed you like a pound of chocolate."

Her head looked like it was on a spring, it bobbed in agreement so hard.

"And when I come back," he added "we're gonna have a dance-off and I'm going to kick your butt."

Evangeline burst out in a fit of giggles. Raffael was fully aware that he was a tragically bad dancer.

"You think you're so good just cause you started dance lessons?" He said.

"Better than you!" the words came out in between peels of laughter as he left the room.

In less than five minutes he was back. The window was open and Evangeline was gone.

~

Evangeline jumped off the sill onto the living room carpet and began to mouth along to Metallica's *Enter Sandman*, which had started. She knew most of the words. She had heard the song blasting out of Raffael's room most of her short life and at this point in her life whatever Raffael loved, she did too. She bounced around as she sang, relishing how scary the words sounded:

> *Exit light, Enter night*
> *Take my hand*
> *We're off to never-never land*

A particularly loud crash of thunder made her stop. She climbed the sill again and stared outside. The rain was easing up and the wild park lands were silent. She was about to jump down and dance again when a strange urge to slide the window open came over her. With only a slight pause she did so as her thoughts somehow dulled into a blank daze. In her socked feet she climbed out onto the sopping grass, just underneath.

She began to walk, her socks making squishing sounds as she crossed the grass. At one point she stumbled absentmindedly, her hands landing in the sopping, cold mud. Without a thought she got back up and continued walking, vaguely wiping her hands against each other. Her mind failed to register anything around her, even the black-haired girl and the woman in the gown and funeral hat racing away through a far corner of her yard.

Reaching the tree line at the end of what was officially their yard, where the extensive park lands began, Evangeline pushed the branches aside and entered the wilderness. It was a light, just past the tree line, which was attracting her, pulling her towards itself. Evangeline walked. Her brain was still numb, but a tiny backdrop of fear started to make its way in. The fear came from what she was now beginning to see as well as her inability to control her desire to keep moving towards it. She wanted to stop but couldn't. She started to cry at the loss of control over her own limbs.

It was as if a lightning bolt had hit the ground and then, rather than disappearing, it froze in that spot, cut off from the sky and just barely touching the soil. The bolt was slit vertically into two and she felt a powerful surge of electric energy under her feet as she got closer and closer to it. A male form stood in the slit, half his frame out and half somewhere within. He was staring at her and she knew he was the one pulling her towards himself.

With dull, dirty clothing hanging over his frame and a grey complexion he resembled a mad, homeless person, shrivelled from malnutrition and the abuse of the streets. The fact that he held a large sword in a clenched fist only added to the apparent madness. His eyes were fiery and were the only part of him that looked truly alive, their red blaze focused on Evangeline.

Evangeline moved slowly towards him with tears rolling down her face and blending with the raindrops. The man's breathing was becoming more audible now and his frame began to shake while he emitted strange growls.

She heard muffled sounds in some different consciousness. Was it Raffael? She wanted to shout for help as her legs unwillingly stumbled towards the thing in the split bolt of lightning. She forced her mouth open but all that came out was a garbled whisper. Her mind grabbed onto it and tried to repeat it.

"raffael...Raffael...RAFFAEL"

She repeated his name, over and over again, each time louder. The louder it came out the more power her body regained, forcing her legs to slow.

The man made a sound, a noise between a moan and a growl. His eyes bulged out of his face and his sword hand rose and smashed the weapon against the light of the bolt, splitting it open farther. His body tensed as he began to push fully through, simultaneously lowering slightly, like an animal ready to pounce. His eyes focused on their prey and Evangeline was again frozen, mouth open.

Suddenly, something struck the man on the side of his head, and he swerved back, partially into the bolt.

Something else, a misshapen object, bigger than the first, struck hard again before the grey man could recover and his filthy, tattered form was flung back into the lightning, which immediately crashed in on itself. A deafening roar from both the bolt and the man pierced Evangeline's ears as both disappeared with a crash. The energy source of the crashed bolt hit the ground surrounding it with full force. Evangeline was flung backwards, flat on the ground, paralysed, her breath gone. Her head, thrown sideways, gave her a one second view of a pair of bare feet running towards her as she passed out.

~

Evangeline woke up to Raffael carrying her inside the house. He lay her gently on the couch and quickly dialled police and ambulance.

Metallica's "Enter Sandman" was still, or again, playing. *Strange,* Evangeline thought, singing along to the final verse:

Exit light, Enter night
Take my hand
We're off to never-never land

Raffael was shaking as he covered her up with a blanket and cuddled her, staring into her absentminded, singing mouth and waiting.

~

At the hospital Evangeline was told that a strange man out in the storm had lured her out, but luckily Raffael had found her in time and scared the man off by throwing rocks. Unfortunately, at the same time, lighting had struck the ground too close to her and knocked her out.

She was lucky, they told her. She didn't really get hurt, and after a couple of hours of observation she went home with her parents who had also arrived in a state of panic.

When they got back home the police had already combed the surroundings but had found nothing. The heavy rains had erased any evidence on the ground. They promised to return the next day and search a greater area. Her parents and Raffael sat in her room and took turns watching her all night while she lay sleepless.

She was confused and angry at Raffael. He kept repeating the same, stupid story about some stupid intruder over and over again. To the police. To her parents. To the hospital people.

But it wasn't true. Except she didn't know what the truth was. Frustrated at her inability to explain herself she burst into tears. The tears turned to screams and then a full-out fit. Her parents cuddled her, repeating that it was all good now. Everything was normal and safe now.

She stopped crying to make everyone stop telling the lies.

She started having nightmares after that night, reliving the details of it, with the cement-like complexion, grey mouth and bulging, hungry eyes reeling her in.

Initially the nightmares woke her up in fits of screams, bringing her parents running into the room. Then they would tell her again and again that the dream wasn't real and repeat the story that they had all made up.

So, she started a habit of throwing her hands over her mouth as soon as her eyelids got the urge to open in the morning. She would wake up, shaking for a minute or two, stifling her own screams. Then, she would look out the window at the rising sun and know it was over until some other night.

She didn't want to be told that it wasn't real. She didn't want to forget that it was. She held on to the memory with anything she could, even the nightmares of its ugliness. Losing the truth felt like being ripped apart inside and losing something from in there. It was this part of her that began to push for the dreams to return, and whenever they did, after the initial shaking, she felt calm and comforted, singing quietly to herself *"Exit light, Enter night, Take my hand, We're off to never-never land"* until she realized that Raffael had become aware of this little habit and had started observing her nervously, at which point she stopped singing aloud, with only her mind repeating the words.

~

He stood in the door and stared at the woman, his shoulders rigid and his body tense. His lips clenched as he breathed in deeply through his nose with his eyes closed. He couldn't control the shaking of his hands and kept opening and closing his palms.

The woman sat frozen in a chair, which stood on a marble floor in the middle of an expansive room. Intricate bedroom furniture made of dark polished wood with symmetrically perfect carvings and gold edgings, lined the room. The only thing that was missing was the bed. In the spot between two wooden and gold bedside tables, where it should have been, stood a "king sized" cage instead, its silver structure illuminated only by the moonlight, which entered through wall-to-wall and ceiling-to-ceiling windows.

The man swallowed and opened his eyes. His shoulders drooped as his vision refocused on the woman, sitting between the windows and the cage. Every inch of her being was shrivelled. It wasn't the shrivelling of old age. It was as if someone had taken a tomato in its prime and suddenly sucked out all its juices, leaving behind only a loose, thin, mostly colourless membrane with just a minimal amount of shape-defining pulp left inside to make it clear that the thing you now see was once full of life.

He could tolerate looking at her grey, decrepit skin. After all, his was now the same. He could even handle the clothes that she had not changed, even though they reeked of blood and rot.

It was her eyes that he couldn't bear - her eyes and her right hand. Her haggard form sat completely still except for that hand. It held onto a thin strand of hair, one of the only strands left on her head that still retained a golden colour. The rest of her hair was dead grey and fell stiffly down her back like dried up hay, down the length of her stained, ragged gown and with it onto the floor.

That one hand moved like lightning, its fingers twisting that last golden strand in crazed circles without pause, while her eyes stared at nothing, vague and sealed off from the real world.

He stood for some time with his slumped shoulders on top of his tall, grey, shrivelled frame and his burning eyes stared into her vacant ones. Then his hands jerked up and raked through his own black and grey hair with an intensity that was on the brink of ripping chunks of it out.

He opened his lips, furious at what she was making him do. He wanted to shout at her. He wanted to holler and scream, but when his voice came out it was rough and choppy, more afraid than frightening, "Will I have to kill you? Don't make me kill you. Mother."

He crossed the room in one stride, grabbed each side of the chair on which the woman sat and shook it with force, making her shrivelled body flop left and right. But her gaze still didn't budge. Her soul wasn't returning to her eyes.

"They are gone. They have left us. They won't return." His shrivelled face pressed into hers, their misshapen noses almost touching as the fire in his eyes darted from side to side, trying to find some sort of recognition in hers.

"You MUST deal with it...you can deal with it. I know you can. You need something to hold on to. If I kill you it will destroy everyone. Your death will destroy your children. Hold on to that if you must."

The woman blinked and, with her mouth slightly open, focused her eyes on him. The film that had covered her pupils lifted ever so slightly. She still didn't appear to be fully in the present, but she wasn't fully blank anymore either. He watched her hand let go of the gold strand of hair, letting it flop down with the rest, and his body crumpled to the ground. He held on to the sides of the chair for steadiness while his head slumped down in between them and he dry heaved. He didn't know how much more of this he could take.

"There are other humans," she whispered, so softly it was almost a sigh "Beyond the lightning."

He straightened himself out and his eyes narrowed, focusing again on hers.

"I see them." she said and her face distorted, the cheeks pulling the skin from the corners of her mouth upwards into something that he could still remember used to be a smile.

"The door came to a girl," she continued, only partially aware of him, "Only a young child. Maybe six or seven, but it looked for her. Come, see her with me. She's so...alive."

He calculated the evidence, turning the ring on his pinkie as he thought. He told himself that her half-filmy eyes looked serene, rather than insane. He didn't have to kill her.

"Show her to me, mother."

Chapter 6

TRUTHS

Once Evangeline had settled down, Raffael drove to his parent's house to get her a proper pair of pajamas, glad that his parents had missed the show she had put on.

He reached the house feeling ill at ease. His legs seemed to weigh more with each step he took up the stairs to Evangeline's room. Raffael knew that Evangeline never believed his explanation of that night. But, he had explained it to her in the only way that explained it to himself.

Then, she started drawing *him*. And then, she started drawing more of *them*.

"Are these people you have seen somewhere?" Raffael had asked her nervously the first time he saw the pictures of the others.

"No. I just dreamt about them," she had answered, her eyes wide, looking at him as if expecting some admission or recognition.

He just breathed deeply, forced a smile and told her she had talent. Then he offered to buy her some professional supplies. He didn't know why he did that. Maybe to make her new hobby seem normal?

When he entered Evangeline's room now, he walked directly to the dresser and poked through the drawers, trying to avoid any personal items he didn't want to know his little sister possessed. Finally, he found some pyjamas and turned back towards the door, his eyes avoiding the paintings. In the doorway he stopped.

He stood, leaning his head on the door frame. Raffael felt all the dead eyes staring at his back from each canvas and his body unwillingly turned around. He looked from painting to painting until he came to the largest one. It was of the man in the storm, the canvas almost two meters tall and now a number of years old. He knew this was it and he knew he could just turn around and leave, pretending to have never heard Evangeline. But his feet moved towards the painting as if they didn't belong to the rest of his body. When he reached it, he wasn't sure what to do. He lifted it slightly, but it was oddly heavy. He placed the painting back down and walked around to the back of it. He stared at its canvas covered back. Canvas had been stretched all around, completely covering the cavity that the thick wooden frame formed in the back.

Feeling in his pockets he pulled out a small, Swiss army knife and clicked it open. His arm hesitated, then he struck the back of the canvas with a sharp stroke and slashed downwards. A gaping hole flapped open and something shone inside.

Raffael knew immediately what it was. He had never forgotten that sword. That jewel: a scarlet stone seemingly melting out of the metal of the actual blade, its shimmering beauty a glaring contrast to the hungering drabness of the man that had been holding it.

~

Why did he have to watch Evangeline with me today, of all days? The woman thought as she pulled her mind from Evangeline's hospital room and refocused her eyes on the present.

She refused to let him see that she was affected in any way and kept her back straight in the chair and her grey mouth in as normal an expression as she could pull together. She serenely slid a dry strand of hair off her face and smoothed it back down with the rest of the grey mass which fell down and collected just above the floor.

His elbow rested on a wooden table, and he was pressing the ball of his palm into the middle of his cracked, lifeless forehead. The jewel on his pinkie ring shone even in the dark as his arm twisted left and right. She couldn't see the expression on his face, but his chest was moving up and down in what could be spasms of misery or shakes of laughter.

"Eros, I know that was...an unfortunate sight."

"Actually mother, it has been decades since I've been this amused." He put his arm down and raised his face up. He was smiling with just the right side of his mouth. She knew that was his derisive smile. Had he always been *this* scoffing? It was hard for even a mother to handle him.

"Evangeline is sick Eros. We both know that she reacted to the medicine," she said, chin up and looking directly at him.

"Or are we hoping?" he responded, his eyes narrowed as his smile widened. "Half of her usual clothing suggests that she is a prostitute. I was wondering what tier for some time now but today I will be generous and put her in the upper one due to her obvious training in the art of dance."

"Ero-"

"Although, for an upper tier entertainer a little less behind is usually the custom prior to payment."

"Eros, enough!" She really did have enough of him this time. If he were a little smaller she would have whacked him over the head, but unfortunately, he had outgrown her reach many decades ago, "It is not our world or our culture. Everyone in her world wears those clothes and you know that after twenty-four years of watching."

"Exactly, mother. Twenty-four years," he let his arms drop and threw his head back, "we have watched her for twelve years of her life and twenty-four of ours. Somehow you made this connection with her, but it means nothing. She...that...is not fate. It is not destiny. We've discussed this, mother. She will change nothing."

"Then why are you here, watching?" she saw his eyes dart around her face momentarily and she knew there was a part of him that believed her, even if he didn't want to, "You think I need something to hold on to, so I hold on to her. But, she came to *you* today. *She* is looking for *us*. She *wants* to find us. She will find a way in soon and she will bring Lola. I can feel it. I am not insane and you know that by now."

"You are not insane, mother, but you do need to hold on to something. Don't bother to deny it. So, the question is: does she really want to find us or are you making her want it?" his voice was not derisive anymore. It was a quiet force. A brutally honest demand. She preferred the derision. It was easier to answer to. To defend against. He waited only a second before continuing, "and if she does come, mother?... You have watched her for twenty-four years. You have grown to care for her, perhaps to love her. Are you willing to sacrifice her?"

"She is not a sacrifice, Eros" She made her voice strong but couldn't stop her bottom lip from quivering.

"Whoever sees her first will be the one to kill her. You know this. What if that is you?"

Chapter 7

PNH

"Let me get this straight," Evangeline stated after listening to the description of her blood disorder provided by Dr. Mike Buchanan, a pudgy, balding man with an overdose of freckles, "it's called what?"

"Paroxysmal Nocturnal Hemoglobinuria. PNH for short," Dr. Buchanan answered.

"Okay. It's going to take me about a week just to remember the name. Soooo... my red blood cells are produced mutated, so my immune system doesn't recognize them as part of my body and kills them off because it thinks that my blood is actually a disease and it's trying to get rid of it. Right?"

"In a nutshell."

"So why aren't I dead?"

Her parents both looked at her in shock. *Okay, not my smoothest moment*, Evangeline thought and tried to figure out a way to explain herself better. Raffael saved her the trouble by entering the conversation.

"Not all your blood is mutated Evangeline," he was sitting in a chair a little to the left of her parents and Dr. Buchanan. A monstrous bag lay under his feet, "some of your blood is produced normal, but some of it is not."

"How much is normal and how much mutated?" Her father asked, his eyes suddenly bright "I'm sure not much of it is mutated...she feels good most of the time."

"Dad," Raffael looked at their father with the most adult look Evangeline had ever seen on his face, "the percentage of mutated blood varies from patient to patient. Evangeline will need a special test done to determine the exact percentage of mutated blood. If its low, little treatment is required beyond observation and some steroids for the occasional attacks of pain. If the mutated blood goes above fifty percent, daily blood thinners will need to be considered."

"Why do I get the pain attacks? And why only sometimes?" Evangeline asked. This time Dr. Buchanan answered.

"Red blood cells die and are replaced regularly in all of us. The dead blood cells come out via our urine. But, in your case, if for example, if you have a cold and your immune system is trying to fight it off it ends up killing more of your red blood cells as well. And, when there are too many dead blood cells too quickly your body doesn't have enough time to clear them out and you end up getting blood clots." Dr. Buchanan began to write out a prescription as he continued, "To start off with, we will give you a prescription for Prednisone, a type of steroid which will alleviate the pain and slow down the immune system, when necessary. You don't need it all the time, but keep it with you. If you start to feel the symptomatic pain, you can take a pill once a day until the pain subsides. Tomorrow a haematologist will stop by and meet with you to discuss the details. Do you have any other questions for now though?"

"What is the cure?" her dad asked, straightening up and looking ready for some action.

"There is no cure, dad," Raffael answered. "it's genetic. But there is treatment. Evangeline's life for the most part will be uncompromised."

"What do you mean it's genetic? Do we have it? Is it from us?" her mom looked like she was about to cry and Evangeline felt suddenly agitated. She was the one with the mutated blood. Meanwhile, she felt as if she was supposed to be calming her parents down, with her dad going into fits of unwarranted optimism on one side and her mom falling apart on the other. Then, feeling instantaneously guilty she reached out and rubbed her mom's shoulder.

"Mom, I'm sure you're not the one to blame for my X-Men blood."

"Skipping the X-Men part Evangeline is right," Dr. Buchanan said, "This is a genetic disorder, but it's not inherited. She didn't get it from anyone, and her kids can't get it from her. The mutation is only in her. The disease is very rare and no one knows much about it. We just know that it suddenly appears. In Evangeline's case it seems to have been around since childhood, since she's always had below par blood work. It just came out fully during puberty."

Evangeline zoned out while Raffael and Dr. Buchanan continued pacifying her parents. She was thinking about the split lightning and the man in it. He appeared around the time her blood started to go weird as a kid. And the worse the blood, the clearer the dreams...

She suddenly heard Raffael clear his throat "Mom, dad, why don't we go outside and talk. Evangeline looks beat and I'm sure she needs a little time to think and deal with things, right?"

Evangeline smiled at Raffael "Thanks Raffael but...can you stay just a little? I just want to clarify some information with you...make sure I understand it correctly. You guys can leave. It's okay."

Her parents and Dr. Buchanan left the room and Raffael shut the door behind them. Then he put an ear to the door and Evangeline raised her eyebrows at him.

"You never know with them," he said, "they might burst back in, ready to support you again."

Evangeline grinned, "so, are they gone?"

"Yeah. It's safe."

Evangeline's eyes wandered around the room and then stared out the window. Raffael was visibly waiting for her to speak first but it suddenly felt impossible to break the silence. She focused her eyes on his face. She decided. She wouldn't let him off the hook this time.

"You know this all started around the same time as the lightning."

"Before we go on, I need to understand," Raffael said, lips tight and eyes boring back into hers, "Why this fucking, crazy obsession with one weird thing that happened more than ten years ago?"

Evangeline's heart was pounding and she had a sudden urge to slap him, "Why don't you be honest, at least with yourself? Maybe that's why you haven't kept a girlfriend for longer than what? A second? You have no idea how to have an honest relationship with others because you refuse to be honest with yourself?"

Raffael was quiet. His face was red and his whole body looked like an elastic pulled tight and about to snap. She didn't care.

"It's all related. We *both* know it! The sicker I am, the clearer the dreams become and when I almost died, I heard THEM."

Raffael stared at her silently. Finally, he exhaled and let his body loosen. Then he began tapping his fingers on the back of the chair.

"I'm not crazy," she said, not sure if trying to convince him or herself.

"I know" Raffael replied simply and unzipped the massive bag, pulling it towards the bed. Evangeline looked at his face then turned her head down to peer inside the bag.

"Sorry, I think I ruined the painting when I was getting it out."

"It's okay," she said quietly. She reached out and moved a pile of clothes and some pots and pans aside and stroked the jewel of the sword, "I wasn't sure…but I thought I told you about it when I was high on those drugs."

"You did but…I'd be careful who else you tell, Evangeline. Do you remember the men that came with the police after the incident?"

"Yeah, they wouldn't leave. When I looked back on it later it seemed strange that so much effort was put into finding one creep in the bushes. They know something we don't know and I feel like it's the answer to my blood."

"Hmm. I think we disagree on the last point. PNH is a medical condition, not a magic malady. But I do think they wanted what you have." He pointedly looked at the sword, "so, what now Evangeline? What do you plan to do to emotionally balance me out so I can have human relationships?"

"I'm sorry, Raffael. I may have a slightly explosive temper."

Raffael's lip curled up, "Unfortunately, some of your rant was true, as much as I hate hearing it come out of the mouth of a teenager. I may have a VERY large rug that I like to shove things under."

Evangeline grinned, feeling a closeness to her brother that had been missing for years, "so... tell me, why is there a bunch of pots with the sword? Are we 'cooking up a plan'?" She snickered at Raffael's appalled expression.

"I'm going to pretend that I didn't just hear the most God-awful pun ever," he said, "I just needed an excuse to carry a mother-ass bag out of parents' home. I told them I took up a cooking class and needed to borrow some gear. Look, I don't know why I brought this" - He pointed down at the sword — "I just felt like...when you asked me to find it...maybe I owed you that after all these years...so...now you tell me, what's brewing in that head?"

"I want to find the man we saw." Evangeline met Raffael's eyes.

"I somehow knew this, and yet ... why?"

"I feel like he's important...maybe even my cure."

"Evangeline, I'm not denying the sword or the man anymore here, but yet again, your 'cure' is the Haematologist and whatever treatment she decides on."

"No. I think those...people, have the answers. They know something."

"Look, 'they' don't exist. They were all just dreams, which all started after the man in the lightning. Those people are just nightmarish manifestations of the one man. Only the one man was a real person," Raffael said.

"I want to find him. You don't need to help," Evangeline said, and although she knew she looked like a stubborn kid she crossed her arms nevertheless.

"He looked like he wanted to kill you, not chat with you...and how do you plan on finding him? I personally don't have a clue how to jump into a bolt of lighting without dying, do you?"

Evangeline was quiet, her eyes on some spot on the wall.

"What's your plan?" Raffael said, his eyes narrowing.

"Well...there was the lightning bolt, and the sword was inside it ... and in my dream they said the names Lola and ... Bambi. I have the sword so maybe the next step is Bambi ..."

"Before I even move on to asking who Bambi might be, how did you actually manage to get the sword anyways?"

~

There were no visible injuries on Evangeline's six-year-old body and she returned home from the hospital the same night. Her parents put her immediately to bed where she just lay and stared at the ceiling while they sat around her bed and stared at her.

She had to go back into the forest, but she knew they would never let her outside now. There had been police walking in circles around their house and strange men in suits. They didn't find anything, but they would return tomorrow in the daytime, her parents reassured her. She had to go back in the forest before they did.

She closed her eyes, rolled over into the fetal position and pretended to sleep. She remembered Raffael telling her something about sleep cycles and rhythmic breathing. She wasn't sure what rhythmic breathing meant but tried to breathe as rhythmically as possible.

Finally, her dad told her mom and brother to go to bed while he stayed. She smiled but quickly caught herself and readjusted her lips. Her dad could never stay awake in her rocking chair and soon enough she heard a snore. Evangeline opened one eye. She whispered "daddy?" and receiving no answer slowly rose and tiptoed out of her room and down the stairs.

Evangeline saw the glow of flashlights outside in their backyard and hid behind a sofa chair. She would sneak out the front and go around. She clicked open the locks silently and climbed out in bare feet. They hit the cold, wet mud with a soft sloshing sound and she snuck around to the back, squishing mud with every step.

The men in suits were still there but having a silent cigarette. Evangeline crept around the outer edge of the yard where the trees separated it from the park, hiding in their cover. She passed behind their storage shed towards the spot where the lightning had been and stopped, looking around in confusion. She squinted her eyes and stared at the dark ground around her in every direction until she saw a large drop in the ground filled with muddy water. She slipped to her knees and scooched to it and with an unsure hand slowly reached into the mud until her whole arm was submersed.

Her hand finally felt something hard and cold and with part of her face in the muck now, she grabbed at it with her other hand and began to pull. The object was extremely heavy, and her scrawny arms could barely budge it. The two men began to walk and mud squished around twigs which cracked with each step they took. She stopped, muddy water dripping from her face. They turned and walked in a different direction and when the sound of their voices and feet finally began to mute she braced her heels against a rock and pulled with her entire, skinny body.

Unable to lift her treasure she dragged it along the ground, inch by inch, until she reached the storage shed. Completely out of breath she pushed the sword into a space underneath the shed using the strength of her whole upper body to do so. Then she snuck back into the house and stared at her mud-covered pajamas in the full length mirror by the door. Remembering that her mom had just done the laundry she tip-toe-ran to the laundry room and changed into clean pajamas, wiping herself clean with the old ones. She bundled them up and shoved them under the couch, tiptoeing as quickly as she could back into her room and her bed. She would sneak the pajamas to the bottom of the laundry bin tomorrow, she thought to herself, and the men wouldn't find her sword anymore. They wouldn't steal the truth from her.

Chapter 8

ERIC'S THE MAN

Val stomped down the hospital hallway with Cynthia somehow managing to simultaneously huff to keep up and smile back at Ian and Eric with demure apology plastered on her face. Val really didn't care if she lost some or all of them. Cynthia had called her for a ride to the hospital without the added explanation that Ian and that snivelling worm Eric were waiting at her house to jump in also.

Eric had dropped to the lowest ranking of the most revolting insect category in Val's books during the play-out following Evangeline's passing out. Rather than worrying about getting help for Evangeline, his concern had been his reputation and the repercussions that might land on him if Evangeline had overdosed on something. Val saw that had the others at the party been willing to, he would have chucked Evangeline out on the street and pretended not to know her.

She had no issues with Ian but couldn't comprehend why he was here either as he clearly had no interest in Cynthia and barely knew Evangeline. She saw Cynthia give her a pointed look to slow down and responded with a tight-lipped scowl and an even faster gait.

"She's running ahead to warn Evangeline. You know chicks want to make themselves look good, even in the hospital," Eric smirked over at Ian as the distance between them and the girls grew. Ian made a "hmm" sound.

Ian knew the only reason Eric was at the hospital was because it drove him insane that a woman didn't adore him. As far as friends went for Ian, Eric was just there, playing rugby on the same team, okay to have an occasional beer with when his personality was diluted within a group environment. One-on-one Eric's loudly and repeatedly proclaimed delusions of self-grandeur went past amusing and into the mentally draining category. However, Eric's delusions of social and sexual grandeur also made it impossible for Ian to resist seeing Evangeline shoot Eric down miserably…again.

Ian had followed Eric and Evangeline around the party, patiently enduring Cynthia's glossed on personality and the bizarre, demure act she was putting on, just so he could watch the play by play, and it was frankly awesome. He had to be there for the finale. On that note, he wondered how much he would have to hint his complete lack of interest to Cynthia before he would need to shoot her down miserably. He knew coming along for this trip didn't really help his situation. He wondered if he was as big an ass as Eric for being here for his own, personal, slightly evil, amusement.

"How can you not get it?" Eric obviously mistook his silence as wanting to hear more, "Chicks love that night-in-shining-armour shit. She's on her deathbed with some cancer or some crap. She's completely insecure and vulnerable, thinking that no guy will wanna bang her before she dies. All I need is to look like some compassionate, dumb, dick and she'll be eating out of my hands."

"Yeah, I can see the compassion just oozing out of you." Ian said, "By the way, she doesn't have cancer. She has a disorder called PNH."

"How do you know?"

"Well, let's see. I asked Cynthia and then I actually looked it up. I figured that if you go visit someone in the hospital you should actually know what's wrong with them so you don't look like a stupid, jackass. Oh, wait, I mean, a 'compassionate' shit for brains."

Eric looked a bit stumped but quickly recovered, "alright. Give me the three second summary on PHJ."

"PNH. Oh, and sorry. Looks like we are here so you and your compassion are on your own." Ian couldn't help smiling.

~

Evangeline was on her laptop, looking up otherworld portals and feeling like an idiot for doing it.

She closed her laptop and put her head down over it, swallowing down nausea. Her parents had taken her to eat her first solid food since Friday at the hospital cafeteria and she realized she had overdone it.

Val stalked into her room with Cynthia running behind her while Evangeline was rocking back and forth, pondering if she needed the vomit tray.

"What do you mean Ian and Eric are here? Whyyyyy?" Evangeline moaned.

"Ask your pal Cynthia," Val said, leaning against the wall and crossing her arms across her chest.

Evangeline looked at Cynthia, "Since you brought them, you can tell them to go away."

"I am not-," a knock on the door interrupted Cynthia's protest and her voice changed to sugar, "hey! Come in!"

"Hi. Can we see the sick beauty?"

Evangeline didn't think she could get any more nauseous but the sentence which had just come out of Eric's mouth proved otherwise. She threw her head back on the pillow and looked straight up at the ceiling.

"You really *didn't* need to come," was all she could bring herself to say.

Eric was apparently not thrown off at all by her lacklustre response to his entry. He whipped a small, decorative box of expensive chocolates out of his jacket and held them out for her to take. His face now took on a simper, "these made me think of you. The box has an intricate kind of beauty."

Evangeline knew she should be semi polite and take the chocolates but her hand just didn't want to.

"Oh, how perfect!" Cynthia grabbed the box of chocolates hastily, "I'll just open them up for her. She's still a little weak."

Cynthia took out a chocolate and shoved it without warning into Evangeline's mouth as Evangeline's eyes popped out in shock.

"How is it? It looks absolutely delicious," Cynthia smiled sweetly.

As much as she wanted to, Evangeline knew that spitting out the chocolate was beyond rude, even where Eric was concerned. She forced herself to chew minimally enough to swallow and looked at Eric for the first time since he entered, "Thank you."

Unfortunately, that was more than enough encouragement and he grabbed a chair and swung it over to her bedside, reaching over to take her hand, "I've been doing a lot of research on PNH. I really admire your bravery, Evangeline."

"Uh, thanks," Evangeline said, pretending she wanted more chocolates in order to keep her hands away from his grasp, "I didn't do much except pass out and lie in bed for two days. So, anyways, what did you learn about my blood?"

She forced the second chocolate in her mouth and passed the box around to the others. Eric looked confused,

"Your blood?"

"Yes, PNH, my blood disorder?" she looked at him with a grimace.

"Oh...yeah, of course -"

Evangeline didn't hear the rest because the nausea began to climb up her throat and she felt her face going green. The last chocolate did it. She began to droop her head down and loll it back and forth, trying to calm the nausea.

"I'm sorry, look, I don't think this is the best time...I'm just not-"

Her garbled explanation was interrupted by Eric's chair legs scratching against the floor as he suddenly started inching it away from her bedside, "you said blood disease? Like an STD? Is it contagious?"

Val quickly grabbed a small tray and ran over to Evangeline. She stood partially between Evangeline and Eric and aimed the tray under Evangeline's mouth, but the stupidity of Eric's question gave Evangeline an urge for vengeance.

She quickly raised herself up in the general direction of the tray but pushing her body up she aimed her head as far over the tray as she could and projectile vomited over the tray and onto Eric. Her aim was perfect and he shot out of the chair,

"Shit!" Eric hollered as a half-chewed piece of chocolate slid off his vomit soiled pant crotch.

Val held a napkin out for Evangeline and after a bit more dry-heaving Evangeline wiped her mouth and looked up. Eric was swearing while Cynthia was trying to wipe him down with some towels. Ian was just sitting silently with a bemused look on his face in the opposite corner of the room.

"Sorry Eric," Evangeline said, not at all apologetically, "I guess the chocolates made me nauseous, or maybe it was just your conversation. By the way, it *is* contagious. Passed on through fluids."

"Is she serious? Is she fucking serious?" Eric's holler was half enraged and half terrified.

"Very serious," Evangeline smiled, "You should RUN. You can grab some diapers from the nurses' station on your way out since you do look like you shit your pants."

"Are you completely demented?!" Eric shouted, pointing at his filthy crotch. Val couldn't help it and burst out laughing and even Ian hollered with laughter. Eric stormed out of the room and without any other insult to throw back at Evangeline, shouted "fucking psycho!" from the doorway.

Vomiting up the unwanted dessert had a miraculous effect on Evangeline and she threw her head back and laughed along with Val and Ian. Cynthia stood in the middle of the room red faced and open mouthed, holding her filthy towels.

"Don't worry, Cynthia," Ian said through his laughter, "It's impossible to inflict any lasting damage to Eric's ego through his thick head."

"I thought you guys were friends. I felt a little bad," Evangeline said.

Ian responded with a shrug, "He's on my team but generally speaking he's an ass. Ironically women never seem to get the full gist of his nauseating personality because he's just sooooo hot. But I never lost hope. I knew the right projectile vomiting woman was out there somewhere."

Evangeline smiled. She definitely preferred Ian's slim frame and intelligent eyes to Eric's ostentatious build and whimpering looks. And Cynthia was right, he did have literally beautiful, olive skin.

Her thoughts were pulled to the sound of Cynthia chucking the dirty towels in the laundry and stalking over to the adjoining bathroom, shutting the door behind her. Why was she so mad? Shouldn't she be happy that Ian couldn't care less about Eric's reaction?

"So, aren't you scared of my STD infested blood?" Evangeline said.

"Sorry to disappoint," Ian said, "I actually did real research before coming here. The only thing your blood likes to kill is itself. It's interesting. And it's nocturnal, which apparently means it always gets worse at night."

"Yeah, she's like a night stalker. The vampire chick," Val said and plopped into a chair.

Evangeline's mind suddenly trailed off. A thought came to her head. Vampire wannabes. Her school had a whole herd of them. They must have gone nuts researching portals, other worlds and whatever else they attempt to summon. And then there was Bambi. She was one of them.

"That is the face of a very deep thought or no thought at all," Ian said, "I have that face constantly in religion class. To this day Mrs. Constantine can't decide if I'm vigorously pondering my mortality or sleeping with my eyes open."

"Actually...I was thinking that since I busted up Eric's party, maybe I should have one of my own. What do you guys think? Keep with Eric's theme? Small and VIP, but of course not invite Eric..and...I was thinking of a totally different type of VIP. I bumped into Bambi the other day at school and it made me wonder what her and the death clan do at parties..."

Val looked at her dubiously, "I personally wonder what you wonder about."

"Oh, come on," Evangeline said, "We could do a Halloween thing. Get some creepy basement, a couple death clan members, some Ouija boards, or whatever they use, definitely some drinks and see what the darkness brings...I heard they are into opening portals to other worlds. It would be hilarious."

"I heard the Death Clanners don't associate with non-members" Ian said.

"We can...I don't know...infiltrate by befriending them?" Evangeline said, trying to grin nonchalantly.

"Huh?" Val said with sarcasm, "What are you going to do? Go funeral hat shopping with Bambi?"

Evangeline laughed at the closeness of Val's guess.

"Alright," Ian said in a definitive tone, "I think me and Val are pretty unsure about the success of this but I'm up for it. Come on Val. You will look hot in a funeral hat. Maybe you can get a sporty one."

Ian laughed as Cynthia re-entered.

"Am I missing out on more vomit humour?" Cynthia frowned.

Evangeline suddenly realized that Cynthia felt hurt because she felt left out, not because of Eric's fate. She smiled at her, "We're having a Halloween, VIP event. You are one of the VIPs of course."

"Sounds like a blast," Cynthia said blandly, "Well, it seems like you are suddenly feeling better Evangeline so I'm gonna head out. Hope you don't mind. Tons of homework for tomorrow. If you want to stay longer Val, I'll catch the bus. No worries."

Cynthia grabbed her coat, looked at Ian and cleared her throat.

"Oh, sorry Cynthia," Ian stood up, "I have some cash. Let me call a taxi for you."

Cynthia's head moved slightly back and her lips mouthed an "oh" apparently taken aback by the way her hint had been taken.

Chapter 9

PLASTIC MAN

Evangeline turned off the lights in her hospital room, yawned and closed her eyes.

The black of sleep turned to red. The red narrowed to a stream of blood that ran down a grey wall in trickles and drops. Evangeline's line of vision travelled up it, as if swimming up a waterfall. At the top, on the harsh rock surface of the wall, was the body of a girl. Her hair was dark and lustrous, falling in waves down the wall, the blood dripping through it. She wore a gown, like something from a medieval movie, long folds and layers of rich fabrics tossed around her, their colours soiled with the colour of her blood. She couldn't have been more than thirteen or fourteen and her lifeless eyes stared into Evangeline's.

~

When the Haematologist, a tall, slim and slightly mousy looking lady named Dr. Monica Benini, came the next morning Evangeline was fully dressed in her regular clothes and yawning in a chair. She had called her parents quite early, lying that her back was killing from being in bed so long. She had in fact had horrifying nightmares all night and was trying to not sleep.

Her mom arrived almost immediately, going on about her guilt for having turned into a basket case during the diagnosis. She was here to make it up. Evangeline was thankful. She knew she wouldn't fall asleep with her mom chattering incessantly in an attempt to provide "positive support".

Dr. Benini had little new to say and Evangeline began to zone out. Meanwhile her dad was torturing the poor woman with piles of information he had printed out. Raffael, who did not need to be polite, or professional, like Dr. Benini, was quickly skimming through their dad's papers, ditching the garbage and focusing her father on the couple of credible sources of information that he had found. Dr. Benini's brown eyes were smiling at Raffael.

A man sat silently beside Dr. Benini, awaiting his turn to speak. He was representing some PNH support group. He was average built with blond, three-quarter parted hair, over a slightly round, pudgy face that would have been cute in middle school but by adulthood turned his appearance into one of those plastic politicians on TV that could easily be imagined torturing puppies while still smiling at the crowd. While he sat in the chair, he smiled his plastic smile, his fingers running smoothly up and down a pen as if it was some cherished object. Evangeline kept thinking of Golum from Lord of the Rings and wanted to gargle out "myyy precious" as she watched his rhythmical movements over that ratty, chewed up pen.

The man cleared his throat and looked at Dr. Benini, "unfortunately I need to go soon Monica."

"Oh, yes. Sorry Daniel," Dr. Benini said, "Actually, I think we covered all the important aspects, but you can email me at any time Mr. Kennedy."

She directed the last part at Evangeline's father and Evangeline almost choked and shot a look at Raffael whose chest moved with a stifled laugh. Dr. Benini had to be a sucker for punishment if she actually chose to give their dad access to her personal email.

"You may of course contact me also," Dr. Benini turned to give Raffael her business card, then paused and wrote something on the back before handing it to him, "I added my personal number."

"Oh, thanks." Raffael seemed pleased though slightly confused and Evangeline thought she saw Dr. Benini blush as she moved towards the door, giving last minute advice.

"We'll have the blood results in a couple of days, Evangeline," Dr. Benini was saying, "If less than fifty percent of the blood is mutated we will just monitor and give prednisone when necessary. If it's above fifty percent, we'll have to discuss further treatment."

"Okay. Let's see," Evangeline responded with a tight-lipped smile. Monica Benini smiled back gently and added, "and don't forget to keep your prednisone on you."

"Got my babies right here." Evangeline rattled her bottle of pills.

"Don't go nuts," Raffael said, "you know that prednisone is a steroid."

"Yeah, I know. I've always wanted a beard and I heard it does wonders at the Olympics." Evangeline gave Raffael a criminal grin and shook the bottle like a maraca. Raffael narrowed his eyes, but Dr. Benini laughed out loud. She sounded like a female Santa Claus as she waved on her way out.

Daniel joined in with his own version of a laugh, followed by a clearing of his throat.

"Alright, Evangeline," Daniel's smile couldn't possibly stretch any farther, "You know that Dr. Benini's office is in Hamilton, which is around forty-five minutes from your house. Dr. Benini was too modest to point out though that Hamilton houses the best PNH experts in Canada. A lot of research is being conducted into your blood disorder. It's quite fascinating."

"Thanks" She raised her eyebrows at him. He coughed again and she wondered if that was his go-to reaction.

"What I mean is that your blood structure and activity may provide important insights into other blood diseases. Possible cures. You could be part of something amazing."

Evangeline's dad perked up at the word "cure" and Daniel's smile turned in his direction. Evangeline hated him.

"Our PNH support group currently has fourteen members. There are even online members from around the world."

"What does the support group have to do with your research?" Evangeline asked.

"It is about the sharing and dissemination of information. You would be part of the national PNH registry and we would have access to your blood results as well as treatment information. We might also suggest other treatments that could fit each particular case."

"Of course she will join. This is absolutely wonderful!" Her father was all over it. Daniel was snaking in just the right words for her father to grab on to.

"I'll see. Thanks for the information Daniel. So ... bye ..." Evangeline finished with a wave of her hand in his direction and a tight, superbly wide smile which she hoped matched his. Her father's face turned red and Raffael's teeth clenched. On a bright note, Daniel actually stopped smiling.

"I apologize Daniel. We really appreciate your visit. Evangeline has a lot to deal with right now, but I am *positive* you will see her at the next meeting," Raffael looked pointedly at her.

"Great. Why don't I get your card Raffael...and Mr. Kennedy? I will email the details. Evangeline?" Daniel said.

"That's fine. My dad will let me know." There was absolutely no way he was getting her contact details.

Finally, Daniel gathered his things, put away his chewed-up pen and play-doh smile and left. The moment the door closed behind him Evangeline braced herself for a mental whooping from her family.

~

It felt amazing to be home and in her room...alone. After a lengthy argument about her rash decision making, rash first impressions and rash, illogical temper Raffael stated that he knew she would join the PNH support group like any other intelligent human being after she sat down and thought about it logically.

At the end he gave her a stiff hug goodbye and headed back to his own life and practice in Toronto.

Her father continued the liturgy all the way home in the car, sprinkled with guilt inspiring phrases of "You wouldn't be so selfish as to deny knowledge that could potentially cure people." But she knew that Daniel had just fed her father the fake hope of a cure for her.

Only her mom remained silent. She was thankful for at least that.

Evangeline threw herself on her bed, looked around at the paintings and closed her eyes. A second later her eyes popped open and she shot up out of bed. She stumbled to the large painting of the morbid face and looked around to the back at the gaping, empty hole. Taking her mobile phone out of her pocket she began to type a text to Raffael and stopped midway.

Strange, she didn't feel comfortable writing it out in clear words. As if someone might read the phrase "where'd you put my enchanted sword?" and rob her of it. She wrote,

Hey Raffael, where'd you put my things from the hospital?

The reply came a second later,

Sorry, must have forgotten to put them back. Don't worry. I'll return them to you when we meet up at the PNH support group.

Evangeline's face went hot as she stomped in fuming circles around her room. In the middle of a raging, inner monologue she suddenly smiled. She looked at the phone in her hand and typed,

Hey Raffael. No problem. I don't need it. I have some other stuff.

She had gotten the sword. She could possess anything for all he knew. It would drive him nuts.

~

"She's bluffing. That little, blond, afro shit," Raffael was steaming more than the cup of coffee he had just poured himself back at his flat.

Yes, they had seen something strange and perhaps even outside of the natural and he admitted it. But she had told him he couldn't deal with things and yet it was obviously her that wasn't dealing. She couldn't accept that her blood disorder was something real and permanent that she would live with long term. She wanted to cure herself by imagining that it had some supernatural connection to one, strange, childhood incident.

He sat down on the living room couch, which cornered one of the windows and looked down, out into the street. It was a cloudy day and the sun was obstructed, making evening arrive sooner than usual. A man stood on the corner. He picked up a phone call on his cell and fishing a pen out of his shoulder bag hastily wrote something on the palm of his hand. The man hung up and stood pondering the writing on his hands, flipping his pen between his fingers as he did so. Finally, he put the pen away and walked down the street.

Raffael watched the man disappear with a feeling of agitation; like when he heard a piece of a song and knew he knew it but couldn't remember the name. Something was suddenly driving him nuts. He put his coffee down and began to pace. He paced so long that his coffee went cold. Frustrated he made another cup but still his mind was blank.

Chapter 10

THE NIGHT SHE TOOK THE HAT OFF

Bambi woke each evening alone in the basement and waited for her mother to return. She was only six, but she knew to be quiet and never leave the darkness of their hiding place. It was what she had been doing for months, or possibly years, as far as her child's mind could piece together.

Bambi pushed the coffee table towards a cabinet and stacking some books on it made her nightly stairway to the small window near the ceiling of the room. The window was exactly at ground level and so small that she could see nothing except a little gravel surrounding it and a patch of grass beyond. She stared through the window nightly until her mother returned home with dinner.

Her mother would return each night, some hours after the sky went fully dark, with plates of delicious things, many of which Bambi had never tasted before. Her mother never ate with her. She always declined when Bambi offered and said she had eaten on the way. She must have, Bambi reasoned, because she seemed so much better than before. Some nights she returned almost glowing and she made those strange growling noises so much less.

In that other dark room that they ran away from Bambi remembered feeling as if she had slept endlessly every time she woke to its dripping cold, black walls. And when she woke up she was always starving in the putrid smelling darkness, never knowing when her mother would return. When she did, she never had more for her than something hard, dry or mouldy. In this room, her mother returned every, single night and they were never hungry and always discovering new things.

They found a box one night. It was like a painting that lit up with images of different worlds and people when they poked at some buttons on a little contraption lying beside it. They sat many nights experimenting with the buttons after that and learned to click them in the right way so the box would let them watch worlds of light and greenery flash by. Strange buildings and oddly dressed people filled the worlds in the box and they understood bits and pieces of the things they did and talked about, their worlds and languages similar, yet different.

One night the box showed them a little room with a seat with a hole that had water at the bottom, and they learned that people go to the bathroom by sitting on this seat. They were excited because that same room was attached to their own, little, underground dwelling and Bambi could finally relieve herself in cleanliness there. There was even a tub with water coming out of the wall and Bambi filled it nightly and sat in it until the water went cold. She loved the feeling of cleanliness, the scent of her skin freshly washed each night, never again smelling like dirt, mould and feces.

But the most wonderful thing was the light. It had been another one of those magical discoveries in that box that showed them how to turn on the lights. Her mother screamed and hid in terror the first time they did it. Then she slowly rose from her crumpled position and stared at it in wonder, feeling it on her hands. Afterwards she forbade Bambi from lighting it again in the room because of the low windows through which it might be seen. But, the tub room had no windows and they would enter it each night, shut the door, turn on the light and sit happily in its brightness, Bambi in the tub and her mother on the closed toilet seat. But even in this warm comfort her mother never took the dark veiled hat off her face.

Each night her mother seemed healthier and more glowing, and each night Bambi hoped she might get just a little closer. She longed for her mother's arms and the comforting beat of her heart. She would attempt to sit just a little closer when they watched the magic box or brush her hand across her mother's when her mother passed her the towel after a bath. Each night, with the same sad patience, her mother distanced herself without a word.

After some nights her mother began to change again. She was restless on the bathroom seat and paced back and forth under the glow of the light. She started leaving multiple times per night and when she moved away from Bambi's attempts at intimacy, she did so with more and more harshness.

Bambi was confused and focused more and more on that green patch of grass. Her mother forbade her from pushing the small curtains aside, but she just couldn't help herself. Each night she pushed them open just slightly and watched that little patch of grass. She thought of the little, blond girl with the wet socks and how the wet grass had felt.

She didn't remember why they stopped going outside. Each time she asked her mother her mind suddenly went blank and she woke up an unknown time later. She had stopped asking after a couple of times, terrified of the strange loss of time and memory which the question always brought.

She heard a click somewhere above her, pushed the curtains closed and jumped down to the couch. Tonight Bambi decided she would ask again. She collected her courage, stood up and approached her mother.

"Mamma?"

"Yes, *cara*." Although *cara* meant sweetheart, tonight her mother said it without any warmth; a word used impatiently and out of habit. It did not dissolve Bambi's resolution.

"Mamma, let's go out in the sun today. It will make you more calm. You don't have to be scared. I will hold your hand." Bambi reached over and took her mother's hand firmly in her own, looking into her eyes as best as she could through the darkness of the veil. It was only a second before her mother's surprise turned to fury. She ripped her hand out of Bambi's and flung Bambi away with a strength that made Bambi fly across the room and smash down on the couch, knocking the whole thing over backwards. Her mother then began to take random objects and smash them on the surrounding walls, screaming,

"Why?! Why do you have to keep trying to touch me and hold me with your stupid, little human hands?! Stop touching me! Stop touching me! *Stupida! Idiota!*"

Bambi had rolled backwards off the crashed couch and was now cowering behind it, crying uncontrollably. Her mother grabbed a vase and facing Bambi now, aimed the large object directly at her child, lifting her arm to throw. With her eyes wide open, Bambi was frozen in shock, her little head sticking out from behind the cover of the couch.

Just as the arm was about to fling the vase it stopped, as did her mother's screams. For a second she simply stood there, still and silent, staring at the terrified Bambi. Then, slowly, she put the vase down and began to shake. Without a word she walked up the stairs and out the basement door, clicking it shut. Bambi didn't move. She only cried silently in the darkness, waiting and hoping for her mother to return.

It was right before dawn when her mother came back. Bambi was still behind the fallen couch. Her tears had stopped some hours back, but her confusion and terror had kept her rooted to the spot on the floor.

The door slid open and her mother stepped silently down the stairs. She walked slowly, her shoulders shaking as she approached Bambi and held out her hand to her. Bambi took it uncertainly. Her mother looked down at the little hand inside her own and knelt down. Then she did the one thing Bambi had wanted for so long; she put her arms around Bambi and holding her tightly against herself picked her up.

She carried Bambi, hugging her against herself, up the stairs and towards the basement door, which she had left open for the first time since they had arrived. Bambi stared at the open door, wide eyed. She felt that she should be happy but suddenly could only feel fear.

"Mamma?"

"We can go outside now Bambi. You can see the sun."

Bambi did not respond but held her breath and her mother. Right as they walked through the doorway, her mother took Bambi's chin in one of her hands, as she still held her up against herself with the other hand, and turned Bambi's face to her own, looking straight into her eyes. Bambi thought she saw a flash of red as things went momentarily blank. Then everything was back to normal and they entered the main level of the house.

They came out of the basement into the hallway between the living room and the kitchen. The house was empty and silent, all it's surfaces uncommonly clean, to the point of sparkling perfection.

They walked through the hall and then through the kitchen, which led to the front door, and Bambi stared down from her mother's arms at the shining floors, while her mother walked slowly, in an uneven trail, as if avoiding unseen objects on the floor. Bambi scrunched up her nose at the horrifically putrid smell of the house, which did not at all match its spotless surfaces, and burrowed her face in the shoulder folds of her mother's long, dark gown.

Finally, Bambi heard a door squeak open and lifted her face to breathe in the fresh air. The air smelled of drying grass, the smell of ending summer. She lifted her head as much over her mother's shoulder as it would go, staring wide eyed at her surroundings.

High placed streetlights, on top of long poles, dispersed the darkness around them, which had a misty feel to it. The street was clean, with houses that looked like they were made of little, neatly stacked blocks with well-organized trees and greenery surrounding them.

There was no one outside in the neighbourhood, it's silence that of the sleepiness of the pre-morning hours.

Bambi's mother put her down, barely breathing. She took Bambi's hand and began to walk straight ahead, silently. Her gait was that of purpose as she walked, never once looking at Bambi's face, which kept turning towards her mother with curiosity as she was pulled silently along.

They walked for a while, taking a couple of purposeful turns which Bambi did not take notice of. She was engrossed in her surroundings as well as the fear that snaked through her body at the strangely slow determination with which her mother walked.

At last they stopped at a corner and Bambi's mother turned to Bambi and placed a hand on her cheek.

"Walk in this direction. Straight ahead. There will be people and noise but you don't need to be frightened. Give them this letter." She handed Bambi a folded note. Bambi took it suspiciously.

"Where are you going, mamma?"

"I have to go elsewhere right now, but I will watch you and make sure you are safe."

"I don't want to go. I want to go with you."

Her mother's chest seemed to heave for a second, then she bent down and kissed Bambi's forehead shakily through her veil, "I love you. Trust me. This is where the sunlight is waiting for you."

Putting her hands on Bambi's shoulders she turned Bambi away from herself in the direction in which she wanted her to walk. Bambi swallowed and took a couple of steps forward then stopped and spun around. The street was empty. Her mother had disappeared into thin air.

Terrified, Bambi began to scream, running backwards, but there was nothing. Bewildered she spun around and ran back again to the corner. With tears falling wildly she ran in the direction which her mother had pointed her in, shouting, "mamma! Come back!"

She ran blindly until sounds began to reach her ears: people talking, sirens blaring. Then, hands were grabbing her. She was manic with terror and confusion as machines with the words Police on them surrounded her and people in blue clothes grabbed at her. She tore away and ran, frantically trying to escape, running and climbing into the back of a white machine as hands tried to pull her down and out of it.

Bambi grabbed onto a white sheet and pulled, trying to pull herself up and inside the machine, away from the grabbing, shouting people. The sheet was not secured and tore off as she pulled, revealing a small, white body beneath.

It was a girl, so much like herself, with long black hair and pale face, lying dead and still with only blotches of blood splattered on her, still red, signifying the life that had been in her not long ago.

Bambi shrieked in terror, closing her eyes and letting go of the sheet, letting herself fall into the hands of the people surrounding her. With eyes tightly shut and her face hidden in someone's chest she stretched out the hand with the letter crumpled in it.

"Take it. Take it. Mamma, come back."

The voices where indistinguishable, their large number and speed blending them together in her ears. She felt a hand taking the letter out of hers as another large arm cradled her to a warm, comforting chest until things finally went soothingly silent and blank.

Bambi remembered little else of the chaos and confusion of that night. What she did remember was her first ray of sun. It woke her up, its warmth landing on her face through the windows of the police car whose sirens had been silenced. She was lying in the back with a burly, older man sitting beside her and making soothing sounds towards her when she opened her eyes. The morning sun streamed in through the glass and she pressed her face to the window, wanting nothing more than to feel each and every ray on her skin.

~

A younger officer found the black, funeral hat and brought it to the detective in charge of the case, asking if he thought this was part of the evidence. He had found it on the sidewalk, halfway between the crime scene and the basement where the strange, little girl had been held captive. The detective looked at it and shifted his burly frame. The style of the hat matched the bizarre outfit of the girl when she had run to them in terror and passed out in his arms. It most likely was part of the evidence but... "No, looks like a useless piece of dropped junk. Just... chuck it here."

They found Bambi's place of captivity from the directions in the letter, and though some pieces came together many remained unanswered. The strange girl's responses were a mixture of Italian and English and were not plausible or even logical.

The therapist decided the girl must have been mentally or physically abused as well as brain washed to the point of not being able to distinguish reality from the strange tales she had obviously been told or made up in her own head in order to emotionally survive.

The detective could not get that little creature out of his head: that strange letter she had passed to them and the face that looked so much like the murdered girl's.

Some days later the detective made his way to the foster home where Bambi was being cared for. She was sitting in a playroom, on a small chair, staring at dolls with blank eyes.

"Is this yours? Would you like it?" He spoke softly, crouching slowly to her level. He didn't know why he was here with this weird, black hat in his hands as he watched her head turn and stare silently at it. Somehow, he had felt that maybe she needed it. It was the only thing they had found that just might be hers.

She finally nodded, not taking her eyes off the hat.

She was wearing regular kid's clothing now, but seemed to him much more awkward in the jeans and t-shirt than she had been in the Amish style frock that they had found her in.

He stuck his hand out, bringing the hat towards her. Silently she took it and cradled it to her chest. Then she stood up, walked to a corner and crouching in it pressed her face into the hat. She remained there, motionless, until he left.

Chapter 11

WANTED AND UNWANTED FRIENDS

Evangeline sat in the passenger side seat, her mom having insisted on driving her to school on her first day back.

"I forgot to tell you; I called the language institute and they are willing to have you do the Italian language test this coming weekend if you are up for it." Her mom said as she fumbled through her purse with one hand, while driving with the other.

"Oh yeah. I forgot about that. Thanks mom. So... anything I can help you find?"

"No. Got it!" Her mom pulled out a tiny, decorative mint box with the letter E engraved on it and placed it on Evangeline's lap.

"I was at one of those shee-shee bakeries with some profs and they had these there. I thought it was quite pretty and might make carrying Prednisone around more…classy? It should fit five or six pills…"

Evangeline clicked the tiny mint box open and closed. Then she pulled a crumpled up, zipped sandwich bag out of her backpack, which she had stuffed some Prednisone pills into, and began to swap its contents with those of the mint box.

"Thanks mom. It really is pretty. I like it. You know…you've been great."

Breathing in deeply, her mom looked over at her, "No, but thank you, Evangeline."

"Huh?"

"I know I haven't been great. Thanks for saying I have been. I'm not good with this emotional stuff. You know, nerdy, socially awkward professor," her mom smiled, "I just want you to know that I do understand about you not wanting to be in a support group. I probably wouldn't either, even though I probably look like I need one," she laughed and looked over at Evangeline with slightly smeared makeup, "And…I've been amazed at how you've been handling everything…even your father."

Evangeline groaned in response.

~

Evangeline was late for class, having had to politely wade her way through people who genuinely asked about her health and those that just wanted gossip. She finally joined Cynthia and Val in history where Mr. Fernandez' voice boomed out at them.

"We are starting partner projects today. Everyone remembers?"

No one did. The three of them looked at each other and Cynthia instinctively put her arms on her hips as Val inched over to Evangeline. But, Evangeline got up and started to walk away saying, "You guys be partners this time."

"Huh?" Val looked at Cynthia and then followed the direction of Evangeline's gait with her eyes, "Oh, damn. Look, it's her party plans in action."

Evangeline approached a clump of students, generally called The Death Clan. *What's their thing anyways?* She wondered. *Death, vampires, zombies? A bit of all of the above? It's almost impressive how even their uniforms look morbid.* She raised her eyebrows at the multiple layers of depressing makeup and the purposely ratty additions of even more depressing accessories.

They didn't realize Evangeline was approaching them until she was right in their circle, at which point they just stared at her. Evangeline looked straight at Bambi in their midst, "Do you want to be partners?"

Bambi stood stock still with a frown on her face and for a second Evangeline thought she would turn around and leave. Then, emotionless, Bambi said, "Okay" and simply plopped down in a seat.

When everyone was seated Mr. Fernandez passed around written instructions and Bambi skimmed through, summarizing, "You and your partner create presentations....ten to fifteen minutes...political and economic changes of one particular country in the twentieth century and how they paralleled, contributed to or brought on changes in that particular society's mores and values...countries are first come first serve. You can read the rest yourself."

Bambi passed the paper over to Evangeline, who skimmed it and then looked up, "How about doing Italy?"

Before Evangeline could blink Bambi was already at Mr. Fernandez' desk, scribbling their choice down furiously.

The class made its way to a reserved period at the library where Evangeline surfed the web for information while Bambi looked through a book she had found on social-economic changes in Europe. Evangeline was having a hard time concentrating because Bambi stared at her more than at her book.

"So, you said you're partly Italian? I thought you were adopted...and a vampire," she said, trying to take Bambi's unnerving attention off of herself.

"I'm not a vampire. My mother was."

"Okay...so, your father was Italian then?" Evangeline was trying to stay serious but the smirk and eyebrows were not obeying. Bambi didn't seem to have the same issue and replied in a monotone, "I don't know anything about my father. But my mother sometimes mixed Italian with English."

"Did you know your mother? I'm sorry...did she die?" Evangeline asked seriously, forgetting the whole vampire bit. Bambi was quick to refresh her memory.

"Vampires don't die."

"Okay. So... did she fly away?" At this Bambi just stared back into her book. *What was I supposed to say?* Evangeline thought and went back to her computer screen, blandly skimming pages *Dammit, I'm partners with walking death here because I heard something that sounded like Bambi's name in a dream. Well, what the hell. At this point I might as well go all the way.*

Evangeline lifted her head, sighed and said, "I'm going to have a party. Do you want to come?"

"Why? Are you looking for a token freak?" Bambi's voice was without any actual malice.

"Uhm... no. I want to get a small bunch of people together and try some rituals. Maybe Ouija boards and stuff. I figured you'd know what to do."

Bambi looked at her blankly. "Ouija boards are stupid."

"Well...I'm actually more interested in portals."

"Why?" Bambi looked at Evangeline with an intensity that was creepy.

"I don't...know. It's a personal thing I guess." Evangeline furrowed her forehead as she backed her face a bit away from Bambi's.

"Me too." Bambi said, not taking her eyes off Evangeline. Evangeline was now positive that all of this was a bad idea but decided it was too late to quit. At least the party would be memorable.

"So, you're coming to the party then?"

"Yes."

~

Evangeline didn't realize that her party invitation to Bambi was also a lunch buddy invitation. She wasn't surprised that Cynthia ditched her and Val as soon as she realized who would be eating with them. She was surprised though that Ian not only decided to join them but was also trying to hit it off with Bambi, who, until his arrival, had sat at the table and just stared at Evangeline.

"You know, I definitely think that there are things beyond the ordinary," Ian said, after Bambi explained her belief in other worlds and species, "otherwise...well...life would be fucking boring if this was all there was."

Evangeline smiled and wondered if she was smiling too much. She put some more food in her mouth and chewed obsessively.

"They say that the universe is like a folded piece of paper," Bambi spoke slowly, in between her miniature bites from beneath her funeral hat, "it has indefinite folds like an accordion and each fold is a different space or time dimension. If you could make a rip between the folds you could jump into another fold."

"You're talking about wormholes," Evangeline said, "the whole concept that when the world started the huge ball of energy split into matter and antimatter. Our world is made of matter and no one knows where the antimatter went. I used to have this theory that antimatter created twin worlds to the matter worlds. When I was a kid I believed that lightning was a doorway to the other worlds."

Evangeline didn't know why she shared the last part, nor did she have a clue why Bambi was staring at her in paralyzed enthrallment.

"Yes," Bambi said, "A wormhole and portal are the same thing. So, you can say we want to open a wormhole. The problem is, wormholes are supposed to fold in on themselves almost immediately. I think you need a connection to keep it open. Something from that other world. It has to be something significant that connects with it and that would suck you through the wormhole to the other side."

"How would you get something from another world if you're in this world?" Val said, looking up from her mobile.

"I think there are things around us...things that don't belong here. Unexplainable objects. For example, the Stonehenge." Bambi said.

Val laughed aloud, the drink almost coming out of her nose, "So the plan is to inconspicuously sneak off a piece of the Stonehenge and bring it to the party?"

"What do you have, Bambi?" Evangeline said, "Sounds like you've tried this before."

Bambi shrugged, "I have my hat."

They all stared at Bambi, waiting for her to continue.

"It's the only thing I have from my real mother when she left me."

"I'm...really sorry," Ian said genuinely, "I thought my mother was an asshole for leaving my dad because he didn't make as much money as she wanted. I guess that's why I like to pick out the real people now...the ones that don't try to smother their insecurities by living out a fake life."

Evangeline could feel his eyes on her and knew that half of this was a statement about Cynthia. Her heart began to beat louder both from excitement and guilt. She felt that she should somehow show that there was more to Cynthia and yet didn't know how since it was only on rare occasions that even herself or Val got glimpses of it. Thankfully Bambi spoke,

"Really? That's worse. My mother only left to save me."

"From what?" Ian asked.

"I don't know. The answers are on the other side of the portal."

Chapter 12

THE PEN

Raffael felt annoyed. What was it? It was something important, but what was it? He was in his office late and sitting at his desk he took a pen in his hand and stared at it. He lifted it up in front of his face. Nothing. Then he tried to remember the man in the rain below his apartment; to recall his precise action. He began to glide his fingers up and down the pen and suddenly his eyes widened. He remembered.

~

Why is there so much police interest in this? Raffael wondered, standing and looking out of his parents' living room window. His sister was up in her bed by now with their parents watching over her. It had been hours since the lightning incident. They had already been to the hospital and back and yet the cops were still here.

The cops looked like they were finally starting to clear out. Her parents had been all thankfulness at the attention the police had taken in searching the grounds, but Raffael found it odd. He felt there must be more to that creep in their yard than the cops let on. He wondered how bad it was. Was it some serial criminal they didn't want the media to know about? He cringed at the though that his six-year-old sister had gotten so close to that semi-human thing.

He began to turn away from the window when he noticed the two men. They wore some unremarkable suits and were gesturing intermittently to the cops. They stood at the far edge of their yard, exchanging a word or two every now and then. Their faces were not fully clear in the darkness but he could see from their moonlit profiles that they were both clean-cut, dull, guys; the types that would blend into any crowd. One seemed to be constantly smiling and wouldn't stop repetitively flicking something in his right hand...twirling something? Rubbing the thing up and down? It made Raffael think of an ex-smoker's obsession with fiddling with objects in their predominant hand.

Raffael squinted for a second but couldn't identify the object. Losing interest as well as alertness he yawned, turned and finally went up the stairs to bed.

~

Evangeline saw the new message arrive from Raffael on her phone.

Great, Dad's cheerleader is writing, she thought, pounding the message open with her finger.

I'm sorry, the message said, *I'll bring your stuff back as soon as I can. BTW. Don't go to the support group until we talk.*

She had stopped walking without realizing it and just stared at the phone, re-reading the message. She should feel happy to be validated and yet she felt worried. Raffael substantiating her theories meant that there actually was something substantial in them.

Raffael insisted on talking in person but due to his gruelling call schedule couldn't get into town for a while. When he finally made it in they drove out to some trails along the Grand River and he told her about plastic Daniel as they walked.

"How positive are you that it was plastic Daniel?" Evangeline asked, skipping some stones off the edge of the river.

"Positive. His plastered-on smile and porny, pre-occupation with writing objects is unmistakable" Raffael responded, picking up a stone and skipping it beside hers.

"Gross."

"Anyways, based on Daniel's appearance and now reappearance in our lives at this particular time I do agree that there's a connection, but...I'm not you," Raffael said, scratching the back of his neck and rising, "I know that what we saw wasn't just a man. I know it wasn't what we know as normal. But that doesn't make it magic. In my world, there is no such thing."

"So, what is in your world then?" Evangeline grinned at him, pre-amused at whatever scientific explanation he was about to give her.

"There's a connection between the police, what we saw and your blood disorder. Your blood condition is somehow related to the man in the lightning."

Evangeline stopped smiling. She didn't notice before but now she saw it on his face. He was terrified that somehow her blood and that man's blood might have something in common.

Raffael continued, "I'm trying to figure out if there's a way to get some more info on the support group participants without you actually joining...Daniel's emailed me repeatedly now about getting you in there...stay away for the time being."

"No arguments there. Although, now I'm actually slightly curious about the support group."

"I heard your blood results came in by the way. Forty-nine percent mutated. Not particularly great luck. Monica emailed and said dad was quite pushy with getting you on every med known to man but mom's keeping him in line and Monica won't pressure you into anything for now either."

"Monica? Oh, Dr. Benini?" Evangeline grinned, "So when did you get to a first name basis with my Haematologist?"

"We're both doctors. We don't need to keep regurgitating the title to each other, you little shit."

Evangeline looked at Raffael and grinned wider. He looked at her and rolled his eyes, shaking his head as if dealing with an obnoxious child. She laughed.

"You know, *Monica* mentioned that her parents used to live in Kitchener and her family still owns a house in town," Raffael said, "It's been sitting empty for years though. Supposedly a bit dilapidated. It seemed like the perfect, private, slightly creepy place for your party. Definitely better option than parents' basement...I was going to ask her if you could use it until you started annoying the crap out of me."

Evangeline's mouth opened and shut and now Raffael grinned.

Evangeline's party was turning out to be *the* party to go to. The fact that Evangeline had managed to get the Death Clan to come via Bambi was apparently an admirable feat that most people wanted to witness. Even Cynthia was back to her thrilled self at having the IT party.

So, after visibly enjoying his sister's begging spree for a couple of minutes, Raffael gave in with certain conditions.

"Look, not that I don't trust you but...it's a high school party and it's your doctor's house. I'll need to be there. Monica probably too. Don't worry. We'll be inconspicuous. I actually prefer *not* to be seen around drinking minors for legal reasons. And don't even pretend you won't drink. Tell parents you are having a "spooky" Halloween sleepover with a couple gal pals at Monica's place and if the shit hits the fan at any point during the party I will personally call the cops...right before disappearing and pretending I was never there. You, my friend, are fully responsible for any crap that happens."

Evangeline did a soldier salute. She couldn't believe she had just been handed a whole, entire, private, party house. Raffael sighed and shook his head, "What is this new preoccupation with this Bambi character by the way?"

"I don't know Raffael. She looks at me really strangely...and those dream people saying her name...I mean, not exactly a common name. I don't really know what the point of her is. I just feel like I want to get closer...and then *she* brought up the portal opening. It was eerie."

"So, you think she knows how to open a worm-hole portal? Seriously?"

"No... but...I don't know. I feel like she knows...something."

"Okay. Well, not to encourage you but your vampire-wanna-be friend had only part of the theory." Raffael stretched and began to walk again with Evangeline stepping beside him, "If an object belonged in another space or time fold, it might be pulled towards it, trying to avoid annihilation. Remember that matter and antimatter annihilate each other when they come into contact. But then you'd need exotic matter to keep the portal open."

"Exotic matter?" Evangeline tried to remember the theories Raffael had taught her years ago, "Wait. Okay. Matter and anti-matter are same but opposite. You bring them together and they annihilate themselves. Exotic matter has negative energy. You bring it into contact with either matter or anti-matter and you get a complete nothing."

"Exactly," Raffael said, "Exotic matter is like the in-between, between matter and anti-matter. It would be the thing to stabilize a wormhole. So, you need anti-matter to open a wormhole and exotic matter to keep it open...so...what do you have?"

"A funeral hat and a sword?"

Raffael raised his eyebrows, "and what are you going to do? Chant in a circle around it?"

"Well...we might" Evangeline looked away embarrassed and they both burst out laughing.

They were back at the car and Raffael changed topics, "I heard you got into the level two Italian."

"Yeah. The test wasn't too hard."

"You're smarter than me. I never weaselled an exchange year out of parents. All I got was six miserable years of German."

"Your fault. You never complained. You just skipped class behind their backs."

"Yeah, some of us love their parents enough to keep them happy with lies."

Chapter 13

BAMBI AND THE SWORD

It was the night of the party and Evangeline was nervous. Forget the blood disorder, the sword, Daniel and opening some crazy outer world portal. She was suddenly terrified of having a completely crappy party. It would definitely make Eric happy if he heard she had the most useless event of the year.

They had decided to skip cheesy Halloween costumes and just keep the theme to "dark". Evangeline was wearing black pants and a black top, both quite a lot tighter than her usual and she stared in the mirror for a while before deciding that she hadn't crossed the line between sexy-cool and needy-for-attention.

Val came to pick her up and as they drove her mind inadvertently went to Ian's reaction to her outfit and then to guilty thoughts of Cynthia. A voice kept telling her there was no need to feel guilty; Cynthia had never actually dated Ian and Evangeline wasn't actually dating him either. But the guilt was still there because somehow it felt wrong that they both wanted to.

They arrived in front of Dr. Benini's house at the same time as Raffael. As they all got out they saw Bambi standing in front of the slightly dilapidated front door, wearing a long black gown, with her hat for once in her hands, rather than on her head.

"Impressive," Raffael said under his breath, "So Morticia Addams over there is your guide to the extraordinary?"

"Shut it," Evangeline whispered back as they approached Bambi.

"Hey Bambi, Monica's not in the house?"

"I don't know. I didn't knock. I just stood here."

"Ahhhh," was all that Val could think to say.

"I'm Raffael, Evangeline's brother."

"Yes. It's a pleasure," Bambi said and Raffael raised his brows as he rang the doorbell. Evangeline couldn't help grinning when Monica Benini opened the door. She still looked just as gawky but had apparently tried to "sex herself up" with a corduroy skirt and fitted turtleneck, which kind of made her look like a librarian gone wild. However, the way Raffael said "Hello" to Monica and smiled widely gave Evangeline the impression that the sexy librarian thing was doing something for him. She wasn't sure if to give him a high five or to be slightly grossed out, never actually having seen her brother around women due to their large age difference.

As they started to clean up the house Monica veered away from shop talk and was an amazing hostess. She had even convinced Raffael to get them twice the secretly promised alcohol.

"They're high school seniors Raffael. What would Evangeline look like if she hosted a party with one bottle of wine?" Monica said as she pulled out bottles of wine that looked slightly too classy for a high school crowd.

"Wow. Monica, my loser brother needs a lesson in coolness from you," Evangeline said jokingly but Monica seemed to blush, apparently flattered. Evangeline smiled wholeheartedly and liked Monica all the more for this dorky sweetness. Even Raffael grinned.

Both Cynthia and Ian arrived shortly after and all got to work cleaning up and putting up some black curtains and other additions in various sections of the house. Ian was being a particularly good household helper as well as a very polite and muted version of himself. Unfortunately, his behaviour made Raffael eye him suspiciously, which made Ian nervous. This quickly became a cycle that led to intense clumsiness from Ian's side, resulting in a crashed curtain rod which almost smashed into Raffael.

Evangeline knew she would get quizzed if Raffael found the chance to catch her alone so she stuck like glue to anyone she could. At one point Raffael almost got her as she was arranging some sitting spaces, but she saw Bambi passing through the hallway and immediately called out, "Hey Bambi, I never told you, I found something that might rival your hat for the portal opening. Wanna see?"

Raffael brought the massive bag into the house and they all gathered in an old, downstairs office, which contained a stately, hulking work table in the middle. The table hadn't been dusted yet but Val took care of that with her sleeve while Monica unsuccessfully attempted to hide her shock. Raffael noticed and laughed out loud.

"So? Still feeling good about getting all those nice bottles of wine for this rif-raf?"

"Okay," Evangeline said, "let's add rif-raf to our list of forbidden vocabulary, along with, I believe you once called this party a 'shindig'?"

"No need to wipe off the dust Val," Raffael grinned as he spoke and Evangeline knew he was about to say something stupid, "might as well keep some bacteria around. It's the only 'culture' here."

In between everyone's groans Val said, "Okay, let's bring this thing out."

Raffael put the duffel bag down on the floor and opened it. Then he took the sword in both hands, lifted it up and placed it slowly down in the middle of the table. Everyone stepped a little closer to it and stared at the jewels.

"Is this an actual artifact? I didn't know you had this." Val said, looking over at Evangeline.

"This thing looks...real. Where did your family get it?" Ian said.

"Apparently it was just lying around in our backyard," Raffael said and looked over at Evangeline. Before anyone had time to comment

Val reached over to try and pick up the sword, at which Bambi shrieked, "Don't touch it!"

Val almost tripped over herself while everyone else spun and stared at Bambi, whose eyes were fixated on the sword. Her whole body was quivering.

"Don't...I mean...it's...it looks fragile. We should just...be careful with it," Bambi said, her eyes glued to the blade.

"Yeah, sure Bambi. Why don't you guard it?" Cynthia said.

"Yes. I will guard it," Bambi said in the tone of a soldier on duty.

"Allllright then," Val said, "people are going to start arriving. Let's finish off and Bambi, you guard the sword so we are alllll safe." She elongated the last part as if speaking to a slow child.

Raffael placed the huge bag on the table, put the sword back in it and zipped it up, saying that he had no intention of a having a drunk teen attempt ninja moves with it. He then placed it in an inconspicuous corner of the room, while Bambi took up command in the doorway.

Everyone made their way out of the office, looking over their shoulders at Bambi whose eyes never left the corner with the sword.

"Well, she seems pretty excited about the sword," Raffael said once they were all out of the office, looking at Evangeline.

"Do you think she's going to steal it? Should we watch her?" Evangeline thought aloud.

Ian scratched his head, "I say we pass by the office door every now and then...in teams of two."

Although they all laughed, they stuck to the plan.

Even when people arrived Bambi did not move and became a spectacle at the party. People began to call her the Swiss Guard and took turns posing for photos with her and betting on who could make her speak or move.

Meanwhile, Raffael and Monica, having devised a private mini-lounge in one of the upstairs rooms, retired to it with two of the best bottles of wine.

The party was a surprising success. The Death Clan had all shown up with the hopes of making the rest of the world see their passions. Meanwhile, the rest of the invitees had enough expensive alcohol in them to be honestly fascinated with the Death Clan.

At one point Val exclaimed, as she shuddered, "Ohhhh. That's just grotesque."

Evangeline looked over to where Val was staring and saw one of the most popular guys from school making out with a guy with extremely long, greasy, black hair and pallid complexion.

"Maybe to a drunken mind he appears brooding?" Evangeline said and Val shuddered again.

"Come on," Val said, "let's go upstairs and start the portal 'ceremony'. I think I've had enough alcohol now to do this and last time I saw her, Bambi was starting to look a little woozy from standing in the doorway so long."

Val and Evangeline grabbed the couple of people that would be involved in their personal attempt at wormhole opening and made their way to the office. Raffael told Evangeline early on in the night that since Bambi did not appear to be a picture of stability he preferred to be present for whatever she decided to do with a humongous sword. Him and Monica were therefore at this point also dragged away from their enjoyable private party.

Evangeline noticed that some of the other rooms along the way had filled up with the everyday crowd being led by Death Clan members in whatever conjuring they decided to lead them in.

Other than Bambi, Val, Raffael and Monica, their personal group consisted of Liza, a friend of Bambi's, Ian, Cynthia, and Mark and Jack; friends of Ian and the most unalike fraternal twins Evangeline could ever imagine, with Mark looking just like his slim, fair-skinned and fair-haired mom and Jack being a photocopy of his bulky-muscled and dark skinned Korean dad. Cynthia entered last. She appeared bored and unwilling, mumbling under her breath "this is going to be pathetic but if I don't come most definitely something will actually happen."

Evangeline noticed Cynthia narrow her eyes briefly when Ian placed himself beside Evangeline, but regained her normal facial appearance as soon as Mark smiled at her very tiny, black outfit across the table.

Raffael was across the table from Evangeline and Ian, and didn't bother to un-narrow his eyes as he stared at them. Evangeline felt Ian's hand playing with hers under the table, his fingers brushing occasionally up against her thigh. Her lips turned up into a smile. She knew Raffael couldn't see anything, but her grin would drive him crazy. She didn't mind. This would be a little revenge for the fact that he had somehow miraculously showed up whenever Ian had come within five feet of her all night.

Everyone knew at this point that Bambi was planning some crazy ritual so no introductions were necessary. As soon as each person had picked a spot around the table Raffael opened the bag, pulled out the sword and simply said, "Alright Bambi, you're the boss."

"Everyone has to put their drinks down. Then raise your hands," Bambi said.

Mark, a brilliant guy academically who seemed to lose his brain cell capabilities as soon as he left the classroom, shot his hands up above his dirty blond head as if he were being threatened at gun point and even Bambi looked at him as if he were crazy.

"*Not* like that," Bambi's friend Liza, a tiny thing with platinum blond hair and pale blue eyes who looked like a miniature elf, demonstrated with her hands. She bent her arms at their elbows, lifted the bottom half of her arms as if to touch her shoulders with her hands, but then flipped her palms out. Evangeline was slightly disappointed that her "hand time" with Ian was suddenly over but had no choice but to follow suit with everyone else as they brought their hands up and held them almost palm to palm with a person on each side of them.

"I will begin the calling," Bambi continued, "I will repeat it many times. Try to lose yourself in it as if you're meditating. Some phrases will repeat so join in when you can. Just remember to not actually touch anyone around you. The palms are close, but separate."

Bambi began to chant in what sounded like a strange mixture of Italian, English and some other middle earth language she had probably conjured up, with Liza joining in.

"Can I join now?" Mark said loudly and Bambi stopped to give him the look of death while the rest of them laughed under their breath. Even Monica giggled. Bambi ignored the laughter and restarted, while Mark mumbled a "sorry".

"Apre. Porta noi back. Porta noi. We have il tuo. Porta noi."

The chant started to repeat and after some time felt like a terribly ungrammatical, multilingual meditation. Evangeline began to lose herself in it and unconsciously repeat it. She wasn't sure if she were imagining it but it felt as if a current of energy was passing between her fingers and those of Val and Ian, the two people she was palm to palm with. She couldn't feel how much time was passing but Monica's cough signalled that it was too much.

"I'm sorry, Bambi," Monica said, "but I really need to go to the bathroom. Can we take a break?"

"Thank God," Jack said and flopped both his bulky arms and head down, groaning.

Everyone else started to put their arms down and shake them out and Cynthia said, "Okay, that was pretty uneventful. Is it over?"

"No!" Bambi began to quiver and her eyes filled up with tears. Mark, standing beside her, awkwardly patted her shoulder, looking around at everyone as if begging for assistance, "It's Okay Bambi. We can try it again. It's kind of...relaxing. Right guys?" Jack snorted at his brother. While Mark had a dopey kind of kindness Jack had a colder kind of smarts. Mark was the reason everyone liked them and Jack was the reason Mark had survived till now.

"Alright. One last time," Raffael sighed, "let me just grab some chips while Monica goes to the bathroom. I think I heard some mention of food in the chant... Everyone else stay. We'll be back in two."

Cynthia groaned audibly as Raffael and Monica left. Meanwhile, Val and Jack quickly grabbed for their drinks and began to chug before the chanting recommenced.

Evangeline rolled her neck in a circle. She didn't feel bored like the others seemed to be though. In fact, the chant had somehow made her feel mellow. She looked at the sword on the desk. Strangely, although she had had it for many years she had barely touched it. She had hidden it in various spots as time passed, always terrified to pull it out in case anyone saw. Eventually it became encased in the painting and remained completely out of sight for years.

Absentmindedly, she reached out to touch the gleaming, red jewel that melted out of the centre of its blade. But, as her hand approached the blade Bambi screamed "No! You will ruin the ritual!" and threw herself madly at Evangeline with her whole body. Instead of managing to pull the bewildered Evangeline away from the sword though, she pushed her right on top of it, Evangeline's hands landing in front of her in protection, right on the large, flat blade.

Bambi landed on Evangeline's back, her face right in Evangeline's huge mass of hair. Panting for breath and trying to get out of Evangeline's hair, Bambi flung her arms over Evangeline and onto the desk in an attempt to lift the top half of her body back up. As she groped the table for some stability Bambi's hands landed right above Evangeline's, on top of the cold, smooth surface of the flat part of the blade.

The gust of energy between the three of them - the blade, Bambi and Evangeline – was so harsh that it shot a current of pain right through the length of their arms and the two of them simultaneously screamed and tried to get their hands off the sword, scrambling to get off of each other and away from the blade.

It was at that moment that the thunder struck. It came straight through the roof and the full height of the house and landed at the very tip of the blade, where it simply stopped in mid air. The room was breathless, everybody in it frozen. Evangeline stared at the shimmering bolt, feeling as if transported back to her backyard, years before. She rolled slowly away from the sword, her hands sliding off of it.

As soon as Evangeline's hands left the blade, the bolt began to retreat, like the spark off a lit match, fizzing down to nothing. Except that this spark was moving upwards, as if returning back to hide in the sky. Evangeline gulped in a large breath of air and mouthed, "Shit. No," as she tried to get to her feet.

Bambi was faster. She pulled herself up on top of the desk in a jump and grabbed the hilt of the sword. She attempted to chuck the sword upwards into the quickly retreating bolt but it was too heavy and she stumbled over on the desk with it, desperately trying to get back up.

Evangeline grasped the concept and jumped on top of the desk as well. She threw her hands around Bambi's on the sword handle in order to help her get the sword up and into the bolt. Evangeline's reaction was so focused that she didn't notice a third pair of hands also on the sword with them.

As soon as Evangeline's fingers touched the sword again, the thunder bolt shot back down, directly to the tip of the blade, and the three of them flung the sword tip right inside the bolt, slicing it open.

There was no time to think. Half the sword was inside the bolt, disappearing somewhere within, and it was taking their combined strength to keep holding on to it as the thunder was pressing up against it from both sides, trying to close in on itself, not particularly caring if it sucked the sword in or spat it back out.

"Push it open!" Evangeline screamed and the three of them pushed all their weight against the large blade, forcing a small gap in the bolt. Pushing their full weight meant that they practically ran at the gap in the bolt, shoving the sword through it. As the full length of the sword entered, the resistance un-anticipatedly disappeared and all three stumbled over themselves and directly into the lightning.

Chapter 14

THE FIRST NIGHT

Their feet came off the office desk, slid through the lightning bolt and landed on hard dirt.

It was suffocatingly dark around them, not a single thing visible anywhere, except the millions of stars in a black sky. Evangeline's eyes were barely adjusting to the darkness when she heard Bambi scream in hysterics, wrenching the sword out of their hands. Evangeline spun her head around confused and saw the dark silhouette of Cynthia's face, dumbfounded, beside her, stumbling backwards as both her and Evangeline's hands came off the sword handle.

Before Evangeline had time to come to grips with anything that was happening, Bambi threw herself, with the sword in front of her, back into the lightning, screaming and crying in absolute horror as she did so.

"What the f-" Cynthia didn't finish her sentence. The lightning shut in on itself and shot backwards into the sky. A rush of its leftover current hit the ground and hurtled its electric shock at them through the dirt, throwing the two of them off their feet.

Evangeline felt two hands on her shoulders shaking her back to consciousness, "Get up! Get up! Oh my God. Don't be dead. You can't leave me here alone!"

Cynthia's hysterical voice was ringing in her ears as she opened her eyes. She could barely see anything in the all-encompassing blackness except those unrealistically bright twinkles of stars above her. Cynthia's face was just a shadow and Evangeline blinked and stared from side to side, still searching for her breath while simultaneously trying to adjust her eyes.

"Oh, thank God. I was starting to freak out. Where are we? I can't see anything. This freaky joke of Bambi's has lost its humour, not that it ever had any to begin with. It's a bit too real, except that I don't believe in any of this portal or witchcraft crap. I mean, seriously, she just screamed like some banshee and ran off and left us. Is this supposed to be part of the scary experience? Because I'm not impressed. It's just pitch-black and freezing and I am ready to go back and be done with this. There's nothing cool about this. So how do we get back?"

Evangeline was sitting up by now and just staring at Cynthia flabbergasted, trying to absorb at least some of the meaning of Cynthia's verbal diarrhoea. After her last question Cynthia stared back at her, obviously expecting an answer, but all she got from Evangeline was a "What?"

"What? What do you mean what? I want to get the hell out of here. I can't see shit and I'm freezing. How do we G-E-T O-U-T O-F H-E-R-E?"

"I don't know how to get out of here. I don't know where we are," Evangeline said quietly, rubbing her forehead with both hands, in a confusion of thoughts. She hadn't told any of them the truth. Cynthia knew nothing. It wasn't Bambi's fault that they were here. It was hers. She dragged herself and Cynthia into this...whatever this dark coldness was...except that she hadn't dragged Cynthia. Cynthia had kind of pushed her way in. Why? And after all this talk of how she wanted a portal why did Bambi jump back screaming? Why did she leave them here stranded?

The questions spun through her mind as her eyes adjusted enough to see that there was nothing around them to be seen. The ground appeared flat and barren under the night sky and seemed to go off and dissolve in that same flat and barren way into the surrounding darkness as far as her eyes could see, which wasn't very far.

"I don't believe this bullshit. This is *your* party." Cynthia said.

"The house got crashed by thunder, we shoved through a lightning bolt, got electrocuted and ended up in the middle of nowhere in the pitch black of night. If you don't believe in this 'bullshit' then I don't really know what to tell you," Evangeline said.

"Well, I suggest you think of something since this was your grand plan,"

"My grand plan?" Evangeline said, "Okay then. Why'd you follow it? Why'd you jump on the table and grab the sword, Cynthia?"

The air was silent as Cynthia opened her mouth and then closed it again. Then, looking away, she said, "Without me you'd be here all alone after Bambi, your new pal, left you. So, fuck you."

Evangeline looked at Cynthia's face and even in the grey shadows she could see that Cynthia's lips were pressed tightly together and her face was close to tears. She felt bad and angry at the same time.

"You didn't really answer the question" Evangeline didn't know why she was pushing, but couldn't stop herself. Nothing was making sense.

Cynthia remained silent and sitting on the cold ground cradled her knees to herself, staring ahead. They remained motionless this way for a couple of seconds when Evangeline absentmindedly reached into her back pocket to pull out her cell phone. Her eyes went wide as she realized that they hadn't even tried to use their phones. Her hand reached inside and felt a cracked shell.

"Shit," Evangeline said, pulling out her demolished phone, "it completely smashed when we got thrown by the shock. Where's your phone?"

She squinted over at Cynthia in the darkness and Cynthia lifted up her own cell phone towards Evangeline, "It's not picking up any networks. I tried to call for help when you weren't getting up."

"Oh."

They sat silently again for some more seconds.

"So, what are we going to do?" Cynthia finally asked into the darkness, "sit here till we turn blue from the cold?"

"I don't know," Evangeline pondered their options, "Raffael will for sure try to find us and if the portal re-opens it might be likely to be in the same spot? So maybe we should wait, at least until it gets light out. I mean, we can't really stumble around in this pitch blackness and it can't stay dark forever, right?"

The last part was a very uncertain question and they were both silent. Cynthia was again the first to voice her thoughts, "Okay, if this actually worked (which I still refuse to admit) it should have just transported us somewhere in the vicinity of where the party was. We are probably in some forest within a couple miles of the city."

"How do you figure that?" Evangeline asked.

"From the info online you would have to be an extremely powerful spell caster to create portals to other dimensions," Cynthia said, "most attempts lead to movement between small distances."

Evangeline looked at Cynthia surprised, "You actually researched this online? I thought that you thought this portal stuff was sooooo stupid."

"I still think it's stupid," Cynthia said, "but you guys were so into it. I didn't want to look dumb...like I apparently always do."

Evangeline, surprised at Cynthia's vulnerability, looked at her through the darkness, "Well, you are one step ahead of me now."

Again, they sat silently shivering, Evangeline turning her head from side to side, hoping to see something. Anything.

"I feel creepy here," she finally said, inching towards Cynthia.

Cynthia didn't protest, "Yeah, I know. It's like some weird Lord of The Rings Mordor land or something."

"I was kind of thinking we should just start shouting for help but I'm a little freaked out about what might show up in the dark." Evangeline said.

"I'm cool with staying really quiet until it gets light out." Cynthia responded.

"I don't think we'll be here all night," Evangeline said, "I mean, Raffael was there and Bambi jumped or flew back or something. I am guessing she ended up back at the house, meaning that Raffael will hold her down and make her do the chant thing again."

"Assuming this is actually real, what are the chances of it working again?" Cynthia said.

"Actually...I am guessing they are pretty certain," Evangeline's eyebrows creased as she analyzed the train of events. "The lightning bolt was retracting and then the sword brought it back...It's like the sword is the thing that actually did something...Bambi ran off on us but she took the sword with her." Evangeline smiled and breathed out in relief. Actually, she was now certain the portal could be reopened because she had seen it opened before. The only thing she hadn't known before was that the sword was the key to it. Should she tell Cynthia? How would she explain it? Her smile slowly turned to a frown and she bit her lip. She didn't know how to start, or if she should. She looked apprehensively at Cynthia, thankful that Cynthia had not thought to ask why Evangeline had picked this one object to use for the portal opening.

"Yes," Cynthia said, "there's no way Raffael would leave you in the middle of nowhere." Cynthia sat up straighter and began to smooth her hair with her hand and moisten her lips with her tongue, apparently for her upcoming rescue. Evangeline watched her incredulously and tried not to laugh as a sharp wind swept repeatedly in from the same direction, sending their teeth chattering and Cynthia's hair back to its previous mess.

Then, suddenly, Evangeline thought of Ian and feeling stupid tried to inconspicuously comb her fingers through her own hair. Cynthia didn't even look at her when she commented, "Good luck with that."

"Thanks," Evangeline put her hand down and cocked her head at Cynthia, "So you watched Lord of The Rings?"

"Huh?"

"You said that this place looked like Mordor."

"Maybe."

Evangeline snickered, "I love Lord of The Rings. What's the big deal?"

"Apparently none for you," Cynthia said with an audible snort, "you can smear horse crap on yourself and they'll say it's the new Gucci perfume. I'm sure Ian will say your hair looks 'windswept' when you get back."

Evangeline looked at Cynthia out of the corner of her eye and chose not to answer. She felt a pang of guilt, as she wondered how much Cynthia had noticed between her and Ian. A sense of frustration and anger was intertwined with the guilt though. Cynthia had been interested in every, single, semi-decent guy at the school over the course of the last four years. Why was Ian such a big deal, even if she had noticed something?

Having nothing but her mixed thoughts and the cold blackness around them to occupy her, Evangeline began to feel inside her other jean pocket. She found only her miniature mint box. She pulled it out and flipped it between her fingers.

"What, you have mints? I'm starving," Cynthia said.

"It's not mints. It's my prednisone."

Cynthia sighed.

Evangeline rubbed her lips together and realized that thirst was beginning to accompany the hunger and cold. She scooted over again, pressing up against Cynthia.

"Can we do the body heat thing? I think even my toes are chattering," Evangeline said.

Cynthia pressed her shoulders to Evangeline's in agreement and said, "When are they going to be here?" Evangeline had no answer.

They sat shoulder to shoulder, backs towards the wind, their bodies shivering and their eyes staring ahead into the black void around them. Evangeline began to have a nauseous feeling, as if the vomit were moving ever so slowly upwards towards her mouth.

"I think I'm scared shitless," Evangeline said quietly. She heard Cynthia whisper, "me too."

Chapter 15

THE FIRST DAY

Evangeline opened her eyes. The hard, barren ground she had passed out on, and the cold which had penetrated all the way into her bones, had only allowed her a short burst of fear-filled sleep. She lifted her head and noticed that the darkness was thinner, now a dreary grey. She put her wrist close to her face to see the time on her watch. Cynthia, roused by Evangeline's movements, shot straight up and began to look around.

"It's almost 5:00 a.m. earth time," Evangeline said in a groggy voice, "I think dawn is coming."

She stood painfully up and looked around. Through the misty greyness their surroundings looked even more desolate than in the dark. The ground was in fact scorched, as if a fire had swept through. A rare, mostly obliterated tree stump could be seen here and there, but even those were scarce and singed to just tiny leftovers, with barren, dusty earth and gravelly rocks filling their line of view.

They both turned in circles. At first Evangeline thought there was nothing else besides the emptiness on which they stood. However, as her eyes adjusted to the dimness and the dimness began to give way to rare rays of sun, she saw a line. It looked like it might be the beginning of a forest, very far in one direction. Meanwhile, in the opposite direction, jagged mountains loomed like an impenetrable wall, with a patch of what appeared to be a town beneath them. It was so far off that it would not even have been visible if not for the absolute flatness between them and it.

They seemed to be closer to the mountains and after looking from one direction to the other Cynthia said, "There's obviously only one direction to choose." Without another word she began to determinedly walk towards the mountains. Evangeline stood, rooted to the ground, unable to move. She suddenly felt an urge to run to the forest. Cynthia stopped, noticing that she was not being followed and turned towards Evangeline.

There was no way out. Cynthia was right. There was nothing logical about going into the woods and hiding when all they wanted was to be found. Right?

~

They trudged along the gravel and dust covered terrain in silence. After some time Evangeline forgot her hunger and could feel only her thirst. The thirst became a constant burn and the dirt caked all over her body and clothes made every inch of Evangeline feel even dryer and more water deprived.

Raffael didn't come. Why didn't he save us? Why didn't he reopen the portal? Where is he? What happened? Evangeline could think of little else.

Cynthia's tight lipped facial expression kept moving between confusion and fear, her eyes widening and narrowing repeatedly, and Evangeline knew the same thoughts were going through her head. But, neither one of them said anything aloud. Somehow it felt more terrifying to voice it.

There was nothing to do but keep walking silently, their destination seeming to remain just as far away with each passing hour as it had been the hour before.

The rising sun, at first a welcome warmth, became quickly hateful, with nowhere to hide from its beating intensity. After around three hours of walking Cynthia dropped to her knees. Evangeline thought she was passing out, but Cynthia put a finger to her lips with one hand and pulled Evangeline down to the ground with the other. Was that the sound of water? Not much of a sound. A trickle really.

Cynthia was crawling at full speed, putting her ear to the ground every couple of knee-scraped paces to verify the direction. Evangeline followed closely behind and as the sound became clearer she rose to her feet and looked ahead. There was a tiny stream just in front of them.

Evangeline ran over to it and dropped to her knees again when she reached it. It was miniscule. Just a twisting, skinny worm of water which appeared to be coming from the town and going towards the forest in a curved way.

Cynthia was now beside her and tried to scoop whatever actual water she could from the tiny stream. Evangeline joined her, but having little luck extracting the water with her hands she stuck her face in the dirt and tried to get whatever she could straight out by sucking at it. Cynthia, without even flinching, did the same.

It was hard to say if they managed to drink much but even some liquid on their faces and cheeks refreshed them enough for them to get up and begin to walk again. With the now scorching afternoon sun and burning hunger, the trek was manageable only due to the addition of the muddy water stops.

At around 2:00 p.m., more than ten hours after they had started walking, they both fell over by a puddle slightly larger than the rest. Cynthia, rolling over on her back, suggested that they just nap for an hour.

Evangeline was tempted. She could barely feel her limbs. After a minute's consideration she forced herself up though.

"No," Evangeline said, "we have to reach the city before the sun goes down."

"There's lights in towns," Cynthia said.

"Not in this town," Evangeline grabbed Cynthia's hand and pulled her up. "otherwise we would have seen them last night. There was nothing blocking the view."

Cynthia pondered this and her face looked slightly uncomfortable. They looked at each other and began to walk again.

Another hour later and Cynthia exclaimed in sudden exhilaration "Look! A leftover road! Maybe this was like some gold town that got deserted. Oh, God, I hope there's a redneck with a phone left."

It was true. There were remnants of a cobblestone road, however, it did not go to the city, but rather alongside it, coming from somewhere to their left. Regular cobblestone roads had small, regular rocks forming them though. This was like a cobblestone highway. Unrealistically huge slabs of stones formed the road, flattened to a massive, round perfection.

The road ended near the stream where it had apparently at one point opened up into some type of cobblestone-slab courtyard. Standing in the barren leftovers of the courtyard the question lay in whether to follow the stream or leave it for the road.

The closer they got to the city the clearer they could see that there was a massive wall surrounding it in medieval style. The only reason the city was even visible was because it rose gradually up the cliffs beyond it, allowing a slight view of its higher positioned dwellings when seen from a distance. And there was that one building, taller than all the rest, the tips of its massive roofs coming up above the wall. The only thing they could tell about it from this distance was that it was a light grey, almost white in the sun, with multitudes of towers and turrets.

The wall surrounding the city was truly humongous and though still far off, the ground leading to it was flat and let them see that it was very intact looking and thus, for the two of them, impenetrable. If the structure followed the regular medieval city layout there would be a main gate. What would generally lead to the main gate would be a road. So, knowing it was the logical thing to do, they unwillingly left the stream to follow the road.

They walked alongside the looming wall for another forty-five minutes before the road reached a T-intersection with an even larger cobblestone slab highway. The left arm of the T went towards the forest, while the right arm directed them straight to the city. Evangeline stood in the middle of this cobblestone highway and turned in a full circle, looking from the forest along the road and towards the city.

It was a sight which held on to the afterthought of magnificence. She still saw the awe-inspiring beauty of this amazing road, leading straight to thundering rock mountains, along which snaked an incredible wall, higher than any wall she had ever seen in movies or life. Even through her intense fatigue and dehydration she thought of how breathtaking this would have looked if the ground around it for many days worth of walking were not a horrible wasteland.

The magnificence of what they were seeing gave them a small perk of energy and they trekked towards the wall, now along the main road. They could see a difference in the wall's surface at the ending of the road and hoped it was the outline of a gate.

Suddenly Cynthia scratched her head and turned towards the forest, "It's weird. The burned ground seems to end almost in a straight line along the forest, doesn't it? It's like someone drew a line and then burned from it towards the city."

Evangeline looked around and nodded a "hmm" in agreement, too tired for any other comment. She turned around again and continued walking forwards.

As they neared the wall, their steps slowed. They began to clearly see that there was in fact some sort of gate and it was most definitely shut. Eventually, they stood at the gate dumbfounded; the gate was a rock gate. Two humongous slabs of stone, each one over five meters in height and at least three meters in width, looking as if carved straight from a mountain, were placed side by side, closing off a square opening in the wall.

"How the fuck are you supposed to open that?" Cynthia's voice was shaking, "Who lives here? Giants?"

"It looks like no one is supposed to open this," Evangeline said dully.

"Fuck that. They're letting us in. I can't walk anymore. I can't…" Cynthia began to cry and banged her fists on the huge rocks, shouting at the wall to open.

"Cynthia, stop," Evangeline said, barely audibly. The hope of an entrance into this place was what had kept her walking with no food and barely any water. Now, with that hope gone she felt as if her feet would crumble into dust beneath her.

Cynthia had now apparently lost it and was kicking the wall and screaming. Evangeline tiredly grabbed her from behind and tried to pull her away from the wall, resulting in the two of them falling down on the dusty road.

"Cynthia, stop." Evangeline tried to sound strict as Cynthia sobbed into her hands. "If there is anyone inside I doubt they can even hear us pounding on these rocks. There's no point. We have to think of something else."

"What? What?! I don't want to think of anything else. Where the fuck are we? What is this?!" Cynthia sobbed loudly and Evangeline put her arms around her and they both rocked slowly back and forth.

Evangeline was staring at the dust around them as they rocked. She didn't know how to mentally combine this place, her dreams, and the sword that had brought them here. She wanted advice. She wanted to say everything she was thinking. She wanted to think *with* someone. But Cynthia wasn't the person. Not only had she gotten them into this without warning Cynthia, never thinking it would actually work, but Cynthia could barely handle what was happening, without even knowing the other details.

She kept rocking Cynthia and after some minutes Cynthia seemed calmer and the sobs became small, intermittent chokes. Evangeline let her go and got to her feet warily. They had to keep moving. Find something. She took Cynthia's arm and Cynthia let herself be pulled up as she wiped the dirty tears off her face with her other hand.

"Let's walk along the wall back to the stream," Evangeline said.

Cynthia only whispered "Okay" and obediently began to barely trudge behind Evangeline. The trip along the wall back towards the stream was a slow, painful, assault with each step. They finally reached the stream again at the point where it trickled out from beneath the great wall. It had apparently at one point been a slightly larger water source as the space through which it came out from under the wall had been a bit greater but had at some point also been covered with rocks. The rocks were fitted tightly together, allowing only that bare trickle of water through.

"I think we can move a couple of these," Evangeline said, getting down on her knees and grabbing at a rock, "These aren't that large. Come on, Cynthia." Evangeline said as she pulled on a rock. It was heavier that it looked and it took all her strength to budge it. Cynthia sighed and crawled over. She grabbed the rock with Evangeline and their combined strength fully dislodged it. After shuffling a couple more rocks they made a hole big enough for them to squeeze through, one at a time. They took turns looking into it but it was impossible to see much through the tight space. Other than the sound of water, only cemetery-like silence reached their ears.

"Let's sneak in quietly," Cynthia said, looking at Evangeline bug-eyed.

Evangeline nodded in agreement. They could get in, hide somewhere and observe what was going on it this bizarre, walled-off world of silence.

"Want me to go first?" Evangeline said, more out of some sense of guilt than willingness.

"Hell yes."

Evangeline squeezed her body into the stream-filled hole in the wall and yelped from the cold, plummeting into deeper water as soon as she pushed through to the other side. Here the messy stream turned into a little, manicured canal, both its sides and bottom lined with yet more perfectly flattened rocks. She pushed herself up the rock sides and stepped out of the water. As soon as she was out, she crouched down and hugged herself both for warmth and a sense of security. Shivering, she looked around.

The structures surrounding her were medieval in architecture, though with a certain twist, which probably came from the fact that they all had a coat of colourful paint covering them. The shades were mild in hue and gave the place an antique fisherman's village feel, with their sunset blues, and mild greens and yellows.

Everything around her was impeccable...and dead. It reminded her of a pioneer amusement village – a fake town, stylized in the fashion of what used to be, now shut down for the season. She wobbled over in her crouched position as close to the hole as she could get without re-entering the freezing water and holler-whispered through it to Cynthia "It's completely empty. Come on."

"Okay." Evangeline heard the sound of splashing water as well as some muted swear words and knew the cold of the stream had hit Cynthia. Soon enough Cynthia's head popped out through the constrictive opening and grabbing onto Cynthia's arm, Evangeline helped her crawl out. They both crouched, shivering for another minute, looking around silently.

The canal went towards a simple, turned off water fountain and spread out around it in a circle, then it narrowed slightly again and went off to the left. The spot where the fountain stood was like a roundabout which opened up in a circular cobbled space with five cobbled streets leading out of it. The smallest and shortest street was the one that led towards the wall and them, and it was more a park alley than a street actually. A couple of small benches, carved out of rock, sat alongside of it and lined the miniscule canal. Grass stretched out to the left and right of the path.

"The grass didn't burn here," Evangeline said as she stood up and her shoes squished into the green.

"I guess the wall stopped the fire," Cynthia responded, looking down and around them. "It's not very long though. It looks like it's been cut. Do you think there's someone left in here? Like some sort of caretaker?" Cynthia's voice began to rise in excitement but Evangeline put her fingers to her lips.

"Shh..." Evangeline said, "I was kind of thinking initially that this looks like one of those pioneer villages that they make for tourists. Doesn't it? Everything is perfectly manicured...but there's no one here...like it's got that creepy 'Shining' feel to it...like some psychotic caretaker is going to pop out any minute..."

"Okay, unfortunately I saw that movie" Cynthia whispered, "like I wasn't freaked out enough before.

They walked quietly towards the fountain, looking left and right every couple of seconds. From the fountain emerged the other four streets: two streets ran left and right paralleling the wall, the third street followed the canal ahead and the last went off slightly to the right of it. Painted, single, double and triple story buildings ran alongside each street and all streets looked about the size of a one-way road, with raised, cobbled sidewalks lining their sides.

They were about to stick to the canal road, which seemed to lead to the heart of the silent city, when Evangeline twisted her head towards the far right-angled street, "Is it me, or did you hear something this way?"

The two of them walked a couple of steps into the right-hand road. Evangeline craned her neck. Nothing could be heard besides the muted trickling of water through the wall when suddenly a far-off screech reached them. It was impossible to know if it was animal, machine or human through the muted distance. However, it was a sound.

They looked at each other and with wordless comprehension walked soundlessly down the right-hand road. As they entered further into the street, Evangeline thought she saw a pair of curtains shuffle in one of the buildings across the street. She squinted her eyes at the windows but all was unmoving. Cynthia gave her a questioning look but she just shook her head in dismissal and they continued their tiptoed walk.

Evangeline had no urge to enter any of the houses, even though it made sense to. They felt forbidding, the sunlit street somehow feeling safer than whatever darkness lay behind all the thick, opaque curtains which covered each and every window. Cynthia said nothing, only hugged her arms around herself as they walked and Evangeline was pretty sure she felt the same.

After a while they began to hear some more dispersed sounds. It was still hard to tell what they were exactly but now they definitely sounded more animal in nature. It was like a distant clucking with occasional, louder oinking. They gave each other confused looks and continued. The closer they got, the more certain it became that there were chickens and pigs in the vicinity, and lots of them. Suddenly they both froze and Evangeline stared, open mouthed.

The road had turned a corner and opened up into a square, at one end of which she saw metal. It sparkled with a strange sheen in the late afternoon sun and seemed to flow, as one uninterrupted web, which formed itself into an intricate fence that stood ludicrously high, and beyond which they saw the largest chicken farm that either had ever witnessed in their lives.

The farm stretched on, all the way to the mountain wall, still quite far away, with thousands of chickens neatly separated into small, square feeding grounds, each ground with its own little coop. A small trail ran from square patch to square patch, as far as the eye could see, in organized, controlled perfection. And still, there was not a human in sight.

Evangeline walked to the fence and laid her hand on it. The metal gave her a tingly feeling for a second. She looked at her hand against it and saw that where she touched it, the metal let off a pinkish sheen. She removed her hand and the pink disappeared from the metal. Cynthia came up beside her and did the same.

"Look...over there," Cynthia pointed, "There's some pigs...that's it. Chickens and pigs..." Cynthia looked at Evangeline and furrowed her brows, "Do you know how to kill a chicken?"

"My grandmother had some," Evangeline said, "I think she just chopped their heads off because I remember one of the chickens running around with no head for like a minute..."

Cynthia gave her a revolted look. They were both weak with hunger but not quite yet at the point of chopping chicken heads.

"I don't even know what to think...," Evangeline said after a minute of standing and listening to the chickens cluck horrendously, with an occasional oink of an annoyed pig adding to the chorus. She looked to her side. Cynthia had disappeared. She spun in a terrified circle and breathed a sigh of confused relief when she saw Cynthia climbing a tree in a circular patch of greenery in the middle of the open square.

"What the-" Evangeline stopped short when she heard teeth crunching on food. She ran over to Cynthia and almost got knocked on the head by a fruit that Cynthia chucked at her. Evangeline stumbled backwards but caught the fruit and looked at it. It was a regular apple. She bit in hungrily.

Cynthia climbed down off the small tree and together they examined the other trees in the patch. They were a mix of apple and pear and after they finished their apples they picked off a pear each. Evangeline stared at her pear in between bites, wondering if it was really this spectacularly tasty or if she was simply starving.

"Damn, how do we take some more with us?" Evangeline pondered as they both filled their hands with fruit that they had nowhere to put due to the tightness of their now dishevelled party outfits.

"Okay. Let's just go into one of the houses," Cynthia said, "There has to be something in them. It's going to be dark soon anyways. We need to go in somewhere."

"Alright," Evangeline breathed out slowly as they both looked at the closest houses facing them. She may have gotten a slight sugar rush from the fruit but she was still feeling wary about entering any of the fully curtained, perfectly manicured buildings.

Cynthia seemed to have lost her fear though, "Come *on*. There's *nothing* here," she said in a frustrated tone, "like no one and nothing. So, let's get the hell inside, stay quiet and see if anyone comes out to feed the chickens, right?"

"Alright. That one," Evangeline pointed to a house ahead, which had a larger set of ground level windows than the others, though dark curtains were still drawn tightly closed over them from within, just like everywhere else.

"Okay," was all that Cynthia said as she managed to stretch her shirt over a couple of pears. Holding her fruit in her t-shirt-basket she walked briskly to the house in question. Evangeline put the fruits she had been holding gently down on the ground, wiped her hands on her pants and slowly followed Cynthia.

Cynthia put her hand on the old-style handle of the large, wooden door and they looked at each other when it simply clicked open. Without any resistance or even the tiniest of creeks, the door swung smoothly in. Light streamed in from the outside to illuminate a small corridor with a sitting area to the left of it.

"Close the door," Cynthia whispered, entering, "we don't want anyone to know we are in here for now, right? At least until we know that the caretaker from 'The Shining' isn't the one feeding the chickens and trimming the grass."

"Wait," Evangeline said, stepping in also, "Find a light switch first. It's going to be pitch black in here if we shut the door."

They both scanned the walls around them but saw only an unused oil lamp hanging near the doorway. Evangeline stepped into the barely lit sitting room to their left, pulling open one of the thick curtains as she entered. "Let's open this for a sec…"

She was cut off by the sound of a swoosh and the slamming of a door. She screamed and Cynthia jumped back against the wall to the right of the entrance, dropping her fruit.

"Holy shit," Cynthia said, as the pears rolled around her feet.

Evangeline stood, covered by the light streaming in from the now open window. She scanned the room with her eyes. There was a small door in a far corner of it which was creaked slightly open. She looked over at Cynthia and signalled with a finger on her mouth for Cynthia to be silent.

"Hello...Who's in here? You Okay?" Evangeline called gently at the creak. She slowly put her hand on the other curtain and inched her way towards the door while simultaneously pulling the curtain open with her arm, lighting up the second half of the room.

The front door of the house was still open as well and it was hard to be sure over the sounds of the thousands of chicken clucks from across the square, but she thought she heard breathing, or possibly a garbled moan from behind the small door. As she neared the door, with the light from beyond the curtain following her, the creak kept diminishing until the door was almost completely shut.

"Maybe it's scared. Maybe it's hiding like us..." Cynthia half whispered, "close the curtain a little?"

Evangeline nodded slightly and began to slowly retreat in the same manner in which she had approached, holding on to the curtain and closing it slowly with each backwards step. The dark door began to open ever so slowly back up and the sound of deep breathing became more audible.

Evangeline had now closed the second half of the curtain back up and moved to the edge of the first half, about to close it also. Her eyes moved to the fading light outside and then back to the inside of the room. The light seemed to be some sort of controlling factor and she decided she didn't want to completely lose it. Rather than closing the first half of the curtain she stepped out of the light of the open half, and inched in the darkness towards the small door, along the closed curtain. Her right hand was behind her back, ready to grab the curtain and pull it open.

As she walked further and further away from the stream of light and into the dark corner where the door lay, the door began to open more, first just a little and then finally it flowed soundlessly open the entire way and the shape of a human-like creature stared at her, crouched in a dark corridor beyond.

It began to breathe aloud, the sound filling the room above the clucks and oinks from beyond the square. It was a man's voice, carried from the dark body like a sound carried by the wind.

"I'm so hungry. The smell is so good."

Cynthia, still by the front door, echoed through the room, "It's the fruit. Come out, we'll give you some."

Though she had used her normal voice, it sounded like a loud explosion in comparison to the windy sigh of the shadowed creature and inadvertently Evangeline turned her head towards Cynthia and away from the dark door. As she did so, the sigh of the voice turned to an animalistic growl and the thing partially leapt through the air at an inhuman velocity, straight at her.

Evangeline had no time to see it, its movements a blur, like a fan twirling on its highest level so that the individual blades can't be distinguished.

It grabbed her with both its hands, one ripping at her hair and the other around her waist as it tore her feet off the floor. Through her terrified screams she instinctively grabbed at the material at her fingertips and as the creature flung her with itself towards the back door the curtain in her clenched hand ripped off its rod and crashed down to the floor. As it did so, the light exploded into the room and on the two of them. The creature dropped Evangeline mid air with a horrendous howl of pain and she thought she heard a hissing sound, like that of boiling water, as it flung itself behind the door, the slam echoing throughout the house.

Chapter 16

THE GILDED CAGE

At first all Evangeline heard was ringing in her ears and everything spun as she tried to lift herself off the ground but fell back down. Her hand shakily grasped at her scalp where the thing had ripped at her hair and she was surprised to feel it still there beneath her fingers. She lifted herself up again and as her surroundings began to refocus, ear piercing screams registered from the front door.

Looking towards the sound of the scream in a state of confusion she saw that it was Cynthia, pressed against the wall with her back, shrieking at the top of her lungs with her eyes bulging out and appearing frozen in the open position.

Seeing Evangeline rise up, Cynthia's screams began to die down and turn into sporadic outbursts. Evangeline spun her head towards the corner door and saw that it was thankfully still closed shut and the torn off curtain completely illuminated it now. The door, like the rest of the room, the house and the city, was perfectly maintained, a new coat of paint covering its antique wood, which matched that of two little tables strewn about the room, each one with a matching, wooden chair beside it. There was nothing else in the immaculate interior.

Evangeline stood shakily and still facing the back door began to inch away from it backwards, towards Cynthia and the exit. When she stepped on her left foot though, her ankle gave way and she stumbled down in pain, grabbing at it. Her shock was now slightly subsiding and she was beginning to feel pain everywhere. Her foot was definitely badly sprained, if not broken.

Evangeline screamed as she felt two hands grab her from behind. She heard a female shriek echoed back in her ears and spun her head to see that it was Cynthia who had grabbed her under her arms and was pulling her backwards, out of the room and the house.

They got back to the middle of the square, Cynthia's face covered in dirty, tear-stained streaks and Evangeline still too shocked to feel much of anything besides her throbbing scalp and ankle.

Evangeline's eyes went up to the sky. She grabbed Cynthia's arm, "We need to hide. It's afraid of the light, Cynthia."

Cynthia looked up at the sky with realization on her face and grabbed Evangeline under her armpit, looping her arm around her back for support. The sun wasn't far from setting. They had to get as far away from the thing in the house as possible before they lost the safety of the light.

"Where? What if there's more of them?" Cynthia spun in a terrified half circle, pulling Evangeline around with her.

"I don't know," Evangeline responded, her breath raspy with fear.

"They could be in every house, Evangeline," Cynthia said, "We can't go in the houses."

Evangeline's head was spinning as she looked at the animals behind the strange fence, "what if we hide with the chickens? There's thousands of them."

Cynthia looked at the animals. "No…" she said, her chest heaving intermittently as she spoke, "They're some sort of cannibal freaks… and that's the only live meat here…except us. They're all coming here after dark. That's why the chickens are freaking."

Evangeline looked more closely at the chickens and saw that Cynthia was right. The more the sun descended, the more agitated they became. The pigs, though not as manic as the chickens, seemed to be oinking and squealing more pathetically also. She looked back at Cynthia, "How do you know they're cannibals?"

Cynthia swallowed hard and her body shook, "I saw his face when he jumped. It wasn't normal. Not normal human...It wanted to eat you."

Cynthia's face began to scrunch and she swallowed again, this time in a loud gulp, visibly trying to control the crying. "It was trying to eat you," she repeated, "like really eat you. We can't leave, Evangeline. They know we're here now. Even if we get out of this town, they'll find us in the dirt outside the wall. There's nowhere to hide."

"The castle?" Evangeline said and looked towards the peaks visible against the mountains, over the rooftops of the houses.

"You mean that church thing?" Cynthia said, looking the same way.

"Yes. Castle. Church. I don't know."

Evangeline began to pull Cynthia towards a street leading from the square in the direction of the building in question, leaning on her for support. She could barely step on her quickly swelling foot.

"Why wouldn't they be in there also?" Cynthia garbled out, as she let herself be pulled.

"I don't know. Churches are sanctuaries, right? Maybe you're right. Maybe it's a church. And it's big. We can find something to hide inside of. Or maybe there'll be something on the way. Let's go. Away from the animals at least."

Evangeline tugged at Cynthia harder. Cynthia looked from the animals to the house of horror they had just gotten out of and nodded, picking up her pace.

They ran down the cobbled street as if in a three-legged race with Evangeline using Cynthia as support. The light was leaving quickly now and their urgency grew with each step and each fading ray. They were barely paying attention to their surroundings, looking around only for something...anything other than one of the houses...that might shelter them.

Suddenly a flash of red caught Evangeline's eye and she turned her face to see a white house with flowers all around it. Their various red, yellow, orange and blue petals almost sparkled in the evening rays and their intense numbers up and down each level of the house's balconies made her body freeze, almost making the two of them fall over as Cynthia pulled against the resistance.

"What are you doing? Did you see something?" Cynthia said breathlessly.

Evangeline shook her head and began to run again with Cynthia's support, but her face was glued backwards to that house. The house from the hospital dream. Then, as her face turned in almost unreal slow-motion forwards again, the silhouette of the monstrous, architectural wonder rose out from beyond a twist in the road. She saw its walls, exactly as in her dream. The towers and turrets all came into view and the memory of the dead, bleeding girl at the top of one of those walls began to pound in her head like a hammer. Her breath became harsher and harsher as they ran straight to the building and her body started convulsing as Cynthia pulled her through an expansive open square and up the building steps, directly to its front doors.

Cynthia looked at Evangeline's shaking body, "Do not crack. I can't keep it together in this place without you. You're the weird one that acts like surreal situations are perfectly typical. You can't start acting like a regular human being now, freaking out in situations like this. This is the time for you to stay weird."

Evangeline was hunched over, breathing in and out loudly like an asthmatic and shaking from head to toe. Her mind was focused on the vision of that dead girl...she might still be at the top of this building...and...and the woman with that extremely long, grey hair...and the man. If everything was real then so where they. In her dreams they hadn't wanted to eat her or tear her apart like that thing in the house. In her dreams they were here, inside this building.

Her breathing calmed slightly at this thought and she looked up at Cynthia who had apparently been repeating the same thing for a while, "Do not crack. You are not allowed to crack. Do not crack."

"Okay," Evangeline responded and nodded at Cynthia. She straightened out and put her hand on the massive door, looked upwards towards the peaks of the building and stopped, "This is the Milan Duomo."

"What?" Cynthia asked.

"The church in Bambi's book about Italy. The one she kept staring at for days," Evangeline said.

"I don't remember," Cynthia said, "but this isn't a church. I thought it was from far away, but it's a castle."

Evangeline stared up. It was true. It was like they had taken a photograph of the Milan Duomo and stretched it left and right, adding flat, long, corridorial parts and turning the stained glass into simple, clear panes, somehow taking the main pieces of the church and reconstructing them into a living space. But they hadn't taken just any church. It was the main church in Milan. It was an icon in Italy.

"It's true," Evangeline said, "It's not the same, but...so similar. Like a remastered copy."

"Okay. The only thing I can hear is that this has something to do with Bambi," Cynthia said, "that means she might be inside here for me to kill. So, I'm keeping that thought as my going point right now. Ready?"

Cynthia put her hands on the ancient handle of the huge, engraved door and looked at Evangeline expectantly. Evangeline put her own hands on top of Cynthia's and nodded. They both pulled the door with their combined strength. Just like the door of the house, it was unlocked, and its massive weight began to slide open slowly. When the crack was just large enough for them to squeeze through they stopped pulling and squished together to look inside.

There was a large, open space with rows of pillars on each side, leading from the doors to what had to be the pulpit, just like in the actual Italian church that Evangeline had looked at in the books. The pews were not there though and through the darkness she could make out that the raised, pulpit area in the back also seemed to be missing an altar and instead held only some large chairs. Not much else was visible in the small stream of light.

"We can't go in there in the darkness," Cynthia said, "Are there curtains?"

They forced the door open more and stuck their heads in slightly farther. In fact, most of the walls seemed to be covered by a rich material, the length of which they had never before seen, as it went all the way from the ceilings, which were around fifteen metres high, down to the floors.

Evangeline looked both left and right and suddenly had a strange urge to voice, "Lola?"

"What?" Cynthia asked.

"Nothing. Sorry...look, there's curtains everywhere...left or right?"

"I don't know," Cynthia looked from side to side, "Left?"

"Okay," Evangeline said.

They pulled one half of the substantial door open as far as it would go, letting in a stream of slowly dying light, which in its tired glow illuminated only a small, front strip of the inside space.

Cynthia put her arm around Evangeline again, Evangeline let out a deep breath and they began to sprint.

They were half-way to their goal when she heard breathing behind them. Or was it all around them? She screamed and Cynthia's scream joined hers as a flash of dark material whirled in front of them. She kept running, screaming as she raced, when Cynthia was suddenly ripped away from her and Evangeline fell to the ground, still shrieking.

She tried to get herself up, her head spinning in circles, looking for Cynthia, when she was lifted up into the air by something from behind. She flew backwards through the interior of the building at lightning speed, her screams filling the air. Everything was whisking by and she tried to turn herself towards whatever was carrying her. She felt a metal hard hand on the back of her shirt and was spun forwards and again flung down to crash onto a hard surface in a heap of pain.

Evangeline lifted her head and saw Cynthia lying in a similar heap beside her, sobbing and shrieking, her hands encircling her head for protection.

Something clanged right by her feet and a woman's windchime-like voice spoke in a tone that was both authoritative and desperate, "Lock it. NOW."

They both turned their faces towards the voice but all they saw was a swoosh of long, white hair disappearing into the darkness. For a second there was a sound of a man howling in the distance and then there was nothing left except the still darkness surrounding their sobs and shakes.

Evangeline lifted herself up into an unsteady sitting position and saw that they were actually in what appeared to be a vast, metal cage in the middle of a dark room. Each side of the cage was made of bars which seemed to entwine themselves like vines into a perfectly rectangular shape, just like the ones surrounding the animals in the town. The bars completely surrounded them, even continuing above them to form a ceiling and under the platform that had been placed within the cage, and which they were sitting on.

Without thinking, Evangeline crawled frantically to the walls of the cage, groping in the dark for a way out. She found the open door and grabbed at Cynthia, pulling her towards it. In her confused terror, she would have flung them both out and run without purpose in any direction if Cynthia hadn't hurled herself at her at the last moment. Cynthia crawled right over her and stuck a key inside the cage door, quickly locking it.

"The woman threw the cage key to us," Cynthia said, "They aren't keeping us in. They are trying to keep something out."

It took Evangeline a second to absorb this and as she was doing so the same man's holler echoed through the building and they flung themselves towards each other in renewed terror. They sat silently, tightly squeezed against each other until the hollering slowly died out. When nothing could be heard anymore, Evangeline moved slightly away from Cynthia and turned her head in a slow, jagged circle, grasping their surroundings and trying to piece together their situation. She quietly voiced her one preoccupying thought, "But...if she's trying to keep something out then why isn't she in the cage with us?"

Chapter 17

REOPENING

The bowl of chips crashed down and Raffael shouted obscenities, rushing at the bolt of lighting through which his sister had just disappeared. He jumped on the table, his hands out, ready to try to grab at it when Bambi was flung at him back from within the bolt. She was holding the sword clenched in both fists and screaming with her eyes closed. The sword was too heavy for her to lift fully up or she would have skewered Raffael with it. Instead, it pointed downwards and barely missed one of his legs.

Raffael grabbed her around the shoulders with both hands, trying to save his limbs, and they both stumbled off the edge of the desk, crashing into Ian and Mark, who had run towards the desk as well.

Bambi opened her eyes, manically skimmed the faces around her, and went silent. Everyone was stock still for a second, just staring at her.

Raffael recovered himself first and looked back to the bolt to see it slowly retreat upwards before his eyes. His head spun towards Bambi and with his hands still around her shoulders he flung her towards the table, shouting, "Open it! Get them out!"

At being brought closer to the bolt Bambi went into hysterics. Her eyes bulged out at the sword, still in her hands and she thrust it as far as she could across the floor and away from herself, wrenching herself out of Raffael's grip. The sword skated across the floor and smashed into a wall, just missing Val's ankles and making her topple over. The crash of the sword was met with an equal crash coming from the bolt of lighting as it suddenly collapsed in on itself and disappeared.

Raffael's furious scream was muffled by the sound of all of them being flung across the room in various directions as the electric surge of the collapsed bolt ran through the floor.

They lifted themselves up slowly, everyone in shock. Monica must have re entered the room right behind Raffael and slammed the door shut because now they heard some knocks and confused enquiries coming through it at them. Monica stared at the door, then at Raffael. Shakily, she pressed her back against the door, still in the sitting position. Ian got up and shouted out at the door, "Go away. Find your own Ouija board!" Raffael looked at him and Ian said, "It's the only thing I could think of. We don't want them coming in, right?"

The banging on the door stopped as Raffael got up and stumbled over back to Bambi, who was whimpering in a corner in the fetal position and did not even look up. Raffael grabbed Bambi, pulled her roughly to her feet and dragged her towards the table.

"Open it," His voice was slow and dangerously even. No one moved or made a sound, except Bambi, who whimpered in his grip. "Open it," he repeated. His breathing became rough when she refused to do or say anything besides whimper. Monica grabbed one of his arms,

"Raffael, stop. Let her go. She can barely stand. What happened Bambi?"

With that, Monica began pulling Raffael's hands off of Bambi. As Raffael's grip loosened, Bambi looked up at his face, "It's too late already." Her voice was barely more than a whisper.

"What? It's not too late. You just did it. Do it again," Raffael turned away from her and went to the table. He jumped up on top of it, joining Val, who was already standing on it and staring up at the ceiling. Only a perfect, thin slit could be seen where the lightning had entered and then slid slightly open. Nothing else was even touched.

"It's too late," Bambi repeated. She lowered herself to the floor and silently cried, her eyes staring off at nothing, "They are dead now."

Everyone froze.

"Okay. I'm done here. This is fucking crazy. I was never here. Leave me the fuck out of it," Jack stated and he went for the door before anyone could stop him.

As he opened the door and ran out the sound of police car sirens came into range and everyone in the room looked from one to the other. *What had been seen from the outside?* Raffael thought. *The party wasn't loud. Who had called the police? Why?*

As far as their parents knew, Raffael wasn't here. Evangeline had been given the keys to the house to host a small get together. This was also the story she had passed around to the party guests and since, except for the people in the room, no one knew who Raffael was, it wasn't hard.

Now, besides not being fond of the idea of himself or Monica being arrested, charged with giving alcohol to minors and potentially losing his medical license, Raffael had no time to get involved with the police. They needed to reopen the portal and a cop would not be likely to help them with a chanting circle.

He looked around and his eyes fell on where the sword had been on the floor to see that Ian was holding it up. He ran over and pulled it out of Ian's hands. Dragging the sword with one arm, he grabbed Bambi with the other and pulled both to the duffel bag. He put the sword back in and noticing Bambi's funeral hat on the floor, grabbed that also and shoved it into the bag. Looking over at the others in the room he said,

"The police will think you're insane if you tell them any of this. Just leave. You saw nothing. I'll get them back." He looked at Bambi in his grip "*You* are coming with me," and then at Monica off to the side "I'm sorry for everything. I'll drive you to your car."

Bambi, shaking in his grip, let herself be dragged at a running pace, out of the room and out the back door. Monica followed them, seemingly at a temporary loss for words. They ran through the back yard and out a back alley where Raffael had re-parked his car earlier. While they ran he kept hollering at the quivering Bambi, "What did you see? You said it's too late. Did something happen to them? Did you see something happen?"

"I didn't see it," Bambi said, "but I know where they are. No one can survive there. No one. It's all...dead people..."

"What?!" Raffael stopped momentarily and shoved his face into Bambi's, "I know you are into this vampire, goth bullshit but this isn't the time!"

"Bambi, this is serious," Monica interjected breathlessly as she ran behind them, "Raffael is right. No one wants to hear this right now."

They reached the car and Bambi just looked at the two of them dejectedly, her ghastly, white makeup a tear-stained mess and her mouth slightly open.

Raffael dug in his pocket for the car keys, frustrated, but opting for heavier questioning as soon as they got away from the party and the police cars. He knew what he saw. He had now seen it twice. But he didn't need this useless, fantasy crap from the new generation of goth-teen. He just needed to find Evangeline, right now.

He clicked the car open and spun around at the sound of heavy breathing behind them. He was almost relieved to see Ian, and not a cop, standing by the car with Val, Mark and Liza running up right behind him.

"This is incredible!" Mark said breathlessly, "You didn't think you could ditch us?"

"Where'd you really get that sword?" Ian asked and Raffael looked at his face to find that Ian's eyebrows were raised at him. What did this kid want?

"There's no point trying to un-involve us," Ian continued, "We are all involved and it's kind of hard to forget what we saw. The cops might come out back, so open the car and let's go."

There was no time to argue. Raffael opened the door, and giving Ian a harsh look, motioned for all of them to get in. Monica and Raffael were in the front, with Bambi and the others squashed and piled on top of each other in the back.

Everyone was mostly silent, barely able to breathe in their pile, as they made their way to Monica's car, a bit further down the road. They drove slowly through an intersection near the party house to get to it, all looking out the window at the cops assembled outside.

"That's a lot of cops for a noise complaint," Val commented barely audibly, her cheek squashed up against the window. Raffael mentally counted four cop cars.

"What the fuck?" he said, staring at the last police vehicle. He turned to Monica, "Monica, why is Daniel here?"

"What? Who?"

"Daniel. There. From the PNH support."

Raffael pointed to a figure sitting in the last cop car, apparently trying to stay out of view.

"There?" Monica stretched her neck past him to try and see, "That's strange...it definitely looks like him."

Daniel's face began to turn towards them and Raffael quickly turned his own face away and pressed on the gas, getting the car through the intersection and out of view.

"What? Why are you hiding from him?" Monica asked, "What's going on?"

Raffael didn't respond, suddenly wondering how Monica was part of all of this and what her involvement with Daniel was. He looked at her face. She was looking at him open-mouthed, in utter confusion. He breathed out slowly and slightly relaxed.

They reached Monica's car and now had to split into two groups, which seemed to suddenly wake everyone out of their individual stupors.

"What's going on Raffael?" was Monica's first question, followed by Ian, Mark and Val speaking over each other, with Raffael being able to decipher only a percentage of what was said,

"What happened to Evangeline? Where did she go? Is she Okay?" Val kept asking.

"That was so fucking incredible. I can't wait to open that thing up again! I should have jumped on the table. I can't believe they went and I stayed!" Mark kept exclaiming.

"Why aren't you surprised about what happened? You are upset, but not surprised. It's like splitting lighting is a normal sight for you." Ian and Monika kept interjecting.

Only the scrawny Liza remained silent, not moving from the car where she sat right beside Bambi, looking at her as if at an object of great fragility and importance.

Raffael sighed and threw up his hands slightly, "People, we need to split up. Half of you with me – that half includes Bambi – and half with Monica. We can't stay here. We need to find a place to reopen the portal."

Ian and Val simultaneously opened their mouths to interject but he quickly put up his hand, "Stop. I will explain. Let's just get out of here first...Okay., Homer Watson Park. I'll go down Wilson Road to the dead end. We can talk there."

When they all scampered out of the cars at the end of Wilson Road, Monica's phone rang. Everyone looked at her. It was doubtful to Raffael that it could be anyone besides the police this late at night. She picked up the call, mouthing a confirmation, "It's the police."

A shush went over the group as they listened to her half of the conversation.

"Oh...yes...I allowed my friend's little sister to have a get-together with some friends...what? No. I had absolutely no idea. Is everyone alright?...What about the house? Everything is Okay...The girl's name? Yes, Evangeline Kennedy. Let me try her cell phone...no, not necessary to call her parents if no harm was done. I will talk to her...I am in Hamilton right now. It will take an hour for me to get there...Okay., sure. I am on my way."

When she finally hung up Raffael smiled earnestly at her, "Thanks Monica. Really," he said.

Monica smiled and shrugged a little. Even after everything that had just happened Raffael thought he could discern her blushing in the darkness.

"It's your sister," Monica said, "We have about an hour to an hour and a half before I should be at the house if I'm driving from Hamilton. There's going to be a police man still there, apparently waiting for me to sign some forms."

"Don't let on that you saw Daniel," Raffael said, "to anyone. Especially to Daniel."

"Alright, Raffael, but, this is the time when you tell us what just happened."

It was the first time Raffael had recounted to anyone what had actually happened to them twelve years ago. It felt good, albeit strange to state it all, the way it actually was, without justifying it or attempting to make it sound "normal".

While he was talking he realized that it was acceptable for someone like Bambi to talk about seeing aliens, vampires or portals. That was her "package". Hearing a professional, grown man say the same things sounded frightening and he noticed that even Mark, who till this point had been annoyingly excited, now looked uncomfortable.

When he finished the story in as brief a mode as possible, Val was the first to speak. Rather than sounding disbelieving, she sounded hollow, "So all those paintings in her room...those were people you saw...she saw. All those years. She never said a word to me."

Raffael shrugged.

"Why didn't she say anything?" Val looked at him accusingly.

"Come on. Before today, would you have believed her?" Ian answered for Raffael.

"Yeah...no. But all this? She *knew* what she was getting *all* of us into. That lightening might have killed us. She knew that. *You* knew that," Val's eyes bore into Raffael's face and he felt a sense of guilt, though it was quickly overshadowed by frustration at every delay to reopening the portal.

"Val, we didn't think any of this would work. I only joined you so that no one would skewer themselves with the sword, and to get Evangeline off my back. Neither one of us thought that Bambi was actually 'authentic'. No offence, Bambi." He looked over at Bambi and shrugged his shoulders non-apologetically. She only shrugged back.

"Alright," Ian said, "now you tell us about this portal opening, Bambi."

Bambi seemed to cower in a ball within herself again, "I don't know," she sobbed, "It never worked before. I just thought...maybe with...but...I tried so many times before..."

"Why didn't they come back with you?" Monica asked.

"Why would you leave them?" Raffael added, anger again building up inside him. This set off a new stream of tears and started Bambi's hysterics again, "I know it's my fault. But you can't go there. They are dead and it's my fault. But, I won't kill all of you!"

"You just said you saw nothing!" Raffael hollered and Bambi began to scream through her tears.

Raffael shook his head, opened the car door and threw the duffel bag out onto the ground, determined to get this thing started whether Bambi assisted willingly or not. He opened the bag and Bambi, looking over and seeing the gleam of the sword started shrieking again, and spinning on her heels made a run for it.

Mark, the closest to her, caught her in three large leaps, pounced on her and threw her down on the ground. With her face in the dirt, she continued shrieking. Ian and Monica ran over and Ian put his hand tightly over Bambi's mouth while Mark held her down.

Bambi was struggling but Ian and Mark kept their grips while Monica paced around them, repeating in a worried tone, "Okay. Just don't hurt her. Keep her down, but gently. Don't hurt her."

Ian suddenly narrowed his eyes, looked down at Bami and said "Bambi, you've seen this sword before, haven't you?"

Bambi stopped shrieking and Ian let go of her mouth, got up and walked over to the duffel bag. He dragged the sword out a bit and looked pointedly at Bambi. She immediately started quivering at the sight of the object. But, as they waited, she refused to utter a single word.

"She's not going to tell us, "Val said, "So, let's just do this."

Raffael looked at Val. Her voice was completely toneless.

"Okay," Mark said, his voice full of excited purpose again, even though he was still restraining Bambi, "until Bambi talks, why don't we try to redo this ourselves? I can remember part of that chant thing. So, let's start from the beginning. Come on. The weird, no-touching circle first." He looked down at his victim, "Okay, I'm letting you go now, but don't start freaking out again. Okay?" Bambi nodded and sat up on the ground as Mark let her go and stood up.

"Lindsay? Lorry?" Mark looked at the miniature Liza, squinting his eyes, "You. Yes, you. Just sit with her and keep her relaxed, Okay?" Liza nodded and walking over, sat down beside Bambi, still not having said a single word.

Mark pulled the duffel bag slightly further from the car and motioned for Ian, Val, Monica and Raffael to stand around it with him. Raffael rubbed his chin and squinted his eyes at Mark, not particularly full of confidence with this new-found leader, but followed suit anyways.

They redid the stance with their hands almost touching and began to re-chant the repeated bits and pieces of Bambi's chant that they remembered, with Mark attempting to sound as Bambi had, but instead coming out like a wailing dog.

After some time Raffael couldn't take it anymore and dropped his hands, grunting.

"Come on!" Mark said, "Oh...wait. This is what happened last time too. We all stopped and then Bambi and Evangeline threw themselves on the sword," saying this Mark threw himself on the opened duffel bag.

"God, I can't believe we are friends," Ian grunted as he went down on his knees and dropped on top of Mark and the sword. Val was getting down on her knees as well and Raffael threw up his hands, about to join unwillingly when he heard the rustle of leaves and the crack of a stick on the ground. He looked over and saw that both Bambi and Liza had made a run for it. Only a tiny flash of Bambi's white makeup could still be seen through the trees.

"Fuck. Catch them!" Raffael shouted and all of them scrambled up to run after them.

It was too late. In the darkness and cover of the trees there was no way they would find Bambi and Liza.

After a couple of minutes of running in circles Raffael stopped and began kicking at a tree. Then, terrified that they had been double duped he ran full speed back to the car. Only momentarily relieved to find the duffel bag still there with both the sword and hat inside, he plopped down on the ground and put his hands around his head, not knowing what to do now.

"Raffael," Ian said, arriving beside him, "Liza had a cell on her. I saw it. They will call for a ride and get home somehow. I'm sure. We can find them tomorrow."

"Where? Do you know where they live?" Raffael looked up at Ian with a trace of hope.

"Uhh. No. Actually, honestly, I don't even know Bambi's last name... but I can check last year's yearbook. We can go to her house tomorrow. She has to tell us something sooner or later. Anyways...look, It's Evangeline. She can do this."

"Bambi saw nothing," Val added, "we know that. She just went hysterical."

"Yeah, there was probably just too much sunlight on the other side and she thought she would turn to ash" Ian smirked at Raffael.

Raffael looked up at Ian, took his hand off his head and stretched it out towards him. Taking it, Ian helped Raffael up to his feet.

"Thanks," Raffael said.

"No problem," Ian smiled, "I'm just kissing ass so you won't kill me when I date Evangeline after she gets back."

Ian's dumb-ass smirk as well as the imbecilic joke in the middle of a serious situation were so precisely like something that Evangeline would do that Raffael had to snort in reply, "Well, you both have an idiotic sense of humour."

It was early morning by the time Raffael dropped off Val at her car and Ian and Mark at their homes. He wanted them to grab that yearbook and locate Bambi's last name and address immediately but knew it wasn't going to happen. All the respective parents would be up soon and would definitely not allow their teenage kids out in the early morning with a weird man. Even if they got Bambi's address and went to her home, assuming she had made it there safely, there would be no way to get past her parents.

There was nothing to do but go to his own parents' place and wait.

Evangeline and Cynthia were supposed to be sleeping over at Val's after the party so for now nothing would have to be explained to his parents. However, tomorrow the portal would have to be reopened or else both Cynthia and Evangeline would be found to be missing.

Monica, Ian and Mark were on board but Val was strangely non-committal, only shrugging and saying "fine" to everything. Raffael felt betrayed on behalf of Evangeline. He had always thought of Val as someone who would stand by a friend.

Monica told the police that the girls had simply run off scared when the cops came. She placed a couple of phone calls to Evangeline's and Cynthia's numbers so if they checked her phone there'd be a record of communication. As they all predicted, those phone calls went unanswered If Cynthia and Evangeline were found to be missing the next day, Val agreed to say that Evangeline had stomach pains so her and Cynthia had cancelled on the sleepover, caught cabs home and that was the last she had heard from them. *At least she's agreeing to go along with the coverup*, Raffael thought.

In terms of Jack and what he would do, Mark seemed confident. Though Mark's confidence was not something Raffael trusted, Jack was Mark's brother and according to Mark they always had each others backs.

Only Liza and Bambi remained the wild cards.

~

Bambi hadn't meant to leave Evangeline and Cynthia.

Before the party she had had memories that she had held on to. They were the reason she had tried for years to re-open that portal. But, she hadn't known that not all memories are real.

She remembered a time when her mother was impeccably beautiful with dark, glowing skin and long, black hair. She remembered the castle where they lived, her mother working at the side of an ailing and withering queen who seemed always to be in fear when her husband was close. The king was an ugly, short bear of a man with frantic eyes, and her mother always made sure Bambi was out of sight when he was near.

The king's son though, a young man with incredible, dark beauty and steely eyes, was a different story. Bambi's mother made sure that Bambi always looked her best whenever the prince appeared and always wanted Bambi to be seen by him. Bambi didn't like that. He terrified her as much as his father. His eyes were not suspicious like the king's but instead full of piercing derision and mockery, sometimes mingled with a flash of pity. She didn't understand why and only wanted to be away from him.

Her mother would not allow it though. She wanted Bambi to be near him and seen by him and to courtesy and smile to him as a proper lady of the court should, at every opportunity.

Outside of the king and prince and the strange, terrified queen everything was beautiful though: the castle, the gardens, the flowers, the food, the people.

Then, the holes in her mind began to appear. Jumps and skips through time until day after day after endless, dark day were filled with one, dark, cold, damp and putrid room in a suffocating space somewhere. She wondered now why her mother had let her remember that room at all and wondered if it was simply too much, even for whatever power her mother had, to hide a complete, continuous and endlessly black reality.

After that the hole in her memory grew huge and complete, except for a glimpse of a sword and a flash of the beautiful jewel within it as it struck lightning and her mother and her slid right through it. Then the newness of this world, the house on the suburban street and the return to warm, albeit dark, comfort. The sense of warmth and hope mingled with the strange, recurring nervousness she felt around, and for, her mother. The last thing Bambi remembered was the night when her mother had left her on the street and disappeared forever.

All her life Bambi had held on to those glimpses of past memories and ignored the holes and the mists in her mind. She missed her beautiful, strange mother and couldn't come to grips with this dull world that she had somehow been stranded in. She believed to her core that if she could open that doorway in the lightning she could go back to the fairy tale that she remembered and in it would be the mother she remembered.

But, when she stepped back through the portal, the film that had been placed over her childhood memories fell off. Anything that had been too glossy, any memory that was too strangely smooth, had suddenly had that shiny coating lifted off of it to reveal what was truly there.

There was her mother, but not as she was supposed to be. She was a ragged creature with burning eyes and grey, shrivelled, hideous skin. There were corpses everywhere with limbs missing and their bodies shrivelled like raisins, all the blood sucked out of them. Then the barren ground and the fires. Everything scorched. A ragged, growling man in the clothes of a king and a tiny girl, her little locks of auburn hair bouncing around her greying face.

All the images and scenes passed by in a flash and she saw the sword gleaming as it struck the lightning in the hands of that dishevelled man and the girl. Then there was a ripping sound and screaming. Was it the girl's? It wasn't a frightened scream though. It was an enraged and furious shriek. And then her mother's hand, always gliding over Bambi's face as she stared into her brown eyes with her red ones. That glide and that stare, always in the middle of the terror and each time it happened a film slid over the world and everything went blank for a second. Then all the terror was gone, wiped away to reveal a cartoon-glossy world that her mother wanted her to see.

In that one moment when her feet slid through the bolt with Evangeline she remembered everything all at once, as it really was. The horror was so overwhelming and complete, she thought she would never stop screaming.

Bambi didn't even fully recall jumping back through the bolt. She had panicked, closed her eyes and ran blindly. It was only when Raffael's face was staring into hers that she realized she was safe again.

She was a panicky idiot. A gutless, panicky freak who had managed to leave Evangeline and Cynthia. And now, a day later, she sat in her room, paralysed with terror and suffocating remorse.

She had known the minute she laid eyes on the sword that it was the key, but even long before that night, long before she spoke two words to Evangeline she had known that Evangeline would be the one to bring her a key, if there was one to be brought. She had used

Evangeline to follow her false memories and then left her with the consequences. Now, the only way to save Evangeline, if she was even still alive, was to open up a portal to a world that could completely eat up this one. It was Evangeline's and Cynthia's lives versus every life in this world.

The choice stabbed at everything inside of her. But, it was the only choice she could make. Evangeline and Cynthia had to be left to die.

Chapter 18

MEET THE FAMILY

"Why isn't she in the cage with us?" Evangeline repeated, pressing hard against Cynthia as the sounds of the hollering man became audible once more.

This time the hollering was followed by the howling and wailing of uncountable voices, seemingly coming from everywhere. The sounds felt as if they would tear the building to shreds and Evangeline thought she could feel the floors below them shaking.

She huddled with Cynthia, silently terrified, in the middle of the cage. The shrieks became louder and more numerous and after a minute she pushed her hands over her ears as hard as she could and with eyelids clenched tightly closed, she sat, shaking.

After an undefined amount of time their dark world went slowly silent, with only occasional, suppressed wails coming and going. Evangeline slowly took her hands off her ears, straightened out a little and began to look around. It wasn't possible for her eyes to fully accustom to the extreme darkness and she could make out only the shadows of Cynthia's face, moving slowly from side to side as well and the vague outline of their enclosure, with some dark shapes of objects around them. Past that, there was nothing but black.

Evangeline jumped slightly and Cynthia slid backwards when a door from a far end of the room slid smoothly open and a dim light filtered in to marginally illuminate their surroundings.

She now saw that their massive cage was in a type of bedroom and stood where a very large bed should have been, with the shadows of small, carved bedside cabinets on both sides of it. One end of the cage was pressed against the wall between the cabinets. A wardrobe stood against a further wall to the left, with a vanity table and chair beside it. An oblong table with a couple of chairs sat in the middle of the expansive room. The entire wall opposite the bed was covered by the same, massive curtains that had covered the main portion of the building where they had initially entered.

Evangeline grasped only the main aspects of her vague surrounding before her eyes were drawn to the three sets of footprints that entered through the doorway at a pace only barely above slow motion.

The first set belonged to the shadowy figure of a tall woman in a long gown. Then came a man of larger build, even taller than the woman, and what appeared to be a boy, slim in build and reaching a bit below the man's shoulders. The boy was the only one of the three that Evangeline had never seen before. Her breath caught in her throat as she stared at the other two.

The man spoke in a deep tone that didn't ask for comments or questions, "Laura, shut the door." At this, the door began to slide closed behind the three of them, taking the miniscule amount of light with it. Evangeline made out only the flash of a red eye and the tip of a hand on the other side of the door before it shut fully, with a click.

The darkness was complete once more. Evangeline felt her sense of terror growing again as she heard the figures approach but could see almost nothing past their black outlines. Cynthia, pressing against her with increased intensity, let out a tiny whimper.

Suddenly the footsteps stopped and they heard the man groan in frustration. Then, a swoosh, like a breeze flew past them, and the enormous curtains were flung open to both the right and left, revealing floor to ceiling windows in clear glass with some sorts of images etched within the panes.

Moonlight streamed in, illuminating the figure of the tall man and Evangeline knew she had been right – she had painted him too many times to confuse him with anyone else. The ring on his finger glowed almost as bright as his eyes, those two things being the only ones that could be considered glowing about him. The rest of him was shrivelled and raggedy, with hair that looked like dark straw, hanging limp against his face. His cheekbones showed the hints of a face that was maybe once full of character, but now was only grey and shrivelled.

She heard Cynthia utter, "Oh God, Oh God," as she swallowed sobs. The man's hands let go of the curtain edge and he looked at both of them in turn. Even through his decrepit grotesqueness, his disdain was clearly visible.

"Our visitors need the moonlight to see, mother," he said in an accented English that sounded like a mix of German sounds with an Italian flow, "apparently the tiny wench in the tiny shirt is looking for God in my handsome face, now that she is able to witness its glory."

Cynthia, with eyes bulging, quickly covered her chest and Evangeline thought the man actually snorted at this. Meanwhile, the woman, with that unforgettable raggedy, white hair down to her knees approached the cage and breathing in deeply began to quiver and shake. She attempted to compose her body and moved away again, making her way to the oblong table which she used to steady her stance.

"Sit, mother. You wouldn't want to eat our saviours." The man said.

"Stop," the woman responded in the same, strangely accented English with that voice that sounded like chimes in the wind. She put her hand up to silence what was apparently her son and looked directly at Evangeline.

"I apologize for your welcome. My son, even now, is slightly 'classist' as you might say. But…I am happy you have come Evangeline. You have come…and survived."

Cynthia spun her head towards Evangeline. Evangeline swallowed, staring back at the woman, her mind completely void of any comprehensible thought. The woman looked from Evangeline to Cynthia and attempted a smile which made her face look like a stretched-out skeleton.

"I...what...who...are you?" Evangeline managed to stammer out.

The woman looked slightly taken aback by this question but composing her face answered, "I am sorry, Evangeline. I did not introduce myself. I am Julia, the queen of Latina, this land, and these are my sons, Eros and Ehvan," Julia pointed first to the older man and then to the boyish creature which stood still near the door. She then continued, "This is your friend Cynthia. I have seen her in your mind. Hello Cynthia. I thought...well, I had spoken to you so many times, Evangeline. I thought you knew us and heard us when you repeated Lola's name...and came when I asked you to."

"What is she talking about?" Cynthia's whole body shook as she stared at Evangeline, "We came here on purpose?"

"No. Well...yes. I wanted to come here but I didn't know here was...here. I didn't know anything, Cynthia," Evangeline said, looking at Cynthia's horrified face. She turned to Julia, "I just heard the name Lola, that's all." The last was almost a whisper.

"Didn't you come with Lola like I asked? Lola was meant to come back and save us." Julia looked from Cynthia to Evangeline, confusion mingled with hope in her grey features.

"I don't know Lola, I just heard her name and repeated it," Evangeline said again, in a voice that was barely audible.

Eros broke out in a laugh, "Well, although she didn't bring Lola, at least she brought a proper meal, mother."

Julia did not respond to Eros' comment, but stared silently at the girls. Eros seemed to take this as a cue that he could continue and straightened himself to his full height, which was a head above Julia's. He then made his way with a slow step to the edge of the cage where he cocked his head to one side and looked through the bars at Cynthia, "You have seen me before...honey."

Cynthia stared at him, seemingly frozen and he grinned and moved his eyes slowly towards Evangeline, drawing Cynthia's eyes to follow him.

"Your weird paintings," Cynthia whispered, turning to Evangeline, "this...thing," she pointed to Eros, not noticing him flinch, "he's the one in your paintings. You know him. And *she* knows you," Cynthia's voice was rising. She now pointed at Julia, who still sat in silent reverie, "She said you came here because she told you to."

Evangeline's non-functional foot prevented her from fully standing up but she straightened herself as much as she could, the ceiling of the cage still far above her, and looked at Cynthia.

"I don't know what or who they are," Evangeline said in as direct and stable voice as she could, her mind for some reason racing to keep Cynthia on her side, her eyes veering towards Eros in anger, "It's complicated. I've seen them in my dreams. It's true. But it was just dreams. I didn't think it was actually real. I didn't plan *this*."

"Didn't you, Evangeline?" Eros asked while staring into Cynthia's face, "you did say the name 'Lola' as you opened the door to our home. It is a shame that you didn't think your friends were smart enough to understand, so you didn't tell them where you were opening a door to."

It was obvious. Eros was trying to divide and conquer, and looking from Eros' face to Cynthia's Evangeline could not believe that Cynthia was dumb enough to fall for it. She could feel the blood rushing to her face, and she momentarily forgot her terror as her fists seemed to clench themselves in Eros' direction. His eyes narrowed, noticing her clenched hands.

"Stop, Eros," Julia's voice chimed "we will not destroy them. There is a reason why they are here. We have been waiting twenty-four years for someone to save us."

"To save us? Two common wenches? You simply managed to convince them to come. Stop the-" Eros began but was suddenly interrupted,

"I'm hungry" Ehvan stated quietly from his unmoving stance. He was staring at Evangeline as he spoke and his wanting glare made her terror quickly return.

"What is wrong with you? Why are you like this?" Cynthia burst out.

"Like what?" Eros said slowly, "Grotesque looking, blood drinking *things*? Vampires? I believe you earthlings would call our Condition? Yes. This is our 'condition' And *you* are useless to us. This is what we have been waiting for, mother? Our saviours are two, weak, commoners? They don't even know *what* we are. We are *all* hungry."

As he voiced the last sentence his stare travelled intently through the cage from Evangeline to Cynthia. His eyes burned just like those of the man Evangeline had seen as a child and just like when she was a child, that glare entered her and pulled her, making her body move to approach him against her will. Her breathing became harsh as her mind tried to force her body to keep away from the bars of the cage. Julia's voice brought her back to reality, "Eros, no," Julia approached him and placed her hand in front of his eyes, cutting off his glare.

As she snapped out of her trance, Evangeline saw Cynthia, almost right at the bars, her hand open to reveal the key within. She grabbed Cynthia's hand and snapped it shut with her own, pulling her back into the middle of the cage. Cynthia, coming out of her trance more slowly, began to cry, pushing Evangeline away from herself, "Let me go home. I never wanted to do this. It was just Evangeline and Bambi."

Eros and Julia suddenly froze and both looked at Cynthia.

"You came with Bambi? Where is she?" Eros stated, rather than asked.

Evangeline almost threw herself at Cynthia to cover Cynthia's mouth with her hand before Cynthia could say that Bambi was nowhere that was reachable as far as they knew.

"Tell me. Now." Eros' voice was both enraged and shocked, as if he wasn't used to not being given an answer to any question he chose to ask.

"No," Evangeline lifted her head up to look him straight in the face, "Let us out of here first."

His voice came out as snarls when he replied, "Of course my sweet. You have the key. Open up the door and come right out."

Evangeline swallowed hard and didn't move. Eros laughed aloud, "What? Don't you want to come out of your little room? We can even wait till the sun rises. Then you can take a sprint and see how far you get before this whole entire world wakes in the evening and follows your lovely scent, now that we have picked it up. After all, there's not much clothing hiding it."

He spread out his arms in emphasis when he said, "whole world" and laughed bitterly. Evangeline instinctively tried to cover her fitted top with her arms and saw that Cynthia was doing the same. Her eyes darting to Julia, Evangeline saw more clearly that Julia's clothes comprised of a gown, long and flowing, only barely outlining her shrivelled, female curves.

Eros snorted in what was apparently his usual disdain at their reaction and at the sound of his snort Evangeline's anger came back to the surface and she forced herself to put her arms down and look at him directly.

"If we came here then we can figure out how to leave," she said, "You obviously can't. You need Bambi and Lola, which means you need to figure out a way to keep us alive in order to get them. So, figure out a way to let us go alive and we will tell you where Bambi is."

Eros' eyes shone a bright red at her words and Julia placed an arm in front of them yet again. She looked at Evangeline and Cynthia and spoke calmly, but with force, "Yes, we do need you alive and I want you alive, but that doesn't mean we won't kill you. Drinking chicken blood for twenty-four years does not quench our hunger, Evangeline. It only keeps us alive."

Cynthia flinched at the word "alive".

"Yes, we are alive, Cynthia" Julia said, "Unlike what your earthling tales seem to tell of this Condition."

"Why are you all this way?" Evangeline asked, the questions in her head tumbling one over another, "you were a regular human before? How did you come into my dreams and how do you know Bambi? Why is she your saviour?"

Julia had no time to even begin to respond to Evangeline's questions before Cynthia started to add her own set.

"You said this whole world will smell us," Cynthia said, "This entire world is vampires? What is this place? Isn't this earth?" She turned her head pleadingly towards Eros, as if trying to win his sympathy and he smiled at her, focusing his gaze straight into her eyes again.

"You are scared and tired, aren't you, *cara*?" Eros said, almost gently, "Tired...tired of always being in the shadow of Evangeline and her mystery? But it's not mystery. It's just lies and secrets, isn't it? And your friend Valerie, if she weren't wealthy, everyone would see her lack of class and femininity. And yet they think they are doing you a favour by letting you be with them…"

Not knowing how, Evangeline somehow pulled off her shoe and flinging herself towards the edge of the cage, hurled it through the bars, straight at Eros' head. As the heel hit him directly in the forehead Eros grabbed at her throwing hand and would have pulled her whole body and smashed her into the cage if his own arm hadn't banged one of the bars first.

A hissing sound came from the strange metal and his holler filled the room as his raggedy flesh burned like wildfire at the touch of the bar, making his grip momentarily loosen. Evangeline pulled away and threw herself back to the middle of the cage, grabbing hold of her arm as she banged into Cynthia. They both fell, shaking and breathing hard as they stared at Eros' burning flesh.

Then Evangeline's attention was pulled to her own arm which he had grabbed with immense strength. It was throbbing hard, her thumb not able to move. She tried not to cry from the pain of what felt like a crushed bone.

Eros simply looked at her and smiled as he clenched his own fist and the flesh slowly began to heal to its previous greyness, in front of their eyes, "Simpletons are just as simple on their earth as on ours."

Evangeline was frightened, in pain, tired, and malnourished and she hated Eros more with every passing minute. With no way to fight him she blurted out the only thing that came to her mind, "At least I wasn't stupid enough to get my whole world turned into vampires."

Eros' whole body suddenly shook and his breathing became fierce. Evangeline was sure he was about to hurl himself at the cage, not caring if it would burn every inch of him.

It was Ehvan, with slow but purposeful movements, who stepped in front of Eros this time.

"I am hungry. I want chicken," Ehvan took Eros' shaking hand in his own and looked into his face, trying to pull him away. Julia approached and added her own strength to that of Ehvan's.

"We need to eat more, Eros," Julia said, "We cannot talk this way. None of us can. And I will come back *alone* next time."

Julia nodded at Evangeline and Cynthia then looked into Eros' eyes. Finally, with one deep breath, Eros let Julia and Ehvan guide him to the darkness of the door. His eyes blazed as he looked over at Evangeline one, last time, "I will have no mercy on you."

~

Raffael never got the chance to get to Bambi before Evangeline and Cynthia were noticed to be missing. Ian had quickly located Bambi's last name and address and texted Raffael with it but by then, it was already chaos. Police were questioning them all and when

Raffael tried to get to Bambi's place he found that there were always police circling it. Why? How did they know what a huge part Bambi played in this? The only thing he was sure of was that Daniel was definitely involved.

Their entire group seemed to be watched. He couldn't get to any one of those teenagers now without attracting attention. The only person he could inconspicuously talk to was Monica. They easily told the police they were dating so it was normal that they were together. She got an introduction to his family much earlier than either of them had hoped, coming to his parents' house to give her apologies and hopes that Evangeline would be quickly found.

His parents didn't blame Monica. They blamed him. He knew it from the way they silently looked at him, as if wondering why these things always happened to Evangeline when he was in some way responsible for her. A part of him screamed inside in frustration at the unfair blame, while another part told him they were right. Both times he should have been there. Right there. Both times it was the moment he wasn't paying attention. He could have stopped it. At the least he should be wherever his sister now was. Not here. And he felt like he couldn't leave his parents' house, even though they barely spoke. So, he stayed there, moving between the living room, backyard deck and his old bedroom. Monica stayed with him.

The night of the party she had come back in the early hours of the morning and they had gone to another bushy forest just outside the city where they tried over and over again to repeat whatever Bambi had done. The sword just lay there and he felt that it was taunting him. He wanted to kick it and smash it into nothing.

And now his parents were sitting out on the cold deck, waiting for a police call he knew would never come. Evangeline had heard Bambi's name in one of her dreams. She had purposely searched Bambi out. It was Bambi. He had to get to Bambi.

~

Dark emptiness again filled the room and Evangeline felt herself shaking. She turned her head and whispered, "Cynthia."

Cynthia didn't turn her face towards Evangeline, but Evangeline could see the tears sliding down her cheeks. Looking into the darkness, Cynthia said, "I hate you."

It wasn't the usual Cynthia drama. It was a statement uttered in quiet determination.

"I didn't know any of this," Evangeline didn't know how to defend herself, "I didn't plan for this to happen. I never said anything because it sounded stupid...and crazy."

"Sure. Except we were here for a whole night and a whole day and you still said nothing. You pretended to know nothing, just like me. You thought I was too stupid to get it," Cynthia talked without a single pause, "You let us come here. He's right. You're just a liar. You think I'm too stupid to know about you and Ian too?"

"What? How is this about Ian?"

"It's about you being a liar."

"I'm not a liar. I didn't say anything because-"

"Because you thought you were being so nice to dense Cynthia? No point talking to me like an equal? At least Val is honest about the fact that she thinks I'm below the two of you."

"I don't-"

"Yes, you do. Fuck you." Cynthia turned her face away and Evangeline, with mouth open, stared at her.

Maybe it's true, Evangeline thought, *Maybe I am a shitty friend*. But Cynthia had never been a true friend. Cynthia had never given much of herself and now hated Evangeline for not having given much back?... Or maybe if Evangeline had given more to Cynthia out of her own accord, Cynthia would have opened up more and been a better friend from her end? But, shouldn't they be sticking together now and trying to figure out a way out instead of fighting about crazy bullshit? Evangeline's mouth closed and her lips tightened. She had made mistakes but this, this was Eros. This was his plan. Why couldn't Cynthia see it?

She heard a slow creak and quiet, slow footsteps, along with a chicken's clucking. Then, Ehvan was standing in front of the cage. In one hand he held a dead chicken by the neck and in the other he held a flailing, live one by its legs. She could feel Cynthia staring at the sight along with her.

After a long, awkward silence, Ehvan spoke softly, shyly, "I didn't know what you preferred. We like to drink them while they are alive, but maybe you prefer them pre-wrung?"

"Oh my God," Cynthia stuttered out, while Evangeline just stared, still trying to grasp the concept that this was to be their meal.

"We...humans...can't, I mean, don't, really eat raw meat or drink blood." Evangeline finally said, trying to sound nice, feeling a strange empathy for the sad looking boy-monster who seemed to be almost crushed by his failed attempt at "feeding" his guests.

"We like fruit!" Cynthia piped in and Evangeline's mouth went dry with the sudden memory.

"There's fruit trees near the chicken cages," Evangeline said, seeing the boy's confusion, "and water! We drink water...from the stream."

Ehvan looked abashed at the livery in his hands and put his head down, "I don't remember what I ate before."

"No," Evangeline squiggled to the edge of the cage closest to him, then backed away slightly as he obviously smelled her and growled, his eyes turning from sad to hungry, "I mean, don't be sorry. You are...really nice. That was really nice of you. Do you think maybe you could just bring us some fruit and water? I'm so sorry we can't eat the chicken. It looks...yummy though."

Ehvan looked at the two of them and nodded slightly. Without a word he turned around and left, closing the door behind himself. For a second they heard some more clucking. Then with one, loud screech it stopped.

Chapter 19

TERRA NOVA

The next time they heard the door open it was Julia who entered, a large platter filled with various fruits in her arms. She approached the cage and placed the platter right beside the bars.

"You will have to pull the fruit through the bars. I apologize, but opening the door would be unwise at any time during the night," Julia said, "We cannot see through our hunger at times and" - her eyes veered towards Evangeline, then quickly away- "I cannot watch Eros' every move, nor those of all the other inhabitants. It has been difficult keeping them away from you."

"Is that why there was so much screaming before?" Evangeline asked.

"It is the most difficult at sunset, before our meal, and it was the first time we had smelled a human in decades." Julia stepped away from the food and moved to the door. "Laura, leave the water and move away," she said through the door. Then, after waiting a second she opened the door. "When I close the door," she said to Evangeline and Cynthia, "take as much fruit as you want through the bars. I will knock when I am about to re-enter with the water."

As soon as Julia closed the door, Cynthia rushed to the bars and pulled fruit out of the bowl and into the cage. Evangeline did the same, though with more difficulty, with both a swollen foot and hand. She made a painful sound when she pressed on her ankle by accident and Cynthia shuffled some fruit over to her without a word.

After a minute they heard a knock on the door and moved back to the middle of the cage. Julia re-entered with goblets of water, which she also placed by the bars. Evangeline didn't dare approach them and satisfied herself with the juiciness of the fruit, as did Cynthia.

The fruit was nothing out of the ordinary, consisting of apples and pears, figs, plums, peaches and grapes with a couple of out of place cucumbers dispersed throughout. The only odd thing about the fruit was its perfection. Each piece was immaculate, of perfect size, shape, colour and taste.

Evangeline ate with relish until she noticed Julia staring at them curiously. She slowed down her bites, feeling awkward.

"I hope you like the fruits...and vegetable. It is what we have kept up planting. Luckily, it is our harvest time" Julia said, then paused, "I have not seen the joy that comes with eating in twenty-four years."

"You...eat," Evangeline said.

"The thirst for blood is unquenchable. Drinking provides momentary relief, like putting a bandage over a wound. It is always there though, itching, hurting, never healing, having only become more manageable with the temporary cover. There is no joy in it."

"We don't understand anything Julia," Evangeline took a deep breath. The sight of Julia in the flesh terrified her but this monstrous woman was so far the only one willing to help them. Evangeline had to compose herself and speak openly. "I know how we got here, but not really. And I don't understand where or what this is and what happened to you or how us or Bambi can save you. Or even how you know her." Evangeline blurted everything out in one long breath, adding at the very end, "Please tell us something."

"You know Bambi because she is one of you. Isn't she? She always said she was a vampire. At least one person was not a liar." Cynthia said to Julia.

"Yes and no, Cynthia," Julia said, "Bambi is in fact from our world, but she is not one of us. She is the only, single human that we know of that escaped to your world, with the help of her mother, Lola."

"Bambi's adopted," Evangeline said.

Julia was silent for a second, then answered, "That would explain why I have not entered Lola's thoughts in so many years. She is gone."

"Bambi's mother really died saving her?" Evangeline asked.

"No, she must have killed herself to save her," Julia stated, and Evangeline and Cynthia's fruit-filled hands froze.

"Let me tell you everything in as brief a time as possible so that you might understand where you are as well as hopefully trust me a little. Then, maybe you can help us and in turn help yourselves stay alive," Julia said, and focusing her bloodshot eyes on them began her story.

"This world you can call Terra Nova and this country is that of Latina. I have seen much through your eyes, Evangeline. Our warfare and technology could be that of yours some hundreds of years ago. Yet, in terms of advancements of the mind and self growth, we are far beyond you and it sometimes seems that your world is moving backwards.

"There were a number of kingdoms in this world but Latina was one of the two main ones on this side of the ocean waters. The other was Sadamanta, to the north. We shared common economic interests and co-existed in relative peace for a number of centuries, even sharing a common, free port town. That was until the mad prince of Sadamanta, Mamnoon.

"Mamnoon was short, dumpy, and childishly spiteful and possessive. Though he was the elder prince, the king preferred his younger brother Ezekiel who was everything Mamnoon wasn't: handsome, personable and intelligent. Mamnoon lived in jealous hatred and fear that the kingdom would be passed over him to Ezekiel. Until one day both Ezekiel and the king fell ill simultaneously and died within days.

"Though no proof was found, many suspected Mamnoon was somehow involved in their deaths and Mamnoon's sudden kingship was like a fragile thread, ready to break. To secure his hold he began to turn the people's suspicions outwards, rather than in. Suddenly, groups, what you might call 'terrorist groups' mysteriously and yet conveniently grew in numbers, constantly having to be feared and fought all over Sadamanta, creating suspicion of Latina.

"Whether Mamnoon was always mad or whether these games turned him mad is hard to say, but the older he became the more mad he turned, and his wife, the old and crumpled Sadalia, resorted to hiding terrified in the shadows.

"Meanwhile, Mamnoon's son, Daoud (of an age similar to Eros) became a man. Beauty had passed over Mamnoon, but it was unparalleled in Daoud. I would not say Daoud was evil in nature, though perhaps not the best candidate for kingship. All who saw him, desired him and unfortunately he easily fed off other people's desires.

"This is where Lola comes in. Lola was the bastard child of Ezekiel, born of a prince and a woman of royal pleasure."

Cynthia furrowed her forehead at the description and Julia smiled.

"In your words, Lola's mother was a prostitute, though perhaps more precisely speaking, a royal escort. Why Mamnoon kept her alive is beyond us. Perhaps some sense of guilt? Or perhaps just a thrill at the degradation of Ezekiel's offspring, as he let Lola live and work in the castle as a common lady-in-waiting for the terrified queen.

"Lola was our link. I had met her when she was a child, before Mamnoon had completely cut the kingdom's ties. We grew fond of each other and secretly kept in touch until the very end..."

Julia stopped with her lips partially open and stared off into the distance for a second. Then she took a deep breath, blinked and turned back towards the girls.

"Lola was intelligent and highly perceptive, seeing what others failed to notice. Through Lola we learned of a secret that was haunting Daoud. There were times when he would collapse in pain and then not be seen for days.

"Whatever the problem with Daoud's health was, it was kept hidden, but that secret kept Mamnoon awake at night. From what Lola pieced together, Mamnoon feared losing the kingdom. His fear was doubled through Eros who would be the opposing ruler to Daoud in the future. Mamnoon's goal then became to completely conquer Latina during his own reign.

"During this time Lola found an abandoned infant girl (as you can guess, Bambi). She asked for permission to raise the girl as the next lady-in-waiting and Mamnoon couldn't have cared less. However, had he looked closely at the child he would have noticed that Bambi resembled Lola much too closely. Whether he would have thrown Lola out of the castle for birthing another bastard or killed the child, fearing a continuation of that lineage, was something that Lola was not willing to find out and she made sure he never did look at Bambi closely, just as she had made sure to hide her pregnancy well, beneath her gowns. Who Bambi's father was, was unknown even to me, as Lola would never utter aloud that the child came from her own womb.

"War between our countries started in full and the prince began to be seen less and less. One night, during a thunderstorm, Lola snuck in to see what was happening to the prince and through a crack in the door saw him in his chambers, pale, almost blue, heaving slowly as if giving up. He was bent against his bed with his mother shaking beside him in despair.

"That was the night the lightning split.

"It was from your world that the creature entered ours. It was a child, yet with skin shrivelled and dishevelled like an old woman's and eyes burning red with hunger. Lola saw her through a side window as she hid in the shadows of the hallway. The child creature slid through the bolt of lightning, just as you did, and landed outside, near the room of the prince. Two guards saw her and utterly confused about what had just happened, attacked. But instead of fear, Lola said, the child's face lit up in pure glee and as the guards surrounded her, her crumpled body turned faster than light and in less than a minute she had left nothing but bones and skin of the guards. They did not even have time to shout as she twisted their necks and then sucked all the blood from their bodies.

"Lola was too petrified to move. Her eyes were glued to the girl creature, whose skin suddenly smoothed to a glowing perfection. She patted her lovely, brown locks around her face, wiped her bloody hands with slow purpose on the clothes of the dead guards and skipped away into the darkness.

"Lola said nothing to anyone, terrified of either being blamed for the murders or thought completely mad, and the desecrated bodies were found and blamed on the enemies of Sadamanta."

Cynthia and Evangeline were sitting motionless, a piece of fruit hanging halfway out of Cynthia's mouth as she listened. She took it fully out now with her hand.

"So, vampires come from our world? As in, there's living dead actually wandering the streets eternally?" Cynthia said and Julia cleared her throat audibly.

"We are not dead, Cynthia," Julia said, "and the term vampire is a name your world has created. We call this our Condition. Something we believe is curable. We are not lifeless creatures. Our hearts still beat and as to eternal, that still remains to be seen."

"So, you don't know if you can live forever? What about being killed? Do the stakes really work?" Evangeline asked and Julia smiled her skeletal smile at her.

"It will be a while before I trust you enough to give you directions on how to kill me," Julia said and Evangeline suddenly realized that the only way for them to survive might have to be to kill. She swallowed as she saw Julia's eyes on her own. She averted them, not wanting her thoughts known.

Julia looked away and continued.

"During war, unexplained deaths go simply unexplained. Until one day, one of Mamnoon's royal guards, having disappeared for days, returned to the castle at night in a very strange state. He was confused at his surroundings and breathing harshly, though his skin glowed of a health it had never had before. When his fiancée ran to him, he howled like a deranged animal and in front of everyone ripped her throat apart, drinking the blood in relish until the other guards, unable to tear him from the woman, threw fire at him and burned him to ashes.

"In this process, he bit one of the other guards who fell suddenly ill and out of fear was placed in a guarded cell where he shrieked and howled in pain. Within a day he developed the same madness as the first guard and he also was burned from fear of transmission of whatever strange disease he had gotten.

"Though Mamnoon had ordered the burnings, he had not been blind to the fact that the guards, while mad and blood thirsty, were also stronger than ten large men.

"But it was Lola who traced the child creature. She did not realize the king's desires and thought only to save the prince, who had been the only member of the royal family who had ever given her any kindness or attention. Seeing the health and perfection that came upon the infected guards she convinced herself that it would do so for Daoud. Lola remembered that happy skip of the girl creature going off into the night and believed that not all with the Condition went mad.

"In secret she snuck from the castle and sought out unexplained deaths across the country, knowing from the simple look of the dehydrated bodies, when it was the work of the child creature. For the child was not un-intelligent and made sure to kill all her meals properly. It was only the one guard who had somehow managed to escape.

"Lola followed the death trail to a corner of the city and there waited in the night for the child to find her. The girl finally appeared, playing an innocent child lost in the night. Lola spoke immediately and made her simple offer before the child had time to approach: Turn the king's son to be like her and in return gain royal protection and free blood.

"The child came with Lola to the castle. The rest you can partially guess. Daoud was turned and his life was saved. Mamnoon was pleased at Daoud's health and strength, not caring that it meant Daoud was now a blood sucking creature of the night.

"Unfortunately, Mamnoon was too pleased. In return for blood he got the girl to turn not just Daoud, but also the whole army. It was at this time that an important thing about this Condition was discovered: the eternal thirst will drive all who have it insane, eventually turning them into nothing beyond a hungry, instinctual animal. Once that happens, there is no return to humanity. Therefore, those who have our Condition are lost, unless, they hold on to something within; this must be a purpose coming from their human selves that is strong enough to keep their humanity within them. It must hold thoughts beyond hunger. For that, the purpose must be great.

"In times of war the purpose is clear. The soldiers became an army bred to kill. With the help of humans, they could travel covered through the day, attacking and feeding on their enemies at night.

"Lola, seeing what had been created, travelled in secret with Bambi to warn us and told us all she knew. Unfortunately, my husband, may his soul rest in peace, believed that the only way to defeat Mamnoon was to create an army equal to his. I begged him not to, but all was falling apart and Eros agreed with his father. They would not be deterred and our army, faithful to their leaders and seeing

Mamnoon's destruction all around them, volunteered their lives for this purpose. Lola left, more terrified than when she came, promising me that she would again seek out the child creature and gain a solution.

"Eros and my husband managed to capture a Sadamanta soldier with the Condition and began the creation of our own army from hell. But, the soldiers were not as careful as the child creature had been and did not always finish their 'meals'. You know what happens to a human who is bitten and not fully killed..."

Julia smiled vaguely as she said this, looking through both Evangeline and Cynthia. They waited silently, Evangeline feeling that whatever Julia was remembering, she did not want to ask about. Finally, Julia began to speak again.

"The unwanted creatures had no purpose other than to feed and create more unwanted creatures. And the more people there are with the Condition, the more blood is needed. There began to be more blood creatures than humans and as human blood became scarce, war stopped to matter.

"We tried to destroy them but they had grown too many. The sunlight could not protect us from the nights ahead, and even these cages, made from a molten metal which as you have seen is deadly to us, could only hold so many and be produced so fast. One by one, each died or turned till there was no one left as far as we can see."

Chapter 20

THE HOPE

Cynthia shook, "How is this helping us to survive?"

"I said, there was no one left, as far as we can see," Julia said, "Eros saw the end was near. When the Grand Duke, my husband's best friend, drank my husband's blood until there was no life left in him, Eros, about to impale the Duke, looked at the Duke's face and saw pain in his eyes at what he had done to his lifelong companion. Eros could feel there was still humanity within the Duke and gained the Duke's promise to help him save who they could.

"Our Condition allows us to run at around three times the speed and distance of a regular human. So, the remaining humans started to run in the morning. You have seen the scorched ground around our kingdom. While the humans ran, they burned behind them. When the night came, Eros and the leftover army, along with the Duke and those with the Condition who were still half-sane, tried to slow those who were chasing the humans down. Meanwhile the humans continued to run and burn.

"The ground surrounding us is mainly rock; not good for digging or hiding from the sun. Without blood for two days, we will not die, but we become slow and weak. Many, so many, were killed during the escape. But not all. Some made it. Having burned over a five-day distance in each direction the humans prevented us from following. They chose a direction away from both Latina and Sadamanta where they would be safe, until a human from the kingdom came to inform them that all those with the Condition were either cured, or time enough had passed for us all to starve.

"Neither of those things has yet happened. However, every couple of years, just as new life returns to the earth surrounding the city, a fire starts and re-burns everything. Perhaps it is coincidence, but I feel in my soul, just as I still feel that you were meant to come here, that the humans are still alive."

"Why didn't you escape with the humans?" Evangeline suddenly asked and just as suddenly realized that it was a stupid question. Without waiting for an answer, she just said, "oh".

"As Eros prepared for that final battle and escape, he hid us, me and Ehvan...he couldn't bring himself to kill us..." Julia said, "he thought that somehow, after all the others had been destroyed, he would find a way to cure us. To bring us back. But, he didn't need to worry. The final battle was lost...as you can see."

They were all silent for a while with hundreds of questions swimming inside Evangeline's head. It was Cynthia who asked the first, "Why didn't you lose your mind?"

Julia smiled at Cynthia, as if happy at the question. "We force ourselves to have hope," she said, "to plan and prepare for the future. That stems from Lola. She made it back to Sadamanta, though no longer a human. However, Bambi survived and kept Lola's human soul within her. Lola stayed human inside to save Bambi. She hid Bambi in a deep, secret dungeon and kept her alive as she searched for a cure. Much of what happened is not fully known to me, but we communicated what we could through our minds.

"You see, many from Terra Nova possess the power to penetrate minds. We are not mind readers. We can communicate with the minds of others when those others allow it...or occasionally when they are in states of deep relaxation, such as sleep or drugs. You, Evangeline, know this from experience. Though you were a special case. I have not beforehand been able to communicate with anyone from your world. My connection with you was weak, but nevertheless, it existed. I believe your encounter with the portal and with Daoud was what enabled me to reach you. Your brother, I tried him also, but he did not want it and the connection was shut."

Cynthia stared at Evangeline and Evangeline's eyes widened slowly, "The man with the sword that tried to come through the portal when I was six...that was Daoud?"

"Yes, I saw him many times in your dreams. It must have been then that Lola and Bambi also went through to your world," Julia said, "We do not all possess the same strength of mind but Lola and myself were at times able to speak to each other and I learned that the fate of their country was worse than ours.

"Mamnoon, having no more need for the child creature once he learned that his own soldier creatures could now turn other humans, quickly decided to dispose of the girl, as she was subordinate to no one. But the child creature escaped and in a fury infected all the Lords and Ladies who had been Mamnoon's supporters only out of fear. Then, she watched as those who were once blue-blooded gentlemen and ladies ripped apart their hated king.

"Some time after this the fires began to rage through their lands. I assume it was the escaped humans who started those fires as well. Sadamanta's position is not the same as ours. There is no wall surrounding it, and the inside of the city was completely destroyed. There were no known humans left in Sadamanta by that time (with the exception of Bambi) and many with the Condition were wiped out by the fires. However, enough survived, hiding like rats in brick cellars or dirt holes.

"Lola also survived, as did Daoud and the child. Surprisingly, the child creature did not seek to destroy Daoud, seemingly having fallen in love with his beauty, and even went as far as to bring him his 'food'. They were secretive together and Lola, who had by now long-ago hidden Bambi and pretended she had disappeared like so many others, was borne by the prince and his ghoulish companion, but not entrusted into their confidences.

"Though not admitted into their circle, she served the child creature as she had always served the prince, in hopes of learning something of value. She was sure the child knew things which we did not. And finally, one conversation saved her...or at least Bambi.

"Daoud and the child's Condition was different for some reason. Though they craved blood, they seemed somehow...less mad from the desire. More slowly affected. And they would scheme, with the child creature pacing and repeating 'They know on the other side.'

"One day, while Lola was cleaning the dead, bloodless rats off the floor, which were now their only meals, she heard the girl creature utter the words 'Tonight my prince, I will bring you to my home. And they will either cure us or feed us.'

"It was the last time I heard from Lola. After that night she disappeared from my thoughts and I can only assume that she died while Bambi made it to your world. What happened to Daoud and the child creature is unknown. However, you pushed Daoud back into our world and over the years I have felt a slight connection with him and assume he is in Sadamanta still."

Julia's face seemed to relax and her eyes grew less focused on the darkness around them and Evangeline felt the story was at its end. She tried to organize all the pieces in her head.

"So... the cure is on our side, not yours," Evangeline began to sum up, "there are humans somewhere here. Daoud and the kid creature will know how to open the portal and... you think Bambi has the cure...or perhaps some vital information her mother passed on to her."

"Yes," Julia said, "so you see...where is Bambi? She can not be killed. You can't let her stay out there."

Evangeline and Cynthia were both silent. Cynthia looked over at Evangeline.

"Is she already dead?...What have you concealed?" Julia asked in a deathly slow tone.

"She's not dead," Evangeline said and Julia stared at her, waiting for more, when the door opened and Eros walked in, "And yet she is nowhere to be found and you are shaking with fear at the thought of telling us why," he said, "It appears that the one and only chip that was deterring me from eating you is not yours to play with anymore."

Evangeline knew Eros already hated her. Without knowing it, she had hit the nail right on the mark with her comment about his failure to protect his country. She wanted to keep her mouth shut. Now that the reality around them was sinking in, fear felt like it was eating a hole in her stomach. She should shut up. But his sneer and his condescension had an effect on her that was stronger than her terror of him.

"Actually, these bars are deterring you. Unless you want to barbecue and eat yourself."

"We will see for how long these bars will save you, peasant wench, when we stop feeding you," Half of Eros' lip curled up as he watched Cynthia clutch a fruit in her hands and Evangeline inadvertently stared down at the goblet of water outside the cage. She pulled herself together and looked at Julia, "I am sorry, we were about to tell you about Bambi when the little prince stormed in, in his usual state of tantrum."

Out of the corner of her eye Evangeline saw that Eros liked being told he was a spoiled prince about as much as she liked being repeatedly called a wench. Without giving him time to respond and ignoring Cynthia's look of terror at her purposefully irritating him, Evangeline continued, "Bambi came with us through the portal but when we let go of the sword it seemed to suck her back through." She hadn't planned this partial lie, but as soon as she said it, felt that she was on the right track and continued, "My brother was with us as well as some other close people. They will be trying to reopen the portal again to find us. But it was the first time we had ever done this. It might take them some time to figure out how to use the sword again."

"What sword?" Eros said.

"Daoud's sword. He dropped it. It was what opened the portal." Evangeline said.

Julia looked at Eros and said, "I saw the sword in your dreams, Evangeline but thought it was only a memory."

"No. I have it. It's what opened the portal," Evangeline put a sureness into her voice that she didn't fully feel.

"Is that why Daoud never re-opened the portal?" Cynthia asked and they all looked at her. She looked nervous, however sizing up their pondering faces seemed to gain enough confidence to continue, "well, I mean, from what you say he never reopened the portal which seems weird because if he had opened it once and knew he could get out of here....wouldn't he have just reopened it again? Unless, he couldn't…"

"Right," Julia said and her eyes brightened. Eros rubbed his chin with one hand. Evangeline looked at Cynthia with pure relief. That one comment convinced not only Julia, but also Eros, that Bambi would come back.

"But the portal," Julia's voice was suddenly anxious, "It seems to seek out Evangeline for some reason, Eros. It can not open here. They must move away from the town. Otherwise, whoever comes through will die. It was a fool's chance that they arrived when the winds were blowing away from the town and didn't bring their scent in immediately. And it was a miracle that I was able to save them…even from myself."

The room was silent until Eros finally cocked his head towards the huge windows, "It is almost time for the sun, mother. Leave them enough water until the next night. There's still much to find out…though if we do have to get them out of the town, I don't see how both would manage. One could maybe survive if the other were used as a… distraction."

Eros turned and silently moved towards the door. Walking through it he turned towards the cage and said, "How many of those pills do you have left Evangeline? It seems that you may be as good as dead anyways..."

With that he disappeared into the darkness beyond the door and Evangeline sat silently, staring ahead. Julia stood up and moved towards the door also, but stopped for a second and with a serious look at both of them, spoke, "We hold on to our humanity as best as we can. But it has been twenty-four years. Eros... his talent as a leader of humans was pushing others' minds in the right directions.... and it is still his talent now, just as mine is seeing into those minds. I have little control over what he will say or do...little control over the actions of those with the Condition, including my own. We will find a way to take you away from the city...but you must find a way to not let us destroy you first."

She followed Eros into the darkness, with the door shutting softly behind her. Evangeline knew she had tried to inform them and help them, but nothing could take away the effect of Eros' words, nor the fact that although he had spoken to Evangeline, he had looked directly at Cynthia. Evangeline knew that if one of them were to escape he would make sure it wasn't her. She turned her face towards the windows and sat silently, waiting for the sun to rise, not wanting to see Cynthia's face or guess at her thoughts.

Right before sunrise they heard the creak of the door and Ehvan's head came sliding through. He looked at the large windows with the curtains pulled open and did not fully enter. Instead, he pushed blankets and pillows through, as far as he could. Then he slid in a massive basin of water, that looked much too large for him to push, yet he seemed to have no trouble with.

"Mother says she is sorry," Ehvan spoke, "She forgot that regular humans feel cold. The water is for washing. She says she will have a warm bath for you tomorrow...and that big chest there" - he pointed to what looked like a decorated chest in a small enclave in a far corner of the room - "mother says regular humans sometimes need to use that after eating. And these, she says, are for wiping" - he slid a decorated box full of cloth napkins inside the room and scratched his head - "usually the maid brings us things but mother says it's not safe. She doesn't trust Laura's control. Mother was a little embarrassed to bring the wiping cloths but I don't mind...I am not sure what you wipe with those..."

Ehvan looked from Cynthia to Evangeline as if hoping for an answer, but Evangeline just tried to smile. After some time staring at them with no result he finally shrugged, "The windows are big so you can come out and stretch once the sun rises but mother says to not leave the room because there's too many shadows everywhere else...I think you are pretty. Mother says not all regular humans are pretty like you. I am happy you came. I hope I don't eat you."

With that he closed the door and disappeared.

Chapter 21

THE GAME

He could not rest in the darkness of his room. The simultaneous hunger for blood and the desire to touch real human flesh kept Eros pacing back and forth furiously. She had called him stupid for being turned into this. If she could feel what it felt like to watch every single human that you should have protected, be killed or turned...yes, he had done this... but if she knew that pain. And if she knew the pain of dying by being drained of your blood and ripped apart; the torture of your body feeling as if it were shredded from within as it turned into this. It had been twenty-four years, and he still remembered every detail.

For years he had seen glimpses of her common life through his mother's gift. The only thing special about her was that for some reason the portal chose to open near her. But, she had only survived her meeting with Daoud with the help of her brother.

Her brother, he would have been more useful: older, stronger. Yet, she had been stronger than most children at the age of six. Children could never resist the pull of those with the Condition. Even adults found it hard to resist. *Or maybe she hadn't resisted Daoud. Maybe she simply wouldn't shut up until he jumped back through the portal to get away from her,* Eros thought wryly, stopping to take a breath and control his shaking body.

The little wench did not know when to shut her mouth. She spoke not only to royalty, but also those who owned her life, as if they were one of her little, school friends. One of those stupid, little boys like that one idiot Eric that she had put in his place.

Does she think she is putting me in my place now?

He grabbed the side of a chair and cracked it with one hand, seeing her neck between his fingers. Then he took his shaky hand off the broken chair and looked at it. His hand slowly moved back to the chair and ran its length while his eyes closed and his mind saw her long, soft neck beneath his fingers. That supple skin. The blood in contrast to that lovely, slim paleness as its drops slid smoothly down around his teeth while they sank in and ripped through her flesh. His left hand grabbing at her wild hair and pulling her head back, her mouth open in a scream and her eyes closed. His right hand ripping at the tight material around her chest and roughly grabbing the breast beneath...Eros' eyes opened and he threw the chair across the room, shattering it completely. He stared at the pieces, his lungs taking in deep, choppy breaths. God, what he wouldn't do to have her out of that cage.

~

The sun finally filled the room and Evangeline looked silently around with Cynthia. Their cage had literally replaced an immense bed and its bars were just like those around the chicken farm.

She was sitting with her legs squeezed tight, having realized as soon as Ehvan pointed to the chest in the far nook that she hadn't been to the bathroom in a very long time.

She skimmed the room and saw that it was not only beautiful, but also spotless. The floors looked like marble and the furniture was an intricately carved, polished wood with marble toppings and gold edgings. Even the dark curtains were a gorgeous, deep, red, velvet. Her eyes reached the chest and saw that its bottom was marble as well, ornate with flowers and birds, while the top was of simple, polished wood. The contraption was quite large and the nook in which it stood had a curtain that could be pulled for privacy. She was terrified to leave the cage but also terrified of her bladder letting go inside of it and Eros' comments to that.

"I need to go pee. I can't hold it anymore. Can I have the key?" Evangeline asked.

Cynthia looked at her, opened the cage and put the key back in her pocket. Evangeline looked at Cynthia nervously.

"You saw Daoud," Cynthia said, looking into her eyes, "as in he actually came to your house?"

"Yes. I was six years old. Nobody believed me. Even Raffael told me I was imagining things..."

"I know it's true," Cynthia kept staring into her eyes, her mouth set and her eyes narrowed, "I know I wouldn't have believed you and would have thought you were even weirder than I generally think you are...still...how many things don't I know that you do? So, don't give me that suspicious look. I don't deserve it. You do."

Evangeline was about to argue but stopped. She looked back into Cynthia's eyes, "You're right." She slid over to the cage door, mentally repeating, *I trust her. She won't lock me out and use me as bait.*

Evangeline pulled the door open and placed her legs slowly on the floor. Pushing herself off she placed her weight on them and screamed in pain, toppling forwards.

"Fuck," was the only thing she could voice as she slowly lifted up her leg to look at it. So much had happened that she had forgotten it. In the bright light of day it looked even worse than the night before, so swollen that the ankle was spilling over her one shoe that she hadn't thrown. It definitely looked like a break. She looked at the arm that Eros had grabbed and saw that its condition wasn't much better.

Groaning, Evangeline hobbled to the chest, relieved that it was in fact a medieval style toilet as she lifted the wooden lid. She pulled the curtains closed around herself and sighed in relief.

When she reopened the curtains Cynthia was sitting on the edge of the cage. Looking at Evangeline she seemed relieved and stood up and walked fully out, towards the windows. Evangeline hobbled over to join her and when she looked out, she felt a momentary wonder, for that second, forgetting all else.

Latina was massive. They were lucky they had entered it at the spot where they did as at that spot the slabs of immense mountains behind the city curled in, creating a thinner section. In other directions the mountains went backwards, with the city following them and increasing in size immensely.

They were high up, not in a tower, but what seemed to be a whole upper level of the castle and the kingdom below was soundless, empty, and absolutely immaculate. White-washed buildings and villas lined the streets in every direction, with mutely coloured ones filling in various spaces. The city was not only streets but also gardens and what appeared to be orchards and parks. And everything shone in well-groomed perfection in the light of the sun.

From their position, the mountains rose up to the left, their jagged surfaces both beautiful and frightening, misty from the distance. Where the mountain trail ended, the wall began, the desolation beyond it blending into the distance.

"I didn't realize we climbed up," Evangeline said, having no comment suitable to what she was seeing.

"I felt like I was flying. Do you think they fly?" Cynthia asked.

"I don't think so...I think they're just really fast," Evangeline said and looked downwards. There was a narrow terrace below their window. She put her hands on the glass and looked from left to right, trying to find a door to the outside. Cynthia found it first; a small, glass handle to a pure glass doorway that blended in with the rest of the panes. She pulled on it but it was locked. She turned to look at the rest of the room and walked over to the basin of water. Evangeline moved slowly towards the basin as well and put a hand in. It was freezing and she was cold as it was. Feeling the clean water made her realize though how disgustingly filthy she was. She hobbled over to the large mirror on top of the vanity table and plopped into the chair in front of it. She cringed. Cynthia came over and looked as well. They both had wild, dishevelled hair, dirt and tear-stained makeup smeared all over their faces and their previously black clothes were grey and ragged, torn in more than one spot.

"No wonder he kept calling us peasants," sitting in front of the mirror and seeing herself not only made Evangeline realize how horrible she looked, but also how tired she was inside. She pulled herself together and made her way back to the numbingly cold basin. She might hate Eros and his snobbishness, but he still couldn't be allowed to think they were useless peasants or he would eat them alive. Literally.

She knelt down in front of the basin, pulled her shirt off and picked out a thin blanket to use as a towel and a rough bar of soap from the pile that Ehvan had left. Then, she took a deep breath and dunked her whole head in the basin as Cynthia shrieked. She pulled her head out as fast as she stuck it in, shivering uncontrollably, then looking over at Cynthia's horrified face, laughed.

"I dare you," Evangeline said.

"I'm not doing it."

"It's the quickest way," Evangeline said and took another head plunge, forcing herself to stay under just long enough to rub at her hair with the bar for a second. Cynthia came over and tried to wash herself by scooping tiny handfuls of water. She cringed at each icy splash and finally sighing in defeat threw her whole head in just like Evangeline. After they finished, they did what they could with their hair, poking through the pile on the floor as well as the mirror cabinet to find a large comb and some oils that Evangeline ran through her haystack to try and calm it.

Then they peeled off their shoes and socks and stuck their feet in, trying to get rid of the dirt and stench. The cold water felt amazing over Evangeline's ankle and she lay on the floor, wrapped in her blanket, with her swollen foot lifted up and in the basin for some time.

Meanwhile, Cynthia sat in front of the mirror, also wrapped in a blanket, poking through the drawer and pulling out various powders and oils, sniffing them and trying some on her face and hair.

"They really were royalty," Evangeline heard Cynthia mumble as she raised herself up. She sniffed at her shirt in disgust but had no choice except to get back into it. There was no point trying to put on the shoes though. Nothing would fit back over her swollen foot. She pulled her putrid socks back on, grabbed some blankets and a pillow and crawled back to the cage.

"I need to lie down and warm up. Are you coming back in?" Evangeline asked Cynthia, burrowing into her blanket in utter relief.

"No. Not ready to crawl back into my chicken coop again. I'll come in later."

"Okay" Evangeline mumbled from under her pile. Julia said the portal sought her for some reason. Her and Cynthia had to get away from the city. They had to escape. They had to talk. Think of a plan...but in an hour...maybe two. She'd just rest of a bit.

Every part of her body was sore from either being thrown, bent or from simple exhaustion. She lay still, her head in a pillow and her body wrapped in warmth. All her muscles let go and she suddenly felt like she was melting into the floor, her eyes shutting closed of their own accord.

~

Cynthia turned and watched Evangeline sleeping for a minute. *I shouldn't even feel betrayed*, she thought. It was always Evangeline and Val. Val was rich and athletic. Evangeline was quirky and sweetly innocent looking. And she, Cynthia, was just average.

Why should I have been told anything? Evangeline was full of crap when she said that no one knew any of this. Val knew everything. She was sure of it. Raffael was there when Daoud apparently visited them so he obviously knew everything too. Even Ian probably knew.

Cynthia lividly flung powder from the brush she was holding at the mirror when she thought of Ian. *God, I tried my butt off; picking out perfect outfits, perfect smiles and just being perfectly, fucking charming. Meanwhile, he literally trampled over me so that he could drool over Evangeline, who told stupid jokes from underneath her stupid bird nest hair.*

So, I'm the unimportant extra who didn't need to know she was risking her life, being flung into some insane, alter universe and thrown in an animal cage. Then again, I wasn't even supposed to have been here. Stupid Cynthia was just supposed to help open the portal like Mark and Jack and the other extras. I wasn't actually supposed to come through it or ever do anything of significance...

"What if you are to be the significant one here? Who says only Evangeline has to be of significance in this story?" A voice spoke inside her head. It was seemingly her thought and yet it didn't feel as if it was coming from her. Cynthia sat completely still and stared at her own, confused reflection in the mirror.

"I'm going insane," she said under her breath and stood up, about to make her way back to the cage. A sudden longing came over her and she turned her face towards the large wardrobe. She walked to it and opened its doors. A long row of gowns met her eyes. Her hand went out and ran down the length of a particularly exquisite looking dress, pulling it slowly out.

The outfit consisted of two gowns, one being a sort of undergown and the other an overgown. She pulled the white undergown on first, fastening the fitted, long, white sleeves with their gold embellished cuffs. Then, she pulled on the deep, red overgown, watching in wonder as the crushed velvet reacted with the light of the sun to offer various shades. She lifted an arm and examined the long, trailing sleeves.

I look like I'm in the middle ages, she thought.

"A princess in a kingdom in the middle ages," the foreign thought spoke in her head, "all women are average without clothes and makeup," the voice prodded her and she walked to the makeup cabinet again and carefully fixed her hair and applied various products to her face, suddenly knowing what each was for.

She looked in the mirror at the final effect.

"Look at Evangeline. Who is average now? You can be exquisite. Why are you so sure that you were not meant to be the star in this story? The princess of a kingdom that needs only to be seen from behind the veil. *You* can see," her thought spoke.

Cynthia turned her head towards the window and walked absentmindedly towards it. With the long gown trailing all around her she stood in the sunlight in front of the wall length windows and looked out. A market lay below, full of people chattering and bartering. In the streets beyond, children laughed and ran while carriages rolled through and men on horses rode alongside them.

There was a touch on her shoulder and she turned her head and saw Eros standing beside her. She knew it was him, though he resembled nothing of the ragged creature she had seen earlier. Wavy, black hair fell around his equally black eyes, surrounded by a dark complexion and dark beard. He smiled at her and took her hand in his, lifting it and pressing it to his lips.

~

Evangeline groggily lifted her head and looked around her, not knowing where she was. Her eyes scanned the surroundings in the dimming light of the evening sun and she quickly recalled her present fate. She looked beside her, expecting to find Cynthia but she was alone and the cage door was still wide open.

Evangeline's head rushed from side to side, scanning the length of the room and landed on what appeared to be Cynthia, dressed in a long, red gown, in a chair with her head on her arm on top of the makeup table, sleeping.

Was she imagining it or did she hear noises beyond their door? Evangeline scrambled up as fast as her sore body would allow and whisper-shouted "Cynthia! Get up! Cynthia!"

Nothing.

Toppling out of the cage she hobbled to Cynthia and shook her hard.

"Wha-?" Cynthia lifted up her arms in front of her, confused.

"Get up. Get in the cage. Now!" Evangeline tried not to scream as she definitely heard sounds now. Cynthia suddenly shot up and looked at the almost dark room in the setting sun. They rushed back to the cage when Cynthia stopped and started turning in frantic, terrified circles.

"What are you doing?! Get in!" Evangeline cried, pulling on Cynthia and making both of them fall into the cage in a heap.

"The keys! They are in my jeans!" Cynthia now screamed back, trying to pull herself out of Evangeline's grip.

"What? Where? You are wearing your jeans!" Evangeline pointed at a jean leg popping out from under the gown that had flown upwards when Cynthia fell over.

"Oh..." Cynthia said, seeming confused as she pulled up the folds of the dress quickly, fumbling under them to get to her jean pockets. Evangeline grabbed the cage door and pulled it closed as Cynthia pulled out the key. Evangeline grabbed it from her hand and stuck it in the lock just as the door to the room clicked open.

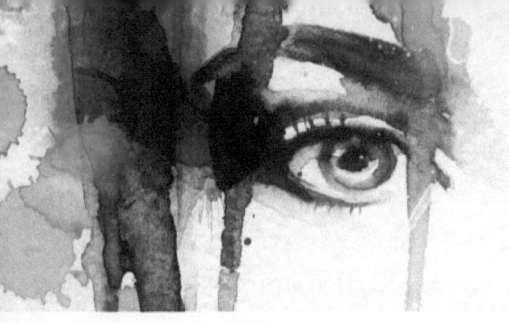

Chapter 22

LIFE IN A GILDED CAGE

The door clicked open and Eros stepped in with his mother and Ehvan behind him. His eyes were on Evangeline's hand as she flicked the key out of the lock, put it back in Cynthia's hand and slid away from the bars.

"That was very dangerous. What made you wait so long?" Julia asked as she placed a fresh bowl of fruit near the cage and stepped away.

"They have made themselves at home," Eros answered, eyeing Cynthia's apparel, "we may now be what you earthlings have come to call 'vampires' but that is *still* my mother's gown."

"I... I'm sorry... I," Cynthia searched for words.

"She was just cold," Evangeline interjected, "our clothes are thin. We were just looking for something more to wear. We're sorry... Julia, are we in your room?"

"Not anymore," Julia said quietly, "this was my room before I turned. That cage was an attempt to protect me in my last days...I have moved to a darker room now. One with fewer memories. You are welcome to keep the gown Cynthia. It is a bit long for you but overall fits you quite well. I apologize for the stain along the neckline."

Evangeline looked at the gown's gold neckline and the dry, brownish stain on one side. She cringed wondering if that was the gown Julia had been bitten in.

"I suppose we should get you some clothes as well. You smell foul," Eros' looked at Evangeline's dirty, socked feet and his face cringed, "at least the smell distracts from the hunger," he grumbled as a side note.

Evangeline instinctively tried to fold her feet under her butt but her swollen foot wouldn't allow it. She looked up at Eros' dull coloured, long shirt, which looked like it may have been white at some point, falling over equally dull, fitted pants, completed by a long pair of well kept, but still old, dull, leather boots.

"What about you? Didn't you wear the same clothes yesterday? And potentially all of this century?" Evangeline asked, imitating his derisive tone back at him.

His eyes, the only thing about him that hadn't lost its luster, blazed in response, "We don't sweat and we don't stink." With that he turned and left the room. The door reopened almost immediately and Eros re-entered with some fabrics in his hand. He approached the cage closer than usual and chucked the fabrics at Evangeline through the space between the bars without a word.

Evangeline tried to grab the clothes and pull them fully into the cage. As she neared the bars Eros breathed in deeply and his face changed from the usual derision to the uncontrolled, growling hunger. He stepped away sharply, looking away from both her and Cynthia.

"These clothes belonged to the squire," he said, "he had a big mouth too, until he was eaten. They will fit you perfectly."

"Where you always this pleasant or is this a special, undead charm that you've acquired?" Evangeline said and Eros' shoulders tensed. Without turning around he said, "I will go and feed now, mother."

As the door was about to close behind Eros, Cynthia called out, "Thank you sire. You are too kind." Eros put his head back in through the crack in the door, gave Cynthia a once over and shut the door.

Evangeline looked at Cynthia with narrowed eyes, "*Sire?* You are too kind?"

"Well, since you didn't thank him for the clothes. It isn't his fault you don't know how to act ladylike," Cynthia straightened and smoothed her gown as she spoke in a tone that was prim yet smugly demure.

"You know, he will treat you how you act. If you act like an insecure servant then-" Evangeline began.

"And if you act like a bitch then? You seem to be the one in servants' clothes." Cynthia was looking away with her chin up, both fury and smugness passing over her face.

Someone coughed and they realized that Julia and Ehvan were still there. Evangeline's face went red.

"We have to go and eat also," Julia said politely, "I will return later and...it is alright. Being in a cage does things to you. I know. Try to remember what reality is." Julia turned and walked to the door, waving her hand at Ehvan to follow.

Ehvan had been standing a little off to the side, simply staring in his usual, pondering silence and now moved to follow his mother out. When Julia opened the door, Ehvan stopped and looked wide eyed at Evangeline, as if trying to say something, but like the previous night, not particularly knowing the art of casual communication. After a couple of seconds of stare-filled silence he finally said, "I don't think it is undead charm. Mother says Eros was always tedious like that."

Eros must have been waiting for Julia and Ehvan not far off, because they suddenly heard something between a growl and groan and both Evangeline and Cynthia burst out laughing. Even Julia couldn't stop a loud chortle. Only poor Ehvan stood, staring in complete confusion from person to person.

"Come Ehvan. It's alright. You made a joke. That is a good thing," Julia smiled, patted Ehvan's head and led him out the door.

~

Cynthia laughed for a couple of extra seconds, then met Evangeline's eyes. They looked at each other in depth for the first time since being thrown into the cage. Cynthia exhaled and then, feeling as if coming out of a daze, she looked around the room and down at her elaborate gown, "I look ridiculous. I am in a cage dressed up for the prom."

"You look beautiful actually," Evangeline said.

"I am insecure," Cynthia didn't know why she was opening up.

"Isn't everyone?" Evangeline shrugged and smiled.

Cynthia smiled back a little and bit her lip. She wanted to tell Evangeline about the thoughts in her head and the alive city she had seen while Evangeline had slept, but didn't know how to start. And what would she say? Is that how Evangeline had felt after she saw the portal: lonely and wanting to tell someone but not knowing how? Cynthia felt stupid. Again. Her usual, daily feeling. Turning away she reached through the bars for a fresh plum.

Evangeline continued looking at her, literally twiddling her thumbs. Cynthia knew they should make peace. They needed each other. But there was a rock that just wouldn't leave the pit of her stomach whenever she looked at Evangeline.

"I am sorry, Cynthia," Evangeline said, "I know it's not enough. It's all I've got. If we...when we get out of here, I will figure out a way to make it up."

"How?" Cynthia couldn't help laughing, "By waving bye to me at my community college on your way to study abroad at University?"

"What?"

"You and Val think this whole high school thing is bullshit. The time of your lives is going to start after. What about me? I am literally book stupid. I'll get into some half-ass college, get some half-ass job, live a boring, half-ass life in the suburbs like my parents.... High school may be the best I've got and I hate you for looking down on that. You're popular without deserving it and you think you're better because you don't give a shit."

Evangeline opened her mouth and stopped. Looking straight at Cynthia she said, "You're right. I guess we did think we were better, but I never thought you were half-ass...you look pretty extraordinary now, of all times," she had a sheepish smile on her face.

Cynthia looked down at her gown and ran her hand over its rich smoothness, "Yeah, that's what the voices inside my head said."

"Huh?"

"Nothing."

Evangeline gave her a quizzical look and she shrugged offhandedly, "It's like Julia said, this place makes you a little crazy."

"Hmmm. Well, Queen Cynthia, let us get your squire ready," Evangeline said. She looked around, flexing her neck to hear if anyone was coming then quickly peeled off her clothes and started replacing them with the ones Eros had chucked at her. Cynthia couldn't stop laughing at the frills of the sleeves on the shirt, doubled up with the high socks with leather ties on top. Evangeline joined her.

"You know, after four years of knowing you, I finally feel like I actually see *you*," Evangeline suddenly said. Cynthia stopped laughing, "yeah, I think we might be becoming actual friends...You wanna know the sad reason why I followed you into the lightning-" Cynthia began but was cut off by the sounds of shrieking piercing the walls of the castle. It was coming from the outside. The main sound was a man, hollering and shrieking in something that was not fully English. Other, intermittent howls from men and women interrupted every now and then.

Evangeline dropped her breeches and they pressed against each other back-to-back, grabbing at each others' hands. Their breathing came in harsh gulps as the horrendous sounds continued for what felt like hours. Eventually, only one man's hollering continued intermittently and their grasps on each others' hands loosened.

Evangeline whispered, "We need to get out of here. Somehow. Julia said the portal seems to seek me out. We can't let it open here. If it does, everyone will die. Everyone."

They both sat silently, no solution presenting itself. The only reason they were still alive was because they were in a cage. But if they didn't leave the cage anyone coming to save them would die, meaning that eventually they would too.

"Do you think they will actually come back through the portal for us?" Cynthia asked after some time.

"Yes," Evangeline stated conclusively.

Cynthia turned her head slightly towards Evangeline, "But what if it won't open again? Not for decades. Julia said something about being like this for over twenty-four years? That doesn't even make sense. You were six, you said. That's twelve years ago. That doesn't add up."

"That depends how you count, little princess," Cynthia turned her head, surprised to see Eros inside the room. They hadn't heard him enter. It was hard to tell whether his tone towards her was genuine or derisive and her face turned red as he looked over her gown again before turning his face towards Evangeline. He cocked his head and raised his eyebrows and Evangeline grabbed the breeches, trying to cover herself. She was still in only a long shirt and stockings, never having finished getting dressed before the screaming began.

"Turn around." Cynthia demanded. Eros' eyes flashed at her, but he turned around nevertheless. Evangeline gave her a grin and hastily put on the rest of her medieval attire. Cynthia helped with shaky hands. She wasn't sure why she was standing up to Eros rather than kissing his ass – her usual go to with people she needed; and they definitely needed Eros. Yet, going against him felt clearer. As if she remembered who she was this way.

The door opened audibly this time and Ehvan entered, holding a large tray full of odours that immediately filled the room. Cynthia's fingers stopped fastening the last tie on Evangeline's corseted leggings and she breathed in deeply, as did Evangeline. Her eyes widened at the smell of real, cooked food.

Ehvan approached the cage cringing his nose slightly, put the covered tray on the floor and tried to slide it closer to the cage with his foot. Eros sighed, seemed to hold his breath, picked up the tray and placed it right beside the cage bars, immediately stepping away again.

"The royal chef is dead," Eros said, "One of the townswomen volunteered to make this for you. She hasn't cooked in twenty-four years and we have no taste for spices anymore so you will have to be happy with whatever she managed to concoct."

They both nodded. Cynthia sat, wide eyed, not knowing if she should approach the cage bars with Eros and Ehvan in the room but not able to concentrate on anything besides the smell of whatever was on the tray. Eros walked towards the door, giving Ehvan a shove to follow him.

"Eat," Eros said at the door, "We will return in half and hour. You put your pants on needlessly, Evangeline. Were you not about to practice saving our world by flashing your behind at it, just like at the hospital?"

~

Evangeline sat, her face red, her mind flabbergasted. Eros was gone before she could even begin thinking of a response. She hadn't clicked in until now that he had apparently seen *everything* at the hospital. Obviously, he wanted her to know in order to humiliate her. And yes, it was definitely humiliating, but beyond that, it was disturbing.

Cynthia was completely absorbed by the food, "Well, I guess I shouldn't be surprised that it's chicken," she said, lifting the tray lid and pulling a chicken leg into the cage through the bars. She bit into it hungrily. Evangeline grabbed one and began to chew on it as well. It was quite good, the townswoman in question obviously having retained some memory of how to cook.

Cynthia was back to her usual self while eating, attempting to not get her gown greasy and to sit and eat properly, even if it was with her fingers. Evangeline sighed. She had already gotten grease on her squire uniform.

"I can't believe he saw you do that crazy dance at the hospital," Cynthia said between mouthfuls, "What if there's people or things seeing us and watching us all the time?" She said nonchalantly.

"Yeah, like now," Evangeline said, her voice slow and pointed. Didn't Cynthia see the importance of this? "How are we going to escape? What if they hear everything?"

"We don't hear everything. But we do hear well," they heard Ehvan's small voice at the door, followed by a delayed knock. He stepped into the room just as another holler pierced the air. It had been quiet for a while and Cynthia screamed in surprise, dropping the chicken on her gown.

"What is that?" Evangeline asked, "What's happening outside?"

"It's Okay," Ehvan's voice was calm, "he won't hurt you. He's in a cage just like yours, except outside. He's waiting for the sun to rise and burn him to ash." He said this plainly and matter-of-factly, as if it were a perfectly normal occurrence.

Evangeline and Cynthia stared at him. He didn't seem to notice that they were waiting for more of an explanation and in turn stared at their chicken.

"How do you eat it? Can I watch?" Ehvan asked.

Evangeline put a piece of chicken to her lips and bit it slowly.

"I want to know how to eat when I'm human again," Ehvan said and Evangeline felt a pang inside, looking at this grey boy who was something between a lost child and deadly creature.

"And how will you turn human again?" Cynthia asked, trying to wipe the grease from her dress. Not even looking at Ehvan. Evangeline looked over at her. Was this some sort of trick question for Ehvan or was Cynthia insensibly taunting him?

"Mother says Evangeline will turn us human," Ehvan answered happily, "Lola heard from the girl creature that the portal looks for something when it opens, but she couldn't understand what. It opened twice by Evangeline. Mother says its important. And Bambi was led to Evangeline. All of that means Evangeline is here to turn us human so we have to make sure she lives and we can't eat her," Ehvan recited the words as if they were a poem memorized at school.

Evangeline tried to push aside the feeling of disturbance over the fact that apparently if she didn't find a way to save them the alternative was being eaten. "Why is that man outside going to burn to ashes?" she asked, shifting the topic.

"That's what happens when we aren't human inside anymore," Ehvan stated and again Evangeline stared at him along with Cynthia. He stared back. Finally, in a slightly frustrated tone, Cynthia asked, "Can you explain?"

"Oh...we need blood," Ehvan said, raising his eyes to the ceiling as if pondering, "We need it so much we lose all our other thoughts slowly. When we lose all our thoughts we go mad. Eros says we turn into animals with only instinct remaining. We can never turn back to human then. So, the mad ones go in the cage outside and the sun turns them to ash so that they don't turn everyone else mad. It's the only way to protect as many citizens as possible and keep them human inside."

"But your mother said that you all hold on to something to keep you human," Cynthia said, "So, why did that man lose his humanity?"

Ehvan cocked his head to one side and after a second of pondering answered, "We study and train every night. We train to be as many things as possible. Then, if one of us gets eliminated another can take over. And, to think is to be, Eros says. The more we learn and the more we think, the longer we can be. Mother says when we were human we were always trying to learn about the world and our own nature, but it's hard to study for twenty-four years, because all I want is blood. Every now and then someone…gives in to that want. To the blood. I suppose it re-motivates me to keep studying." Ehvan sighed, cocked his head in the other direction and stared at them curiously, "Can normal humans lose their humanity?"

"Some people lose themselves I guess. They forget who and what they are. If you lose yourself inside then in a way you lose your humanity," Evangeline pondered in response and noticed that Cynthia's hands were shaking and she dropped a piece of greasy chicken. She picked it up again quickly and bit into it. Evangeline turned back to Ehvan, "But you have so much curiosity and so much humanity. I don't know if I could last that long. Julia said over two decades?"

"Almost twenty-five years," Ehvan said.

"But Daoud came to my house only twelve years ago. Were you infected for thirteen years before that?"

"No. One year. Daoud came to your house twelve years ago your time and twenty-four years ago our time. Eros calculated that time in our world moves twice as fast, after he watched you for some years."

Evangeline frowned. Was her whole life Eros' comedy?

Ehvan stared at her with his huge eyes and then as if understanding her human thoughts smiled proudly, "Eros doesn't have mother's talents. He could only see you when mother let him join her. And, mother could only visit you through your subconscious and sort of other states of mind, she said, like your dreams or when you had a fever -"

"Or when I was almost dying…or…on drugs at the hospital," Evangeline finished, sighing a breath of relief, "but I've never seen you, Ehvan."

"I only watched you one time. You were younger than me…when I was young *verus*. Mother said I screamed and almost went mad for many days after that. Eros said I could not reconcile in my child's mind what I was and what I turned into. I wanted to be human so much. I was not allowed to watch again…There are almost no children left. Most didn't survive the bites and the others went mad very quickly. They say for children it's better not to remember the before...They almost didn't let me see you now, but I promised that I was stronger in my mind. I like to watch you. Except I want to drink you and that makes me upset. But, please don't tell mother or they won't let me see you again," Ehvan finished quickly, looking at them with desperation.

"Cross my heart and hope to...yeah, just cross my heart," Evangeline said.

Ehvan smiled and breathed in. At the smell of their blood his face turned animalistic and he stepped quickly back, returning to normal but looking ashamed. Evangeline felt an aching sadness, along with the obvious terror. She quickly thought of something to say, "By the way, Ehvan, I didn't understand what you said at the beginning. Something like 'when I was young *verus*?'"

The door opened and Eros entered with Julia, "I wouldn't expect our dirty princess to understand the word" - his eyes skirted over Cynthia's stained gown and turned to Evangeline - "but, I would have thought *you* would have figured that out. Isn't that what your parents are paying for?"

Verus. Evangeline thought. *It sounds like the Italian "vero", meaning "real" and obviously Eros knows her parents were paying for Italian lessons.*

"It means 'real', so you said, 'when I was young for real'. But that's not really Italian." She said.

"Italian is your language," Julia said, "Latin was our language. It is the original language of Latina."

"Which entered your world and then you bastardized it into the thousands of slangs which you earthlings call languages," Eros added.

"And English entered our world and became the tongue of the educated, and I am sure we bastardized it in our own way," Julia said in a reprimanding tone and Eros cleared his throat but said nothing further.

"As you may have noticed, thoughts and therefore ideas somehow move between our worlds," Julia continued, "We are interconnected.

Your 'antimatter twin' as you like to think of us," she smiled at Evangeline, "Is that confusing?"

Evangeline and Cynthia were both quiet. Evangeline thought of the outside of the castle and how it looked so much like the Duomo in Milan, "Yes and no," she said. Eros snorted.

Evangeline rolled her eyes and looked away from him. There were more important things now than getting into something with him again. When Ehvan had stated that time ran twice as fast in Latina than on earth she had been momentarily ecstatic. This meant that while this was their third night here, only one and a half nights had passed on earth. Realistically, she told herself, it had probably taken their friends at least a couple of hours, if not a day to get over the shock of what happened and now they were regrouping and trying to figure out how to reopen the portal. *So, me and Cynthia still have time to save everyone as long as we get away from the city fast. I have to get to the point with Julia, now.*

"How do we get out of the city without being eaten, Julia?" Evangeline said simply.

Cynthia gasped, "That is extremely offensive."

Evangeline looked over at Cynthia, who had gone silent when Eros and Julia had entered and again had that bizarre, demure air about her.

"We can't even hope to help them if we are dead, Cynthia," Evangeline said.

"And we can't honestly hope for you to help us once you leave," Eros laughed.

Evangeline gave him a dirty look but didn't know what to say. The truth was that all this time she had been thinking of saving Raffael, Val and everyone else from *this*. She hadn't been thinking about how to save Julia, Ehvan and especially not Eros. He was right.

"Sire, we would not abandon you," Cynthia said, bowing her head while Eros just stared at her.

Evangeline gave Cynthia an uneasy look but then saw Ehvan's face and swallowed. Ehvan's monstrous features looked crushed by Eros' words.

"I don't really know how to save you," Evangeline said, looking into Ehvan's confused eyes, "but I promise to try and never give up, just like you haven't."

Ehvan's eyes turned thankful but Eros coughed, "False promises create crushed hopes, which, as you can guess, in our case can kill. Where is Lola? She also promised to return. Give me a good reason why we should risk ourselves to help you get out of the city alive?"

"I don't have one," Evangeline looked at his face, "except that you definitely have nothing if you kill us."

"I will have one, good meal," Eros said, smiling his gruesome smile at her, "which is the only use I see you as having after watching your entire, useless life." he leaned over to the cage and breathed in, letting her see the horrific hunger on his face. Instinctively Evangeline shrunk away from him and inadvertently let out a small shriek. Forcing herself to straighten up she said, "A whole, useless life and you had nothing better to do than stare at it?"

Eros straightened up and turned to Julia, "Let me know when you tire of keeping them alive. We both know there is no way out for them anyways, unless one uses the other as bait," He turned his face to Cynthia momentarily and walked out of the room.

Cynthia was looking down at the stains on her dress in distress, as if nothing else had gone on in the room. His gaze visibly surprised her. She stared after him as he left, while Evangeline stared at her.

When the door clicked Evangeline turned to Julia with a thought, "Julia, you said that Eros and the Duke held back the vampires so that the citizens could escape. Couldn't you do that now?"

"We could," Julia said, though she shook her head no, "but half of the remaining human citizens were caught and eaten during the escape. Half of the two of you, means that only one of you will make it out alive...and that is only if you are lucky. During the original escape there was still a human army left."

"Then is there any way for us to get out of the city alive?" Evangeline's heart beat faster.

"You came in alive so there has to be a way to get you out alive," Julia answered, "and after we figure out a way to get you out alive, I hope you will return.

Chapter 23

WHAT'S HAPPENING?

Once they were alone Evangeline approached the subject of their escape with Cynthia.

"Why do you keep speaking about them as though they are blood thirsty killers?" Cynthia said in the decorous tone while huffily attempting to smudge her gown clean with one of the blankets in the cage.

"I know they don't want to kill us, but they *are* blood thirsty and they *will* kill us if we don't escape. That's why?" *What is wrong with Cynthia?* Evangeline thought. *She keeps swinging between being herself and acting like she stepped out of some southern belle, soap opera. It's beyond regular Cynthia drama. Maybe she's unable to handle this reality and this is some sort of coping mechanism?* Evangeline breathed out slowly to calm herself. If this was some sort of coping mechanism then maybe she needed to be gentler.

"I'm sorry, Cynthia," Evangeline said looking directly into Cynthia's face, "I know this is hard. I am barely handling it myself. It's insanely hard for me too."

"It's *insanely* hard for you? How is that? You are a squire. You cannot see what a princess sees," Cynthia huffed, pulled out the cage key and decidedly stuck it in the lock, turning it open.

"What are you doing? What the hell is wrong with you?!" Evangeline tried to grab at Cynthia but she was already out of the cage and walking purposefully to the door of the room. Evangeline, ignoring the scorching pain in her leg, jumped out and threw herself after Cynthia, managing to grab the back of her gown. Cynthia tried to pull herself away forcefully and the gown ripped with a loud tear as Cynthia shrieked in anger, "How dare you! How dare you lay your fingers on me. Let me go! I must change out of this dirty gown before my prince returns!"

"Are you insane?" Evangeline shouted, terrified that their shrieks and bangs would bring the whole family to the room. With all her might she tried to pull the screaming and flailing Cynthia back towards the cage but it was useless. Cynthia was equally strong and with her damaged arm and foot there was no way Evangeline could win this battle.

Evangeline was desperate. She let go of Cynthia, pulled her arm back, and slapped Cynthia across the face as hard as she could. Cynthia crashed backwards against the bars of the cage in shock. She grabbed at the back of her head shakily and feeling the wetness of blood burst out in tears.

Evangeline felt shock at what she had done but there was no time. She grabbed the disoriented Cynthia under her arms and pulled her into the cage, quickly fishing out the key from a fold in Cynthia's dress, where she had seen her place it, and shoving it in the lock.

Eros walked in less than a second later, looking unimpressed "The maid heard you shrieking half-way across the castle and made me return from-" He stopped short and began to shake. Then, he hurdled at the cage. His body hit the bars full force and the sizzle of immediately burning flesh filled the room. He didn't seem to care or perhaps wasn't in a state to care, snarling and hollering as he tried to shove his arms through the bars, his flesh ripping and burning off of them as Cynthia and Evangeline screamed in horror, trying to get as far from the reach of his arms as possible.

"Sire! Stop! Do not hurt yourself! Get rid of it!" A woman's voice shouted, her hands tearing Eros back from the bars and simultaneously gesticulating at the blood on Cynthia's hands.

The woman, with her dead hair pulled back in an up-do and her shrivelled, grey skin covering a petite figure in a dark, plain gown, roused Eros enough for him to regain partial control of himself. Stumbling out of the room, with the woman's hands still pulling at him, he grabbed at Ehvan who had now also arrived and pulled him back out. He repeated the woman's words, in half snarls as he slammed the door behind himself, "Get rid of it. Cover it."

When the door shut, only the hungry wails of Ehvan could be heard over Cynthia's sobs in the corner of the cage. Evangeline was shaking beside her.

"What's going on?" Cynthia cried.

"Cynthia, we are in Latina. We are in a city of vampires. You know this." Evangeline grabbed Cynthia by the shoulders and tried to steady her, putting her face close to Cynthia's.

"No. I mean, what's going on with me? What is happening to me? I see things Evangeline...and they're not real but...I think they are. It's like...I see what I want to see," Cynthia kept sobbing, shaking like a leaf. Evangeline brought her closer to herself, putting her arms around her.

"It's just a coping mechanism," Evangeline said, "All this...it's all crazy. It's not normal. Your mind is trying to cope. To make it normal. You see what feels normal, or good. It's Okay. It's going to be Okay."

They rocked back and forth for a while then Cynthia let go and pushed herself slightly away. She looked down at her dress again and taking the part that had torn, ripped it fully off and pressed it to the back of her head. Evangeline helped her secure it in a knot and then took a goblet of water that was sitting inside the cage and gestured for Cynthia to stick her hands out. She poured the water on them to clean the blood off and looked around for something to wipe with but the towels were outside the cage.

Cynthia took the hem of her gown and pulled hard, ripping another huge piece off.

"You're going haywire on Julia's dress," Evangeline said.

"I know, but it feels good," Cynthia said, "I wish I had my own clothes. I feel more normal getting rid of anything that makes me look like a mad royal."

"Still better than looking like a deranged squire," Evangeline said and Cynthia laughed through her tears. She grabbed one of Evangeline's sleeves and ripped it fully off. Then she took the frill-laden material in both hands and blew her nose in it loudly. Evangeline laughed out loud, half crying.

"They're going to be back. Don't tell them. They can't think I'm crazy. They will get rid of us," Cynthia begged. There was no way Evangeline would tell Eros anything. He would be thrilled at the thought that they were going mad in the cage and would be his dinner soon. But, maybe Julia should know? She wanted to keep them alive, after all.

"Evangeline, no," Cynthia shook her head forcefully, as if guessing her thoughts, "Nobody. Let's just say we got in a fight or I tripped or something."

"Okay, I promise," Evangeline said.

~

There was a knock on the door and this time Julia entered. She looked at Cynthia's wrapped up head and their ripped clothing. Her face made it clear that she wasn't convinced by their explanation of slipping on spilled water, but she didn't argue and only called through the door for Laura to bring new clothes.

Laura, the woman who had been serving from outside the door until now, was also the woman who had pulled Eros out of the room. She was one of the few, surviving servants. She had been born to a royal servant and had spent her entire life in the castle. The one thing stronger than Laura's thirst was her protective instinct towards Eros, whom she had grown up with. Taking care of him was apparently her link to humanity.

At this moment, Eros was no longer a danger to himself so Laura's thirst was again her priority. She was apparently a much simpler type of person, and being simpler had fewer needs and less control over those needs. She could therefore barely step into the room without losing herself and could only introduce herself through a small crack before going off to fulfil Julia's orders.

Julia seemed agitated, her eyes darting around the room vaguely the short time she was in it, leaving quickly after everything was sorted. Evangeline wondered if she could still smell the blood they had wiped up and was trying to control herself as well. Or perhaps she was angry at them for the damage their stupidity had caused her son. Despite her generally uncordial feelings towards Eros, even Evangeline felt bad for the amount of scorching his skin had suffered on the cage bars.

"Vampires are definitely not the beautiful creatures modern media portrays them as," Evangeline whispered when Julia was hopefully far out of hearing range.

"According to them, they aren't vampires. They have a 'Condition' which they think is healable, but meanwhile can be barbecued with strange metals," Cynthia added, "too bad we can't ride our way out in this cage. Like put wheels on it and get pulled out by some horses...because they ate the horses."

"Hmmm...yeah, I don't think we can train chickens to pull a wagon," Evangeline said while absentmindedly pulling on one of the bars of the cage. The cage had to be incredibly heavy if Eros couldn't knock it over when he threw himself at it.

There was a loud bang out in the corridor, followed by a couple of pounds on their door. Eros then flung the door open and along with Ehvan lifted up a tub, almost the size of a modern bathtub, with steam coming out of it. They placed it in the room.

"My mother thinks you need a proper bath to restore your spirits," Eros said, "Fortunately for you, I think you need it to restore a hygienic smell to this room, which is the only reason I carried this up here."

"What's that?" Evangeline asked.

"More spiritual rejuvenation," Eros responded dryly, "we have sealed many things to prevent drying and ageing."

Ehvan had instantaneously left the room and returned with a sachet full of some objects and an armful of clothes. He tried to throw them towards the cage but apparently was out of practice with throwing gently and everyone jumped as the clothes smashed against the cage bars. Eros shook his head towards Ehvan, "Leave it. They can get them when the light comes out."

"Okay," Ehvan said quietly and eyed the approaching dawn through the windows. He then looked back towards Evangeline and Cynthia and said, "The red is for you Cynthia and the blue is for you Evangeline."

Evangeline looked at the gowns. Ehvan, perhaps slowly becoming aware of human expressions, looked at her and stated, "Eros says so. He chose them."

Evangeline looked up at Eros and for a second thought his grey cheeks got a tinge of colour in them, but his answer was typical Eros, "Blood is apparently your choice colour and you appear to enjoy being only partially dressed," he said at each of them respectively, finishing off with a pointed look at Evangeline's ripped off sleeves.

"You changed your clothes also," Cynthia said to Eros and Evangeline looked more closely at him.

"My clothes burned off," Eros said.

"Oh...How is your skin?" Evangeline asked. He seemed mostly healed but his face still had a mild, burn outline across one side from one of the cage bars. She couldn't help feeling guilty and could see from Cynthia's slightly huddled position that she felt the same way.

Eros gave her a quizzical look, as if not trusting anything nice coming out of her mouth. Then he narrowed his eyes and said, "It's nothing that a drink of blood can't fix." He turned towards the door as Laura came in, holding a massive tray, bigger than herself. She started shaking uncontrollably as soon as she entered and Eros had to grab her and the tray. He placed it quickly down on the ground with one arm while the other arm wrapped around Laura and covered her nose as he pulled her backwards and out of the room. Ehvan followed them out as Evangeline scooched over to the side of the cage closest to them and shouted out, "What about discussing an exit plan? Where is Julia?"

"If you have a plan we will be thrilled to hear it tomorrow night, that is if you can refrain from ripping *our* clothes to shreds, bleeding all over the room and wasting half the night." Eros said stepping out of the room.

"I'm sorry," Cynthia whispered and as the door shut they heard him snort, "Just make yourself pretty, little princess."

Chapter 24

THE BAIT

When the sun rose the shrieks of the man began again. They knew he was burning alive and neither Evangeline nor Cynthia said a word. They waited silently, their bodies tense, until the deathly hush returned to the city. It seemed to return almost too quickly.

Evangeline and Cynthia now took turns bathing in the large tub; the sachet which Ehvan brought being full of beauty products.

"Do you think they don't bathe at all anymore?" Cynthia asked, smelling a liquidy lotion which seemed to bubble with water and therefore she was using it as shampoo. They were taking partially educated guesses with some of the liquids and solids since none were labelled in the modern way.

"I don't know," Evangeline said, "Apparently they don't change clothes much but don't stink so they must not sweat. I guess if all they drink is blood maybe they don't even go to the bathroom?"

"What if they over-drink?" Cynthia asked.

"You think they pee it out?" Evangeline's face contorted, "Eww. I dare you to ask Eros. Let's see his reaction." She grinned while combing her hair out. She was sitting cross-legged on the floor, wrapped up in a mountain of blankets to keep warm until Cynthia could help her with her gown.

"Don't you dare," Cynthia said in her old, appalled tone, "he would probably eat us on the spot."

"Yeah, and then pee us out," Evangeline laughed at Cynthia's disgusted face.

Although every now and then Cynthia would get a faraway look, she was acting on the whole more like the typical Cynthia than she had acted since their jump through the portal. *Maybe I would have gone just as crazy initially if I hadn't already seen Daoud as a kid,* Evangeline's thought gave her a sense of relief and she began to eye the massive tray of food. Cynthia had insisted that they have a proper, civilized meal once they were fully washed and dressed.

Whoever had prepared today's meal had given it their all. There was of course chicken, but in more than one format: chicken stuffed with dates and plums, chicken stir-fried with peppers, potatoes and beans and even chicken with what looked like apple sauce. On the side was again a medley of fruit. Evangeline wondered why and how they had done all this. Did the whole city believe that her and Cynthia would save them? The thought was more worrisome than comforting.

Cynthia finally climbed out of the tub and they helped each other on with all the undergarments and layers of the gowns.

"Fuck, he has a sick sense of humour, doesn't he?" Evangeline said, looking at the final effect in the mirror. While Cynthia's dress was a royal looking, red gown which flowed all around her, Evangeline had been given what could only be described as a gown for a royal hooker. The material was fabulous and the sleeves long and trailing, however, they came fully off the shoulders with the front of the gown being ridiculously low.

Cynthia looked at herself with dreamy eyes and then disapprovingly at Evangeline, "Why does he want to see your flesh when he has a princess?"

"Cynthia...?" Evangeline spun around to face Cynthia but then Cynthia said in her usual tone, "I'm starving. Let's eat. You look like a medieval whore. Glad that unlike you, I know when to keep my mouth shut."

Throughout their meal Cynthia kept quiet, seemingly intent on keeping her gown clean this time. She wasn't saying anything out-of-place so Evangeline decided it was time to bring up the topic of escape. The idea of the wheels on the cage was obviously not workable but at least it was an idea. Meaning they could definitely come up with others.

Cynthia seemed perturbed when Evangeline tried to start up the topic though and after breathing in and out deeply a couple of times she grabbed her stomach. "I think their cooking may be a bit out of practice after all. I need to go on the box toilet *now*. It's going to be completely humiliating when they empty that thing out."

When Cynthia curtained herself into the toilet niche, Evangeline hobbled to the windows and stared out at the empty world around them. She tried the balcony door again for no particular reason. Even if the door did open the only thing that would accomplish would be to allow them to plummet to their death off the balcony rather than being eaten. She sighed and leaned her head on the glass.

Cynthia had now repeatedly referred to herself as a princess whenever she seemed to go loopy. The fact that Eros had also repeatedly, albeit sarcastically, referred to Cynthia as princess did not escape Evangeline's notice. Was he doing something to Cynthia? Although Eros and Julia had never entered her regular thoughts, they had been in her dreams and subconscious. Was Eros getting inside Cynthia's mind somehow? She would have to tell Julia.

~

Cynthia sat on the closed toilet with the thick curtains drawn around her. Her head was in her hands and she was rubbing her temples with her palms.

She could tell when she was in reality, but then another world would open up around her and what she thought she knew was real suddenly became doubtful. At first she had simply let it happen. It made everything so perfect... But, it was as if something was trying to destroy her. Every time, it would give her reasons to leave safety.

And it wanted to know their thoughts and plans. She could feel it. So whatever Evangeline was thinking in terms of escaping, Cynthia didn't want to hear it.

She was forcing herself to remember what was real now. She kept touching the back of her head every couple of minutes and letting it rouse her mind. But, the alien thoughts kept trying to force their way in. They even led her to things.

While Evangeline was taking the food out of the large tray and setting it up on the small, wooden table Cynthia had walked over to the balcony. Her eyes were led to the rightmost pane of glass and the wall that it touched. She stared at the specific spot but refused to go near it. If she did, the voice would be proven right and she would lose herself again.

"You know this castle because it is yours," she heard inside her mind. She was fighting the voice, refusing to obey it and in its desperation the voice told her more. More than it wanted to.

Maybe Evangeline was right. Maybe they should tell Julia. Cynthia sat on the toilet and tried not to cry. She wouldn't survive the day. Her mind was becoming sleepy and she knew she would lose reality the moment she closed her eyes to sleep and they would both die because or her.

"You are not the extra, Cynthia," the voice kept repeating.

"You are right," Cynthia whispered.

~

"Cynthia, are you Okay in there?" Evangeline said at the curtain.

"Yes, I'm fine. Don't walk in. Are you crazy?"

"Sorry, I was getting worried about you."

Evangeline heard shuffling behind the curtains and finally they were pulled open and Cynthia came out. She didn't look at Evangeline and shuffled over to the cage. She climbed into it and immediately lay down, pulling the blankets over herself.

"My stomach is in complete knots. I need to lie down. I'm sorry. We have to escape. We have to find a way, I know. Just let me rest a bit. You look dead yourself."

"Yeah, but-"

"We haven't slept all night," Cynthia interrupted, "Maybe that's why I'm queasy. My body isn't used to the day-night flip. You've got the cage key and I'm in the cage. Relax."

Cynthia closed her eyes immediately and Evangeline began to wobble-pace the room. There had to be a way out and they needed to figure it out now. Even if time moved 2:1 for them versus Raffael, they were still running out of it. She had an urge to shake Cynthia awake and voiced, "Cynthia. Cynthia," a couple of times, but all she got in response was a snore.

Annoyed, Evangeline climbed into the cage and locked the door. She lay down beside Cynthia and stared at the ceiling, waiting for Cynthia to wake up.

~

"Evangeline," Evangeline heard the sound of her name through a dreamy cloud.

"Evangeline," the sound repeated and her eyes opened. When had she fallen asleep? She had been determined to stay awake. Shit, had they slept through the day again?

She looked beside herself but Cynthia wasn't there. She was standing beside the door to the room, her face pale and her hand on the handle. Evangeline jumped up and grabbed for the cage door but it was locked. She reached in the folds of the dress where she had placed the key but of course it wasn't there anymore. She grabbed the bars, putting her face right up to them, "No," was all she could say.

Cynthia stood perfectly still, looking at her.

"I never told you why I followed you into the lightning," Cynthia said quietly, "I hated you for being popular. You didn't even try. You didn't deserve it. Val just loved you so you got everything handed to you. I was always trying so hard to be where the action was, but everything always happened to you instead, so I followed you because I wanted to be there when it happened. I knew if I didn't grab the sword then something amazing would happen to you again. I just wanted something to happen to me. I just wanted to be the main character of a story."

"Cynthia, I'm sorry, but are you crazy?" Evangeline was desperately trying to think of what the right thing to say was, to get Cynthia safely back in the cage. She gripped at any words that might bring her back, "You are a main character. In my story. In Val's story and totally at the school."

Cynthia wasn't listening, "They're in my head," she said, staring out the window, "They know...they know what I want. They show it to me and tell me it's real. I know it's not but I can't make it stop, because I want it."

"Cynthia, let's just-"

"No. Eros was right. Only one of us can get out of this alive and it won't be me. If you die, they'll kill me, because this isn't my story. I wasn't supposed to be here, but I am here so I can have a role too. A real role. Not just the fake friend who follows you around out of spite."

Cynthia's hand tightened around the door handle and Evangeline screamed, "Cynthia! No, stop!"

"I won't last through the day" Cynthia said calmly, "It's early afternoon. I'm sorry it doesn't give you much time."

"Stop. Stop," Evangeline's mind was going in circles but all it produced was a whirling blur.

"I will distract them. You go to the window. The right wall. Pull. On the balcony go left."

"Stop, Cynthia. Come back. Please."

"Keep left. The key is under the pillow." Cynthia pulled open the door and Evangeline started screaming as she frantically threw the pillows aside, found the key and shoved it in the lock. It wasn't fast enough. The door had already clicked shut behind Cynthia by the time she threw the cage open and sprinted to the door. Even before she had made the couple strides to it she heard the screaming. She froze momentarily but then forced herself forwards. She had to try and save Cynthia. Her hand went to the handle, but just as she was about to turn it there was a crash against the door and the screaming stopped. Evangeline's whole body shook in spasms as blood flowed in from under the door, towards her feet.

Chapter 25

THE ESCAPE

Evangeline was hyperventilating. She knew what the silence and the blood meant, but her brain refused to fully grasp it. She shuffled backwards, tripping over herself and fell as she tried to get away from the blood. She couldn't even scream. Trying to control the dizziness and nausea that overtook her she started frantically repeating what Cynthia had said, in between desperate gulps of air, "The balcony. The right wall. Left."

She half stumbled and half crawled to the right wall of the balcony and stared at it, starting to cry.

"Where? What? Why did you do this?" She groped up the wall which linked the window. Her hand hit a perfectly straight, narrow crevice, which she never noticed before due to its shallowness and precise match with the walls surrounding it. She put her face close to it and slid her fingers inside, feeling around. She pushed, then pulled and with surprising ease a little square piece of wall came out with the pull and she heard a click as the balcony door opened.

Evangeline swallowed her tears and steadied herself. She stepped shakily onto the balcony. The bright glare of the sun blinded her momentarily and focusing her eyes she looked to the left. There was nothing there except the end of the balcony. She hobbled over to the left-most barrier and looked out at the great distance below. Was she supposed to jump?

She turned in a circle confused and saw a small window in the wall, half on the balcony and half past it's barrier. The balcony apparently stretched slightly beyond the bedroom and the window was to some other location. Its glass panes opened easily and she leaned over the barrier to look inside. Within, was a tight, winding stairwell.

Evangeline looked around herself, looked back into the room at the cage and the blood that had seeped in and taking a deep breath pulled herself up on the barrier. Her swollen foot was unsteady and she gripped at the cracks of the wall, forcing herself not to look down. She climbed inside the tiny window and stepped onto the narrow stairwell. Her legs crumbled beneath her and she fell on her knees shakily.

Cynthia had seen this...but why didn't she escape with her? Why? Why did she walk out that door? What was in her mind? What did it do to her?

Evangeline stared at the rock walls around her. Did Cynthia really see a secret escape or had she been allowed to see this on purpose, in order to be lured in here? Whatever the answer, Cynthia did this for her.

The stairwell was fully illuminated by light which entered through small windows going up and down the winding passage. Evangeline gripped at the walls, forcing her limbs back to life and pulling herself back up.

The way out had to be down, she thought and crept silently down past windows and small, closed exit doors. The lower she went the more bars the windows had on them. She took the door handle of the final door and pushed it open slowly.

She entered an expansive kitchen area with cupboards, hanging pots and pans and multiple wood ovens. To one side an area looked as if it had been recently used and she guessed it was where their last meal had been made. The small staircase must have been how they used to bring food up to various levels of the castle inconspicuously.

The windows in the kitchen were narrow and lined just the very top of a single, long wall, far above the cabinets. They were not curtained, probably because of their height and the limited light they let in. Evangeline tried to stay in the miniscule spots of light as she crept through the room to a massive set of doors at the end. She pushed them open.

A large, dark eating hall lay ahead, its tables and chairs covered in shadow, closed curtains lining each wall. The light that entered in through the kitchen barely illuminated their existence. Doors lined two opposing walls of this room and Evangeline decided to stick left according to her instructions from Cynthia. She ran, ignoring her throbbing leg, to the first set of curtains and pulled on them, but the ceilings were immensely high and the curtains barely budged, letting in only a thin stream of light through the middle of the room. There must have been some sort of mechanism installed to slide the curtains open but other than darting her head from left to right she had no time to figure out where it was.

She clenched her fists and frantically sprinted through the darkness to the leftmost door. She was about to open it and run through when a voice stopped her mid step,

"Don't you think I can smell you? I know where you are...always. Get...back...in... the...cage."

The sound of Eros' voice made the blood pound in her brain, her mind both screaming in rage and crying in terror.

"Go!" The final shout came just as the door she had been aiming for flung open. Evangeline saw his silhouette in the darkness and stumbled backwards with a scream. His pace was closer to soaring than running and he would have had her if the ray of light hadn't struck him as he went through it. With a holler he crashed to the ground but in a split second was up again and after her. She had reached the kitchen though and ran into a stream of light by a cupboard.

Eros stopped short in the doorway and like a prowling animal began to slowly circle the room, staying in the shade. His breathing was heavy and his eyes focused on her with bloody intensity. Evangeline grabbed at a pot on a shelf behind her and flung it at him. He caught it mid air. Screaming she grabbed another pot and flung again. Then she was throwing everything at him that her hands could reach; pots, pans containers of old, dry spices, plates, goblets and utensils. She could barely see through the furious hatred and couldn't hear the words she was shrieking at him, "I hate you! What? You're still hungry? Fuck you! I'll kill you! Monster!"

Evangeline wasn't sure how she made it back to the stairwell alive. It was like a car crash, when things happen so fast the person can only remember glimpses of the events. She scrambled back up the stairs, tripping and falling every couple of steps and sobbing uncontrollably. When she got back out the window and onto the balcony ledge again she toppled down on the balcony floor and heaving uncontrollably, began to vomit through her tears.

After some time the retching stopped and another while later so did the heaving and crying. Now only numbness remained. Barely pushing her body away from the vomit, she lay there, curled in the fetal position, unmoving for hours.

At some point Evangeline began to feel the cold air and notice the sun slowly setting. She didn't bother to try and get up and crawled back through the room and into the cage. Her eyes inadvertently went to where the blood had seeped into the room, but all that was left was a watery smear.

Evangeline lay against the bars of the cage, staring at the smear until the shadows began to creep into the room. Then she locked the door with painful slowness, curled her frame into a ball and stared at the wall.

It was Eros. He had gone inside Cynthia's head, telling her she was a princess and making her go insane. And now he was standing outside the cage, silently staring at Evangeline through the darkness.

Without a word Eros picked up the tray and the tub from the night before and carried them back out. He came back, replaced the towels and put a new, small tray of food on the floor. He looked at Evangeline one more time, but her eyes didn't move from the wall and he silently left.

Hours passed and no one else came. At the beginning of the night there were some wails and hollers from somewhere within the castle, and then only silence as usual. Eventually Evangeline sat up and turned her face to the windows. She thought that the night must be close to finishing.

Why hadn't Julia come? *She gave up. She knows there's no escape,* Evangeline thought, *I will eventually die in this cage, being fed and watered and kept like an unwanted pet, just like Eros said.*

Cynthia had uselessly sacrificed herself, thinking that she could save her. Evangeline realized in that moment that death had always been inevitable for the two of them. It could be a drawn-out misery or quick and done. And there was still Raffael and the sword. If he ever managed to reopen the portal it would find her... but only if she were still alive.

She sat in the cage, waiting.

Just before sunrise Eros came again. After the usual knock he entered and looked at the untouched tray, then at Evangeline. She looked back at him now, meeting his eyes. *Maybe it's good that it's him,* she thought, *it will kill him if I come out willingly. No mind games and no begging for mercy. I won't make a single scream. He won't get that satisfaction.*

"Do you plan to starve yourself to death? In that case why not just come out and get it over with?" Eros said dryly and she smiled. She pulled out the cage key and put it in the lock without saying a word.

"Do you think this is amusing, wench? There are no pots to throw here," he said in his usual tone but she paid no attention to the condescension now. She turned the key.

"Close it. Don't be stupid," Though still huffy, his voice began to rise slowly. He began to back away but the harshness of his breathing gave away his desire.

"I guess you are always hungry," Evangeline said and stepped out of the cage. She toppled a bit. Her foot was now swollen more than ever. She straightened herself up and ignored the pain, forcing herself to step on it normally as she moved towards Eros.

"Finish this. You know you want to," Evangeline's voice was calm, a mixture of authoritative and luring, "You know I can't escape. Cynthia was just one course. You know you want my blood...The only thing I want is to never be like you."

She's gone mad just like Cynthia, Eros thought, backing away from her smell. And then she said that last sentence and with it stepped just too close for him to resist.

Eros grabbed Evangeline by the shoulders, spun her, and pushed her against the wall with such force that he could hear the air burst out of her mouth as it was knocked out of her. His face was right in front of hers and he could see that her determination was being replaced by terror. Her breath turned shallow and quick and then only gasps came out of her open lips.

"You will *beg* to be just like me," Eros harshly whispered into Evangeline's face. He grabbed her by the back of her hair and forced her head backwards. All night, he had heard every word she had shouted at him in the kitchen. Every accusation and insult…

Pressing towards her neck as she breathed in terrified gasps he opened his mouth to bite, but then, he felt the skin on his lips. His teeth grazed it and his lips began to move down her neck of their own accord, towards the exposed cleavage. He inhaled her smell and the hunger fully took over.

His teeth ripped through the flesh of her breast; he could barely hear her screams. They were a thousand miles away. The more he tasted the more he had to have and the less he sensed anything around him. She was fighting now; screaming and swinging her arms, beating and ripping at him with her fingers. But nothing mattered. Eros let go of Evangeline's head and wrapped his arms around her, his mouth never letting go of her flesh until she stopped moving, and even then, he kept going.

~

Evangeline had thought she could do this bravely but his face…it's grotesque, crumpled greyness with that animalistic hunger made it hard to breathe when pressed right against hers. She couldn't look and yet her eyes wouldn't budge to look away. She was frozen as he placed his teeth to her neck. Then, suddenly, it was as if he were almost kissing her, moving downwards.

Evangeline started to instinctively fight. What was happening? Was he raping her? Could he?

She had less than a second to ponder before she felt the teeth rip through her skin. The pain was unbearable. She could feel the blood inside her being forced upwards towards the pressure of his mouth. He was taking every drop, ripping it out of her, right from her toes, and everything inside her burned and seared. Not even in the hospital had she felt pain like this.

Evangeline's resolve to not let out a single scream was gone. She was screaming uncontrollably now, ripping his shirt and his skin with her nails and smashing her fists uselessly against his face and head as her legs swung, kicking him incessantly.

Then everything started to disappear. The pain was there, but somewhere in the background, like everything else. Like the voices she now heard.

There was Julia screaming "No!" perhaps right beside her or perhaps miles away. Ehvan simultaneously growling in hunger and wailing in piteous misery.

And then, nothing was left.

Chapter 26

WHAT IS IT?

Julia heard Evangeline's screams but it was too late. There was no saving someone once the bite had started. Either the person would die or become one of them. Julia ran back out of the room, covering her mouth. The blood smelled too good. She couldn't do this. She couldn't. She couldn't live with herself if this was how little strength and humanity was left inside her.

She ran into Ehvan who pushed past her, screaming at the top of his lungs, and ran into the bedroom. She knew Ehvan would join Eros. They would finish Evangeline. Julia couldn't follow him. She couldn't watch Ehvan, her sweet, dreaming child, reduced to this again.

But the sounds from the room were wrong. Ehvan was screaming at Eros to stop and she heard crashing sounds. She ran back into the room and found Ehvan throwing himself repeatedly at Eros, pulling him off the body lying on the ground, which looked to be only a few mouthfuls away from death. Eros was throwing his younger brother off of himself with blind force, setting Ehvan flying and smashing repeatedly into walls and furniture, only to sprint back up and throw himself on Eros again.

"I don't want her to be gone like Cynthia! Don't make her be gone!" Ehvan wailed, finally bringing Eros back to some form of conscious thought. Eros looked at the limp body, grabbed Ehvan as well as Julia and threw all three of them out of the room, shutting the door with a reverberating bang.

"She has to die," Julia was explaining softly to Ehvan who was now cradled in her arms outside the bedroom, "it's too late. She won't be human anymore. She will turn like us. Do you want this for her?"

Ehvan just sobbed, "I don't want her to die."

"She will only turn into one of us," Eros repeated his mother's words, "she won't be the way she was. Now she cannot help us...and we cannot help her."

"She's new," Ehvan continued sobbing, "There is nothing new here. I have nothing more to think about and then I just think about blood. She...makes me think, and if I stop thinking I will stop being human, won't I? And she laughs. I want to learn how to laugh."

That last part broke what was left of Eros' heart to realize that Ehvan hadn't laughed in two and a half decades...and yet...having no recollection of his own laughter, Ehvan still realized that he missed it. Evangeline had to die. But would killing her kill what was left of Ehvan's humanity?

Drinking Evangeline had been an immediate ecstasy followed by blinding remorse and a strange sense of fear. Evangeline brought out his rage. Her words had kept him awake throughout the days, his mind furiously racing in circles because of her. Now there was nothing to hate. Nothing to feel. It would be just like before...except before, he still had her life and dreams to watch. Now there was nothing left to see. But what would she be as one of them? For some reason he couldn't stand the thought.

A scream came through the door and he looked at his mother.

"Eros, she is turning. Finish it. You must," his mother pleaded.

Both his mother and brother stared at him, each begging for the opposite. He felt nauseous. There was no right thing to do and his mother was at fault.

"You know how to finish it as well," Eros said to his mother and standing fully up, turned and walked away.

He meant to walk to the furthest dark corner of the castle he could find, just so that he wouldn't hear her screams for help, but especially so that he wouldn't hear when they ended. But turning a corner he stopped and stood still with his back against the wall and his eyes penetrating the darkness, listening.

He listened to each scream, let it sink in. It was the last he would hear of that voice.

His brother had stopped begging aloud but his weeping continued and still there was no sound of movement from his mother. Ehvan's words must have affected her too, made her see what she had brought on all of them.

Then the hissing began. He had forgotten about the approaching morning. The sun made their choice for them. Evangeline had already started to turn before the sun came out. Now, it would burn her to ashes.

Ehvan let out a horrible wail as Evangeline's screams renewed over the revolting sounds of her burning flesh. It would be over soon. His mother was shushing Ehvan while he cried pitifully.

The minutes passed but the screaming didn't end. It went on and on, as did the hissing. He straightened his shoulders. Something was wrong.

"Mother?" Ehvan whispered.

"Find your brother, tell him he must come. Now," Julia's voice was shaky and Ehvan glided through the hallway, straight into Eros. Eros grabbed his shoulder gently and looked into his face. Ehvan stared back, wide-eyed. They walked quickly back to his mother. She was standing against the wall to the right of the door. Ehvan must have positioned himself behind the door and slightly opened it for his mother to just see inside without being hit by the rays.

"Eros, I don't know what's happening," Julia said, without moving her eyes from the inside of the room. Eros pushed the door gently closed so that the hallway was again in darkness, walked over to his mother and signalled at Ehvan to reopen the door again. He veered back when Evangeline came into view.

Evangeline's body was burning and regenerating over and over again. She was screaming and crying only half consciously as her skin went up in flames and melted off, the raw flesh exposed to the light. Every part of her burned, even her face and head. As parts of the skin burned and melted off, other parts simultaneously regenerated, again covering up the flesh beneath. Then, the process would start to repeat again. The strangest was the hair, which would go up in an explosion of flames before follicles again started to regrow at inhuman speed.

Should they grab her? Pull her out of the sun? But how? She was too far in. Even if he reached her still alive himself, how could he carry her when her whole body was a raging fire? But mainly, what was happening? This wasn't what happened to humans infected with the Condition. What was she?

Evangeline stopped making sounds then. He was uncertain whether she was still alive or dead. Her body lay completely still as the flames continued enveloping her skin and it, in turn, continued to melt and regrow.

Julia stared at him. He knew she expected an opinion, which he always had, but he shook his head at her now and continued to stare at Evangeline.

"I want to see," Ehvan said, rousing him.

Julia again looked at Eros. There were times when she was the queen. The mother. She ruled both the kingdom and her household. This was not one of those times. She was looking to him to make a decision with a face full of grief.

"We don't know what's happening Ehvan. It's ugly. Uglier than the burnings in the market square," Eros answered.

Ehvan swallowed, looking wide-eyed at Eros, "Is she dead?" he asked.

"I don't know," Eros said.

"Then I want to see."

"Close the door," Eros said to Ehvan after a short pause, "mother, go to the handle."

Ehvan shut the door, sealing off the light and him and his mother were about to switch spots when Laura appeared.

"Sire, you have eaten. Both blondes are finished now?" Laura stared at Eros and he motioned for her to come over with Ehvan and she obeyed. Julia opened the door again and Laura screamed. Eros glanced down at Ehvan beside him to see how he was handling it. Ehvan stood with mouth open, mesmerized. They remained like this, taking turns watching her until the early afternoon, at which time the fires slowed, each time becoming less strong while the skin grew back more solid. Then it all stopped and Evangeline just lay there, perfectly still, her clothes burned off but her skin in perfect condition. The hair which had previously been a large haystack was now a tiny one, not having grown back to its full length yet.

Ehvan breathed in loudly, "She doesn't smell like food anymore. Is she one of us now?"

"That isn't how we turned," was the only answer Eros had, "I will watch her until sunset." He signalled for his mother to close the door and Ehvan and Laura to leave and rest. Ehvan stood still and looked up at him. Eros knew he didn't want to miss it if Evangeline opened her eyes, but he also knew that fatigue brought out hunger and Ehvan hadn't slept all day. He raised his eyebrows at Ehvan's shaky stance, "I will call right away if she wakes. Mother, take him to rest."

Julia nodded as she closed the door and led the unwilling Ehvan to his bed. Laura reopened the door for her master and went off into the darkness.

Eros didn't take his eyes off the body on the floor until sunset, hunger burning inside of him by the time the last rays of sun disappeared from the room. Not a limb had moved. Only her hair and nails continued growing slowly. The change in the nails wasn't as perceptible as that of the hair, which was now a larger mess than ever before, lying in a huge, curly disarray all around her.

When it was safe, he slowly approached her and got down on his knees beside her body to feel for a pulse. He didn't need to. He could feel the warmth of her breath when his cheek approached her face. For a second he almost smiled, then his lips tightened at the thought of what she would now be.

Lifting up the body he carried it to a large bedroom and placed her on the bed, covering her up as Laura appeared, holding an armful of screeching chickens. Eros took his allocated amount and nodded a "thank you" at Laura. She bowed and took the carcasses away.

The population would be difficult now. The whole town had been kept at bay in order to keep Evangeline and Cynthia alive, but now, instead of protecting the girls, they themselves had drunk them. It was best for the family not to be seen for a short while, until they figured out how to share this news and handle the citizens.

His mother and Ehvan came shortly after and Julia immediately dressed Evangeline in a long, proper nightgown. *Even after so many years and so much blood, my mother still has the high-bred instinct of decorum*, Eros thought, almost amused.

He looked at Evangeline, lying in some sort of sleeping state and standing beside the bed, pulled the covers slightly down and opened the top of the gown to where he had bitten her. The red marks of his teeth were there…and always would be.

Chapter 27

THE CREATURE

Evangeline's eyes opened with a sense of pain. She felt the driest, most horrible thirst she had ever experienced. Without time to recall what had happened or figure out where she was she began to heave and shout out in rasps, "Drink. Help."

As her surroundings began to focus around her, instead of water she saw a squawking chicken in front of her face and before she could formulate a thought, a hand slashed the chicken's throat and the blood began to drip into a bowl beneath it. Evangeline screamed and flung her arms at the half-decapitated chicken, sending it flying across the room and into a wall.

Her eyes were fully open now and her head was swinging from left to right, trying to take everything in, her thoughts moving at rocket speed. Cynthia. Cynthia was dead. And she had tried to run. Then there was Eros and the bite. The horrible pain. Burning fire. Wait. The bite.

Tears ran down her cheeks as she realized what had truly happened. *I'm not dead. No. No. No. I can't be one of them. NO.*

"NO! No!" Evangeline started shouting and sobbing as she grabbed at where Eros had bit her and looked down to see the glaring redness of the mark. The sight made her scream more. She looked up with her mouth still open and saw Eros standing just a foot away. Except he looked different. He wasn't grey anymore. His skin was a normal colour, dark like the hair that now had none of the greyness of before. He was handsome and young, with outlined cheekbones and a square chin and almost nothing left of the prior decay.

She stared at him, her thoughts blank.

"You need to drink. Laura, give her back the chicken," Eros said. His voice, at least, remained the same, hard tone. Laura came in and picked up the dripping carcass longingly, her appearance exactly as dreary as it had been. Evangeline stared from Laura to Eros in confusion, when the bloody chicken was again shoved in her face. The smell of the blood hit Evangeline's nostrils and she put both hands over her face in revulsion, turning her face away from it. Then she stopped. She slowly looked at Eros, "I don't want blood. I want...water." When Eros didn't move and only stared back at her she repeated, "Water?"

Finally, Eros looked over at Laura but she was mesmerized by the chicken, her hands shaking while she still dangled the half-decapitated thing.

"Just drink it," Eros said to her and she ripped into it, gulping in relish and making Evangeline close her eyes and look away, trying not to gag. She reopened her eyes when the sounds of gulping had finished. This time Eros was holding a goblet of water in front of her face and she took it with shaky hands and put it to her lips.

She took a tentative sip. The water tasted exactly as it always had and she wanted it. She wanted water. Evangeline tipped the whole goblet and greedily chugged down all of it, asking for more as soon as she finished. Eros looked unsure but left and almost instantaneously returned with a refilled goblet which she drank just as quickly. After the third one she finally felt better and putting the goblet down narrowed her eyes at Eros.

"Stop whatever you're doing to my mind," Evangeline said, "I know you don't look like this. You're making me see things just like you did to Cynthia. I'm not stupid. I can see Laura."

"Laura didn't drink you," Eros responded, meeting her eyes.

"What?"

"Chicken blood is not human blood. Those with our Condition need human blood to regenerate. I drank you. Laura did not," He kept looking into her eyes completely without expression. Her eyes moved over his face, taking in his skin, his hair, his youth. It was all from feeding off of her. Her hand instinctively went to the bite mark again and she looked down at it, "I don't feel like a vampire." The statement came out almost as a question and her eyes went back to his.

"I don't think you are."

"What am I?"

"You're...something human, I think."

Evangeline looked at him in shock. What did he mean *I think*?

"YOU did this!" her shout surprised even her and for a second she stopped and then, looking at his face, which only looked at her anger with condescension, she pulled herself up and stumbled out of the bed, "You *think* I'm something human? You *think*?"

Completely blinded by her anger she rushed at Eros and swung her fist. She had never punched anyone in her life and to both her and his shock, Eros blocked the swing a second too late and her knuckles met his nose straight on. A crack reverberated in her ears as his face flew to one side and he toppled backwards against a wall.

Evangeline stood stock still, breathing hard. She looked at her trembling hands and opened and closed her right fist, feeling no expected pain and seeing no damage.

"I'm...I *am* a vampire," Evangeline started to shake again, "I don't want to be. Why didn't you kill me like Cynthia?...You did this on purpose...You wanted to torture me! You turned me into you on purpose." Evangeline's eyes widened and then narrowed with the realization, her voice turning hard and slow.

Eros had bounced back up and his arms and shoulders were tense, his face slightly lowered as he looked at her, his jaw tight in what appeared to be forced patience.

He destroyed Cynthia. He hurt her. But, now, she could hurt him too. He would re-heal but she would break every bone in his body anyways. She clenched her fists and rushed back at him. This time though, she didn't have the advantage of surprise and he easily grabbed her and threw her on the bed, her body crashing into it and flying off the other side. She jumped up, leapt over the bed and rushed at him again. Eros blocked her punch, the expression on his face almost bored as he picked her whole body right up and flung her face down on the floor. He grabbed both of her arms behind her back and pinned her down with his knee, bringing his face down to hers.

"I don't know what you are, but your new strength does not compensate for the fact that you still fight like a little girl," he spoke through gritted teeth while she tried to pull herself out of his grasp, manic with fury. He only pushed her against the floor harder until she stopped screaming and gave up the struggle.

He then let go of her arms and stood up, staring down at her as she lifted herself up with some effort. She felt a bit of pain now, though her anger was nowhere close to subsiding. She stood face-to-face with him, her fists clenched. His lip curled up on one side, watching her breathe heavily.

"Enlighten me as to when you will be finished your tantrum and be ready to behave minimally like the big mouthed wench you generally are."

Evangeline stared at his curled lip and any desire for self control was gone again. She slowly exhaled, unclenching her fists. Then she stepped slowly back and did a half turn as if to walk away from him. She could see out of the corner of her eye that he loosened his shoulders and lightly crossed his arms in front of his chest. She did one quick step forward with her left foot and spun back towards him, her right leg flying up in a half-circle, high-kicking Eros straight in his face.

He flew at a desk and crashed into it, its wooden legs giving way and both him and the desk plummeting to the ground. The sound he made was something between a roar and a growl as he flew up into a standing attack pose. The derisive patience was gone. There was now only livid fury on his face and all his muscles tightened. She stumbled over her feet, trying to back away from Eros when she saw something in the doorway of the room. A loud sob came out of her. Eros turned his head, following her gaze and slowly unclenched his fists. Evangeline stumbled backwards into a corner of the room, her eyes never leaving the doorway. Then she crumpled down.

Julia moved slowly from her position in the doorway. Her footsteps were soft and silent as she approached Evangeline, but to Evangeline's new ears each step sounded like a giant stomp and she stared at the feet, not wanting to look at the face.

When she was a foot away, Julia spoke quietly, "Evangeline."

"Get away from me," Evangeline said, "Liar. Murderer."

Evangeline forced her shaky body up and willed her eyes to stare straight into the smooth, unwrinkled face, with its pinkish glow and long, smooth, golden hair tumbling down around it, that could only signify that Julia too had fed on a human. But, only Eros had fed on her.

"Get away," was the only thing Evangeline could repeat.

A tear came down Julia's face. She backed away, nodded and said, "I understand." Then, she turned and disappeared from the room.

There was still one person left standing in the doorway. Ehvan's hands were clasped together and his face was down. Blond locks fell over his face and she could see his smooth and rosy childish features surrounding the full, pouting lips that quivered. He slowly lifted his face and stared at Evangeline with round, frightened eyes. Evangeline stared back at him.

Eros, moved towards his brother and stood slightly between Ehvan and Evangeline.

"I killed Cynthia too," Ehvan said from behind Eros in a small voice, "I couldn't stop. Am I a murderer?"

Evangeline bit her lip and swallowed, pulling herself together enough to speak to him, "Can you tell me the truth Ehvan? About everything?" She looked at Eros and added, "Alone."

Instead of moving aside, Eros moved even further in front of Ehvan and said, "Do you think I will allow you to be alone with him?"

"I would never hurt *him*."

"I trust Evangeline," Ehvan said, his voice and his eyes hopeful as he stuck his head out towards her from behind his brother.

"I don't," Eros said towards Evangeline "You were unpredictable as a human. Now, we don't even know what you are, but gentility obviously isn't one of your traits." He wiped some leftover blood from his face as he spoke. She had smashed his nose twice in a row and she flinched as he took it in his fingers and quickly cracked it back to its original position, only a flicker of pain crossing his face.

"Fine, then sit outside the door," Evangeline said and Eros snorted, "You are in my room, little girl."

Thrown off guard Evangeline's head spun from side to side. She instinctively covered the top of her nightgown with her hand when she looked at the bed.

"You are not so lucky," Eros said with a sneer, "this was the closest room with a made bed where I could finally cover you up. Your gown burned off. You have a habit of turning your clothes to shreds."

"Thank you for your hospitality," Evangeline said and pushed past him and out the door, without looking at his face, "will you take a walk with me then Ehvan?"

They wandered the dark castle halls, Ehvan manoeuvring the night without any issues while Evangeline stumbled beside him. Eros trailed them from a small distance until finally they came upstairs to an open, viewing area which overlooked the main hall that her and Cynthia had initially run into. Looking down at it, she could see now that it was the throne hall. It looked desolate as Evangeline sat down on the ground, pulling her knees in and staring down at the empty thrones from in between marble pillars.

Ehvan sat down beside her and she looked at him. In their short acquaintance it had become obvious that he either never fully learned to tell anything but the truth or had long forgotten the concept or purpose of lying. He was the only one she could trust. Evangeline's mouth felt like sandpaper, but slowly she began to question him.

Ehvan told her that Julia had watched Evangeline's life for the last twenty-four years. She believed this connection had a purpose. Although Eros did not agree with his mother he often watched Evangeline with her, through her talents of entering minds, which he did not possess. When Evangeline and Cynthia arrived at the castle Julia had every intent of protecting them. She believed Evangeline was the key to something, but then, by accident, she entered Cynthia's mind.

It had been their first day at the castle and Julia couldn't sleep. She stood silently outside their door and kept breathing in the smell of their flesh and blood and listening to their voices. A mind cannot be entered unless it is willing and Cynthia wanted comfort and reassurance so much that she was open to receiving it in any way.

As she listened to Cynthia's voice, Julia slowly started to hear her thoughts and began to answer to them. She told herself she was just making things easier for Cynthia. Making her feel better. But the moment she entered Cynthia's mind she knew deep down inside that the hunger was taking over. Every time she walked into their room from that moment on, she smelled only Cynthia's blood. They were all taking double their allotted daily blood portions just to be able to be in the same room as Evangeline and Cynthia but now that Julia knew that all she had to do was push a little and she would have human blood, nothing was enough.

She didn't tell anyone, both ashamed of what she was doing and afraid that they would stop her if they knew. She tried to stop herself but Cynthia initially made it so easy to keep re-entering. By the time Cynthia tried to stop Julia, Julia's want for her had grown too great.

Eros and Ehvan hadn't seen humans for so long that it was difficult for them to tell what was normal and what wasn't, especially for two women stuck in a cage. Eros began to suspect that something was happening to Cynthia but by the time he put his finger on it, it was too late. Julia was waiting right outside the door.

Evangeline felt that Ehvan's answers should make her feel some sense of pity towards Julia, but she couldn't. All she could do was mourn Cynthia while keeping down the nauseous feeling which crawled up from her stomach every now and then when she watched Ehvan's smooth, innocent face as he spoke.

Ehvan was not supposed to be there. He was only wandering the hallways, looking for his mother, unable to sleep. He never wanted his new friend to become his food, but then Cynthia fell backwards and hit her head on the door and the blood came out. He couldn't remember much of what happened except that his mother had to finally pull him off the dead body. Then, he cried in shock, hiding away in his room, just as his mother was hiding in hers, ashamed and afraid to be seen by Evangeline.

"Why didn't Cynthia turn?" Evangeline asked, then added with widening eyes "Or did she?"

"Eros said she broke her head," Ehvan said, putting his head down, his mouth quivering again, "I begged Eros to fix her. He said what we did was unfixable."

"You're not a murderer, Ehvan," Evangeline said after a long silence, "I just don't know how to feel." The tears were falling again and she put her head in her hands.

Ehvan lifted his head and watched her silently for some time. Then, tilting his head in the usual way that he did when he had a thought, he said, "I did not know I could feel two things at the same time. I am sad. But I am also happy. I am happy that you do not have our Condition."

~

Eros stood a short distance away, his frame concealed by the darkness. Ehvan was right. She was not one of them. They could smell their own kind. Evangeline didn't smell like them. She didn't smell like food either though. And she was missing the hunger. Eros remembered the unbearable pain of the new hunger for blood right after each one of them had turned. They couldn't do anything until they drank. He had seen multitudes of his people shrieking and writhing in pain on the floor like animals. He had been one of them. But Evangeline had no thirst for blood. So, what did she hunger for?

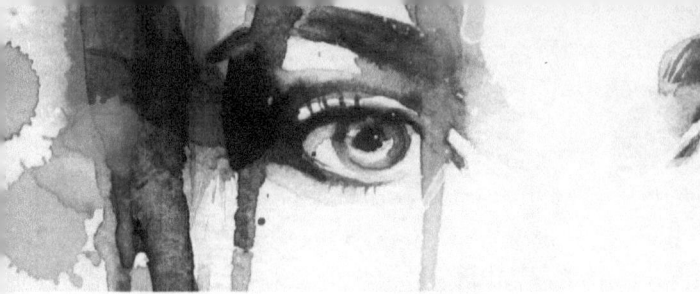

Chapter 28

SEARCHING FOR SOMETHING

The question was, who was Daniel? No search on his name revealed anything and other than googling him, there was nothing else Monica and Raffael could do.

They were still repeatedly being re-questioned by the police and random police vehicles kept popping up in front of the high school, preventing anyone from inconspicuously approaching Bambi. Not that she would have allowed them to, even without the police. It appeared that the weird, little Liza had become her personal bodyguard, warning her whenever Ian, Mark or Val tried to get to her with her mother picking her up right after school.

"Are you sure Daniel has no clue that you were at the house?" Raffael re-asked Monica yet again, sitting on the couch in his living room in Toronto while she sat a cushion seat away. His eyebrows were furrowed and his expression dark. Monica's heart thumped. She wanted to move in a little closer. They were friends now...maybe more? She was an adult. A professional physician. Why did she still feel like the high school dork with a crush on the cool guy?

"Not as far as I know," She responded.

Raffael ran his hands through his hair and narrowed his eyes, "It's just weird that he wouldn't start suspecting you when he obviously suspects me of something. You know they've been trailing me as much as Bambi. And now you are asking him pointed questions. Wouldn't that ring some alarm bells in his head?"

"I don't think so. I think I've been playing the part of 'worried girlfriend' well, but, I can back off if you want." Monica looked at Raffael's expression as she spoke.

Raffael looked at her with complete oblivion, "No. I mean, just be careful. I know you're smart," he said, "It just wouldn't be good for the police to find out that you had been in town the whole time and lied about it. It's for your safety as well."

Monica smiled at him but he was looking through her, "So Daniel was 'shocked' at Evangeline's disappearance? Fucker," Raffael said under his breath and Monica nodded, a bit shocked by the sudden language.

"I pretended to be really upset," Monica said, "I mean...not pretended. You know. Just talked about how I felt responsible because I had let them use the house and now this happened. And how you felt responsible -"

"I am responsible."

"Honestly, I don't think you are Raffael -" Monica began but cut short at the hard look on his face. She changed directions, "So then I asked about the progress of their PNH trials... you know...said I wanted something to take my mind off of things. I asked about the kids that had left the support group and kind of disappeared from my care. How they are doing. He's quite evasive."

"But he had to say something," Raffael stared into her eyes.

"Well, I did find out that they are being taken out of this area," Monica said, "and we know the support group is international."

"We need to find out where they are taken and why," Raffael said, rubbing his slight beard. He hadn't shaved since the party. Monica wondered if it felt rough or soft. He looked at her watching him and she coughed.

"I'm not sure how we can trail Daniel while he is trailing you," she said, "but, I did get a hold of some of the patient histories. Years ago, when Daniel started his work, there were no trends that I could pick up on, but lately the patients that are taken over by Daniel's research team have fifty-fifty blood like Evangeline, or very close to it. Even the support group members have blood that doesn't veer too much from fifty-fifty. But it's once it reaches fifty-fifty that he seems to take them over and they somehow disappear."

"Have you checked on their names? They must be trackable," Raffael said.

"I've only been at the Hamilton clinic for two years. Anything past that seems to have names, locations or contacts missing. It seems as though the files were tampered with to make these people untraceable... or maybe I'm just imaging it. Anyways, I will try to piece things together but it will take time and I need to be inconspicuous." Monica thought for a second and bit her lip slightly, "are you sure you don't want to let Daniel know that we know? What if he simply doesn't trust us, just like we don't trust him? We could pool our knowledge. Maybe he's on the same side as us..."

Raffael's look was full of condescension. "Really?" he said, "You think that? And you're willing to risk my sister on that thought?"

"Okay. Fine," Monica said quietly and looking down picked up her purse to go.

"I'm sorry. Really," Raffael suddenly moved over and put his arms on her shoulders, looking into her face, "You could be right, but he's been around since the first time the lightning opened, twelve years ago! If he knows it opened again why is he still going incognito? What is he? Cop? Doctor? Unless we are sure what he's all about I don't particularly want his help in finding Evangeline just so that he can make her 'disappear' like the other PNH patients."

"I know. I'm sorry too," Monica sighed and smiled, "We've gone over this. Obviously if he knew how to open the portal he wouldn't be following you. I just feel helpless. I keep thinking of what else we can do."

Raffael smiled back, "Thanks Monica. Really. You are doing a lot. Look, if you want, why don't you spend the night here? It's getting late and will take you an hour to get home."

Monica's face flushed, "Oh. Yes, sure. I don't have anything with me...I mean, overnight things."

"That's Okay," Raffael said, "I've got an extra toothbrush somewhere."

An hour later Monica lay alone on Raffael's bed, staring at the bland ceiling, grey shadows running across it as traffic moved along the streets below. She sighed and closed her eyes, looking over at the shut door to the living room, where Raffael had made his bed on the couch.

Chapter 29

LIVING AND BEING ALIVE

It soon became clear that Evangeline hungered for everything and anything, except blood. She started with around a dozen peaches, moved on to a dozen apples and then followed that up with a filler of plums and peppers.

She was trying to appear semi-civilized as she devoured anything placed in front of her, but wasn't sure of her success based on Eros' and Ehvan's awe-struck faces as they watched her, sitting around a large table with her.

While she ate, she found out that she had been unconscious for two nights and two days. She was terrified, immediately thinking of Raffael, but quickly learned that no one had entered and nothing had occurred since she passed out. After a fleeting sense of relief, confusion and fear set in. She had been gone for a total of six days/nights. On earth that would be three. Not that long, but still...

Eros said nothing, but raised an eyebrow as he watched her face.

"Raffael must be having trouble reopening the portal. The first time was a bit of a fluke," she said defensively.

"Flukes are generally occurrences that do not repeat," Eros said.

"He'll come," Evangeline said and started chewing on another plum.

Eros leaned back in his chair and looked at her, "I suppose... you seem to be a repeating fluke in our lives. It is plausible that your brother has the same, genetic talent and determination for repeating mistakes as you do."

Evangeline looked at him with a retort just waiting to be spat out, but she stopped herself. There were questions about him that were nagging at her, first and foremost being why, after making it perfectly clear that her and Cynthia were useless, he had been the one least willing to kill them. She stood up and walked over to one of the few kitchen windows, feeling his eyes follow her every move.

The curtains were slightly pulled open to let in some moonlight, adding to the glow of the candles around which they had been sitting. She pulled one of the curtains open a little more, looked out and gasped.

Outside the window was a courtyard filled with town "citizens". All were grey-skinned, shrivelled beings with clothes that looked as grey and weathered as them. Yet they were also all immaculately clean and tidy, working in an almost robotic manner, each citizen occupied completely and absolutely by one, particular activity; in one spot, a citizen was crawling with slow intent, immersed by the action of picking miniscule pieces of dirt from between the large, cobble-like stones and collecting them, while another citizen followed, scrubbing each rock meticulously. In another spot, a wall was being painted with slow, perfectly rhythmic precision and windows polished to a shine by arms that seemed to move in precisely calculated circles, all seemingly in sync. A large fountain in the middle of the courtyard had four individuals walking through its emptied interior, two brushing out any dust and debris from each tiny crevice of a large, carved female angel in its middle, while the other two scrubbed and polished the surface to perfection.

Evangeline stared in awe, first at the beings and then at the massive angel. The angel's arms stretched out to the heavens and her complete surface sparkled as if millions of tiny fireflies had all climbed just within the rock surface, their tiny glows coming through, just vaguely.

Eros came over beside Evangeline and followed her gaze, "That's the Evening Angel," he said, "a master sculptor spent ten years carving this statue. The rock which he sculpted out of is extremely difficult to work, but has the quality of emitting shine in the moonlight. The Evening Angel is therefore said to be impervious to the powers of darkness. A protector in the night." His grin looked sarcastic and Evangeline turned and looked out at the statue again.

"It's beautiful nevertheless," she said, "But what are they all doing?"

"What do you see them doing? Working," Eros said. "What did you think we do all night long? Devour millions of chickens?"

"Well, no. I just...why? I mean-"

"You mean, what's the point?" Eros crossed his arms lightly, "To stay human" he said, catching her eyes straight on with an almost curious smile. It was a little unnerving to see his face so normal. Evangeline had gotten used to its startling ugliness and seeing him now as relatively handsome and with human expressions was...strange. She cleared her throat and looked back out the window. Did these "human" actions of taking care of the town keep them remembering? Feeling?

"We go to school too," Ehvan piped in, coming up behind them.

"Really?" Evangeline was quite curious now, "What do you learn in school?"

"Everything," Ehvan said excitedly, "we learn from every, single book! Mother says many of the books were reserved for scholars and people of title or special potential before. The regular commoners didn't even read or write. But now we learn everything because empty minds go mad the fastest. So, we fill everyone's mind. It's hard to remember much though because our meals never fill us and the teachers are always hungry too. But sometimes, some things make me think and that's good. When I was learning about the universe I memorized the planets, moons and stars that we know in order of most to least likely to have warm blooded creatures."

Evangeline looked at Ehvan's little, proud face. She knew she probably should be horrified, but seeing that face, brimming with accomplishment at having memorized all edible planets was like something out of a horror movie parody and she burst out laughing. Ehvan looked at her, puzzled.

Perhaps too much had happened, all of it terrifying and confusing and her mind needed to grab onto something to keep going because she suddenly felt that she desperately needed to laugh. She was craving it. She looked at Ehvan's confused face and laughed harder, not quite knowing why.

Eros looked at her with a combination of derision and confusion and then, although it was obvious he was fighting against it, chocked out repeated snorts of laughter.

"I don't understand. Was it not a good, academic accomplishment?" Ehvan asked.

"It was a truly impressive, academic accomplishment, Ehvan," Eros said, clearing his throat.

"I'm sorry, Ehvan," Evangeline added, "adults are just strange. How old are you anyways?"

"When? When I stopped changing or now?" Ehvan asked while Eros snorted at Evangeline's use of the word "adult" directed at herself.

Evangeline rolled her eyes at Eros and turned back to Ehvan, "Uhm, well, when you stopped changing, I guess."

"Ten," Ehvan said.

"Wow. You are really smart for ten," Evangeline looked at him wide-eyed.

"I've been ten a really long time," Ehvan answered, though still looking pleased.

Evangeline smiled at Ehvan, wondering at the strangeness of how this worked. Being stuck an adult was one thing, but being stuck a child meant that although you memorized more, your brain wasn't growing or developing. *It's where Ehvan's strangeness must come from*, she thought, *his adult vocabulary on one hand and his emotional immaturity on the other.*

Without any forethought Evangeline reached out and gently patted Ehvan's hair. He looked up at her hand confused and then sniffed at it. "I like the way you smell now much better," he said.

Evangeline tentatively put her hand back down and looked over at Eros' handsome, but hard face.

"So, what about you? How old are you?" she said.

"Why? Do you think I'm cuuuuute now? Wanna date me?" Eros said, abandoning his strange accent to attempt to imitate hers, still somehow able to add sarcasm to every word.

"You're annoying and pompous actually, and where did you get that cheese-pre-teen-flick vocabulary?"

"Mostly from your head," he answered with a smile.

"When? When I was ten?"

"I cannot be sure, but trust me, your thoughts were never much more 'adult' than that."

"From the tiny amount I allowed you to see," Evangeline said looking straight at him. While she knew he had had limited access to her life she still didn't know the extent of those limits and her face betrayed her and turned red. He brought his own down to meet hers and his smile grew broader.

"You never answered the original question, little girl."

Evangeline knew that if she didn't answer it would confirm in his head that she was enthralled by his new, good looks and he was arrogant enough without that thought. She forced her eyes to meet his and said, "Yes, you are fairly handsome when your skin isn't falling off, but trust me, having now a slight inkling of your personality I would never have the slightest desire to date you, with or without your Condition. And you're avoiding my question. How old are you? Or are you afraid to tell me, old man?"

"Twenty-four," Eros frowned and turned away.

Ehvan was about to say something but Eros just gave him a hard look and Ehvan closed his mouth again. Evangeline looked from one to the other but getting only silence looked back out the window.

"Can I meet them?" She asked, watching the citizens, "Will they talk to me? Can I go outside?"

"No," Eros said and Evangeline was thrown back by the hard tone.

"Why not? I'm not food anymore," she said.

"As far as we know," Eros answered, "No one knows how the others will smell you or react."

"Aren't they all just like you?"

"Alright, we don't know what *you* are."

"You really don't know at all? I'm really not one of you?" Evangeline was both anxious and hopeful but trying not to feel too much of the latter she added, "what if I start turning...more like you, later?"

"No one turns like that," Eros said.

"Then what did I turn into? *Something* happened to me."

"The night is ending soon," Eros said, looking over her and at the sky, "Let's see what the sun tells us. Meanwhile, it is very clear why your blood was not in the mood to turn." He took a tiny, scorched, metal, mint box out of his pocket and handed it to her.

Evangeline stared at the gift from her mom. It had been in the gown and repeatedly engulfed by the fires that enveloped her body, scorching it and destroying its colour and decorations. But, it had survived. She tried not to think about the part of her life that this little box belonged to. She didn't want to cry in front of Eros. Instead, she focused on the PNH.

It made sense. Her blood was already mutated, but not all of it. The mutated parts must have been resilient to the alteration, or perhaps altered in a different way. Meanwhile, the normal parts were infecting her with the Condition, which was why her body kept burning in the sun but then regenerating repeatedly. She had burned for almost twelve hours, according to Eros. She was glad she could remember only the first couple of minutes. Even that much had been unbearable.

She pondered. Had all the normal blood eventually all mutated or burned off? If yes, she was now one hundred percent PNH? What did that mean? Would she die? But she felt alright, better than alright actually. Other than being brutally hungry when she woke up she felt strong and clear. It was as if she saw every detail more clearly and heard every noise more distinctly. But weren't those traits of the Condition? And new blood was constantly being produced in the bone marrow, did that mean that she would burn alive every day? Only the sun would tell.

~

The citizens all left, walking in the same direction, apparently for their morning meal, prior to shutting themselves in for the day. Soon after, the first rays of sun began to arrive, at which point Julia appeared. She stood at a distance, in the doorway of the kitchen area, giving Evangeline the option to ignore her. An option which Evangeline took.

They had re-closed the curtains but still Eros and Ehvan went into a particularly dark corner behind some cupboards. Evangeline walked up to the window, still in her long, old-fashioned nightgown. Eros had (in his usual kind fashion) pointed out that since textile production and trade were at a historical low in Latina, their supply of ready-to-destroy gowns was not unlimited.

Standing in front of the window Evangeline tentatively pulled the thick curtain just barely open. A few rays of sun landed on her hand and it tingled. It was a slightly piercing tingle, bordering on pain, but she kept her hand in the sun and after a few seconds it went away.

More thrilled than she could ever imagine being, Evangeline did a childish bounce for joy, spinning her head in Eros' direction and sticking out her hand to show him. He only stood and watched, though Ehvan clapped and bounced along behind him.

Evangeline turned back to the window and pulled the curtains open more, letting in a belt of light, positioning herself in it.

"Shi...ohhhh" she jumped back out of the light, her whole body piercing and burning. She closed her eyes tightly, her palms sweaty and her teeth gritting against each other and stepped back into the light. The needles pulsated through each and every inch of her skin. She was shaking and sweating, teeth still gritted and eyes closed, forcing herself to remain there, hoping and begging every power above that she was still Evangeline. Still human.

The pain slowly began to subside. Evangeline opened her eyes and watched the rays on her skin, feeling them burn her less each second. Then the burn was all gone and only the feeling of warmth remained. She opened the palms of her hands and lifted her head up to the light, bursting out in ecstatic laughter.

Still laughing, Evangeline turned around and faced Eros and Ehvan again. She could have sworn she saw the hint of a smile on Eros' face before he gestured for her to close the curtains. She nodded but then stood for another minute in the light. She placed her palms against the glass and let the warmth go through and enter her skin, feeling its now gentle sensation. She heard Eros clear his throat and she took her hand off the window, pulling the curtains closed.

The room was now solely illuminated by a couple of large candles and that vague light entering in singular streams through the slit of windows along the edge of the ceiling. Evangeline sighed, preferring the open light of the sun or even moon to this closed off, candle-lit dungeon.

"You're going to sleep now, aren't you? I'll go outside then," she said, addressing no one in particular.

"It's autumn. Perhaps some clothes? Shoes?" Eros said, looking at her bare feet.

"Oh, yeah. I wasn't thinking."

"Hmm. Come," Eros led the way out of the kitchen with Ehvan about to follow. He stopped and turned to him, "It's time for you to eat your meal and rest. You will see Evangeline tomorrow night."

At the sound of the word "meal" Ehvan's eyes protruded and Evangeline barely had time to smile at him before he ran out with his mother behind him.

Eros led Evangeline out the kitchens, through the large eating hall, then through the main doorway to an even larger, open room just behind the throne hall, at the side of which stood a wide, curved, marble and gold staircase. They went upwards and into an open hallway. While they walked Eros looked back every now and then but Evangeline barely paid attention, her mind a blur of joy at being something closer to human than to vampire. She only looked around when they again entered his room.

"I'm going to wear your clothes?" Evangeline asked, looking at him just as he grabbed her from behind, in a locked position, holding both of her wrists hard in his hands. He pushed her face-down on the bed and put himself calculatedly right on top of her. She started screaming and attempted to pull her arms out from under her own body and his grip. He had fighting skills which she completely lacked though, as well as a much larger body mass which he was now using to keep her down and immobilized.

He let go of her with his right hand and used it to reach for something on the edge of the bed, while still holding both her wrists with his left hand. He grabbed whatever he had been groping for and flipping her over on her back at lightning speed, shoved her left wrist into an iron handcuff, clicking it shut.

Chapter 30

TRUST ISSUES

As soon as Eros attached Evangeline to the bed he took his weight off of her and stood up, distancing himself just enough to avoid the free arm that was trying to get at him.

"What the hell?! What -" Evangeline started screaming at Eros and stopped. He was very calmly walking over to a large, leather-bound chair standing along the wall and facing the foot of the bed. Her eyes wide and her mouth open, she watched him sit down and look at her with a placid calm.

"We are not as immune to the sun as you," he said.

"Wha...?" Evangeline looked at him, first confused and then awestruck, "You think I would kill you?" The thought hadn't even crossed her mind. She had been completely engrossed by the joy of not being burned alive that morning. He sat there and continued looking at her as he slowly cocked his head to one side.

"I would...never kill someone," she stammered.

"Why not?"

"What? I don't...I never thought about it. I've never killed anyone. I couldn't."

"You wanted to kill me when you first woke up," Eros smiled slightly.

"No...I... I wasn't really thinking. I wouldn't have killed you. I just...wanted to hurt you a little...a lot." Evangeline finished off quietly and Eros raised his eyebrows. She breathed out and slumped her shoulders, giving up on trying to wrench her wrist out of the cuff. She slowly wriggled and slid herself as much as she could towards the headrest so that she was in a half-sitting position. Looking properly at Eros she bit her lip, "I'm sorry for that. Well, most of it."

Eros grinned for one moment, then turned serious again, "Don't be" he said, "The truth is I would have killed Cynthia if I had found her first."

Evangeline looked at the hard expression on his face and said, "At least you never lied."

"Neither did my mother. Not to you, anyways," Eros was trying to meet her eyes as he spoke, but she looked away, still hating even the thought of Julia. He continued nevertheless, "My mother cannot accept the fact that she is what she is. She lied to herself. She was a great queen. A great human. It is a credit to her that she even managed to get you into the cage without killing you. I wouldn't have. The only reason you survived was because of Ehvan and only because he had fed on Cynthia and the experience shocked him...he only tasted human blood once before...a time he can no longer remember."

His words only partially reached Evangeline. Her mind had gone to a place that was hard to bear.

When Cynthia had died Evangeline had had an emotional breakdown. Since waking up, her emotions were like a squash court, with the ball bouncing from trying to keep Cynthia out of her mind to realizing that with everything else that was happening it was easy to not think about Cynthia at all. This would send Evangeline spiralling into incredible guilt at being able to put Cynthia aside and she would purposely force herself to think about Cynthia again, not be able to emotionally take the rawness of it and run back again to trying to get away from her thoughts.

Right now was one of the moments when she forced herself to bring it to the surface and slowly moving her eyes back to Eros said, "Where's Cynthia?"

"She's in the catacombs below the castle," Eros responded, meeting her gaze, "we put her within a dormium tomb. Some were still left open. Dormium is what your cage was made from. None of us can touch it. Her body won't be...disturbed this way."

"How did you put her in?"

"We managed. Now that it is closed though, we are not able to reopen it without great effort."

"Can I open it? Can I see her?"

Eros looked at Evangeline for a minute before responding, "Do you honestly want to?"

Evangeline's heart was in her throat. No. She had never seen a dead person in her life. She couldn't. Not Cynthia. Not the first time ever. She couldn't handle it.

"No," she finally said, "but can I see where she is?"

Eros nodded, "I will take you tonight."

Evangeline lifted her cuffed hand as much as she could towards him and tilting her head looked at him from beneath, "I'm not going to kill you."

"I prefer to know where you are," Eros responded, not appearing in the slightest bit moved. "Since my mobility is constrained by the light during the day, keeping you within my line of vision appears to be the only option."

"I am NOT going to kill anyone," Evangeline couldn't help groaning as she spoke, "are you going to chain me to your bed every night? You're going to have to trust me."

"Trust is not demanded. It is earned. I do not trust anyone who tells me to trust them."

"You know, you make it hard to like you."

"Rulers are not meant to be liked."

"Well, then you are doing awesome."

"You would do quite well as a queen yourself, wench."

Although Eros' statement was an insult, it had an aspect of compliment to it, which was a first for Eros and Evangeline grinned crookedly. Seeing the grin Eros lifted his eyes to the ceiling, back to his usual condescension.

Evangeline snorted without caring. She wasn't sure if she found him less menacing because his looks were more human for now, or because he actually was less menacing since he stopped having the constant urge to eat her. Apparently Eros preferred to be menacing and with a tight-lipped look turned away from her.

"What's with you anyways?" Evangeline said, "What's your deal with the constant 'wench' and 'commoner' and 'peasant' stuff?"

"You are a wench and a common peasant, are you not?" Eros sucked on his teeth as he spoke.

"I see your highness didn't pride himself on creating an educated, middle class?"

"We are all intellectual geniuses now. Were you not listening to Ehvan?" Eros laughed dryly.

"Seriously. Don't you have anything between royalty and peasants and wenches?"

"Apparently you would be that magnificent middle ground?" Eros gave her his usual look, which generally gave the impression that he was about to snort any minute. She groaned loudly and was the one to roll her eyes to the ceiling this time. Well, if she couldn't move and he would be a jackass all day, she might as well try to sleep. Apparently, she would be living the night life with the rest of the inhabitants.

Manoeuvring her body around the constriction of the handcuff Evangeline crawled under the covers on the bed. Although she had slept for two days straight, her body was still worn out. She yawned, only her head sticking out from beneath the sheets and said offhandedly, "Aren't you going to crawl into a coffin or something?"

"What?" Eros literally barked out. Evangeline couldn't see his face anymore but his tone made her giggle a little wickedly. With her eyes half shut she said, "That's where vampires are supposed to sleep according to our legends."

"That's both revolting and incredibly over-dramatic."

"That's Hollywood," Evangeline yawned again. "So where do you sleep?"

"In my bed. What's Hollywood?"

"A place where they tell revolting and over-dramatic stories," Evangeline mumbled, more to herself than to him, "sorry I took your bed. Oh, wait, you bound me to it. Comfortable dreams in the chair then."

"Consider yourself lucky," Eros retorted, "if I were human you would be begging me to bind you to my bed."

He expected a retort back from Evangeline but got nothing in return. He stood up and walked over to the bed. He stared down at her closed eyes and slightly open mouth, her breath coming out of it in a slow rhythm. After a little while he felt his mother's presence and found her just behind him, watching Evangeline over his shoulder.

"I have not slept in four years. I only rest with my eyes closed," his mother said as she watched Evangeline's calm breathing. Eros did not reply but walked back to his chair and sat down again.

"She is the key that Lola saw in her mind," his mother said, "Lola said 'the one who remains human will have the cure'. I thought she meant Bambi. I always assumed that Bambi would return. But she meant this. She meant Evangeline, except that Evangeline knows even less than us. She will need to find Daoud to find the answers we need. She will need to leave." His mother looked at Evangeline's bound hand.

"Of course she needs to leave. She cannot live in a graveyard," Eros said, then smiled tightly, "and once she leaves, she will never return."

Eros saw his mother open her mouth to speak again and stopped her short, "Let's not start this again, mother. Lola preferred to kill herself rather than come back. *No one* in their right mind returns here if they are able to leave alive."

"She will return, Eros. I can feel it. She reacts differently to us. She sees us as human-"

"You are assuming, just as you are assuming that she will forgive you for Cynthia."

His mother put her head down and her shoulders quivered. Eros sighed. He shouldn't have said that. She had enough pain inside of her for all of their pasts. But the hopes, the attachments, were they keeping them alive at the expense of more pain? He walked over to his mother and they stood side by side looking at Evangeline. *She actually looks sweet*, he thought, *when she's not rolling her eyes or snorting or groaning or...just generally speaking.*

Eros' mouth started to move into the shape of a grin but he caught it and stopped it. "Alright mother", he said, "We can hope but we also have to be realistic. I am highly uncertain whether she will receive a warm welcome if she does manage to reach Sadamanta. On the other hand, if she does find any humans on the way they may take her for one of us and that won't be a very warm welcome either. Even with all her present strength mother, I would be surprised if she managed to fight off a friendly rabbit."

"Well, then you would be the correct person to train her," Julia said and Eros burst out in a laugh. Evangeline stirred slightly and he stopped, lowering his voice.

"You are a regular court jester, mother."

"Are you telling me that you lack the ability?"

"You are trying to work upon my pride."

"And it is working. She will be willing to learn. Let's see what you can do."

They remained silent, watching Evangeline's rhythmic breathing. *My mother is on a mad, hope filled mission again*, Eros thought. He had been renowned for training soldiers and his mother thought she could trick him into proving that he had skill enough to train anyone. He didn't need to prove that. Of course he had the skill to train her. But what would be the point? Why bother?

Evangeline rolled over on her back and the top of her nightgown became visible. He stared at it, his mind inadvertently travelling down the cleavage to the marks left over by his teeth, the only scar that remained on her skin, hidden beneath the bedsheets. His mouth felt dry and his teeth suddenly ached, almost pulsating in his mouth, his mind back in the room with the cage, his teeth running down her skin.

"She must meet the citizens tomorrow," his mother's voice made him start and he looked at her slightly confused.

"We still do not know what she is precisely or what she can do," Eros heard himself say, as if from a distance.

"And we may never know precisely," his mother responded, "The citizens are becoming wary and suspicious. She must be seen. You know she is not dangerous and she is no longer edible. That is all that matters."

Eros did not respond, only frowned his unwilling agreement.

"And on the topic of danger Eros, I believe you need not bind her in the day."

"I had my nose broken repeatedly tonight. Her temper is unpredictable."

"As is yours," his mother shook her head at him in one of those condescendingly motherly moments that still made him grit his teeth. She looked at his face and laughed lightly, "I have often wanted to break your nose myself. I applaud the girl."

Eros looked at his mother and sighed, "There is no hope in chaining her again tomorrow anyways. She will not be stupid enough to get within a mile of me at the break of day. I will remove the handchains from the bed in the evening and Laura can put fresh sheets on the bed before the following morning."

His mother looked at him curiously before responding, "There are many spare bedrooms, perhaps we can ready one of those?"

Eros cleared his throat, "Yes. Of course. I'm tired and hungry. I am going to rest my eyes now for a while."

Rearranging himself slightly on the chair he placed an elbow on one of its armrests, propped his head up on his arm and closed his eyes. He could feel his mother still in the room, watching him for some time. Finally, he heard her footsteps moving towards the door and her sing-song voice say softly, "Have a good rest. I will see you in the evening."

~

"Eros, what pleasure do you gain from this? Stop. Don't answer that," Julia said, standing in the doorway of a room with intricately decorated walls, etched in gold, with a number of chairs and loveseats positioned around small tables.

A young woman was desperately trying to throw her gowns on in embarrassment, her face red and bent low so as not to be seen. Eros stood up from one of the loveseats, running his fingers through his black, wavy hair and casually threw on his shirt, then stood and rubbed his chin.

"You are betrothed. You are in line to be king after your father. What kind of man are you, Eros?" Julia was shaking at the calm stance and amused smile that her son wore on his face, standing there, in front of his mother, half naked with some cleaning or washing girl.

"I am simply a man, mother," Eros replied, his tone frustrated, "it is as simple as that. Do not look at me as if I am Daoud. Do not make me out to be some languid and idle virgin seducer. I do not take my title as a birthright but as an honour which I work hard to deserve. You know this."

The girl had by this time pulled herself mostly together and was standing at the door with her head still down, waiting for her golden-haired queen to unblock the way. Julia did not move, but looked at the girl.

"What is your name and where in the castle are you employed? Lift your head," Julia said, filled with disgust and fury. The girl began trembling again but before she could lift her face, Eros stated in a tone of unquestionable authority, "Keep your head down. Mother, step aside."

Julia could feel her face burning red at his words but she controlled her anger and stepped aside to avoid further confrontation in front of a servant. The girl, still shaking, ran through and disappeared into the hall. Before Julia could turn to Eros in full fury, he shut the door with a bang and faced her, "Do you think she did anything that I did not want her to do?"

Julia's face turned even more crimson, but he continued, completely unabashed, "Did you mean to dismiss her or punish her for doing precisely what we both wanted? I have agreed to do my duty and marry the girl you and father have chosen. The young duchess is of the right breeding and proper training and a beneficial tie. I, in turn, will be a proper husband to her. However, until then...well, future kings betrothed since puberty do not go courting and that is why the world has wenches."

"Well, I suppose I must say that you always do take full responsibility for your actions. I cannot fault you with lack of accountability," Julia said tartly, "however, this is not a light in which any mother wishes to see her son in, Eros."

"Then I suggest knocking."

"You are in the drawing room, Eros. Really. If you must...be a man...can you not do so in your own, private chambers?"

Eros looked around himself and lifted his eyebrows at her, shrugging, "Perhaps this room was not the wisest choice. I apologize. However, I do not bring wenches to my bed under any circumstances. When a woman enters a bed, she does so with the assumption that we may fall asleep together and I have no intention of falling asleep beside someone that I have no desire to wake up beside. I prefer to clearly eliminate the hope that there is any longevity in our encounter."

Chapter 31

THE CHILD THAT DIED

It had only been four days since the lightning but Bambi felt so tired she could barely move. They had all repeated the same story so many times that all of them knew it by heart. Thankfully, news in a high school travels fast so Bambi knew what story she was sticking to. Even Jack, who didn't give a shit about Evangeline or Cynthia stuck to the story, probably figuring this was the best way to get the cops' attention off himself. And there was a lot of attention. Both sets of parents and local police were still searching for clues.

During the party, the other party guests had heard shouts coming from the "portal room" but no one had seen anything out of the ordinary so the group passed it off as Bambi making them do an extra loud chant. Then in the chaos of the police arriving and everyone making a run for it, it was easy to believe that Evangeline and Cynthia got scared for having a party without permission and run off with everyone else.

And that's when the story went blank. No real clues could be found anywhere. They were simply gone and no matter how many times the police re-questioned everyone, none of them told them anything new or different. By the third day they stopped questioning, all of them except one creepy looking police guy who introduced himself as Norm, and who specifically came by Bambi's house. His three-quarter hair part and plastic looking smile made her almost as queasy as his strange, almost knowing questions.

"There was a strange hole in the ceiling, Bambi. Can you tell me anything about it?" He had asked on his first visit to her house.

"I didn't notice. The house was overall pretty dilapidated from what I remember. There must have been lots of holes," Bambi replied in the emotionless, bland tone she was so used to using at school.

"Hmmm," was all he said, staring at her and just smiling for an uncommonly long time, like some deranged serial killer, before continuing, "You like vampires, don't you? Are you a vampire?"

"We're sitting in the sun. So, no."

"But, you like vampires. Were you chanting a special chant to find some? The other kids at school said that you tell them that your birth mother was a vampire?"

"Oh, I just say that to sound cool." Even Bambi knew this statement sounded bizarre, but maybe if the creepy cop had seen some of her death clan friends he might think that amongst their group it was cool to state that your relatives were vampires.

"So... did you find some vampires with your chant, Bambi?"

"No, the cops interrupted our chant. Anyways, I just found that chant stuff on Google."

"Hmmm..." he said and again sat there smiling at her.

He came to her house more than once, each time asking variations of the same questions. Bambi was pretty sure that Norm was the same Daniel that Raffael had pointed out in the car after the party. She wanted to talk to Raffael and warn him but she felt watched. For some reason she was scared of going out alone. Of even taking the bus. She made sure her mom dropped her off at school and picked her up daily and barely left the house without a "chaperone".

Another reason that she didn't search out Raffael was because she knew that if he got the chance to get her alone, he would try to force her to reopen the portal. She had seen him stalk her in his car while

Ian and Mark were cornering her every chance they got at school. Mark even pretended to want to date her. Strangely, Val made only some dull attempts to question her, after which she backed off, though she did get in the habit of giving Bambi dirty looks every occasion she got.

Then there was Liza. Bambi tried to avoid her at all costs, but apparently she was now some sort of dark goddess in Liza's eyes. Before Evangeline's party Bambi hadn't minded Liza, though she knew that the tiny girl was a complete fraud. Liza's general favourite was explaining, while staring at people, that she could suck out the life blood of her enemies with just one look.

Bambi hadn't minded this. Just as she hadn't minded the others in their group, so purposefully anti-establishment that they actually formed an establishment of their own. None of this mattered to Bambi because even though they all probably thought she was just as fake as the rest of them, they at least let her state the truth and pretended to believe her.

But now, Liza had found that Bambi had some sort of real power and kept begging Bambi to reopen the portal secretly with just her. Bambi would always say "maybe", while thinking "never".

At least Liza's tiring adoration was good for two things: she helped Bambi avoid everyone she wanted to avoid and she adamantly agreed with Bambi that the police should know nothing. According to Liza, it was up to them, goddesses of the night, to hide this world from the undeserving common minds.

Bambi was sitting at her desk in her room now, staring out the window at the darkness setting in. She had given up by now on trying to stop the flashbacks. Once her memories had been reopened there seemed to be no way to close them off again. The blanks in her life were refilling themselves with horrific memories out of their own accord now.

Some moments it was so bad that she cowered in the corner and cried for hours, shoving her pillow in her mouth so that her parents wouldn't hear her screams. She waited now. She focused her eyes on the moon, which looked as if its bottom tip were touching the roof of a faraway home and just waited, a pillow ready, firmly in her grasp.

And suddenly, the moon was gone and Bambi was back in the basement of that safe home her mother had found. It was the last night again. Bambi was cowering behind the couch as her mother stood, her body no longer shrivelled and disgusting, but instead filled with a healthy glow and a porcelain sheen that only comes from feeding off the living. Only some red veins, pulsating with dark, rich blood that was not her own, visible in spots beneath her dark, glowing skin, marred her physical perfection.

Her mother had stopped throwing things now and was putting the vase down which she had almost hurled at Bambi. As she did so, a blood red tear slid down her cheek.

The memory went blank and then resurfaced again with her mother returning near the end of the night. She walked over to Bambi and picked her up, holding Bambi close to herself. As she did so, her mother began to shake, her face turning ugly with animalistic desire before she quickly controlled it. She then tightened her hold on Bambi as she approached the threshold of the basement.

As they walked through the doorway her mother took Bambi's chin in one of her hands while still holding her up against herself with the other. She turned Bambi's little face towards her own and looked straight into Bambi's eyes. Bambi saw the flash of red from beneath the mesh of the hat which was meant to make the unwanted things disappear. However, this time they didn't.

They entered the main level of the house, into the hallway between the living room and the kitchen. The house was silent, but its surfaces were no longer clean and sparkling. As they walked through the kitchen towards the front door Bambi stared down from her mother's embrace at the tiled floors. Her mother walked slowly, in an uneven trail, avoiding the dead bodies that lined it. Blood was everywhere: on the shrivelled, desecrated bodies, the furniture and the walls. There were so many men. Had they been the easiest to seduce into the home? The stench of the rotting, sucked out flesh was horrific and Bambi put her face inside the shoulder folds of her mother's long, dark gown so as not to vomit.

They walked down the road and she again felt that disquiet as her mother pushed her forwards alone, her terror when her mother disappeared and her arrival at the scene of a crime and finally the sheet that she pulled off of the dead girl.

She saw the teeth marks on the dead girl this time. Her mother's teeth marks on a child whose face so much resembled her own. Why? Why would her mother purposely kill a girl that looked just like her own daughter?

The memory was gone but her thoughts kept circling. Why? Her mother had killed that girl, most likely imagining that she was killing and feeding off of Bambi. Her own child. Nothing made sense. And after all that, why did she save Bambi in the end? And where did she go?

Bambi stood up shakily and walked out of her room. Her parents were downstairs and she quietly entered their bedroom. She knew exactly what she was looking for. She had stared at this object many times in the past, wondering what it meant. Initially she had found it through accidental snooping but finally her adoptive parents had told her about it.

She walked over to her mom's dresser and opened it, pushing some books aside to lift up the little, flat box underneath. The were some photographs and one letter inside. She flipped slowly through the photographs, all featuring the same girl. Finally, she landed on one which was a close up of her face; the face of the dead, bloodied girl from the stretcher. Her parent's real daughter. She stared at it a long time before opening up the letter and rereading its contents.

To parents who have lost their child, a child who has lost her parents.

Her mother's flowing handwriting looked up at her. Below the single sentence was the address of the house which her and her mother had hidden at and where she had killed so many. The police, after finding all the bodies, had decided that Bambi must have been one of the only surviving victims, too traumatized to remember anything correctly.

What they couldn't figure out was who had written the note. Her parents told her that the police felt it was the killer, feeling a strange pang of temporary remorse that Bambi must have brought on. They assumed, based on the note, that Bambi's "lost" parents were among the victims, yet no one was ever able to trace them. The assumption was that her parents' bodies had been placed in a location that was never discovered.

After years of legal battles, Bambi's adoptive parents, convinced that Bambi had appeared on their lawn in the middle of their own horror for a reason, did obtain adoption rights. Bambi loved her adoptive parents. They were good to her and like they once told her, considered Bambi a sign; a heaven-sent meant for them.

Bambi cried now as she sat on the floor, staring at the photograph of their dead daughter, wondering how they would feel about Bambi if they knew that the parent of their adoptive child was the one who had murdered theirs. And perhaps... their child would not have been killed that night if she hadn't looked so much like the one they now raised.

Chapter 32

WELCOME TO OUR WORLD

Evangeline awoke to Eros shaking her slightly and clearing his throat. She rubbed her eyes and realized that both her hands were free.

"You sleep like an elephant in a coma," Eros said.

Evangeline just groaned, not awake enough for any comebacks. She turned her head slightly and noticed with bleary eyes that Ehvan was bouncing up and down right behind Eros. She rubbed her eyes again and lifted her head up, trying to take a better look at him. He was holding a basket full of something white and as soon as he saw that he had her attention, jumped out from behind Eros.

"Evangeline!" Ehvan said, pushing the basket towards her face, "Look! Josep said the eggs we usually throw away are good for humans! Did you know that you can put eggs in hot water and they turn into human food? Look! I did it all by myself and they turned hard inside. Will you eat it? Can I see it?"

"I would love to," Evangeline chuckled, "You know, I love eggs."

"Oh," Ehvan looked crushed, "you have eaten eggs before?"

Evangeline stifled a laugh, "Well, yes, but, how did you know that eggs were my very favourite? May I?"

She sat up and reached out for the basket and Ehvan eagerly watched her take an egg. Evangeline cracked it against the side of the bed and began peeling. She noticed Eros staring at her as much as

Ehvan and wondered if he secretly enjoyed watching people eat as well.

She placed the peels back in the basket but dropped some between the bedsheets accidentally, the result of which was an exasperated groan from Eros as he looked at the mess on his bed. Evangeline just smiled sweetly up at him before taking a big bite of her egg.

Ehvan's eyes bulged out and he let out a "Wowww," as she chewed and Evangeline burst out laughing with her mouth full. She quickly covered her mouth with her hand so as not to spit up egg all around her, apparently a second too late for Eros. He sucked on his teeth and lifted his eyes to the ceiling, "When you are done turning my sheets into a plate, I will take you to wash up and get dressed. The citizens have been waiting for hours for you to grace them with your presence."

Evangeline swallowed the rest of her egg and looked up at him flabbergasted.

"You wanted to go outside. Did you not?" Eros asked.

"Yes. Of course. I'm just...nothing. Yes!" Evangeline jumped out of bed and kissed Ehvan on the top of his head without thinking, "that egg was awesome. May I have another?"

Ehvan passed the whole basket to her with joy etched all over his face while Eros watched with narrowed eyes that widened ever so slightly at the kiss.

Ehvan ran off to do his schooling, and Evangeline followed Eros out of the room. They walked down the hall and a couple of doorways later Eros opened a room and stepped in. Evangeline remained in the hallway and only craned her neck to look in.

The room was smaller than Eros', with a single bed positioned against the wall opposing the door. This wall was covered by long, deep green curtains which were most likely concealing windows. A large, finely woven rug with complimentary shades of green covered the centre of the room and a wooden wardrobe with the usual gold finishings and handles stood against the wall to the left of the bed.

On the wall to the right was a large mirror with a thick wooden frame and a little table and chair below it. Flowers had been placed in a vase on the table and beside that, a small, pretty basket with combs and other accessories. To the right was a fireplace nook, in which many candles had been placed and lit. A couple candelabras also stood in various spots around the room, and it made Evangeline realize that wall candelabras had been lit along the hallway and that it must have been done solely for her benefit, since neither Eros nor Julia seemed to need any light to see.

"This room is not large, but one of the brightest during the day, as well as the warmest. My mother thought you might find that pleasant. Laura readied the bed for you and mother filled the wardrobe with gowns of your size," Eros opened the door to the wardrobe to display that it was filled to the brim. He re-closed it and walked back out of the room, looking at her and smirking. In the doorway, he motioned gallantly for her to enter and said, "There are no chains."

Evangeline looked at the handle of the door and the keyhole below it, "Are you going to lock me in?"

"I wish," Eros grunted, "make yourself presentable before the night is fully over. You slept through a quarter of it. We will meet you down in the throne hall. You can find your way there."

He walked away, leaving Evangeline alone in the doorway. She stood for another second, double checking that he wasn't still behind some corner, about to pounce. Then she took one step inside and heard a knock on the door frame, just behind her. She turned to find Laura, standing with a basin of water in one hand. Without a word, Laura entered, placed the basin on the table and left. Evangeline voiced a "thank you," and tried to smile, but Laura only stared at her with the expression of a frightened animal and disappeared.

Evangeline walked over to the basin and began to wash her face, looking absentmindedly in the mirror. When she saw her reflection, she stopped.

Her hair was visibly longer than it had been in years, having reached and surpassed its original length in just one day. She approached the mirror closer to stare at her face, which seemed different in some way, and scratched her head. Then, she took her hand off her head and looked at it to see that her nails had also visibly grown in the last twelve hours. She moved her wrist in a circular motion, confused but not knowing why, and suddenly realized that this was the hand which had been damaged and swollen and now was completely healed. So much had happened she hadn't even thought about her injuries, simply not having felt them. Now she stared down at her left foot to find that it, too, was in perfect condition. After more intense self-scrutinizing she found that any freckles that she had acquired in the last eighteen years were completely gone, her skin brand new and alabaster smooth.

Fear started to rise up in her again. If she was human then why was she all porcelain and perfect? Evangeline looked around and noticed a small sliver of wood unevenly protruding from one of the table legs. She bent down, clenched her teeth and ran the palm of her hand over the sliver, hard and fast. Her skin sliced open and she yelped. Lifting the hand shakily to her face she stared at the blood gushing out. It didn't look very appealing. Hesitantly she put her mouth to it and sucked.

The taste of the blood was nauseating and she shuddered in disgust, then smiled in relief and took her mouth off the cut. She had sliced her hand a little more than she had intended to and the blood was not subsiding. Grabbing a small towel from the table she pressed hard on the wound and lifted her arm above her head. As she stood, waiting for the bleeding to stop, she considered the upcoming, official introduction to the citizens. How would they all react to her? Would they be welcoming and hopeful like Julia or more of the Eros types? She wasn't sure which was worse anymore. What if the citizens placed Evangeline on a pedestal as some sort of saviour and she fell off that pedestal? It seemed that this case scenario might be more dangerous than entering a room full of indignant skeptics like Eros to begin with.

On top of everything else chicken fed vampires were grim and desolate looking beings. How would she react to standing in front of a whole group of them? They shouldn't see any shock on her face, she decided. They might be just like Ehvan, at least some of them might be. She couldn't make them feel the horror of what she was seeing.

The blood on Evangeline's hand subsided and she began to wash her face in front of the mirror. She wiped it and then stood and looked in the mirror, pretending she was standing in the square outside of the castle, facing the other citizens. She put on a practice smile. "I look like freaky Daniel," she cringed. She stretched her mouth out and tried to smile more naturally and suddenly wondered how she had even thought of Daniel and put him quickly out of her mind. This was definitely not a good time for thoughts of her old life to swim up to the surface.

Evangeline pulled at her hair, preferring to concentrate on that instead. It was huge and a weird, in-between length and the only thing she could think of doing was to calm it with oils and force it into two tight, French braids on the sides of her head. Then, she opened the wardrobe and stared inside in confusion. She had no clue what gowns were meant for what purpose. To Evangeline they all looked equally medieval and fancy. Finally, she settled on a deep blue gown with gold embroidery along a unique, lower v-cut neckline and fitted sleeves.

Once dressed Evangeline made her way down. The upper hallways of the castle were wide and easily navigated and she found her way to the main throne hall easily enough. The family was waiting in the middle of it, whispering in hushed tones which stopped as she entered. She had not been in the throne hall since the first day when her and Cynthia had run through the darkness. The night before she had only been able to gaze down at it with Ehvan, also in darkness.

Now, candelabras were lit all the way from the main entrance along the path to the large throne at the end, which stood slightly in front of four smaller ones on its sides. The glow of the candlelight wasn't incredibly strong but still managed to reveal the beauty of the room. The marble floors were in perfect condition, the slabs cut in a variety of geometrical shapes which fit each other precisely, and encircled pillars made of multi-coloured marble that led all the way from the main doors to the thrones. The thick curtains covering all walls were in fact not black, but a variety of deep reds and blues, lush yet classically simple, like the wood and gold thrones.

Evangeline wavered a little, straightening her dress and shoulders as she approached them and putting on the smile she had practised.

Ehvan was the first to speak, "Did you eat all your eggs?"

"Oh, I saved some for later," Evangeline answered, smiling a real smile at the thought of the twenty or so eggs that Ehvan had brought her. Apparently being always hungry meant that he had little concept of how much a regular human ate. From the current look on his face, the concept of saving anything edible for later was also foreign to him.

"Hello Evangeline," Julia said with a nod when Evangeline was standing in front of them, "Eros says you are adjusting well. I am happy."

"I'm Okay. Thank you for the room. It's nice," Evangeline forced the words out and they came out stiff and choppy. She wondered if she would ever be able to look at Julia without feeling a stinging sense of betrayal.

Then Evangeline looked at Eros, curious that he had given her any credit when speaking to his mother and noticed that he was looking over her gown. Damn. This was probably not a go-outside gown, but a supper gown or a horseback riding gown or a God-only-knows-what gown and she would get to hear about being a simple peasant and not knowing the difference. He said nothing about it though and lifting his eyes off the dress to her face, stated before turning and leading them towards the entrance, "Ready? That was an effective smile. Let us see if you can hold it."

When they stepped outside Evangeline immediately knew why Eros doubted her ability to hold a happy expression. She had not realized that what appeared to be most of the population of Latina would be all standing, awaiting their appearance. There were not hundreds, but thousands of grey skinned, human-like forms standing freakishly still, in every corner of the square in front of the castle and down each street coming out of it. Those that could not fit were inside the buildings on the balconies, in the windows and even on the roofs.

Their stillness, their intense, burning eyes, and their almost lifeless appearance in such huge numbers under nothing but the light of the stars made Evangeline gasp for air. She froze mid step, unable to move or breathe. Eros turned and smirked slightly before continuing forwards and she forced her body to move towards him, positioning herself between him and Julia.

They were standing at the edge of the very top stair with Ehvan slightly behind them and the silence was extreme. Evangeline knew she must look terrified and no matter how hard she tried, her facial muscles could not be forced into anything resembling a smile now. The best she could do was pull her shoulders back, look at the crowds straight on and try to even out her breathing.

Eros was watching her out of the corner of his eye and apparently being satisfied at the amount of composure she was able pull together, gave Evangeline a slight nod and began to speak to the crowds. Evangeline looked at him confused. He wasn't speaking in the accented English she had become accustomed to, but instead an odd mixture of old-English, Italian and Latin. The citizens listened motionless and she tried to focus on his words but could pick out only the gist of the speech with her limited Italian and Shakespearean skills.

Eros recaptured their history, talking of the original child creature, Lola, Bambi and Daoud, and finished off at the point where Lola and Bambi went through the lightning bolt to Evangeline's earth and Eros and his mother first entered her thoughts. It was obvious from the condensed tone that the citizens had been told this history many times, it being the main hope of a return to humanity which they held on to. After the reiteration Eros went on to state that Evangeline was the one whose scent they had all smelled. She had arrived through the thunder as a human, but her blood had been transformed to that of a mortal whose blood could not feed them, and in turn she didn't need blood to feed on.

"We know two arrived. Where is the other one?" A man, standing in the very front, said in a clear voice which carried through the silence of the streets. Evangeline felt Julia quiver a little but Eros stood still and looking around at the crowds, nodded at the man, about to answer when another voice spoke loudly, "You have fed and you have not given us food."

This voice belonged to a woman, also near the front. She was as grey and shrivelled as the rest of the citizens, but her clothes were bright and fresh with colourful crochet flowers lining the edges of her long, vibrant white sleeves. It wasn't that the other citizens' clothes were dirty. They were simply dull, the whites having long ago faded and each piece of cloth looking as though it had been re-worn and re-washed until everything blended into one, drab ensemble, no one caring anymore about anything except the functionality of whatever they put on. No one, except apparently this woman who spoke with clear resentment. The fierceness in the woman's voice was terrifying, bringing to Evangeline's mind a vision of thousands of enraged, resentful vampires tearing to shreds the three that had to this point kept her more or less alive.

"It was our fault," Evangeline heard herself blurt out. The thousands of eyes that had been burning into Eros were now burning into her and even Eros turned his face to look at her in disbelief. Her mind was racing. Perhaps he had known exactly how to answer to this accusation. Of course he did. He would not have come out here otherwise. Why had she opened her mouth? They were all looking at her now. She had to continue. Say something...something...anything.

"We... uhhhhh... we... we... had mutated blood. Both of us. We weren't safe as humans so we asked the royal family to turn us. We thought we would both turn into...me...but Cynthia (the other girl) didn't survive the change. We asked to be bitten. We knew there was no other way."

Well, some of that was true, though heavily twisted, Evangeline thought. To her relief the faces in the crowd turned from suspicious to curious and she was about to attempt breathing again when the same woman spoke again, "Do you think we can be saved?"

Evangeline stood still. The whole world seemed to be motionlessly waiting for her words. Her mind went blank as she looked from one grey face to another to another to another.

"I think so," she heard herself say as if from a distance, "If my blood could keep me human then there must be a way to alter yours back to human also."

Evangeline hadn't actually thought of this before but the moment it came out of her mouth it just made sense and she smiled a real smile. The effect of the smile was astonishing. It was as if these thousands of beings had forgotten what a smile was and seeing it almost frightened them. Some bulged out their eyes while others recoiled or trembled. Only a few seemed to push forwards, almost fervently trying to get closer to the expression of a feeling and thought beyond hunger and need.

Evangeline wasn't sure what to do. She looked from Eros to Julia in bewilderment, but before either could react the same woman asked, "How can you be here to help us? You are from the same place where this all came from."

"Josepina, Evangeline did not bring this here. The child creature did and in the end we were the ones who let it spread." Eros answered in a clear tone as he looked at the vibrant woman who refused to be appeased.

The majority of the citizens seemed to accept his answer, however, some followed Josepina's suit and kept staring at Evangeline through narrowed eyes. Evangeline met Josepina's gaze and suddenly thought of her friendship with Cynthia. She hadn't given of herself to Cynthia because Cynthia had been walled off. But, maybe the walls wouldn't have come down so late if she had taken hers down first. Evangeline's face relaxed and she tried to pretend that Josepina was not a threat but just a person she knew...a Cynthia,

"I've been told by Eros and Julia that according to Lola the child came from my world, but I've never seen anyone like you in my world, except for Daoud, when he tried to enter it from yours," Josepina seemed to narrow her eyes more and Evangeline realized she must sound as if she were trying to move the blame for all this to Terra Nova and she quickly continued "We do have legends in my world about this kind of transformation, but we always thought they were just fun stories to scare kids. But...they say all legends are based on truth so that would mean that someone must have seen this condition at some point, but it's unclear where it came from and why the child came from us to you. Those are things that only Daoud and the child would know."

"And how do you plan to get to them and obtain the answers from them?" Josepina asked a bit less harshly but still with the afterthought of a sneer. Evangeline completely didn't know how to answer this one since she never considered that she would actually do it. Julia, however, seemed to have been anticipating this question and her answer was ready,

"Evangeline's transformation has given her some of our more positive traits such as strength. She understands the risks but I promise that she will make it. Eros has agreed to train her in battle to prepare her for any potential confrontation with Daoud and whoever else she may encounter in Sadamanta."

Evangeline felt like a cartoon character whose whole jaw just dropped and slammed right into the floor. What she comprehended from Julia's words was that: Evangeline=saviour=take on Daoud= battle-trained-by-Eros, and frankly that whole train of thought was incomprehensible. She distinctly heard Eros choke but Julia seemed unfazed and continued calmly while the crowd silently stared.

"We will need to reorganize some of your duties as well as recommence some of the human ones we have not maintained. Thank you to Lorenzo and Samina for creating the previous nourishment for Evangeline and her lost friend." Julia looked down at the man who had initially spoken and Evangeline followed her gaze, still sweeping her jaw off the ground. The man was tall and his skin was even more wrinkled than that of the others, like that of an obese person who loses extreme amounts of weight, their stretched-out skin just waiting for a surgical body lift. A quite different woman stood beside him, her equally tall height exaggerated by her extreme, wrinkled skinniness, which did not match her profusely round face.

"If you are willing to oblige," Julia continued speaking to the man and woman, "we would ask you to continue creating the human nourishment for Evangeline, while she is with us in Latina."

Lorenzo and Samina both looked at Evangeline as if waiting for her approval and she said, slightly abashed, "It was delicious. Thank you."

Lorenzo and Samina said nothing, but only looked back at Julia. She apparently took this as a yes and continued speaking, back towards the whole crowd, "Some others will be chosen to create food supplies for her journey. We will need to relearn using the smoke house in order to create durable, dried meats and fruits. She will need to have a combination of long-lasting components that a human body requires. We will also need a seamstress or two to create appropriate travel clothing for a woman, mainly from the garments which we currently have. Those who volunteer and are skilled enough will receive additional blood to compensate for the extra energy expense.

Josepina, you were once and still are a fine seamstress. Evangeline is willing to help us. Are you willing to assist her by acting as head seamstress?"

Evangeline wasn't sure if Josepina was at all willing to help her, however, the promise of more blood seemed to bring something resembling an excited smile to her face and she nodded her accord.

The speeches ended shortly after, with Julia finishing off by thanking the citizens for the hospitality she knew they would show their guest while she stayed and explored their city, and announcing that it was now mealtime.

The word meal had an immediate effect, with even Eros and Ehvan suddenly looking like they were itching to run. The rest of the citizens did not even attempt to refrain themselves and seamlessly turned in the same general direction, proceeding down the streets in smooth lines, only looking over their shoulders every now and again at Evangeline.

After the citizens were all way on their way Eros motioned for Evangeline to follow and led the group down a different path away from the castle. Julia kept giving him perturbed looks and after a minute of walking said, "Eros, she does not need to see this."

"This is what we are. You want her prepared, do you not? And on the note of preparation, I did not agree to train her."

"I don't want you training me," Evangeline said and turned to Julia before Eros could respond, her voice spitting out "why did you state that I'm going to find Daoud? You don't have the right to make this promise on my behalf, not to mention without my knowledge. You don't have the right to use me as a scapegoat for your unfounded promises. Is this what you do regularly? Who do you think you are?"

Julia stopped in her tracks and suddenly Eros' face was right in Evangeline's, "I let your initial outburst go when you first awoke and I do not wholly disagree with you for once, but from now on, whatever points you want to make, don't ever use that tone with my family." His voice was dangerously quiet and half of her recoiled while the other wanted to keep pushing. Ehvan ended whatever was about to start with his wide eyes and his lips quivering as he spoke, "You don't want to help, Evangeline? We'll never be human?"

"No," Evangeline said quickly, afraid of what her words might have done to him, "I want to help and I will. It's just..."

"I did not ask Evangeline and made the choice for her. That is wrong," Julia said, touching Ehvan's face consolingly while begging Evangeline with her eyes not to destroy him.

"But you would choose to help us anyways, wouldn't you, Evangeline?" Ehvan looked at Evangeline with his big eyes and she swallowed her anger.

"Yes, you're right," Evangeline said, "I would have chosen to help you no matter what. I just have a quick temper, but it really doesn't make sense to be mad at your mom. I'm sorry," she smiled at Ehvan, but he kept looking at her with the same uncertainty. Not knowing how else to fix this, she said, "I promise, Ehvan and I never break a promise. You keep your promises, don't you?"

"I have never made a promise."

"Promises are something that can't be broken," Evangeline said.

"Mother promised that one day I will grow to be a man, just like Eros."

"And your mother never breaks her promises, does she?"

"No. Never."

"See, I promise also. Just like your mother," while Ehvan was nodding his head at her, looking calmer, Evangeline turned slightly and gave Julia a quick, hard look before facing Eros who silently nodded once and began to lead again.

Julia walked silently beside Eros while Ehvan and Evangeline followed behind. Ehvan began to chatter about his school and training, forgetting his doubts in the excitement of being able to show Evangeline his whole world. He grabbed her hand and holding on, swung it the whole way.

They finally reached the dead end of a side street which was composed of a large wall, presumably made from dormium because Eros did not touch it. Instead, he pulled on a hanging rope on the side, which rang a bell somewhere within. The door opened from the inside and they entered a small space in which stood a citizen. A light suit of armour hid the citizen's entire body while a strange, facial enclosure covered the entire head, excepting the eyes. The bizarre metal mask was so tightly fit to the citizen's skull that it looked as if it were melted directly on.

"He is one of those in charge of handing out the food," Eros said, his gaze resting on Ehvan's hand, still inside Evangeline's, "the armour is in case someone tries to attack him for more food. The helmet prevents the smell of the animals from driving him mad. It is quite insulated. We can easily go without breathing for approximately one hour."

Ehvan started bouncing from foot to foot, still chattering, "Yes, Eros said we learned this after the first group of food handlers went mad and ate half the chickens on the first day. It was chaos and then everyone was *really* hungry until all the baby chickens grew up."

The food handler at that point opened a hatch to a space where someone else must have deposited three live chickens. As soon as the hatch was opened and they smelled their food, their faces began to take on their animalistic looks, not having eaten for a couple of hours, and Evangeline stood stock still, afraid to breathe. It was obvious they were trying to control themselves as they also stood relatively still, though she could see Ehvan's limbs quivering slightly. The food handler pulled out the struggling chickens and they each took one.

Evangeline had already seen Laura devour a chicken and she herself had been bitten, so the sight was endurable, but barely. The hardest was seeing Ehvan, in his childlike state, ripping apart the chicken like a brutal killer. She felt nauseous and slowly looked away, trying not to make her revulsion too obvious.

Julia looked less repulsive but more strange, her ladylike features and obviously upper-crust gestures not fitting the activity at hand. After a quick glance at Julia, Evangeline's eyes went to Eros and she was startled when he met her gaze. His movements were rough but calculated as he held the chicken in a perfect grip, his teeth making sure not a single drop of his meal spilled. Staring directly at Evangeline as he drank, his gaze was slightly glazed over, as if intoxicated, and moved from her face down to the open V-neck of her gown to right above the spot where he had bitten her.

Evangeline was frozen in her spot, his action being somewhere between sexual and terrifying, when suddenly he finished with his chicken and snapping its neck with smooth precision threw it back down the hatch from where it came. Wordlessly he turned away from her and back towards the gate with Ehvan and Julia behind him. The door was reopened and they stepped out into the open darkness.

Chapter 33

CONSCIOUS DECISIONS

They stepped back into the street and Julia and Ehvan nodded to Evangeline and Eros and began to walk away. Evangeline looked after them confused.

"Mother will take Ehvan to his schooling. We will meet them later. I will show you to the main parts of the city, but you will not distance yourself from the castle in the night without us and you will never enter any building without us," Eros spoke as he began to walk.

"Why?" Evangeline said, following after him, "I thought I wasn't edible. I thought they wanted to help."

"They want to help…but they may still kill you," Eros said without looking at her.

"I don't understand," Evangeline started to say, but noticed that in a split-second Eros had managed to be meters ahead of her. When his legs moved he looked like he was walking normally, yet it was as if he were sliding through distances.

"Is this some sort of vampire, speed gait?" Evangeline huffed out of breath as she ran to catch up. Eros stopped, looked at her and restarted walking a bit closer to her pace, "That was my regular gait," he said, "this is my shuffle."

They went down various streets, with Eros explaining the basics of their town functioning while Evangeline tried to keep up with him and keep the turns they took straight in her head as well. Other citizens had also finished their meals and were returning to various jobs and training sessions around the city. Many looked completely unsuited to their lessons, like a scrawny looking girl who was swinging a sword twice her size.

"Everyone is trained to do everything," Eros said, his glance only barely stopping on the scraggly, grey skinned child with the deadly weapon, "if we are cured of this...Condition, we will need the city to be functional, regardless of who survives until then."

A bit further down Evangeline noticed a building with large windows, through which she could see a mixed group of citizens, from tiny women to hefty looking men, all sewing and crocheting in the dark.

"Activity also keeps the mind sane. We have little but time on our hands," Eros said without pausing.

They walked through various neighbourhoods. Those that were closer to the castle consisted of wider streets and taller buildings, which had large, windowed store fronts, now either unused or restructured into training rooms. Further down the neighbourhoods tightened, each street housing humbler buildings, some with small, store front setups and others with just doors. Even in this section though, everything was immaculate, with citizens having nothing but time to perfect their city.

This tighter part of the city was busier and as they walked many of the citizens stopped to look at Evangeline, some going as far as to sniff. On and off people bowed and she bowed back politely, albeit slightly confused.

"Why are they bowing to me?" Evangeline finally whispered to Eros.

"Your behaviour and spoken presentation in front of the castle was commendable," Eros said simply and Evangeline looked at him amazed by the compliment, "though of course you could not keep your mouth shut as, apparently, always," he added and Evangeline laughed aloud to the curiosity of the citizens working around them, as well as Eros.

"Sorry," she whispered, "for a split second I thought that you had been kidnapped and replaced by your identical twin, pleasant Eros."

He cleared his throat and kept walking without bothering to respond. Evangeline snickered and rushed to catch up again.

"How come they aren't bowing to you?" She said, when she managed to reach Eros, "Shouldn't you be the king?"

"First of all, I am the prince. I was never coronated. Second of all, we generally disposed of those formalities approximately twenty-three years ago."

"Yes, it was around the time he learned to crochet with the rest of us," a voice spoke up behind them and Evangeline turned to see Josepina, with her grey face and manic, floral dress. Though exact age was impossible to tell from the citizens' generally crumbling appearance, close up Evangeline could distinguish that Josepina must have been somewhere before middle age when she turned. Between mid twenties and late thirties felt about right.

Josepina's eyes were hungry, but not bland like those of most of the others'. There was a rare amount of both life and shrewdness in them.

"You are quite pretty," Josepina said, her eyes looking as if they were speed reading Evangeline up and down, "just as attractive as our prince was before. Though he has recovered most of his appearance for now." Josepina continued talking but switched into the strange mixture of languages that Eros had used before. Seeing Evangeline's confusion, she stopped.

"You do not use the common tongue? Then you are a finely bred lady, I see," Josepina said almost mockingly and Evangeline was about to protest but Josepina continued in smooth English, "I said that this gown suits you. The dark colour brings out the gold of your hair and the lightness of your skin while the neckline appreciates your bosom. I am no longer surprised that our prince found a way to keep you alive. He always appreciated fine breasts on a slim figure."

Evangeline could only utter "Uhhh," her eyes not sure of where to focus.

"You may have no need to bow to me at present Josepina, but insolence is still punishable," Eros said evenly. Josepina did a low, apologetic bow as a response, though her eyes were still full of mockery.

"I hope I did not lead you to fear our prince. Whatever chastity you have is safe with him. We lust only for blood now. All other lusts buried," Josepina said as she began to back away, then added as an afterthought, "though not forgotten."

"I can handle your prince," Evangeline said after her, "and his lusts don't interest me."

"Then we are both of us lucky," Eros said, his eyes narrow and following Josepina as she disappeared inside a building with a sound that was something between a snort and a laugh.

"Uhm...What was she before?" Evangeline asked, still not quite willing to look at Eros.

"The *star* of the house of ill repute," she heard Josepina's voice vibrate out from somewhere in response.

"The star of the...? Ohhh... ahhh... good friends, were you?" Evangeline snickered, losing her embarrassment as the sight of Eros'.

"I did not visit this street before I was *this*," Eros said, again walking and looking straight ahead.

"Really? Then how is it that you know the lovely Josepina so well?" Evangeline continued grinning and he sucked on his teeth with annoyance.

"The 'lovely' Josepina made it her business to know, or to know about, all men."

"Really? She definitely made it her business to know a lot about you."

"And you seem to think you know me well also. You can handle me, can you?"

"I've handled you so far," Evangeline shrugged offhandedly as they entered a section which had obviously housed some of the wealthiest in the city. The street began to open up, progressively turning into a wide road, lined with villas on extensive properties stretching out around them.

Julia appeared behind them now, having caught up, most likely using the same impossibly swift strides as Eros. Evangeline tensed but tried to act natural, looking with curiosity around her at the surrounding villas, each one in a particular style, reflecting both the wealth and taste of the past owners. It was like a fashion show for houses, ranging from the ostentatious to the creative and the classic.

Walking past villa after villa Evangeline began to get an eerie feeling and finally realized why.

"I don't see any people in the section of the city."

"Not many of the highest standing citizens survived," Julia answered, "they turned but...usually went mad. Many lasted no more than a day or two. The truth is that those who have always had to survive often have more skills to do so, both physically and mentally."

Eros walked silently, his gait slow even for a human, and stared straight ahead.

"So...what about you? You are upper class but you survived and have more humanity than most." Evangeline said to both of them.

"I, as you put it," Eros said, his mouth in a one-sided, mirthless smile, "was stupid enough to get myself and the whole city turned into what it is. And so, I will be here and keep this city and its people functioning, until the very last person turns to ash." He looked ahead to a villa that had the look of a summer cottage about it, with wooden beams used intermittently between bricks for the walls and a lovely red, sloped roof covering a number of joined levels.

"I will visit Duke Karpenski, mother," Eros said, "I will meet you ahead." He picked up his speed to what was apparently his normal one and was immediately gone.

Evangeline now walked awkwardly alongside Julia for some silent seconds thinking about Eros' determination to atone for feeling that he was the cause of all of this. Was this what he held on to? In the end it probably wasn't his or his father's doing. It appeared that Mamnoon had done all the necessary damage before Eros or his father added to it. However, seeing this, knowing that he had a hand to play in this, must kill him inside, she thought, remorse eating at her for what she had said to him in the beginning. He was a pompous ass, her opinion on that didn't waver, but at the same time, he was a lot stronger and wiser than she thought she could ever manage to be in his shoes.

Julia interrupted her thoughts, "Do not mind Eros. This is the house of his fiancée."

"Oh," Evangeline was shocked, her face turned towards a large, whitewashed villa on her left.

"She was one of the first to go. Chiara was a well-bred girl but not of a very strong constitution. We felt she was a good match for Eros, to balance his...slightly stronger personality."

Though the story was sad Evangeline momentarily had to bite her lip to stifle a laugh. Only his mother could smooth over Eros' personality this well. Julia didn't notice Evangeline's slight choke and continued, "Perhaps a different person, more of his equal in strength and intellect, would have been a better choice. Perhaps they would still be here beside him...As it is, he stands alone, having to have been the one to kill his fiancée."

"He...?" Every tiny hair on Evangeline's body was standing straight up. Julia looked at her and smiled a dismal smile.

"The rules were made," Julia said, her eyes slowly moving away from Evangeline's face and to something unseen in the distance, glazing over as she spoke, "For my son, as the one who made those rules for the survival of the city, to break them for anyone, would have meant the end of us all. Could the people follow his rules if he could not? Eros is the leader. He is therefore the one to execute those that are completely lost and threaten the survival of the others. He is always the one to put them to the mercy of the sun. The rules are the same whether it is the simplest of peasants, his fiancée, Ehvan, or me."

Evangeline had no response, morbid thoughts obtrusively going through her head. They walked along in silence, staring at the mostly empty villas and she tried to think of anything that would change this topic.

"Why didn't the other citizens take over these sections?" Evangeline finally asked.

"This part of the city is farther from the food," Julia said.

"Huh," Evangeline supposed that made sense. The population seemed to have little need or desire for grandeur, "I didn't see anyone else eating with you," she realized.

"We eat separately in order to be available to keep order when necessary. The majority of the citizens go to various, designated gates where they are provided their allotted food. I believe you went by the main gate the day you arrived."

They had reached the cottage-like villa where Eros was sitting on a carved chair, watching a short, big-boned man in formal clothing tend flowers in the moonlight. He lifted his head and shakily straightened out to approach Evangeline. Taking out his hand he beckoned for hers, which she slightly hesitantly put in his. He looked at it, then slowly felt the skin as he patted it. After a couple of pats, he looked at her face and lifted a hand to touch her cheek.

Evangeline stood, uncertain of how to react as the man felt her face with both hands and burst into sobs. Eros stood up and came to the man. He put his arms around him and led him back to the chair. Julia followed them and hesitantly Evangeline did also. The man sat, and still shaking, stared at Evangeline.

"Well, I knew it was a bad hair day, but I didn't know it would put people to tears," Evangeline heard herself say and cringed. *Nothing's changed. I still make idiotic jokes in tense situations*, she mentally groaned.

Her words did manage to have some sort of effect on the man though. He stopped shaking and simply stared at her. Julia cleared her throat and spoke, possibly to stop Evangeline from speaking further, "Evangeline, we would like you to meet one of my late husband's closest friends, as well as ours, Sir Leonardo Karpenski."

"It's a pleasure to meet you," Evangeline said, trying to redeem herself. The Duke stood up again and shakily, though quite properly, bowed and officially took her hand in greeting this time. Evangeline smiled and the Duke smiled back, that grey, grotesque smile, before Eros gently led him back into the chair again.

"It is time to go for tonight. You have not eaten," Eros said towards Evangeline, "Lorenzo and Samina should be finished preparing something for you. On the way we will stop by the main educational facility."

Eros nodded at the Duke who nodded back and lifting himself up spoke for the first time, in a quiet, deep tone, "I will be fine, Eros. Thank you, Evangeline. Please come again."

Then he held up a hand for them to wait and walked over to a small tree, picked a fruit off of it and brought it back for Evangeline, "We always had the best fruit trees. They were famous. Lilia had that special touch with plants...This is for you, for the walk back."

Evangeline thanked him, took what was a peach and bit into it. It was delicious and made her realize that she was both starving and thirsty. All she had had all night were eggs and they had been walking for hours.

Both Julia and Eros walked back at a quickened pace and Evangeline had to revert back to running to keep up. She stopped to catch her breath and watched the way their legs moved. Starting up again Evangeline tried to move the way that Eros and Julia were moving.

She began to glide her legs, as if on ice and almost fell over herself, making Eros look back and shake his head. Waiting until he turned around, she tried again. This time it sort of worked. She did it again with her other foot and it worked again. It wasn't that she was walking faster, but rather as if her body were capable of bends and stretches that had previously not been possible. Her feet were gliding, barely touching the ground and she swiftly moved towards Eros and Julia, laughing aloud.

Eros looked around again to find her almost caught up, and seeing her walk said, "hmm," while Julia raised her eyebrows at him.

They reached the educational facility, not far from the castle, though on a different side of it than they had previously been exploring. The facility was an extremely large building, perhaps previously used for some sort of storage, consisting of only one open room within. The room was now set up like a library, books lining all the walls with only miniscule windows along the tops of those walls, right below the ceiling. Evangeline could barely see in here yet the citizens seemed to have no issues with the lighting, sitting at large, wooden tables spread out all through the room and either reading from various volumes or apparently writing volumes in the blackness.

They found Ehvan at one of the tables, immersed in a book which looked bigger than him. He heard them approach and lifted his head, then jumped out of his seat and sprinted over. Ehvan grabbed Evangeline's hand and pulled her to his book, explaining that it was the history of Terra Nova philosophy. He pointed to various passages, which she squinted to see when Ehvan suddenly said, "You are my first friend, Evangeline."

"What do you mean? Don't you have friends?"

"No, there's almost no children left."

"Oh...I remember. Well, I love being your friend but I'm not really a child either, you know."

"Really? Eros calls you a little girl."

Eros didn't even try to hide the wide smile that spread across his face and Ehvan looked to him for an explanation.

"Well, I'm just a bit younger than your brother," Evangeline said, smiling sweetly at Eros, "but it's just that Eros hasn't seen a human woman in so long he's lost some of his famous, previous *experience* with them."

Eros' lips tightened and Evangeline smiled brighter. Ehvan only said "Oh, Okay," but Julia looked from Eros to Evangeline, awaiting further commentary. Neither said anything else though and after a couple more minutes of Ehvan showing her what he was learning they made their way back to the castle where Evangeline was taken into the kitchen.

The smells reached her from far away and she tried not to run at the food, absolutely starving at this point. She was happy that she didn't need to try to look ladylike while she devoured half the kitchen because as soon as she was shown to her meal, everyone, including Lorenzo and Samina, left for their next feeding.

Apparently the citizens fed three times a night in order to stay more or less "balanced". They drank two chickens at the start of the evening, after the hunger of the day, one chicken in the middle of the night, and two more before dawn to get them through the next day. Pigs were saved for special occasions because they grew slower, though Ehvan said were slightly tastier, and specific additional duties were occasionally compensated with extra chickens or a pig.

Evangeline's meal was quite good, though there was a large amount of leftovers even after she had stuffed herself to bursting. Apparently Samina and Lorenzo had little recollection of human appetite as well. She decided to take a platter of leftovers up to her room for the daytime.

Eros knocked on her door only seconds after she put the platter down on her table. She confirmed that the curtains were closed as dawn was approaching and he entered, carrying a candelabra.

"You wanted to see Cynthia's tomb."

Evangeline had partially forgotten about her request during the night, but partially she had not wanted to think about it, perhaps postponing the moment. She only nodded now. He picked up another candelabra from her room and handed it to her. Evangeline followed him, holding the candelabra with a hand that was sweatier with each step.

They walked down to the main throne room, then, once inside, turned into a small, dark hall off to the right of it. It led to a couple of random rooms whose purpose was long put aside as their furniture had mostly been covered, and ended at a round, open area with marble statues of angelic creatures lining its pure white walls. In the middle of the round room was a large, circular staircase, its marble steps leading downwards, below the ground.

Evangeline felt slightly faint and her steps were shaky as she slowly followed Eros down, her nausea threatening to come up.

Their candles illuminated a massive, underground area with hundreds of marble and dormium coffins intermixed in rows throughout. Faraway hallways lead off to potentially more coffins. Eros led her to a section off to the side where mostly open, still empty coffins stood. This only made the realization stronger that the hundreds of closed coffins all around them were filled with bodies, the majority of which were murdered.

The open coffins all appeared to be dormium and Eros led her to one on the edge that was closed. He nodded to it, "Dormium is untouchable to us and it also masks scents, making it easier to resist...her body will be safe here," he said and stood back.

Evangeline sat down on the floor beside the coffin, placing her candelabra beside herself and cradling her knees. The coffin was simple but pretty, with flowers lining its edges, all melted out of the strange metal. She stared up at it, not sure what to feel. The tears that slid down her cheeks were silent and she let them slide, without any urge to wipe her face. Eros stood to the side and waited, his body and face still.

After some time Evangeline stood up, wiped her face and looked at Eros, "It's daytime isn't it? Can I go outside?"

He looked at her for a moment, his face expressionless, then nodded "yes".

Evangeline began to walk back towards the stairs and as she passed him he turned his face to her and said, "Before you go…I appreciate your kindness towards Ehvan. Thank you for not being cruel."

"Why would I be cruel to him?"

Eros only kept looking at her and she bit her lip and said, "I know what he did to Cynthia, but he didn't choose this. He was only a child…and there's so much good in him."

Eros' eyes moved over her face as if trying to find the hidden antagonism behind her words. Finally, he turned away as he said, "Thank you as well for lying to him…about your return."

"What do you mean? I'm not lying."

"You're not lying to him, or to yourself?" Eros didn't wait for her answer, soundlessly walking away amongst the coffins.

Evangeline stood for a second, staring after him, then resumed climbing the stairs. She had left the candelabra on the ground and the darkness overtook her halfway up the stairs. She somehow stumbled back to the throne hall, not quite sure how she got there, and pushed the huge, main doors open with all her strength.

The sun hit her with its full force and she screamed, the needle-like pain jabbing at every inch of her body, just like before, though slightly less strong. She bent down to her knees and squeezed her eyes shut, clenching her fists. She waited. Slowly, the pain began to ease up and after ten or so minutes completely disappeared.

Evangeline opened her eyes and stood back up. She was crying again, but this time for herself. Where was she? What was she? She would have given anything at that moment to just have her mom hold her. She wanted her room, her bed, her world. Anything. Just one single thing that made sense.

Where was Raffael? Why hadn't he come? She wanted a human, even if just for a second.

She looked up at the sun and opened her still-clenched fists to feel the rays on the palms of her hands and suddenly shrieked again. The inside of her hand, where she had cut herself on the sliver of wood, burned with pain. Evangeline instinctively shut her fist closed again, but then, taking a deep breath, slowly reopened it and let the sun burn.

"Fuck. Fuck. Fuck," was all she could say as the pain seared and she watched the wound sizzle. Then, slowly, the pain dwindled and she saw that the skin was healing itself. In another minute her palm was completely healed and she just stared at it. What exactly did this mean? Rather than feeling relieved or curious she felt fear and confusion.

Evangeline began to walk, readjusting her body positioning and movements again to mimic those of Eros and Julia. She was getting smoother and her speed increased with each step. She retraced her and Cynthia's original steps from the castle, through the graveyard- still streets, the square by the main animal gates, down to the fountain with the miniature canals and to the same spot in the wall through which she and Cynthia had entered.

She stood in front of the opening, then, just as before, climbed into the freezing water and squeezed her way back through the wall and out into the barren wasteland beyond. Rising up Evangeline looked into the distance, shivering as water dripped off her hair and gown. She could stay here. If she stayed in Latina they would give her food, clothing and tell her which direction Daoud is in, and supposedly train her to face him. But maybe she had lied to Ehvan. Maybe she didn't want to face him.

She knew there might be humans out there somewhere. She could go into the forest and search for the humans that had possibly survived and with them find shelter. Maybe with their help she might somehow also find a way back to her own home. And no matter what, they would at least be human.

Evangeline's mind went to Ehvan and his small, hopeful face and she swallowed. She was just like Julia. Eros was right. She could see in Ehvan what Julia must have seen in Cynthia; a small, trusting creature that you couldn't bear to hurt but...

But. The but was that Julia could not control what she was. Evangeline could. So, if she hurt Ehvan, wouldn't that make her worse than Julia? Weaker? More awful and pathetic?

"I'm the only one here with a choice," Evangeline said aloud knowing that this was the moment to make it. Up until now she had been aimlessly surviving here. But that made her just like all the citizens of Latina, except that they didn't have a choice. She did.

Evangeline turned around and climbed back into the freezing water. She might get eaten. She might be dead in a week. True. But she would at least try to save someone, even if that someone might not be her.

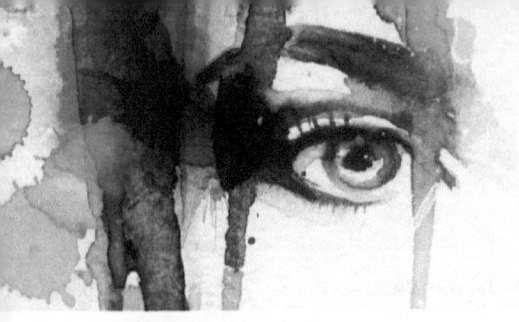

Chapter 34

BREAKING DOWN DEFENCES

Eros sat in the darkness, staring at the words of a book he had re-read hundreds of times now. Decades of trying to appreciate famous poets and he still hated poetry. The boredom of it just made him more hungry.

He put the book aside and walked out of his room, wandering down the dark hallways. Coming up to the door to Evangeline's bedroom he stood in front of it for a second, then pushed it open and entered, knowing the room was empty.

Eros smiled dryly to himself as he slowly walked over to the bed and sat down on it. The nightgown Evangeline had used lay folded on top of the sheets and he picked it up and looked at it. There was a knot in his stomach which felt like something along the lines of disappointment. However, feeling disappointment would signify that he had actually hoped she might stay, so he pushed the knot down, refusing to acknowledge its existence and stood up, straightening his shoulders.

He walked over to the table and randomly began picking up the grooming things on it. Would his mother be crushed? Or perhaps somewhere inside she also knew this was inevitable? Then they would have to think of what to say to Ehvan. They had to keep his hope up. And then they would have to deal with the rest of the city.

He put the hairbrush he had been poking at back down and turned to leave when he smelled her scent outside the door. How? He had been inattentive, forgetting that she had acquired her silent strides that day.

The door opened and Evangeline jumped back in shock at seeing him in front of her. She was soaking wet and shivering, with a mop of ridiculously matted, wet curls.

"What are you doing here?" She sputtered through her chattering teeth, "You scared me to death."

"Why are you sopping wet? You look like a drenched corpse."

"Wow, were you this charming before? Seriously."

"Only to a select few. You have not answered the question," he said.

"Neither have you. Wait," she said, and narrowing her eyes at him put her hands on her hips, "Are you checking up on me?"

"Yes, I am," he responded and smiled, happy to see her thrown off guard, "Why are you soaked through?"

"I... it's a long story."

"Another day in the life of Evangeline? Hmm, well, feel free to help yourself to another gown. I am optimistic that the wardrobe will last you a week?" Eros said and briskly walked past her and out the door. He heard her sarcastically fake-laugh behind him and smiled. He didn't know why he was smiling and realizing that he was in fact smiling, tightened his lips and walked faster.

Back in his room Eros picked up the book again, but didn't even bother to try and read it. He was drumming his fingers on it when light footsteps in the hallway reached his ears. He looked up to the sound of a knock on his door and a blond head popping in.

"Hey, you're not sleeping are you?" Evangeline said from his doorway.

"No, are you alright?" Eros asked, standing up. He could not imagine that she would come to his room simply for a visit.

"Yeah, I'm fine," she said, rubbing one bare foot against the other. She had changed into the nightgown again, and had a blanket wrapped around her shoulders, "I was just...Okay, if I tell you something can you just this one time refrain from your usual ridicule?"

"I have been refraining. This is me at my most *charming*," Eros said.

Evangeline looked at his face and paced for a moment from one foot to the other. Then she bit her lip and said, "It's Okay then. Sorry for bugging you," and pulled her head back out, quickly shutting the door.

"Wha... Stop." Eros called out. He could hear her footsteps scampering away down the hallway and jumped up from his chair, "Stop. Alright, come back," he called at the footsteps, striding towards the door, "I swear to not deride you about whatever it is you want to tell me." Did he just shout at her to come back? Was he finally going mad?

The footsteps stopped and tentatively returned. Evangeline opened the door again and this time came fully into the room.

"Remember...you promised," she said and he only lifted his eyebrows, nodding slightly as he walked back to his chair and sat back down, his eyes on her face.

"Alright," she said, pacing a little again, "It's just weird not having the cage bars or handcuffs or like some ball and chains or something around me. It almost started to feel...you know, kind of safe...I'm just having trouble sleeping in there....and the silence...it's too much...I tried to find Ehvan but he is sleeping with your mom...I thought maybe I could just sit in here for a while? You could call me a wench. I could call you an arrogant ass. The usual fun?"

"You are frightened of being alone?" Eros wasn't sure if to be amused or disbelieving.

"Don't look at me like that," Evangeline crossed her arms and frowned at him, "you are the one who said that people here don't want to kill me, but they will. Now I can't close my eyes. Just let me sit in here for ten minutes. I'll just relax a little and then I'll leave you alone. I promise."

"I could kill you also. Have you noticed?"

"Yes, well, you already did."

"I... huh," Eros rubbed his left temple with his hand, completely stumped for a response. Then he opened his palms up in defeat, "Alright. Can you read?"

"Of course I can read. In English."

"Good. Take this," Eros chucked the poetry book at Evangeline and she stumbled trying to catch it, "One, sit somewhere. Two, read. Three, don't bring me to the brink of insanity as you seem to generally do."

Evangeline looked down at the book and then back at him, "I can't read in the dark."

He groaned, got up and walked over to his large, corner desk which he opened to retrieve some long unused candles. Placing a couple around the room Eros lit them and sat back down in his chair, "I see that you are having issues with part three of my instructions already."

Evangeline, rather than looking in the least bit offended, grinned broadly at him and he had to control the instinct to grin back at the little imp, "See," she said, "you are already insulting me and I am insulting you mentally back as well. Isn't it fun?"

She turned her head and looked around the room, holding her book. The room was spacious but had never been a place where Eros entertained guests. It contained only one, large and comfortable leather chair for himself, as well as an intricately carved, hard, straight-backed chair, created as a gift by a famous artist. The artist had gone a bit overboard with his creativity, the carvings becoming quickly more important than the utility of the chair, the effect being that bumps and ridges protruded in every direction. The chair stood in front of the writing desk and looked more comfortable than it actually was and that was saying a lot since it didn't look remotely comfortable.

Evangeline looked slightly longingly at the leather chair which he was already occupying, then walked to the creatively bizarre, wooden one by the desk. He watched, over the random, new book he had picked up, his lip twitching in amusement as she kept readjusting herself. He was enjoying himself too much to offer her the leather chair. After a couple more attempts at odd poses in the chair Evangeline stood up and tentatively made her way to the bed. She glimpsed at him out of the corner of her eye and he pretended not to notice as she snuck back on the same side of the bed where he had previously kept her captive and sat down cross legged on top of the sheets, the book on her lap.

Eros opened his mouth slightly, about to comment on her comfort level in his bed. But there was no other place to sit. If he made her feel stupid she would just leave. *Good, it's an easy way to get her out of my hair,* he thought, but closed his mouth and said nothing, his eyes inconspicuously moving between his own book and her hair, which was combed out and loose, wildly bouncing around her face, shiny from the oils she had used to apparently try and calm it. It was long now, the way he was used to seeing hair on the women of Latina, yet his fingers had the urge to take the curls and lift them up, make them just as they had been the first day she arrived, a wild helmet just above her long neck.

They were silent for less than two minutes before she started to yawn and again readjust herself repeatedly,

"Do you have any other books? I'm just not that into poetry. You like poetry?"

"No. That's why I gave it to you."

"Oh, thanks," she rolled her eyes at his smirk.

"I didn't bring up much else today. Here's a book about how to work metals." He wasn't sure why he was offering her the most boring books he had, except that it amused him.

"Oh, is there anything about dormium in it?" Evangeline actually looked interested and he nodded slightly. She came over to him and switched books, taking the volume about metals and crawling back on the bed with it, "I was actually wondering how you managed to make all those dormium walls when you can't touch it."

"We could previously," Eros said, "much of the wall separating the animals existed before we turned. It separated the city from the mountain wildlife in one section, in another section it housed stables and race and competition courses and the spot where we fed with you, was the entrance to a prison facility. Dormium is a difficult substance to work, but once melted into its shape by a proper master it is virtually unbreakable and impermeable. Not all of the wall was joined together at the time though. It was by accident that we realized that those who turned could not touch dormium. When this plague started to spread beyond control we attempted to join the wall in order to build a refuge. It was too little, too late. Hundreds could turn in one night. After the final battle, once the city began to slowly organize itself into what it is now, we found ways to finish the job. The pieces were there. We only needed to bring them in contact with each other. Dormium will fuse together with itself under specific conditions. It is almost a living metal."

"Really? That's amazing," Evangeline said and her eyes sparkled with interest as she opened the book. Eros raised his eyebrows and grinned. It would be amusing to see how long she could keep quiet, reading the dull volume.

~

Evangeline was sitting cross-legged on the bed and trying to concentrate on her book. The book was not what she had imagined. She had absolutely no background in metalwork so understood very little to begin with, on top of which, it was in the common tongue which meant a mish-mash of English, Latin and Italian. To top it off it was so detailed, that she couldn't imagine even a metal-work expert caring that much.

She lay down on her side, propping her head up on her elbow and focused on the finely drawn sketches. It was still boring. The sketches made little visual sense, repeatedly showing people molding dormium like blobs of play-doh in various ways.

Evangeline stifled a yawn and looked over at Eros whose eyes were focused on his reading materials. She considered trying to swap books again but was scared of getting booted out of the room.

As bad as life had been in the cage, the bars had provided a sense of safety. Even being chained to the bed was somehow comforting. It had provided a strange sense of boundary as well as the knowledge that Eros was sitting and guarding her while she slept. As snappy as he was, if he had wanted to kill her he could have accomplished that in a hundred different ways by now.

Now, she was suddenly completely alone in that room, with the all-encompassing silence of this world surrounding her. She was breathless with terror at the thought of closing her eyes. She had opened the windows, thinking that the light would make things feel more normal, but its rays somehow made it even worse. Being awake was one thing, but lying down and not knowing who or what would be standing above you if you kept your eyes closed for a second too long and the sun went down was another.

Evangeline readjusted herself again, determined to focus on the book and follow part three of Eros' instructions for as long as she humanly could.

~

Eros looked at Evangeline without lifting his head to see that she had moved to a lying position on her side. She wasn't stifling her yawns very well as her body kept fidgeting over the book. Dormium might be interesting, but five hundred pages on molding it was not. The only reason the book was even up here was because it occasionally helped him to pass out for a couple minutes.

He was waiting for her to start complaining, wondering what flippant commentary she would come up with to get a third book. He had a stack of retorts ready, just waiting to be thrown her way. But she didn't complain and after some time she stopped fidgeting and moving all together.

Eros got up and walked over to the bed. He looked down at Evangeline, passed out with her face on top of the book. Her mouth was slightly open and she was drooling on the page. He shook his head as he pulled the book out from under her face.

Chapter 35

TALENTS

A horrible sound was ringing in Evangeline's ears. She opened her eyes to find Eros standing above her, dangling a large bell.

"Stop! Oh my God. You can just *tell* me to go to my room. I must've passed out. I'm *sorry*. I'll go sleep in my room. I'm going. I'm going."

"You can go and get dressed and ready in your own room," Eros said with a sardonic smile.

"What?" Evangeline asked, bleary-eyed.

"It is the middle of the night, again. We have all had our meal. Yours is waiting for you in the kitchen. Hurry up. The citizens are beginning to think we ate you."

Evangeline sat up and looked at him, "I slept all day? Are you serious?"

"Do I jest much?"

She looked around his bed and then up at him, "I'm...sorry. You had to sleep on the chair."

"No. I slept on my bed," Eros said evenly.

"Oh," Evangeline's eyes went slightly wider and she immediately regretted letting him see her confusion. Eros narrowed his eyes.

"Do you think I seduced you while you were sleeping?" he said, his lips curling down, "I believe Josepina explained the likelihood of that. I rested on the other side of the bed, wench. On top of the covers. We rarely feel cold, except for in extreme temperatures. The covers are for...nostalgia, I suppose. If you choose to hibernate on my bed do not expect me to sit on the chair all night."

"You could have just woken me up, you know," Evangeline said, standing up to go.

"I considered it. However, you had already slobbered on my book and the option of ringing a large bell in your face this evening appealed to me."

Evangeline gave him a dirty look, which had the effect of bringing a wide smile to his face. She was about to leave the room without a word when a thought came to her head and squinting her eyes at him she began to laugh, "Sorry, I was just imagining you seducing someone."

Eros' smile began to lower into a confused frown and she burst out laughing harder, "It's just that, well, how did you do it before? I mean, seduce someone? I can't imagine you being charming for the life of me."

"You would know if I were attempting to seduce you, which means that this is a piece of knowledge that you will not be privy to," Eros responded, his face filling with absolute irritation. Evangeline wasn't sure why it was making her laugh all the harder, except that it was extremely gratifying to see him not so full of himself.

"How did the *boys* at your 'school' do it?" Eros suddenly turned on her, "Did they pretend to find every provoking word you utter amusing, follow you like trained pets and attempt to conceal via idle conversation and shallow compliments that the first and foremost thing on a man's mind is how to undress a woman quickest?"

"Huh. Well...," Evangeline was momentarily taken aback, "that is generally the gist of romance I guess...except I've never heard it summarized that *romantically*. Were those your moves then, your gracious highness?" She bowed extravagantly at him.

"I do not believe in ridiculous performances to get a woman into bed," Eros replied.

"So, what did you do? Just tell them it's time to get it on?" Evangeline joked, expecting a quick retort. Instead, he shrugged his shoulders, looking slightly embarrassed.

"Seriously?"

"It was never an order. It was a statement and they were happy to be chosen."

"Uhhh."

"What, wench?" Eros asked, and Evangeline could see that even though he was trying to sound huffy he was having a hard time meeting her eyes. She folded her hands across her chest and stared harder into his.

"Alright," he said, "it might sound a little flaunting when said this way."

"A *little* flaunting?" Evangeline thought she would choke on her own laughter, "Ohhhh, every woman was just *begging* to be chosen to go to bed with me," She imitated his tone and accent.

"You could only wish to be one of those," he almost growled at her, making her feel even more mischievous. Evangeline stepped towards him and pretended to snuggle up, "Oh, my master. My highness. Oh, pleeease choose me. Please. Let me be the chosen one."

Eros turned to her dangerously and she quickly jumped back, laughing.

"I am on the brink of physically expelling you from my room," he said and she ran towards the door.

"Dress in the clothes laid out on your bed," she heard him say from behind, "They are for your training."

"My training?" Evangeline asked, turning back towards him.

"Yes, your training. I am training you."

"Oh."

Eros' embarrassment was gone and he stood, his head tilted towards her, "You said you can handle me," he said, his grin looking not too friendly, "Let us see how that works out for you. And hurry up. I would like to start before the sun rises again."

~

Evangeline was back in some sort of boy's clothing as she ate her evening breakfast at the huge table. It consisted of the expected eggs, fruit and an unexpected loaf of bread. The bread was greenish in colour, looking and tasting like a vegan bread option, which she supposed made sense since there was no dairy that she could see in the vicinity.

She ate as much as she could, knowing there would be no snacks on the town in between meals. Plus, Samina and Lorenzo just stood in the corner and stared at her and she felt that she might offend their cooking efforts if she didn't eat enough.

They were about as social as Laura, who somehow mysteriously managed to enter and exit Evangeline's room, replacing and tidying whatever needed it without Evangeline knowing when or how she did so. Evangeline had entered her room that evening to get dressed, and in the five seconds she took to pick up the shirt on the bed and look at it, a basin of hot water had appeared behind her for her washing. It was simultaneously impressive and terrifying.

Samina and Lorenzo stared at her now as she chewed and swallowed each bite. When she couldn't eat any more she complimented them on the wonderful breakfast, to which they only nodded and kept staring. She stood up and received a growl from Lorenzo when she picked up a plate to clean up after herself. She quickly placed it back on the table and made her way to her training, a little apprehensive.

Evangeline took a back hallway to end up at an inner courtyard. Trees lined its circumference unevenly, hiding little benches placed beneath them, while an open grass area rested in the middle. Eros stood there, waiting, and seeing her looked up pointedly at the moon and the fact that half the night was already over. Then, he gestured with his pointer finger for her to come over.

Evangeline straightened her shoulders and made her way over to him, hoping that whatever increased senses he had, they did not include hearing her pulse pound nervously. Whatever Eros had in mind for her training there was no way it would be pleasant.

"Let's start with me seeing if you have absolutely any skill to work with," he said as she approached, "I have already witnessed your pot throwing and punching so can safely say that you have no combat training."

"Thanks. I still broke your nose."

"Do it again."

Evangeline stood, looking at Eros. He opened up his palms towards her and raised his eyebrows, waiting. She came closer to him, feeling the sweat accumulating on her own palms and wiping them against her pants.

The truth was that before hitting Eros, Evangeline had never hit anyone in her life. There was one time in grade nine when a group of wanna-be gangster chicks had decided they wanted to kick her ass for some dumb joke she had made, but then Val had arrived with the football guys.

How did Val do this? Evangeline thought and remembered Val just jumping into the action headfirst. So, not having any other plan up her sleeve she swung her fist full force at Eros' face, expecting disaster. She wasn't astonished when Eros blocked her fist with the palm of his hand. However, she was completely bewildered when he kicked her feet out from under her, grabbed one of her ankles with his other arm and completely lifted her off the ground, swinging her upside down in front of himself.

Evangeline knew he was tall, but being tall herself hadn't noticed the extent of his height. It now became quite clear as her hands swung above the ground, unable to touch it. She tried to pull her ankle out of his grasp by shaking her leg. When that had absolutely no effect she tried to pull her top half up to reach his grip on her ankle but Eros simply started to swing her back and forth, making her shriek.

All of a sudden he swung her full force and let go, her body flipping 180 degrees in the air. Evangeline was screaming at the top of her lungs when she felt his hands catch her and place her on her feet, down on the ground. Dizzy and disoriented she wobbled and plopped down on her butt to hear the verdict of, "You're dead," coming from Eros.

Evangeline was blind with rage and without thinking pulled herself up and rushed at Eros again. This time, before she could even take the two steps, he was already behind her. One of his arms grabbed her and wrapped itself fully around her torso and arms, the strength of his grip completely immobilizing her top half. Meanwhile, with his other hand he grabbed her throat tightly.

Eros put his teeth to her throat and Evangeline was suddenly numb with shock and fear. Her eyes were wide open and her breath was coming out in uneven gasps as he ran his teeth slowly up her throat. Then, reaching her ear, he stated in an unexpectedly calm and regular voice, "And you're dead," and let her go.

Evangeline was barely standing, her legs shaking beneath her.

"Are you just doing this for your own amusement?" she said, not looking at him.

"I have to admit, this is the most amusement I have had in the last decade," Eros said, and when she turned to him still shaking, he added, "What is it? Are you not enjoying handling me?"

"So, you've proven the obvious: I've never fought before and I'm not as crazy fast and strong as you," Evangeline said through gritted teeth, "Now are you actually going to train me? Because if you're just going to amuse yourself then tell me now so I can leave."

"And go where?" Eros said, "the irony is, you were lucky to have arrived here. You are right. You know absolutely nothing. If you had just appeared out of nowhere in any type of human village or refuge there is a very good probability that they would have burned you on a pyre, thinking that you were one of us. Humans don't just pop up in these lands. And if you had arrived in Sadamanta, well, the last we heard through Lola, not many were anything but insane and Daoud and the child were not the most welcoming of hosts. Now you know where you are. You understand our world and your fragile position here, but you still don't know what welcome you will receive outside these walls. So, unless you plan to live out your days as half a guest and half a prisoner in Latina, watching every being around you eventually go mad and turn to ash, then you have no choice but to stay in this courtyard with me and do as I say."

Evangeline put her hands on her hips, half in defiance and half because she did not know what to say. He was clearly enjoying his current position of power and she had an urge to kick him in a special spot and leave. But, who else would teach her how to fight? And, since she currently lived in his castle, she'd have to just come back if she stomped off. That would be even more embarrassing.

"Are you going to teach me or just keep amusing yourself at my expense?" she said, refusing to let him win this so completely.

"You are an overconfident bigmouth who likes to amuse herself by purposely satirizing me. So, yes, I will amuse myself at your expense very much," Eros said, shrugging and smiling, "I will enjoy every second of this, wench, but I will also teach you."

"What? *I'm* an overconfident bigmouth? Okay, maybe I am, a bit, but *you*...oh my God, you -"

"Are you certain that you would like to tell me more about me before we are finished today's training?" Eros said, lowering his face slightly towards hers.

"Well, why would I start keeping my big mouth shut now, when you are already planning to throw me around some more?"

Eros grinned momentarily, then pointed to a spot on the grass and tilted his chin up at her, "Pick up the sword, big-mouthed wench."

"What?"

"Pick up the sword."

"You do realize I have no clue how to sword fight, right?"

"I figured as much," Eros said, "we need to find your innate talent. Raw strength is not it. You do not have centuries at your disposal. We must work with whatever is instinctive for you."

"Alright..." Evangeline slowly moved towards the sword then looked at Eros again, "Let's make one deal. If we are stuck with each other for a while, then, I have a name. It's not wench or peasant, Eros."

Eros looked at her for a couple of seconds then simply said, "Alright. Evangeline, pick up the sword."

Unfortunately, the sword was not her innate talent either and it took less than two minutes of her swinging for Eros to determine that.

"Put it down," was all he said.

The bow and arrows, axe and hallberg fared no better. After trying about every weapon imaginable Evangeline was beyond frustrated. She was good at nothing. Not only that, but the truth was that weapons terrified her. She couldn't imagine herself chopping at someone with a sword or shooting an arrow through their heart.

"I can't do this, Eros," she said, completely discouraged, "I'm never going to attack anyone. Okay, maybe just you with some pots, but not with axes and blades. I've never killed anyone or...punctured anyone. I don't want to. I thought I was just learning to defend myself."

"Perhaps she is right, Eros," Julia's voice came from a bench, off to the side, obscured by some trees. Evangeline spun her head towards the voice in surprise.

"I apologize, Evangeline," Julia said, approaching "I came some time ago. I hope my presence didn't startle you too much."

"Oh, no. That's fine," Evangeline lied, actually not particularly thrilled that Julia had witnessed her pathetic-ness. She nodded at Julia and Julia nodded back.

"Evangeline is not going outside on the offensive," Julia said, turning to Eros, "I suppose we can think of her as a peace envoy. She is going to negotiate with whoever she finds. What she needs is defensive skills if negotiations don't go well."

"Hm," Eros was looking at Evangeline through squinted eyes, "alright, we have nothing to lose at this point."

Staring at Evangeline intently Eros' face suddenly took on that terrifying look of primal hunger, "Are you ready?" was all he said to her, and without waiting for a response his body moved into the pose of a jaguar about to go after its selected prey.

Evangeline barely had time to scream before he came at her. Without much thought she turned and ran for her life. She had no plan. Seeing a tree, she ran for it, jumping at its trunk, aiming to catch its lowest branch. To Evangeline's disbelief her legs ran up the trunk, and pushing off the trunk she leapt, her body spun 180 degrees as she did so, and she landed clean on top of the branch that she had been merely hoping to grab.

She sat, poised on the branch, like a cat balancing itself, and looked around completely amazed. Unfortunately, her amazement lasted only a second. The branch she had pounced on was half dead, and her weight was too much for it to handle. The branch snapped and crashed down, Evangeline crashing with it.

Nothing felt broken as Evangeline started to pick herself up, disoriented. She felt Eros' arm around her waist, helping her up and when she was finally standing, she pushed her hair out of her face and said breathlessly, "thanks."

"You're welcome," Eros replied, "by the way, you're dead," Evangeline groaned as he continued, "but, that was the least hopeless I have seen all night."

Evangeline looked up at Eros' face and grinned. She could tell he was trying not to smile back.

"Alright," he said, "wipe the blood from your face."

"What?" Evangeline's hands covered her face, terrified, but neither Eros nor Julia seemed to be poising themselves for attack.

"There is no smell to it, but it is better if we do not have to look at it, nevertheless," Julia said, "in any case, it will heal in a moment."

"Yeah, not until morning," Evangeline said. Eros and Julia looked at her confused and she realized she had not told them what effect the sun had on her. After hearing the explanation Eros rubbed his chin while Julia looked at him.

"We have been thinking of talking to the Jumping Mole. Perhaps we should take Evangeline tomorrow night," Julia said.

"He was already erratic as a regular human," Eros said, still rubbing his chin, "now he is half sensical at best. However, the times he does make some sense are indispensable. Alright, tomorrow. Bring Ehvan as well. He seems to pull the mole out of his contemplation at times."

"The Jumping Mole?" Evangeline asked, wondering if she were about to find out that there were talking animals here.

"In the past, a great scholar, though always a bit mad and half comprehensible," Julia explained, "he came to be called the Mole when he was a child, due to his face being generally buried in books and parchments. The jumping aspect was added after he was affected by our condition. You will see why tomorrow."

"Our condition has made most probably the least alteration in The Mole," Eros said, "If I had not known him previously, I would have thought he had gone mad and caged him in the sun by now. However, as it is, he is only slightly stranger now than he used to be."

"Oh. So you believe he may know something know about my mutation?" Evangeline looked from Julia to Eros.

"No, not precisely," Julia said, "but he may sense things."

Julia's explanation made little sense and Evangeline was about to ask for clarification, but Eros spoke first, looking at Evangeline, "It's time for our mid-night meal. Yours will be in the kitchen laid out. We are finished for today. I will think and formulate a training plan for you with my mother, to start tomorrow. Right now you may change into a gown and amuse yourself as you wish for the rest of the night."

"Oh, you said I can't go outside by myself."

"I said to stay close to the castle and enter no building alone," Eros said, "we will appear every now and then and... check on you."

"Thanks dad," Evangeline smirked and Eros cleared his throat. Walking past Evangeline, he looked up at her hair and said, "I would also suggest doing something to tame the hurricane on your head." With that he flicked a curl off her face with his hand. As the curl fell back down his hand paused, the curl sliding over his fingers on its way. Abruptly he put his arm down and walked away without looking at either Evangeline or Julia. After a second Julia nodded with a polite smile and followed Eros out of the courtyard wordlessly.

Evangeline went to eat and change with her mind obnoxiously replaying the image of Eros' hand in her hair. Were there moments tonight when she had almost had fun with him? Did he actually smile a couple of times? She started thinking about what Josepina said about his looks and if he really looked even better before. For some reason she thought of Eros standing beside Ian, one slim and smiling with kind, deep eyes. The other massive and intense, with eyes full of judgement but also intelligence and loyalty and...and her thoughts weren't making any sense. Evangeline shook her head out, as if physically trying to get rid of them. Eros was still Eros, and doing only what was necessary to get her out of his city in one piece so that he might have some hope of Evangeline finding a cure for them.

Going to the mirror to fix her hair Evangeline inadvertently voiced a "Gahh." No wonder Eros had called her hurricane head. Although it appeared to be slowing down, her hair had grown quite fast in the last two days and was absolutely huge and frizzy. Her nails were similar but at least she could bite them. She had used the oils she had found in her room and tried to put the curls into braids again that morning, but the training had made half of them come out in various sections of her head. It looked like two mad birds had gone to war in their nest.

Evangeline untied what was left of the braids and tried to comb her hair out when Ehvan entered.

"Hello," Ehvan was all smiles, "Eros said you have a one percent chance of learning to fight. That's great!"

Evangeline laughed, "Thanks Ehvan. How's your night?"

"I'm painting a house today," Ehvan shrugged.

"It seems like you know how to do pretty much everything. You wouldn't know how to cut hair by any chance?" Evangeline said jokingly but Ehvan tipped his head and scratched at his own hair in serious consideration.

"No... but...I trim bushes," he said, "Your head looks like a big bush. Would you like me to trim it?"

Evangeline grinned. Apparently bluntness ran in the family. She looked at herself in the mirror again and said, "What the heck. Got some scissors?"

"Yes, I will go get them, but what happened to your cheek?" Ehvan pointed to the scratch on her face and she lifted her hand to feel it. It had scabbed over but was definitely still there, "Oh, I was attacked by a tree."

Seeing Ehvan's confusion she chuckled, "It's just an expression. I fell off a tree."

"Oh, why were you climbing a tree?"

"To escape your brother."

Ehvan considered this for a second, "Was he trying to bite your cheek?" he leaned over and sniffed at her, "He must have been very hungry because your blood smells bad now."

"You know," Evangeline smiled, "That's really great news."

~

Ehvan was so precise in the cutting of each and every curl that he didn't notice he was over forty-five minutes late for his next activity until his mother came looking for him. Julia's face was terror stricken when she saw him with a huge pair of hedge scissors at Evangeline's head. The terror quickly turned to shocked confusion at Evangeline's wide smile.

Apparently, Evangeline's hair did have the consistency of a thick bush because Ehvan did quite a good job with it. Evangeline kept grinning at herself in the mirror as she looked over the final result. It was strange but attractive, something along the lines of an inverted bob with the curls right around her face being cut shorter so that they framed her face without falling into her eyes.

Evangeline was so happy that she picked Ehvan up and swung him around. When she put him down, he stood and stared at her for a moment. Then, his big lips bursting out in a smile he picked Evangeline fully up with his small, skinny frame and swung her around in return.

Evangeline did not expect this and her shrieks of terror brought Julia (who had left the room) running back. When she saw Ehvan swinging Evangeline around at full speed her mouth dropped open and she started running towards them but at that moment Evangeline burst out laughing both at the fact that this skinny creature was flinging her around as if she were a little piece of fuzz, and at Julia's facial expression.

"Okay, Okay, Put me down!" Evangeline shouted, still laughing as Julia shook her head and left the room again, looking precisely like a typical mother who had just seen her kids play some oddball game she didn't even want to try and comprehend. Evangeline and Ehvan looked at each other after Julia had left and this time even Ehvan laughed.

Afterwards, Evangeline walked with Ehvan to the house he was supposed to paint, staying to watch a little. She felt lazy and thought she probably looked lazy too, so took a paintbrush and began to help. However, the citizens were less than pleased. It turned out they were very protective over each daily occupation, with the prospect of losing even a tiny part of an activity and having nothing to do but focus on their hunger a terrifying one. So, the paintbrush in Evangeline's hand was quickly intercepted.

Not having a clue what to do Evangeline left and began to walk aimlessly, though a little nervously. Many of the citizens she passed bowed to her and she bowed back. Many still sniffed, some said hello and a couple asked to touch her. Whatever they did, it included staring. The most unnerving were the children, though there seemed to be less than a handful of them in the whole city. They mostly just looked blank. She would have preferred any sort of expression, rather than the emptiness in their faces. One child began to shriek uncontrollably after seeing her and had to be taken away.

She remembered Ehvan telling her how he almost went mad after he entered Evangeline's thoughts when she was a child, not being able to handle what he was. Evangeline looked, frightened, after this shrieking child, hoping to God she hadn't somehow hurt him. A tall, slim, male citizen appeared right in front of her and pushed her gently away "Go. Walk. No fear." he croaked out as if he hadn't spoken in years. So, she walked, trying to find less populated streets where she wouldn't be so much on display.

Eventually she made her way back to the villa neighbourhood from the day before. She stood and looked at the villa of Eros' fiancée; its walls were pure white with stained glass in multiple colours decorating parts of each window. A number of small towers protruded from the villa with a miniature labyrinth of some strange, exotic-looking flower bushes surrounding it. It was all quite beautiful and yet she didn't particularly like it. Somehow it was too ostentatious, almost to the point of tacky, and she couldn't imagine it fitting Eros.

Evangeline condemned herself for thinking this, or anything mean, about someone's dead fiancée as she walked on, reaching the little cottage villa, which she liked much better. The outside of it was empty today with the Duke nowhere in sight and she continued walking when a voice came up right behind her, making her jump.

"Hello, Evangeline."

"Hello...uh...Sir Karpenski."

He smiled and handed her a peach, "Just Leonardo. This is for you," Leonardo's voice was quiet but deep, it's tone kind, with an almost soothing, though sad undertone.

"Thank you," Evangeline said, taking the peach and smiling down at him. He was a bulky man, looking as if he may have been quite massive in his previous human form. However, in height he was a head below Evangeline.

Evangeline didn't know what else to say and after a minute of silently staring at each other the Duke bowed his head slightly and walked away towards his villa.

His quiet sadness jabbed at her heart and she called out after him, "Would you like to walk with me?"

The Duke turned back towards her and silently began to walk with her, every now and then looking at her face. After some time, Evangeline broke the silence.

"I love your house. It's my favourite on this street."

"Thank you," The Duke said, the happiness in his eyes almost making up for the grotesqueness of the grey smile, "My wife loves it too."

"Oh, is your wife inside?"

"No, my wife escaped. She escaped with my son. I am keeping this house for her just the way she likes it. I don't want her cross at the state of her flowers when she returns."

"Oh, I am sure she will love it all," Evangeline said, not knowing how else to respond, "I have never seen a more beautiful garden." How old would his wife be now if she had actually survived? When did one give up hope? Or was hope something you simply created if there was nothing else?

"Thank you," he responded, the gratitude in his face visible even through its greyness. "Eros' father, he always came to our house," the Duke continued, "It was his favourite also. He was a good friend.

Stubborn and hard on the outside just like his son, but once you had his trust he would die for you."

Leonardo became quiet and preoccupied and Evangeline let him ponder as they walked side by side. After a while the Duke looked deeply into her face as if deciding something in his mind, then spoke even more quietly, "He protected my family even after his own wife and child were turned, but...I could not protect him from myself. Eros...he forgave me. I don't know if I could...if I saw someone do that to my family...but Eros still saved my family after what I did...still comes to visit me..."

Evangeline was barely breathing, listening to him, his eyes boring into hers, making it impossible to avert her gaze. He was the Duke which Julia had told her and Cynthia about. He was the one who had killed Eros' father. Why was he confiding all this to her? She was confused and his face began to look frightened, as if expecting her to scream and run away from him. Evangeline suddenly realized that he had wanted to confess. A confession to a human. To see if he was forgivable. Still able to be accepted as a human being.

What could she say? At a complete loss for words Evangeline tentatively reached for his hand and squeezed it. He squeezed it back and looked at the sky, "I must go back to my house," he said, "morning will soon come. My wife, she loved teas. I still have some leaves. Would you like to come in for tea?"

"Eros said not to go into anyone's house alone." As soon as she said it Evangeline felt like pounding her head on a wall. This man had just confided a guilt to her that he had been carrying for two and a half decades and she followed that up by telling him that she couldn't be alone with him just in case he got hungry.

"I'm sorry. I shouldn't have said that. I-" she stammered out but he gently interrupted.

"No, Evangeline. Do not apologize. Eros' words are wise ones. Thank you for the walk. Perhaps I will see you another night."

"Yes. I would love that."

Chapter 36

VAL

Wednesday was half-way over and again nothing. *That would make it four and a half days now,* Ian thought. What were the chances Evangeline was still Okay, wherever she was? He stared down at the crappy pay-as-you-go cell phone in his hand under the desk so that his teacher wouldn't see. Raffael had snuck a couple of those phones over to him Monday night after the main round of police chaos had ended. Ian was supposed to pass them around to Val and Mark so that they could all communicate without being traced. Except there was nothing to communicate.

Val was sitting a couple rows in front of him, her dark pony-tail bobbing as she scribbled some notes. They had barely spoken since Evangeline's disappearance. She was supposed to be Evangeline's best friend, but it felt like she was barely making an effort here.

Bambi had flat out refused to try and reopen the portal and just that morning she had actually threatened to charge him and Mark with harassment if they didn't leave her alone. *Guess Mark's pick-up lines aren't that great. We really need Val for this,* he thought, staring at the back of her head.

He had tried the friendship card and the guilt trip card but all that seemed to be doing was pissing Val off. *What's her issue?* Ian racked his brain, *she's not a shitty friend... and they were best friends. Almost inseparable.*

Ian looked at the number fifteen on the back of the basketball jersey that Val was wearing today instead of her uniform shirt. He thought of Val on the court; she never bothered trying to trick her opponents. She just went for it. Straight for the goal.

He nodded his head, watching the ponytail, "Exactly."

Everyone was looking at him. *Shit, I said that out loud.* He put his head down and pretended to write. Lunch was in ten minutes. It was time for the goal.

~

Val saw Ian approaching and made a beeline for the bitchiest group of girls in the school, sitting down right beside them in the cafeteria. She loathed them, but so did Ian, and she knew it.

"Hey...Val," Zara said, lifting her painted-on eyebrows, "you don't often join us."

Val had to smirk at the tone in Zara's voice. It didn't matter if Zara or her cronies liked Val. She knew they were too chicken-shit to tell her to leave.

"No, I don't" Val said, not bothering to smile, "I guess today is your lucky day." She pulled out a small bag and started eating without another word. Zara and the clones passed looks around. Val was popular, but definitely not one of them. When Olivia, clone number two, pulled out a designer meal and placed it on the raunchy cafeteria table Val couldn't help herself and belched.

"Oops," Val said and smiled innocently.

"Oh, guess Evangeline's not here anymore to force you to act sort of like a human that's not a lumberjack, right?" Zara said, "wow, two girls missing after just one party. It's good we went to Eric's that night."

"Yes, it's a good thing you never got invited to Evangeline's party," Ian said from behind Val's shoulder. For the first time in days his presence was actually a semi-welcome addition and Val almost smiled at his comment.

"Oh, hi Ian," in the blink of a second Zara had put on her *a man's here looking at me* smoulder, "I'm so sorry. I never meant to sound offensive. You know we are all really shocked and worried. I mean, Evangeline disappeared literally right after her terminal disease was discovered."

"Can I talk to you privately?" Ian completely ignored Zara and looked directly at Val.

"Oh, is there something going on between you two?" Zara must have picked up on the offense because she quickly turned vengeful, "I thought you were spending time with Cynthia? Or maybe Evangeline? Wow, you sure move on fast, Ian."

Val threw her lunch back in its bag and stood to follow Ian out. Anything was better than this, "Yeah, Ian decided to hit me up until you finish raising your grades with the male teachers." Val said over her shoulder and walked out before Zara had time to grasp the meaning.

She made her way out the back doors, through the school parking and into the empty football field before she finally stopped and breathed in deeply. Ian was still right behind her.

"Well, you definitely know how to be a bitch," he said, half smiling.

"Fuck you," Val responded, "so what's your spiel for today? Am I a bad friend? Are innocents dying because of me? What do you want me to do? How exactly do you expect me to open up some intergalactic portal?"

"I don't know what I want you to do," Ian said, staring at her like some disappointed dad, "but I want you to do more than this. I know you're pissed -"

"Wow, you finally clued in?" Val laughed, "she put *everyone* in danger and didn't give a shit. I've known her for years and-"

"And the truth is that what you are most pissed about is not the fact that she lied because it wouldn't have mattered," Ian said, crossing his arms and tilting his head at her mildly. His calm, all-knowing manner was making her want to punch him, but he continued without seeming to notice, "If Evangeline had told you the truth about what she was trying to do, Val, you would have been your typical self and laughed your ass off and gone ahead with it all anyways. Maybe even more so because you would have thought it was hilarious. You're just pissed because you are stuck here without a real friend, eating lunch with bitches named after mass shopping outlets, and meanwhile Cynthia went with Evangeline. You're jealous, Val."

Val's hands were shaking. She knew her face was red and she was about to explode but wasn't sure if in a violent fit of fist punching or tears. She had to wait a couple of seconds before her voice could come out. It came out slowly and quietly, "Don't I have a right to be pissed at that? It's a weird coincidence that Cynthia just jumped on that table and knew what to do. We were supposed to be best friends and I knew nothing. Obviously she didn't want me there with her."

"Seriously Val," Ian said, "You think Evangeline actually chose to go into the unknown with Cynthia as her one and only ally?"

Val shrugged her shoulders, "How did Cynthia know what to do?"

"She didn't," Ian was grinning at her as if she were a kid, jealous over a toy. She felt stupid and kicked at a rock, "come on, Val. Cynthia's talent is knowing when and where anything is about to happen."

Val sighed, "I guess I'm just pissed. I feel like I didn't really know Evangeline as well as I thought I did. And then I'm pissed because Cynthia, fucking Cynthia of all people, gets to go with her and I'm stuck here in bullshit high school. It's like she chose Cynthia over me," Val looked at Ian's still grinning face and punched him in the shoulder, "don't give me that look. I know it's stupid but, I was the one trying to pull Bambi off of her and I got left behind as a reward. Why wasn't I part of it?"

"I don't know," Ian said, "Why wasn't I part of it? You know, I've liked Evangeline since grade nine. You probably don't remember this stupid poetry project in grade nine English. I was pulling myself together to go and ask her to be partners and then *you* literally steamrollered over me to get to her. I mean, you ran like a bulldozer. I almost got flattened."

Val laughed aloud, "I remember. I mean, I don't remember you at all. Sorry. I just thought she looked so gawky. Like a complete nerd. I thought she'd get us a good grade."

"I just thought she looked different…It was like the beginning of high school and everyone was trying to get into the cliques and she was just in her own world, doing her own thing. It was…interesting. Anyways, then you guys ended up best friends and I ended up waiting three more years to get anywhere, like a complete loser. And now I'm here with you, the one who killed it for me to begin with, no offence, and Cynthia gets to go jumping through portals instead of me."

Val could not get over the one thing in the monologue "You waited over three years to make a move? You're joking, right?"

"That was not the most important part of my speech, Val," Ian said.

"Yeah, I know, but seriously. I had no clue you were such a dork. Holy crap. Three years. It's like a tween, rom-com." Val was trying not to laugh but it was impossible.

"Alright, I guess we are not getting off this topic, so let's roll with it," Ian said, throwing his hands up, "so what Val Striker has just learned is that people are multidimensional. For example, we all know you are a rich, jock chick but you probably never even knew yourself that you had a bitchy-jealous-girl streak. Did you ever think you'd be jealous of Cynthia? Perhaps Evangeline knew that about you and perhaps she didn't. So, don't judge her because you didn't know all of her. She'd have to be pretty fucking flat if you did."

"I know," Val breathed out and slumped her shoulders, "I know I wouldn't have believed her if she had told me any of it…and I can't believe I'm jealous of Cynthia," Val furrowed her brows at Ian, "promise me that if we manage to reopen that portal you won't let me get stuck here again. I swear I'll kill you if you go and travel the universe and I'm *still* in high school."

Ian grinned at her, "I'll take that as a 'yes, Val is finally on board for real'?"

"You know it's not like I wasn't helping...it's just...you know. Anyways, Okay, I'm on board for real now. But honestly, I don't know what to do. We need Bambi, but all of us have approached her. Other than kidnapping the bitch, what can we do? And even if we kidnapped her, she can just *not* open the portal. We need her to actually agree."

"Well, the cops still seem to be trailing her," Ian said, "and she's getting her parents to literally chaperone her to and from school along with that Liza chick. Raffael can't get within ten feet or he'll be in jail for harassment of minors, and Mark's pretend infatuation with Bambi almost got us a restraint order. We need *you*."

"If I just harass her like you and Mark, I'll be joining you on the restraint order list, besides, that approach will just draw more attention to us," Val said staring across the field, "We need emotional blackmail."

"It's not working," Ian said, "apparently she doesn't give a shit if Evangeline or Cynthia are dead." They started to walk slowly across the field, distancing themselves from anyone that might think to approach and say 'hi'.

"No," Val said, "I mean...something particular to her. You told me that Raffael later told you something about a dream that Evangeline had had."

"Yeah, apparently Evangeline draws some pretty strange things?" Ian said, "Like dead faces she sees in dreams or something? And one of them said Bambi's name."

"And that's why she chose Bambi to befriend, out of all the death clan freaks..." Val pondered.

"Yeah, pretty much. She thought it had some meaning."

"I can't believe I'm saying this, but...it probably does," Val said slowly, "We figured out Bambi knows those dead people. She's trying to avoid them. So... what if we don't let her? I don't know what it will do, but I bet you it will do something to her...I'll need access to Evangeline's room though. Do you still have those conspiracy theory cellphones that Raffael got?"

"Yeah, here's yours."

Chapter 37

THE JUMPING MOLE

The sun was rising as Evangeline climbed the steps to the castle. She was not sure if she had made Leonardo feel better or worse and decided to go back the next night, no matter what.

She sat on the top step of the castle for some time and watched as the sun slid slowly upwards in the sky, illuminating her new world. She wanted the feel of the rays on her face, to stay out in the light, but was tired after a whole night awake. Her skin burned slightly when the first rays hit, but not as much as before, except for the cut on her cheek, which scorched as it healed.

Perhaps just knowing what to expect made it better, she thought when she realized that she had sat through the burn, unmoving, her eyes open and her face to the sun, simply waiting for the pain to pass. Afterwards, she felt the smoothness of her cheek and sat a little while longer, taking in the absolute silence. This morning, not even the tiniest gust of wind broke it. Finally, she stood up, yawned, and walked inside.

Eros met her two steps in.

Evangeline grinned, "I'm surprised you didn't check up on me till now."

"You watched Ehvan paint, disrupted work, wandered through the eastern section of the city and then went to visit the Duke, who, by the way, is too far from the castle and you know it."

"Oh," Evangeline said.

"My mother will also start training you as of the coming evening. You lack basic survival skills, such as knowing when you are being tracked. I did not even attempt to be quiet."

"You just followed me all night?"

"No," Eros said, "My mother watched you try to steal paintbrushes, Josepina tracked you on and off around the east end as it is in the vicinity of her neighbourhood and I watched you walk with the Duke." Eros' lip curled up in mockery, "I know you need to see the sun, but now go have some food and go to sleep. You will have a full schedule starting tomorrow night."

"Hm. Yeah, Okay," Evangeline said with a frown and turned to go. She still had little urge to sleep in a deathly silent room but she figured it was time to start getting used to it.

"Alright," Eros said.

"Alright what?"

"You can sleep in my room but don't expect me to sit in the chair all night."

Evangeline turned back towards him and looked at his face, confused, "You're on top of the covers?"

"If I choose to lie down, yes. And you are on the left side," Eros said.

"Thank you?" Evangeline wasn't sure how to take his burst of generosity.

"It saves me time checking up on you during the day," Eros said without expression, then took her chin in his hand and turned her face to look at her cheek, "Hmm...good. It healed fully."

"Oh...yeah. I told you."

Eros was still holding on to her chin but his eyes were on her hair now, "I am not sure if I would have had either the courage or absurdity to let Ehvan attack my head with hedge scissors, however"- he suddenly let go of Evangeline's chin and placed his hand on his waist while his other hand ran through his hair- "well, it's not disastrous."

"You know what?" Evangeline smirked at him, "from anyone else that would be an insult. From you, I will take it as a compliment." She bowed extravagantly at him as she began to walk away towards the kitchen and said in a huffy accent, "I will see you upstairs my Lord."

"From anyone else that would be a sign of respect. From you, I will take it as mockery."

"You are a wise ruler, my Lord."

~

About twenty minutes later, Eros heard a knock on the door and Evangeline's head popped in. When he confirmed with a nod of his head and a roll of his eyes that she could come in, Evangeline entered the room with a wicked smile and a plate of food. Before he could protest she jumped on the bed with the plate and stuffed a piece of chicken in her mouth.

"You weren't about to say that I'm not allowed to eat on your bed and turn it into a platter, were you?" she said, her eyes crinkled in laughter even though her mouth was chewing food.

"I am on the verge of revoking the use of your proper name, *Evangeline*, and reverting back to wench."

Evangeline laughed in response, "So, *Eros*, what are we reading today?"

Eros' throat tightened at the sound of his name rolling off her tongue in that soft accent that she had from her world. She was such an aggravating, little imp with her mocking smile and mischievous eyes. And her hair was ridiculous. He threw a random book at her and she missed catching it. The book landed right in the middle of her plate, making half the food fly and land all over his sheets. She mouthed, "Oh shit," and with a sheepish grin started putting everything back on the plate.

He ignored her pathetic attempt at cleaning his bedsheets and looked down at his book. Why did he offer for her to sleep in his bed again? And why did he still keep wanting to bite her? When he smelled the blood on her cheek it held absolutely no appeal and yet he couldn't stop thinking of running his teeth along her body. He knew why, just as Josepina knew, but he refused to admit that he knew it. There was no point. Just keep her alive. Let her leave. Let her live. She would sleep in her own room starting tomorrow.

~

Evangeline finished putting the food back on her plate and climbed under the covers. She leaned against the back of the bed with her knees up and leaned her book against them, flipping its pages with one hand and picking at whatever food was left on the plate with the other. Today's book was full of children's tales. She wondered if Eros was trying to insult her with it, then decided she didn't care. It was better than metalwork.

He was completely ignoring her. His nose was in a book, but from his unmoving gaze it was obvious he wasn't reading. His dark brows were furrowed and she wondered how long they would stay this colour before they started to turn grey again.

"Why didn't you bite me in the kitchen?" Evangeline asked suddenly.

"What?"

"Why didn't you bite me in the kitchen when I was throwing things at you?"

Eros stared at her over his book, then put his face back in it, saying "I didn't want to."

"But you did want to."

"I wanted your blood," he said not looking up from his book, "not your life, but generally one doesn't come without the other."

"I thought you wanted me dead."

"Well, there were moments. There still are." Eros snorted but Evangeline refused to let him off the hook. She continued staring at him seriously until finally he lifted his eyes to meet hers and groaned, "I never wanted you here," he said, putting his book down, "I was furious. I was livid with my mother for pulling you here, lost in her own hopes, and furious with your stupidity at actually going out of your way to come here. What could you accomplish other than driving us to kill you sooner or later? I thought it was better to...get rid of you...before anyone formed any friendships or attachments and made things harder. It's not pleasant regretting murdering someone you cared about for the span of an existence that could be eternal."

Evangeline thought of the Duke and his penitent, regretful existence. As much as she liked Leonardo and felt for him, looking at Eros' face made her wonder if she could forgive someone the way Eros forgave the Duke, even if she understood the reasons. She thought of Julia and her throat tightened.

Eros was still looking at her and she didn't want him to even guess at her thoughts about his mother. She thought of something else, "But you watched me for twenty-four years. Wasn't that already a type of attachment?"

"Which is why I was not precisely happy when you arrived, smelling like my next meal. Still, watching someone through a misty dream is far different than knowing them in person," Eros said. His eyes were on hers and his intensity made Evangeline freeze for a second before he abruptly added, "for one, I had no warning what kind of buffoon I would be dealing with."

Evangeline laughed and giving him a stupid look, did a gorilla imitation. He shook his head and just said, "idiot," before turning his face back down to his book. She stuck another piece of chicken in her mouth, smiling broadly at the smirk on his face that he couldn't fully control.

Eventually Evangeline put her book down and burrowing under the covers said, "Good night," to Eros, who answered, "Good day."

"Oh, yeah," she said and closing her eyes added, "good sleep then."

She always slept like a rock. Thankfully one thing remained the same, she thought as she dozed off.

~

The next night after breakfast Evangeline started her training with Julia, while Eros watched. Julia was convinced that since Evangeline had acquired speed, agility and strength through her transformation, then she must have acquired at least some ability to heighten her other senses also.

Evangeline didn't argue. She knew she could see a bit clearer in the dark now and sounds did seem more prominent. Her skills were far from those of the citizens but she felt she might be able to improve them to some degree.

They started out by sniffing ingredients. Julia then began to hide them somewhere in the kitchen and with her eyes closed Evangeline would sniff them out. It was going much better than the physical training of the night before and they quickly moved from more profound scents to milder ones.

After that they tried sounds. First they let Evangeline listen while one of them walked through the castle to a random room and closed the door. She would then retrace their steps to that exact door. They moved on to softer footsteps and finally to covering her ears when they walked and simply letting her hear the slam of the door and pick the room with only that. The final exercise was too difficult and they moved back to soft footsteps.

Only her eyesight seemed futile. She was simply not able to see any better than she already did in the dark. Apparently that was a talent that only came out with the full Condition.

Training her senses with Julia was mentally draining, every part of Evangeline's mind screaming out for a break. However, it was nothing compared to the physical hell Eros decided would constitute her self-defence training. Part one consisted of increasing her speed which he felt had potential. For long distance stamina he simply made her run for an hour. After that it was time for short distance, raw speed. Eros' idea of improving this was to set a random finish line and give Evangeline a five second head start. After five seconds he sprinted after her. If he reached her before she got to the finish line he did a variety of things, including knocking her feet out from under her and letting her fall on her face in the grass, or tackling her down, full force.

Regardless of how Evangeline ended up with her face in the dirt, each time she did, his teeth were at her throat at which point he would politely smile and say, "You're dead."

One time Evangeline made the mistake of losing her temper and kicking him in the balls as soon as she pulled herself up. He just looked at her and smiled calmly.

"That would have been very effective if I were a regular male," Eros said, "As it is, for us it does little of consequence. However, since I know what you were insolently trying to accomplish..." then he set a small fountain as the next finish line and told her to run. Evangeline suspiciously looked at him but he had already started to count down from five so she turned and sprinted.

Eros caught up with her easily half-way to the fountain, but this time, instead of tackling her, he picked her up by the waist, tore to the fountain and threw her straight into the freezing cold water. Evangeline screamed, as Eros simply stood, watching her, enjoyment etched all over his face, just as he had promised.

She wanted to kick him again, this time in the head, but he was a hundred times stronger than her and not sure she was ready to find out what her next reward for insolence would be she simply stomped out of the fountain and stood in front of him fuming.

"Didn't you forget to say I'm dead?"

"I will have abundant opportunities tomorrow," Eros said evenly, "at present it's time for lunch. We will meet you in the dining hall after you have changed out of your bathing suit.

"Jackass," Evangeline said under her breath.

"From training with my mother, you should know that I can hear that."

"I do."

~

Half way through Evangeline's solo meal, Eros, Julia and Ehvan all appeared. Their meal had finished quickly, as always. Ehvan sat down in a chair and stared at her mouth while she ate, fascinated as always. Julia on the other hand, was interested more in her meal manners.

"You have a different style of eating than we had used, but it is obviously a taught technique nevertheless."

Evangeline looked down at her hands. Their utensils were a bit different: the main utensil was something that resembled a child's chopstick with the two sticks joined for easier use. However, while one end was a sharp, pointy stick the other was a small spoon, making the utensil something of a spork stick. The knives were the same, other than the fact that they all looked like steak knives. She had simply been using the utensils in whatever way worked, not having anyone to use as an example.

"Your parents must be educated," Julia commented, still watching her eating progress.

"Yes, they're both book worms," Evangeline said, smiling. Her smile quickly vanished as her mind instantaneously went back to her own world.

"I am sorry," Julia said, observing Evangeline's face, "it must be difficult for you."

"No, it's fine," Evangeline said, surprised at her own answer and the fact that it was true, "it's just the first time I've spoken about my family since arriving here. It felt strange, but I should get used to it."

"It's alright to admit that you aren't ready to talk about them," Julia said, her wind chime voice soft and quiet, "you don't need to be fine."

"I know," Evangeline said, "but I am fine."

Evangeline took a slow bite of her meal and looked up at Julia. She knew Julia wasn't that different from the Duke. Why couldn't she do what Eros did? "You've made it fine. Thank you...for that," Evangeline said to Julia. It was as much as she could say for now. She tried not to let her eyes wander to Eros, grudgingly thinking that he was a better person than her.

Julia did not respond, only looked at Evangeline's face for a minute. Evangeline eventually looked back down at her food and continued to eat silently.

"Did you know that the Jumping Mole is the only mad person allowed to live?" Ehvan startled Evangeline with his happy, out-of-place comment and her head flew up. Ehvan, as usual didn't notice and continued, "Mother says it's because he is a different kind of mad. For the last ten years he has been trying to create a vegetarian meal for us...it hasn't worked yet."

"Huh?" Evangeline chewed on some food, pondering this. She had never even considered that there could be an option of creating a non-killer, vampire diet. She was suddenly curious about the Mole and finishing off the rest of her food as quickly as possible was ready to head out.

As they were leaving, Samina and Lorenzo re-entered with a basket of provisions for the next meal. Evangeline thanked them for the food as always, and as always they only nodded and stared.

On the way to the Mole's house Eros and Julia began to fill in some of the gaps in Evangeline's knowledge of their world, apparently this being of importance to her comprehending the Mole.

"From what we could see, your world is about machines," Eros said, "You calculate how to create and you create physically. Our world focused on creation with the sixth sense portion of your mind. That is just one small portion of the unused sections of your brain. You must know how little of its mind a human uses. Our society focused on opening the unused portions and creating with those."

"Okay," Evangeline said, not really comprehending what he meant at all. She saw nothing that significantly different in their world, except that they had the technological advances of the middle ages.

Eros smirked and shook his head, "Remember the book about dormium?"

"Oh... uhh,"

"Exactly," Eros said, "the one you used as your pillow. If you managed to look at any of the depictions in the book before you fell asleep on it, you will remember that they showed people molding the dormium with their hands, using equipment only to etch in decorations and such. You know that dormium is hard and almost unbreakable. How do you think anyone can mold it with bare hands?"

"Okay, how?"

"Dormium comes from within the mountains lining this city, an interesting reason for why we never climbed or dug through them, which I am guessing you never pondered," Eros raised his eyebrows at her and she shrugged, having truly never thought of it. He continued, "when dormium is brought out in the sun for the first time, and the first time only, there is a reaction within it. Its particles restructure themselves. It is at that moment that a master of metalwork must be present to focus his mind on those particles and to know precisely how he needs them restructured. He has to bend them to his will. Once he does so, they will stay that way potentially forever, though when brought in contact with other dormium, over time, it is possible to have two dormium objects fuse together. That, is another skill. In any case, working dormium is a timed process that is done with the mind mainly. Our work with the mind is also why my mother was able to communicate with you to a certain degree, throughout your life."

"You haven't communicated like that with me since I arrived...only Cynthia" Evangeline said to Julia, though she looked straight ahead.

"Both sides have to be willing to talk," Julia said, "and both sides must have some ability. You have extremely limited ability, as well as untrained. That is also why I could only enter your mind through your dreams or other states of semi-consciousness, and only to a very limited degree."

"But Cynthia was fully awake," Evangeline said.

"Yes," Julia said, "She wanted me to come in... very much, and then I pushed...very hard. Cynthia also had ability. Great ability actually, for someone completely untrained. She saw inside my mind and let you know about the window off the side of the balcony. That room, it had been mine as you know. I had used that window to sneak into the kitchen in the middle of the night when I was younger...when I opened my mind to enter Cynthia's, she was able to see some of my long-term memories. A rare ability."

"What about you?" Evangeline looked over at Eros, wanting to veer the topic away from Cynthia now.

"Me?" Eros said, "I, as my mother likes to say, have a brain like a pile of dormium, once formed, it solidified in its singular shape. I have absolutely no sixth sense ability of my own. However, I am able to be led to follow others, just as when I followed my mother into your head. If you think back you will recall that you never saw me without my mother, but you have seen her without me."

"It's still a highly rare ability," Julia said, as if trying to defend her son's lack of it, "the majority never develop it to any significant degree and we only specifically train those with visible intrinsic aptitude."

"If developed properly, sixth sense can go beyond mathematical thinking," Eros said, "it can go beyond three or even four-dimensional vision and comprehension."

"And the Mole is an expert at sixth sense thinking, I am guessing?" Evangeline said.

"Yes and no," Julia said, "sixth dimensional thinking must be properly controlled. The Mole was, and still is, a brilliant man, but he lacks control. He, as you will see, is a bit erratic, the various parts of his mind not working very well together, making it hard to tell many times whether he is telling us something useful or not. Turning into what we now are has made things even more difficult. Many who had been efficient at aspects of using their sixth sense portions of their minds are unable to do so or have retained only limited ability through the hunger."

"Maslow's hierarchy of needs," Evangeline said as they continued walking.

"Hmm?" Julia looked at her.

"Oh, he was a sociology researcher in...my world," Evangeline said, "he had this theory about a hierarchy of needs. Needs are stacked like a pyramid and your basic survival needs are at the bottom of it. Above those is the need for safety, then love and belonging and so on. Right at the top of the pyramid is self-actualization. Basically, you can't get to the top of the pyramid and reach self-actualization if your lower needs aren't being met," as Evangeline spoke and explained the theory it began to make clearer sense in her own head, "...you guys are always hungry so you can't think deeper...the constant physical hunger makes it impossible for many of you to think on any level other than the most basic. I think it's amazing that you are able to get past the hunger at all and function so well."

Evangeline saw Eros out of the corner of her eye, observing her face seriously, but it was Julia who spoke, "Hmm...yes...sometimes," Julia said, "but thank you, Evangeline, Sir Maslow described our current situation quite well."

Evangeline smiled at Julia's use of Sir when they suddenly stopped.

"Well, here we are," Eros said as they approached a humble-looking, three-level building in what felt like it must have been a shady area of the city previously, with its tightly wound alleys and cluttered buildings. Now, however, this neighbourhood was perfectly manicured just like everything else.

"The mole's mother was a woman of very high standing, while his father was a labourer," Eros said, as if guessing her thoughts, as he opened the door of the building. This door, like most other doors in the city, was unlocked, "he was her father's labourer to be precise. Needless to say, the Mole was an illegitimate child. His mother died in childbirth and though her family were decent and raised the Mole well, he eventually moved back here, saying that he found his father's neighbourhood and populace much more inspirational to his grasp of human nature."

Eros and Julia entered the building first, with Evangeline and Ehvan behind them. Evangeline smiled in amazement as she stood inside the entrance, letting her eyes adjust to the darkness. The building, which previously must have been a rental style complex of apartments with a staircase in the middle, now very obviously belonged to just one person.

The doors to all the apartments had been removed, as well as some of the walls, revealing rooms and living spaces full of nothing but shelves packed with books, parchments, paintings and sketches. It was like some mad wizard's library. Evangeline loved it, imagining how amazing and magical this place would look in the light.

"Isn't it wonderful?" Ehvan reflected her thoughts, "I am still trying to finish reading all the books in here, but the Jumping Mole won't allow anyone to remove his books from his house and mother won't allow me to come to visit him alone. She says he is too finicky for her liking."

"Romeo," Eros called out, poking his head inside one of the rooms.

"Romeo?" Evangeline said.

"That is his name," Julia answered as they heard a slightly shrill voice coming from a room further down the hall, "Prince, what do I smell? Man. Woman. Child. Food or desire?"

Eros grunted and followed the sound of the Mole's voice with the rest of the group behind him, "Romeo, I have been informed that you are regularly missing from your city duties, as always."

"I have dusted all my bookshelves, your highness. Must we not start from the inside when we clean our lives?" the screechy voice said.

"Start where you are told to start. I want you working in the city. You have more than sufficient time to be in your house between work."

At this point they had entered an expansive room with high bookshelves randomly placed in every possible spot and direction within it, both along the walls and all through the middle. The room had high, slim windows lining one whole wall and it was the only house Evangeline had seen that did not have thick, dark curtains permanently covering each window.

The light of the moon illuminated this area and Evangeline saw an absolutely tiny man crouched right at the very top of a particularly high bookshelf. He looked like he must have been old before he turned as his skin was not only grey but also loose and flappy. The finishing touch was a scraggly beard which unevenly covered his face. Evangeline tried to swallow her laughter but some still managed to escape and she got one of Eros' special looks for it. How could she not laugh when this man's name was Romeo? Where in the world did they come up with these names?

Romeo, aka the Jumping Mole's, beady, little eyes were moving all over the place at lightning speed and when they fell on Evangeline they stopped and bulged out and he started to leap from the top of one bookshelf to another towards her, his skin flapping from side to side. Evangeline gasped as he did a final leap right at her, too surprised to do anything except stumble back. Apparently, Eros was quite used to the Mole's frantic movements and with one quick move of his arm grabbed the Mole by the scruff of his shirt in midair, just as the Mole was right in front of Evangeline's face.

Plopping the Mole down on the ground in front of Evangeline while still holding on to him, Eros said, "Romeo, this is Evangeline. I am sure you are aware of her arrival. Perhaps you would like to introduce yourself?"

The Mole did not respond, but only stared at her, sniffing very audibly. His manic head movements as he sniffed made Evangeline a bit anxious and she backed away slightly, saying uncertainly, "Hello, its uhh... a pleasure to meet you."

Her voice seemed to bring his mind back to the present and as his body movements calmed down, his eyes also became less beady.

"Oh...I'm sorry," he screeched out, "what must you think of me, little princess."

"I'm sorry, my name is Evangeline. Evangeline," she repeated it for good measure, looking at Eros and Julia for some guidance.

"Eeee-van-gehhhh-leeeen," Ehvan articulated loudly, looking up at Evangeline. He smiled at her broadly, apparently satisfied that he had helped.

"Oh. Oh yes. Yes," The mole giggled like a little kid, then, pulling himself together, straightened out and bowed in greeting, "It's a pleasure to meet you, Eeeevangeeeeleeeen," he said, repeating Ehvan's method of pronouncing out her name.

This was the most bizarre encounter Evangeline had had to date and that was saying a lot. She chuckled, making the Mole giggle again, "Yeeess. It is all happy coincidence that you are here, but the other one! Her time here must be limited! Get her back! Out of here!" he shouted, his giggle forgotten and his eyes bulging and beady again.

"Romeo, the other girl has passed away," Julia said. Evangeline inadvertently looked at Julia but Julia's face was facing straight ahead.

"Perhaps you still sense her remains?" Eros asked.

"Whatever it is, take it back to its world. And bring the black haired, royal bastard girl back. Have I not told you what happens when you bring our worlds together?"

Evangeline looked from person to person expectantly, waiting for some sort of explanation. Ehvan looked up at her and said, "The Mole told me that our worlds come from the same, single piece of energy. You cannot bring the worlds together or they explode. But Evangeline didn't explode." Ehvan looked at the Mole in confusion.

The Mole, visibly frustrated took over, "At first the universe was a living energy. This energy wanted to be calm, gentle life, but it was too great and intense. To weaken itself enough to become stable, it split itself, half of its energy creating one universe, and the other half another. Our universes are complimentary and tied together. Thoughts, ideas, even dreams can travel between them. But they can never come in contact with each other. If two compliments should find each other they will again join to become the initial energy which they came from, creating a hole in both planes of existence. No life can come from one to the other! It is dangerous to us all. To all existence. Get them back to where they belong!"

"It is difficult to understand," Julia smiled gently at Evangeline.

"No, I get it," Evangeline said looking at the Mole, "matter and antimatter. They split, forming one matter and one antimatter plane of existence. Bring them back together and it implodes in on itself, turning back to energy. If Bambi met her double in our world, they would implode."

"You and I do not know what a piece of energy chooses to manifest itself in, in each universe," The Mole said, "Some compliments may be doubles but many are not. Bambi's compliment can be anything which is living, a tree, a bird, or...or...a chicken."

The Mole stopped and his head flew from side to side as if looking for something, "is it supper time? Where is my chicken?" then, noticing that the group was still in front of him, he calmed down again and said, "Not time yet, I see. No matter, I hate chicken."

"But, Romeo, I'm not from here either," Evangeline said, "Why isn't it dangerous for me to be here?"

"You are yourself and your compliment. A living being at war with itself. Of both worlds. Energy not split. No one knows how but there are others like you, in our world and yours. The doorway will only open between two true compliments, so it will only open for those like you and it will search out to open near those like you. You may stay where you wish Eeeevaangeleeen because your body will be at war with itself both here and there...though it seems happier now."

"So, I am both matter and antimatter?" Evangeline asked of no one in particular, "Everyone with PNH is both matter and antimatter? Then what was the sword? Exotic matter? That's why it kept the portal open?" A realization was dawning on her. She swallowed. Eros was looking at her, his eyes wide, rather than the narrowed mockery she was used to. She tried to focus on the Mole, not knowing what kind of emotions were passing over her face and which ones she wanted Eros to know.

"I don't know matter and antimatter and whatever is exotic, but you are human energy, battling with itself. You can choose where to belong. Everyone else must go to where they came from," the Mole said.

"What about Bambi's mom, Lola? Isn't she in my world?" Evangeline asked.

"I don't feel Lola's danger, but I sense Bambi's and....and... Cynthia," the Mole said, his face a bit confused as he tried to remember the name. "Get them back to where they came from."

"How?" Eros let go of the Mole's shirt.

"Open the lightning, of course!" the Mole burst out as if it were the most obvious thing on earth, "And burn *him*, Burn him! YOU," he shrieked and looked directly at Evangeline, "burn Daoud. Go there and burn him, but you will need to be faster and jump higher."

"We're training her," Eros said.

"She'll train you one day," the Mole started giggling again. Evangeline, initially amused, was now becoming annoyed; he was telling her to go and burn random people for apparently random reasons. She moved her body weight from one foot to another, folding her arms across her chest. The mole cocked his head to the side as he looked at her,

"You are impatient to go?" he said in his shrill, slightly giggly voice, "Yes, you are here to fulfil others' desires. But they must change forms for that. Jump higher and find Daoud first. But you should make a pit stop on the way," the mole was speaking faster and faster now, like a wheel gaining momentum down a hill, "pit stop. Snack stop. Yes, snack. Can't snack without people. People are good snacks. You are not a good snack. You smell foul. But, I almost perfected my new diet. I just need a little extra...something. You smell foul but most healthy things are a little foul, aren't they? Yes, little princess, a little foul, healthy additive to my diet. I am certain it will do my blood well."

The Mole was looking directly at Evangeline and smacking his lips. Eros grabbed her roughly and threw her behind himself with an "It's time to go." He was standing between Evangeline and the Mole, blocking the Mole from her view completely as his tiny, flabby frame was only about half that of Eros'.

Julia pulled on Evangeline's arm and then pushed her gently in front of herself in the direction of the front door. Evangeline did not question and made her way out of the house as fast as possible.

Chapter 38

PLANS

It was good to be outside, away from the Mole's unpredictable thoughts and movements and Evangeline breathed out deeply.

Ehvan looked back sadly at the building, "There will be no reading today?"

"Not at the Mole's house," Julia answered, patting him gently, "You may go to the learning facility though. Why don't you run now, *caro*. You still have enough time before supper."

Ehvan didn't need convincing and sprinted away from them. Evangeline watched him disappear then looked over at Eros who had come out of the Mole's house with a slightly grim look on his face.

"It is borderline," Eros said, looking at Julia, "he is not much more erratic than usual but he did have the intention of snacking on Evangeline."

"Did he attack?" Julia asked.

"No, he did not even move from his spot. Only continued to lick his lips and talk about requiring a healthy additive."

"He has been attempting to create that vegetarian diet for a decade. Perhaps it is just an extension of that," Julia said.

"Perhaps," Eros looked at the door to the Mole's house.

"What's going on? I don't understand," Evangeline interrupted their discussion, worried by the bleak edge in their voices.

"The law is absolute, Evangeline," Julia said, facing Evangeline, "we cannot control ourselves when we smell human blood, but our own blood both smells foul to us and does not feed our hunger. There is no hope left for any citizen who attacks one of our own."

"You are trying to decide if to kill the Mole or not?" Evangeline asked, her heart dropping like a rock into her gut.

"Yes," Eros said, unapologetically, "Any citizen who attacks another citizen is beyond redemption. We know. We have tried. It is the point where they have lost all their 'higher level thinking' as you put it, and have become no more than a rabid animal. Their human mind has been eaten by the hunger."

"But I'm not a 'citizen'," Evangeline said.

"Your blood holds as much appeal to us now as sucking on dirt. In that sense, you are considered one of us…luckily Romeo did not attack and his conversation made the usual sense…in any case, I believe you are more clear now as to why you have received specific instructions to never enter a building alone, yes?"

"Mmm," Evangeline barely noted his pointed look, preoccupied with the thought of someone dying because of her, "so he won't be killed, right?"

"No, he won't," Eros said, "did you hear anything I said about entering buildings?"

"Yes. Fine," Evangeline breathed out. The mole was not exactly likeable, but she didn't want him burning to death. She couldn't even fathom the concept. She knew they had burned someone on her and Cynthia's first day but she hadn't known them then…and…then they hadn't seemed human.

Eros gave her a tight-lipped look, shook his head and turned to Julia, "It seems that Evangeline should find the humans, rather than heading straight for Daoud."

"Yes, I suppose it makes sense. It also confirms that there are still some alive," Julia said, "It has been a long time since I have been able to get anything sensical out of the Mole about their survival."

Apparently, even at the walking speed of a person with the Condition Latina and Sadamanta (where Daoud was located) were about fifteen days away. The location where Julia and Eros felt any humans might have settled in, was an old training centre for dormium metal workers. It was a very small, isolated spot, with only a couple of small buildings where those with the intrinsic ability to work dormium had been previously trained to use their sixth sense metalwork skills in seclusion.

The training centre would have had some dormium stored there and having dormium available for the working would have provided a sense of safety for the humans. Since the facility already had structure, they would have already had immediate, if inadequate housing. The possibility of them having gone there was also highest as the facility was kept a secret from Sadamanta; dormium development had always been a competing factor between the two countries. Since the facility location was classified, it was never in the line of the war, guaranteeing that none of those with the Condition ended up there purposefully.

The facility was at an angle of a bit more than ninety degrees from both Sadamanta and Latina, the three forming an uneven triangle, with the training facility being the middle point. Therefore, while it would take approximately fifteen days to get directly from Latina to Sadamanta, it would take around ten days to get to the training facility from either. If Evangeline went to the facility on her way to Sadamanta it would increase her journey by only five days, however, it would let her potentially restock supplies and perhaps gain information on Daoud before reaching him.

On the other hand, she would have to find the facility, with only rough instructions from Eros and Julia to guide her. Having absolutely no wildlife or navigational experience she might miss the facility and be left wandering in the forest for an indefinite amount of time, assuming she ever found her way out. Additionally, if the humans which escaped had not settled there or had moved on, she would also have wasted time and resources for nothing.

"But you trust the mole," Evangeline said to both Julia and Eros.

"If you mean in terms of his sixth sense, then yes," Julia answered.

"Then I need to find the training facility, don't I?"

"Well, humans are safer than Daoud," Eros said.

"Why did he keep telling me to burn Daoud?" Evangeline asked Eros.

"He has mentioned Daoud burning on a bi-yearly basis for the past two and a half decades. Perhaps in another decade we may get an explanation," Eros said with a dry smile, "however, as we burn in the sun, we can assume that the Mole wants him dead."

"When do I have to leave?" Evangeline asked, afraid of the answer. On one hand leaving meant the hope of finding something...anything. On the other hand, this city had become her safety and she was frightened to leave it. Without wanting to, each night her brain calculated how long she had been in Terra Nova. Tonight was night number ten. Even with time passing at a ratio of 2:1 between Terra Nova and earth, each night the hopes of Raffael coming for her were bleaker. And now, the Mole's words, if true, sealed it. Raffael wouldn't come because he couldn't without Evangeline. She was the matter/antimatter – PNH anomaly who had to hold the sword and open the portal. Did Eros and Julia realize this? Had they clicked in? She was afraid to look at them and pretended to look up at the dark sky as she spoke.

"We should plan on you wandering the forest for twenty to thirty days, regardless. We have not made much human food, except some basic farming that we use as pig feed, for over two decades," Julia said, as Evangeline continued looking everywhere except their faces, "You cannot travel with fresh fruit, which will quickly rot. You don't know how to hunt. We need to prepare you. We have maintained one of the old smoke houses but it will take some time to dry and preserve meats and fruit, both because we are relearning the process and because it is a lengthy one."

Evangeline's heart thudded in relief. She didn't know how long it took to smoke meat but it seemed like she had many days, if not weeks before going off to wander the world alone.

"Meanwhile, you will practice your other survival skills," Eros said, "speed, defence...do you even know how to start a fire? I am assuming you have never hunted a single animal in your life?"

"You said you are salting meats," Evangeline said.

"And if you run out?" Eros asked, lowering his face slightly to hers.

"Well, apparently I die," Evangeline retorted.

"Not after I'm through with you," Eros said and she looked at him, surprised until he capped off his comment with, "I have not kept you alive, suffering through your impertinence and insolent humour for you to die the day you finally leave."

Evangeline let out a snort, "Good to know you care, blockhead."

Eros looked at her confused and she grinned, "You said your head is like a pile of dormium. Dormium head. Blockhead."

"I see we are back to pet names, dirt face? Since that is where your face happened to be during most of your training." Eros grinned back.

"You know, the Mole said I would be training you one day."

"Yes, then he giggled like a deranged ten-year-old girl."

They both noticed Julia observing them silently and Eros' face returned to its usual seriousness, as he began to walk towards the castle, "Come on blond disaster. Before the sun rises."

When they reached the castle, the night was nearing its end. Dropping Evangeline at the castle door, Eros said, "We are going for our meal now so you go and have your meal too. You need all the energy you can get for getting your face out of the dirt again all evening tomorrow."

Evangeline fake laughed then stopped and shouted, "The Duke!"

"What?" Eros asked in shock while Julia tripped backwards at the shout.

"Sorry. I promised Duke Karpenski that I would visit him tonight." Evangeline began to run down the steps again but Eros grabbed her arm mid step, "I don't think so. The Duke is too far and it is too close to sunrise."

"So? I can come back after sunrise."

"No, it's too far," Eros repeated.

"Too far for what? Ohhh, too far for someone to follow me there and back before the sun rises..."

"Hmm," Eros said.

"Well, since *you* can't follow me then no one else can either, so I will be safe."

"No," Eros said steadily.

"Yes," Evangeline tried to wrench her arm out of his grip unsuccessfully while he just stood and shook his head. "You can't hold me till morning," she said, getting annoyed, "You need to eat and I made a promise, so yes."

Eros was about to retort but Julia put up her hand and looked at him in a rare display of parental discipline, "Eros, let her arm go. Evangeline is right. It is too close to sunrise as well as our meal for anyone to follow her. You need to trust her and we need to feed quickly."

Eros let Evangeline's arm go with a slight grunt and she quickly ran off down the steps.

~

"Eros, she will still have to leave. Remember that," his mother said when Evangeline was out of sight.

"I never forgot, mother," Eros replied and began to walk towards their feeding area. What point was his mother attempting to make? All he was trying to do was make sure Evangeline stayed alive long enough to leave.

"I am sorry, Eros," his mother said, matching his stride, "I simply did not expect you to form such a... closeness so quickly."

"What are you talking about, mother? You do not want me to keep her alive?"

"Where has she been sleeping, Eros?" his mother looked at him pointedly and his lips tightened. Without an answer he turned his face forwards and continued walking.

~

Evangeline sat alone on a little, carved, swinging bench in the front garden of Leonardo Karpenski's house. Flowers surrounded her, half of them closed and half open towards the moon. She had heard of night bloomers but had never seen any before. She rocked back and forth slowly, thinking that this midnight garden was something between romantic and eerie.

All of a sudden, the Duke appeared almost right in front of her and she half shrieked. She definitely needed more sound training.

"Evangeline?" The Duke asked, visibly both surprised and pleased.

"I promised to visit. I'm sorry I'm late."

"Oh, no," the Duke said, "it is I who is late. I had to..."

"Grab a chicken?" Evangeline smiled at him and he smiled back, exhaling as he did so, "Yes, I suppose you could call it that."

The Duke looked up at the sky as if calculating how long he had till sunrise. Then he looked at Evangeline and smiled, "Will you wait here one minute?"

"Of course," she said and he disappeared inside the house. She swung gently as she waited and in a couple short minutes saw him coming out of his home, holding a small, ornate tray on which stood a little teapot and cup.

"I had this ready, just in case you came back," he said as he approached, "you are not opposed to having tea under the stars?"

Evangeline smiled and took the tray from him, positioning it delicately on her lap and pouring herself a cup of tea.

"There is no milk in the city," Leonardo said apologetically, but Evangeline shrugged and said, "I always liked it black."

After a couple of sips of her tea, she looked around them and commented, "I have never seen flowers that bloom in the night."

"It is only certain varieties. I discovered them accidentally over the years," Leonardo said, watching her drink, just as everyone at the castle watched her eat, "They are not what my Lilia, my wife, had originally planted, but she was never opposed to trying different varieties."

The Duke went on to explain some of the varieties to her and they chatted, though for a little while only, as the dawn was quickly approaching now. Leonardo stood up, looking regretful and took the tray from Evangeline, "Thank you for coming. It was nice to talk again," he said, sounding as if he hadn't spoken for many years.

"It was nice to talk to you too," Evangeline said, "Not many people talk to me. They just stare."

"We are all the same here, Evangeline," Leonardo said, gently looking at her over his short, frumpy frame, "our hunger is reflected in each other and it becomes our life. But you, when we see you, we remember...other things. At the beginning it is confusing...for some perhaps too much to handle initially...but in the end, we are all happy to remember..."

They were both at the door of his house now and the Duke bowed his head in farewell, "I hope to see you again."

"Can I come tomorrow?" Evangeline asked, liking the Duke's calm manner and the fact that he actually spoke.

"Every day if you wish," he answered and she laughed, "You shouldn't have said that."

~

Eros appeared behind Evangeline in the dark hallway on the way to her room.

"I'm still alive. Disappointed, your highness?" She said over her shoulder.

"No. If you are to die, I hope for it to be by my hand, you insolent, little..." he stopped mid sentence and breathed out slowly as Evangeline turned to face him, both surprised and amused.

"Just get into your night gown," he said, turning away, "and hurry up. I have no intention of starting to read only to be interrupted half way down the page."

Eros walked away without looking at her and Evangeline entered her room scratching her head. Presumably this meant that she could stay in his room again if she wanted to? Did she want to?

She was feeling calmer after talking with the Duke again. Even the Mole helped in the sense that the more she knew the people here the more human they became. This world was slowly becoming almost...her world...or maybe it was because she knew it might be? What if it was? If she didn't think about her other life, her other world, all those other people she had once known, if she just thought of this world, the way it was, the people she now had here...Julia, Ehvan and...Eros...what she felt was a tingle of nervousness and a warmth travelling from her stomach all the way up to her face.

She changed into her gown, fumbling slightly, picked up the tray with her breakfast and made her way to Eros' room. As she walked, she shrugged her shoulders to the empty hallway in a sign of, "It's no big deal."

He was sitting in his chair as usual and after a small pause in the door, Evangeline walked in and made herself comfortable on the left side of the bed. A couple of books lay on the bedside table beside her and she sifted through them to pick out one that seemed interesting. She began to read quietly while picking at the food on her tray. He continued to read his own book, looking up at her every now and then.

She stayed up as long as she could, wondering where/how he would fall asleep. But he didn't before she passed out.

Chapter 39

THE HAUNTING OF BAMBI

Raffael clicked open the door of his parents' house. After the questions and the searches had come up empty, communication between him and his parents began to dry up. By day four he was avoiding their contact altogether. It was Okay. He didn't begrudge them blaming him anymore. With every day he blamed himself more. He was useless. He hadn't managed to get anywhere in terms of getting his sister back.

He walked in slowly now, knowing that both of his parents were at work. While walking by the living room he glanced sideways at the large sliding window where he had initially almost lost his sister. He turned away and climbed the stairs to her room. Val wanted all of Evangeline's creepiest paintings. The more the better, she had said, and specifically the man with the sword, since Bambi seemed to recognize it, as well as the woman who apparently said Bambi's name in Evangeline's dream. Raffael couldn't take them all. His parents would start asking questions. However, there were enough to choose from without rousing suspicion.

He looked from painting to painting. The painting which portrayed the man with the sword the best was also the painting that the sword had been inside of - meaning the hugest painting in the room. He picked up the large canvas, groaning.

Then, he went around and picked smaller paintings and sketches, a mixture of portrayals of the man with the sword, the woman with the long, raggedy hair and another man with a ring containing a dark, crimson jewel, similar to the one in the sword.

He was about to leave with his stash when, taking one last look around the room, his eye landed on an unfinished work. This was a sketch of the woman with the long hair. It was lying on Evangeline's desk and was quite small in size, though in this sketch, unlike in the others, the woman seemed more active. She was leaning forwards, her hand stretched out as if trying to reach out of the canvas, with eyes so clear that they seemed to be staring at whoever held the picture. He had never seen this work before and wondered if Evangeline had done it after coming home from the hospital.

After a short pause Raffael decided to take this picture also. It wasn't finished, but definitely up at the top in terms of disturbing. It took him a couple trips to the car in order to get the whole stash loaded in it and on its roof. Finally, he left the house and locked the door behind himself.

~

Communicating on their pay-as-you-go cellphones was easy, but inconspicuously passing a mountain of paintings to Val, one of which happened to be massive, was not. In the end, Raffael came up with something he thought sounded semi-plausible.

"Hi. I know your daughter Val is not home. I'm Raffael. Evangeline's brother. Evangeline loved to paint. She made this...uhm...collection of paintings for the art competition at school. If Val could submit these for her, I would really appreciate it."

"Oh, sure. Of course. I'm really sorry about your sister. I can tell Val misses her a lot," Val's father said. He was a freckly man with a pasty office complexion and slightly lethargic looking, office body. Raffael wondered how he had managed to end up with Val's mom – that woman could put Beyoncé to shame with her golden complexion and curves. Meanwhile, the dad's only saving grace were his eyes, which looked just like Val's, bright green and full of energy and intelligence.

"We all believe she will be located...but thank you. In the meantime, I know she really wanted to submit these."

"I'll give them to Val. I'm sure she won't let Evangeline down."

~

"Are you sure your friend wasn't into some sort of drugs?" her dad asked Val as he squinted sideways at Evangeline's paintings.

"Dad, stop," Val said, not even looking at her father as she lifted the pics and canvasses and loaded them into their jeep individually that evening. She had brought the car into the garage and was loading it from the inside, in the off chance the weird, plastic cop was circling her house. For the most part the cops had now left her alone, but she knew they were still trailing Bambi for whatever reason and decided it wasn't worth the risk.

"I'm just saying, these are just really...bizarre."

"They're personal interpretations of the battles of the human spirit," Val said. She had literally just pulled that out of her ass, but it sounded good. She did a mental, self-pat on the back, "anyways, they're really good," she continued, "I think they have a good chance at winning the competition."

"Well, it's nice of you to submit them for the contest for her. She definitely has talent. Her choice of...expression....is just a bit disturbing."

"Well, so is the human spirit."

"Hmm...any new information on her and Cynthia's disappearance?"

Val didn't have to look at her dad to know what he was thinking: two teenage girls in skimpy outfits go missing after going off alone after a party. Only a matter of time before they are found in a gutter or garbage can.

"No," she said stiffly and banged the car door shut.

"Val, I know she was your best friend but-"

"She *is* my best friend dad. Now let it go."

Val walked off, into the house, before her dad could continue. They would open that fucking portal thing again...somehow. Evangeline and Cynthia would be there. Evangeline was probably painting zombie faces and making imbecilic jokes in an alternate universe while Cynthia was torturing alternate living species with her snootiness. And she, Val, would go through that portal and see something fucking amazing. Another world. Another plane of existence, in which Evangeline and Cynthia were alive. Because Bambi was full of shit. They were alive.

~

"I can't believe you are actually friends with the janitor," Val said. Mark and Ian were helping her drag all the paintings into the janitor's room almost an hour and a half before school started.

"What? He was the janitor at my elementary school before," Mark said, "and he always brought me smarties and hung out with me at recess...I was kind of a fat kid."

Val and Ian howled with laughter.

"You started chillin' with the janitor in grade school?" Val asked.

"Sounds a little...Oh, I don't know... Here's a Smartie, little boy," Ian said.

"Come on. He was really nice. Why the fuck am I helping you assholes?" Mark said, dropping one of the paintings down with a thud.

"Okay, Okay, we're sorry. We'll stop. Promise," Val pulled herself together and pointed a warning finger at Ian to stop laughing also.

"Yeah, sorry, Mark. We appreciate the storage space," Ian said and looked at Val, "Okay, so the plan is to.... just creep Bambi out?"

"Sort of. She knew the sword and I think she knows...as in actually *knows*, these...people things. From what Raffael said, he and Evangeline got accidentally intertwined with these creature things and the lightning. Bambi though...well, I asked around a bit. She used to say she came from an alternate place. Apparently, for once she wasn't bullshitting. The point is to evoke something out of her...I have a feeling that seeing her old pals will. Let's watch her reaction and gauge what we do next by it."

Bambi arrived shortly before school started and walked up to her locker cautiously, seeing that there was something stuck to it. Looking directly at the portrait she dropped her backpack with a thud. Seeing people stare at her as well as at the morbid portrait, Bambi quickly picked up her backpack and put in her locker combination with shaky hands. She flipped its door open as fast as possible so that the portrait would be out of anyone's line of vision.

Bambi stood and fumbled inside her locker until almost everyone was gone from the hallway. Then she pushed the door closed again and started ripping the heavy-duty tape off of her locker door, after some minutes managing to dislodge the picture.

"Assholes," she said under her breath. Taking the picture Bambi walked to the closest garbage can and was about to rip it up and chuck it in. Her hands refused though. She just couldn't rip through the face. Looking at its morbid greyness she only scrunched it up and threw it in the can.

Bambi walked back to her locker, clicked it closed and went to her class.

Chapter 40

NIGHT BY NIGHT

Evangeline's nights and days became an odd routine. The evenings started out with the first meal, followed by training, then a midnight meal and free time, during which the family did their individual city duties and Evangeline explored her walled-in world. Often she would practice a bit on her own and then pay one or two visits.

Julia and Eros were still the rulers and still oversaw all citizens and all duties in all sections of their world. This meant that their jobs varied each and every night and Evangeline generally did not see them between training and morning. Ehvan, on the other hand, had a set schedule and was always excited to show her what he did. When he found out that Evangeline used to take dance lessons, Ehvan brought her along to his dance class.

"Dancing isn't really a requirement to restart a regular, human society. How come it's one of the duties?" Evangeline asked Ehvan as they walked down the street to his class, "do you guys just enjoy it?"

"I don't. I think it's stupid, but mother says without culture society loses its heart. I am still not sure what that means but to mother it means that I have to practice and never forget our traditional songs and dances."

"Well, some humans say that culture satisfies even more than food. You can say that your mother wants to make sure you will be well fed when you change to a regular human again."

"Well, it's easier to dance than to find food so maybe it is good to be satisfied by culture," Ehvan said with a frown on his face, "right now dancing is very unexciting though. Eros says it is because I have no memory of how it felt before."

"I love dancing. I'm not allowed to help out around the city but I could learn to dance, couldn't I? Want to teach me Latina's traditional dances? Maybe it will make it more fun for you?"

"Maybe, but I doubt it."

The lesson ended up being more fun than either could have expected. Ehvan felt proud of being the expert, while Evangeline was actually allowed to participate in a Latina duty. Even the dance teacher, Betel, was thrilled. It had been quite a number of years since she had had the chance to start fresh with someone rather than repeating the same moves.

Evangeline had taken a number of dance lessons as a child and was generally coordinated. However, Latina's traditional dances were different from anything she had ever studied.

The most famous dance, was a partner dance in which the partners did something between a tap dance, flamenco and rhythmic ribbon dancing without the actual ribbon, all the while never touching each other.

The dancers stomped their feet in various rhythms, while they moved their arms like waves above their heads and to their sides, each wave being either two or four beats of the feet. Evangeline felt like each part of her body was doing a completely different style of dancing and though she could sort of follow either the arm or leg movements, when she tried to combine them it was disastrous. She felt like she was doing the coordination game where the person tries to rub their stomach and head simultaneously in opposite, circular directions.

During her first hour, Evangeline barely learned one basic step and did not get anywhere close to combining it with a partner. When a partner was added to the dance, the partner's feet didn't always do the same moves, however, they had to make sure to stomp to the same rhythm because their hands, though not touching, intertwined with each other in cohesive waves.

Although Evangeline felt she was pretty horrible, Betel praised her to no end, saying that most didn't get this far on their first day. Even in her grey and wrinkled state Betel managed to look short, plump and round and her whole frame jiggled when she grabbed Evangeline's hand and forced her to promise that she would come again and continue her dance study. Evangeline wondered if Betel really thought she had potential or if she just desperately wanted someone new to train. Still, it was one thing she was allowed to do around the city so she began to join Ehvan whenever he went.

Evangeline's other regular visits consisted of having tea at the Duke's before sunrise. On her third night visiting him, she was stunned to see that he had managed to bring out a whole table and chairs into the garden for them to properly enjoy their tea times.

After the Duke would go inside for the day Evangeline would watch the sun rise and spend some time in the light, often re-exploring her favourite parts of the city in the light. She liked the orchards and gardens the best as they lacked the eerie feel of the still streets, and she could feel completely unwatched and free with no blacked-out windows facing her.

Eventually Evangeline would return to the castle, take her food, change into her gown and go to Eros' room. It became an unspoken arrangement between them that Evangeline stayed in his room during the day. Neither commented nor asked about it.

They would generally read for a while, before Evangeline passed out, though intermittently they also began to talk more and more. Their conversations ranged from the everyday to the more philosophical, with no particular routine in what they discussed. Often Evangeline learned bits and pieces about life in Latina before it turned.

"Why did you choose Josepina to follow me around?" Evangeline asked one day, "I thought she was a lady of pleasure."

"Josepina was in the...profession of men, yes. She was known throughout the kingdoms for her talents. Not the way you think," Eros looked at her face and cocked his head, "Josepina had the specific sixth sense talent for feeling the needs and desires of other people. Again, not the way you think...not completely anyways. She knew when to become a confidante, what was required to placate a vengeful temper or even how to calm the sick and dying. She began to be used in political meetings and was a brilliant addition to intense talks. But yes, she always remained in her initial profession. She seemed to enjoy it. After some time she owned the highest profile courting house probably ever heard of."

"I'm still not quite sure why she's my personal stalker," Evangeline said, "to begin with, I didn't get the impression that she liked me when we first met."

"Our transformation affected the abilities of those who could use their sixth sense. Those who had limited skill lost it completely. Those who had great skill, such as my mother or Josepina, were able to retain some of it. Josepina felt you out when she met you. She was more or less satisfied with you. We use her because she can sense you by tuning into your emotions. She is probably the best...stalker of all of us."

"I didn't know I was that high profile that I get my own sixth sense bodyguards."

"You are that much of a walking disaster," Eros said.

Other nights they talked about life in Evangeline's world, Eros being particularly interested in its political structure.

"You have absolutely no respect for royalty. Tell me about the king in your world," Eros enquired one morning after Evangeline had amused herself more than usual at his expense.

"We have no king. I mean...we're part of the commonwealth, but...anyways, let's just say we have a Prime Minister. We're a democracy."

"What is a democracy?" Eros asked, leaning forward.

Evangeline was not a political genius in any sense but did know the basic governmental structure of a democratic country and explained it to Eros in fairly simple terms.

He thought about it before commenting, "It sounds like a potentially disastrous system. In a politically unstable country wouldn't it just lead to dictators or despots repeatedly taking over? And if the population is stupid I imagine it would be very easy for the most idiotic candidate to obtain votes simply by being the loudest." Evangeline was about to protest but he continued before she could get a word in, "Don't misunderstand, your democracy has great potential. I simply imagine that it only works in a country which is stable and educated to begin with, therefore, you are obviously from a wealthy, stable and relatively educated country."

"Yeah. True. I guess you could say I'm lucky," Evangeline said, thinking a bit before continuing, "and you're right, in some countries in our world democracy is more like demo-crazy. So, what about Latina? Do you think it was ready for democracy, you know...before?"

"No," Eros responded, "but perhaps half-way there. I assume citizens let the monarchy know when they are ready for a new system."

Evangeline gave him a particularly sweet smile and said, "Yes, in our world, when the citizens were ready for democracy they just beheaded or hung most of the royals."

Eros looked at her and ran his tongue over his teeth in a slow, purposeful manner. She coughed and buried her face back in her book.

Eventually Evangeline would fall asleep. She knew that for most of the citizens sleep came rarely with their Condition of constant hunger. They might snooze intermittently throughout the day or simply rest. Eros sometimes rested on top of the sheets beside her and sometimes simply in his chair but no matter how long she stayed up, he always stayed up longer and rose before her. It was always after his first meal that he would return to the room and wake her up for another night of training.

Each evening's training session started out with Julia. Evangeline and Julia worked well together and slowly became cordial, though not close. Julia's previous actions, though understandable, had still created a barrier between them.

Julia's job was to torture Evangeline's senses in order to expand them. They made slow, but noticeable, progress and after some nights they were finally able to move beyond slamming random doors to smelling and tracking individual people. Evangeline would try to smell her way through the darkness, often with eyes covered, to find Eros, Julia and Ehvan in various parts of the castle, while they were silently waiting.

Eros took the activity to more amusing levels by waiting inconspicuously in a bizarre spot such as on top of a wardrobe or even a chandelier, while Evangeline sniffed around confused, knowing that she smelled him but unable to find him. Then when Evangeline least expected it, he would leap at her, and either pick her straight up off the ground or grab her and say the usual "you're dead" just before gripping her neck in his teeth.

Ehvan began to copy his brother, stating one night that "this must be what fun feels like." He did not bite Evangeline like Eros but simply pounced on her all over the castle. One evening Ehvan accidentally got his shirt stuck in the chandelier he was hiding on top of and when he tried to leap down on Evangeline the entire chandelier crashed down.

"That is enough!" It was the first time Evangeline heard Julia shout and she had to admit it was slightly scary. Julia's wind-chime voice definitely held power and Ehvan, who had fallen on his butt, sat frozen amid the crashed pieces of the chandelier, as his mother entered the room like a bolt of lighting, "If you do that one more time...just one more time, I swear young man, I will....I will eat your chicken for a week."

There was no way that Julia would starve her own son, but Ehvan sat paralysed, his eyes wide in terror as he voiced, "no... not my chicken." Evangeline had to put her face down to hide her laughter.

Though Ehvan was forced to stop playing his favourite game, Eros randomly kept up his amusement, often outside of training hours.

After Julia finished numbing Evangeline's senses, the training would move on to Eros and physical numbing. It was very clear that even as a regular human he had been highly trained in combat. Once the skills of his Condition were added to that, he was unbeatable, especially by Evangeline, meaning that, as he had predicted, she did have her face in the dirt for the majority of her time with him.

Eros told Evangeline almost immediately that she was useless at open combat and hopeless with weapons of any sort. "The sharper your weapon," he said, "the sooner you will manage to kill yourself. Your talent is evasion and escape."

It was true. Evangeline felt as if she had turned into a cat. Her slim frame was easy to manoeuvre and squeeze between objects and in just a matter of days she turned from cat to flying squirrel, leaping between branches and trees. Once she got up a tree Eros had no chance of getting her.

Eros then pushed her to climb faster and more difficult surfaces, moving from trees to buildings to almost flat walls. He also continued to torture her with the daily sprints, which always ended with him catching her before the finish line. And although he had pointed out that she was a pathetic fighter he forced her to learn what he considered basic self-defence and escape moves. He regurgitated that in case she were actually captured at close range by someone or something, she would need to find a way to at least temporarily immobilize them and get away in order to get to something she could climb.

Evangeline began to see over time that Eros, like most of the citizens, was not so different from Ehvan; a combination of mature individual as their vampire years dictated and the person he was the day he turned. It was as if in some ways parts of their emotional beings could not grow or develop in this state. The younger a person was when they turned, the more visible this was, such as in Ehvan.

For the most part Evangeline didn't mind this in Eros. She was happy he didn't act as old as his vampire years stated he should, although she wasn't always thrilled with his college frat guy techniques of amusement.

Eros had promised her that he would amuse himself at her expense and he kept his promise a bit too well. As part of "evasion training" when he caught her in a race, he would grab her and bind her in some way. Sometimes he held her hands behind her back with one hand while his other hand made sure she stayed face first in the grass. Other times he grasped her from behind with both of his arms around her upper torso, completely immobilizing her top half. Still other times he chose any of a half a dozen ways to restrain her. Then he would explain techniques of escaping his grip and let her attempt them while he just smiled, apparently entertained.

One time he started the training session off with "Let us see how many times I could kill you tonight."

Evangeline rolled her eyes at him while he slowly rolled his neck. Then, he looked at her and said, "It's time to run. Ready? Five, four, three, two, one."

Evangeline sprinted and Eros proceeded after her. He reached her within seconds and captured her in a tight grip from behind, in a standing position. When he had her, he grabbed her neck with his teeth from every angle imaginable repeatedly and counted in between bites. He reached ten before finally letting go.

By the time Eros had released his grip Evangeline was furious. Eros threw his head back and laughed aloud. When she saw his exposed neck, Evangeline, without thinking, jumped at it and bit hard.

Eros fell back against the tree, his eyes wide open and Evangeline straightened up and said, "You're dead." Eros' eyes moved around Evangeline's grinning face but she had no idea what he would have done because Samina appeared to announce that Evangeline's midnight meal was ready and training was over.

Later, that morning, Eros barely spoke while Evangeline sat on his bed looking at scrolls of lineages and old maps. She could feel him watching her over his book but pretended not to notice, only grinning over the scrolls every now and then. The next night it was as if nothing had ever happened.

Regardless of the tactics, the training was beginning to pay off. After some time, Evangeline began to notice sounds and smells which she hadn't before. One of the first things she caught on to was the fact that Laura was secretly following her around the castle. She brought this up with Julia, feeling a bit unnerved. Apparently though, everyone but Evangeline had always known.

"She is simply protecting her master," Julia said.

"Her master? Eros? She's protecting Eros from me?"

"Laura's mother was my closest lady-in-waiting," Julia said, "Laura has been with us since birth and since Eros' birth. Now, more than ever, he is her everything. Serving him is her purpose for being. It is her link to humanity, Evangeline. Without this purpose she is completely lost. Hurt Eros and you kill Laura."

"Alright, I understand these links between people here, but why and how would I possibly hurt Eros?"

"Hmm, well, you did manage to purposely throw a dirty, dried up, bird nest on his head when you were climbing trees last night."

Evangeline grinned, then immediately tried to pull her grin back in, "I'm sorry. You're his mom. I shouldn't laugh."

"Well, it was actually quite humorous and I am his mother so I know he deserved it," Julia looked at Evangeline and did a rare chuckle. She quickly cleared her throat and resumed her usual, kind but serious countenance, "Evangeline, Laura was the one who saved

Eros from death. She pulled the others off, screaming through her own hunger so that they would not drink him to the absolute end. You are an unknown. You can go out in the sun. You can touch dormium. You can save us or destroy us. Laura is simply doing what she has always done; taking care of Eros."

But how come no one is worried about what she might do to me in her infinite quest for Eros' protection? Evangeline thought, but said nothing.

Chapter 41

A LADY OF PLEASURE

Now that Evangeline could pick out Laura's scent and sound she decided to try something more difficult. Wandering around the city the following night, she tried to locate Josepina, who she knew was still being "hired" to be in Evangeline's vicinity for at least a portion of each night.

The most difficult aspect of this was that she did not remember Josepina's particular scent, having met her before her own senses had been trained. Therefore, what she had to do was wander around Josepina's relative section of the city trying to separate the scents of the citizens in the streets and find one scent that repeated itself in various locations.

After a while she thought she had picked up on something and tried to inconspicuously get closer to it. The citizens were now more used to her and some would even ask about her training progress or tell her proudly about their own duties. Once they learned that Evangeline could not speak their common tongue, they spoke to her in English, which they had all perfected in the last twenty-four years of study, though they still mixed in Latin or Italian words.

Those that had been lucky enough to be given "Evangeline duties" for which they received more blood, were particularly proud and would show off their progress. One of those was Max. He was a square shouldered, square boned and square faced man with an almost feminine voice which contradicted everything else about him. He was in charge of the smoke house and seemed to crave conversation. Having not much else to say he would explain the process of food preservation each time she passed by the smoke house, which was up and running for the first time in two and a half decades.

Most chats were like Max's. Short and focused on the here and now, with most citizens reverting back to their all-encompassing hunger quickly and resuming their robotic duties. However, some people would surprise her, bringing small relics out of their houses and telling her about the people they had once belonged to, the people they had loved and lost or the people they still hoped to see one day. It was sadly beautiful and she tried to smile and give anyone that wanted to talk some time, even those like Max, whose liturgies on meat were excruciatingly dull.

Therefore, being inconspicuous about wandering aimlessly was not hard initially. She simply pretended that she was saying hello and chatting with the citizens as usual. However, after a while the scent began to take her in precise circles and visiting the same group of citizens making horseshoes for long gone horses for the third time in a row began to look strange.

Evangeline smiled at tonight's blacksmith trainees stupidly and turned off into a different street, deciding it was time to ignore the scent. Seeing a small bench around the corner she sat down and sighed. Then, suddenly the scent was back. Looking slowly around she saw absolutely nothing except a couple of citizens repainting an already perfectly painted house. She put her elbows on her knees and rested her face in the palms of her hands, looking down at her feet.

Then, there were two sets of feet beside her and she looked up to see a small girl and a tall boy. Since children were almost nonexistent she immediately knew the girl to be the one who had initially screamed at her sight and the tall boy-looking citizen to be the one who had told her to leave.

They stood now and stared at her and she wasn't sure what to do except stare back.

"We follow you every day," the boy finally said, "you found out."

"Oh...yes," Evangeline said, disappointed that she had been so completely off on her search for Josepina and a little spooked by the child creature staring at her with humongous, empty eyes, "so...why do you follow me?" she asked the boy.

"Sofia wants to. She likes your hair. It's not grey."

"Oh, thank you." Evangeline said and they just stood and stared. "So why didn't you say hello and talk to me?" Evangeline finally asked in order to break the silence.

"You still frighten Sofia. She remembers something when she sees you. I don't know what. She doesn't say."

"I'm sorry Sofia," Evangeline turned to the girl, "If you ever do want to say hi or talk, you can. I promise I'm nice."

"I know," the boy responded in Sofia's stead, "you say hello to everyone. I didn't when I was human."

With that he simply turned and walked away. Sofia followed him, staring over her shoulder at Evangeline.

Evangeline stood up and sighed. She started to walk down the street in the direction of the Duke's house, done her trailing for the night, when she heard a voice behind her, "Did you expect to track someone who is already tracking you?"

She turned to see Josepina standing in the middle of the road in a blue gown with blue and gold embroidery along its hemlines and birds of all sizes and shapes embroidered into every spot and space on it. Looking at the dress Evangeline wondered how Josepina stalked her so inconspicuously. Did she go around town hiding in holes?

"Yeah, I guess I was a little optimistic in my skills," Evangeline said.

"Not a little," Josepina said, "You must know some things about me now. I could lead his highness in eternal circles, Evangeline. You would have more chances tracking him, actually. So why is it that you hoped to find me?"

"Well, I guess I was just practising tracking..." Josepina was looking at her with an amused smile. Evangeline knew that Josepina could sense if she was full of shit. Obviously, Evangeline could have practised on anyone. She changed approaches, "And, I guess I've never known a lady of...pleasure?"

Josepina's smile grew broader, "And what do you hope to learn from me?"

Evangeline's face turned red, "Nothing, actually. I guess I was just curious about you because you have so much more life in you than most people here. You still talk about everything and seem to think about everything. It's.... rare. And your clothes...how do you do it?"

"That is a much more interesting question than I thought you had," Josepina said, "the dress...well, I create them out of hunger during the day with whatever materials I find. Crocheting and embroidering is time consuming. A perfect activity. Dressing up is also time consuming. Another perfect activity. Though I think most find the contrast of the bright clothing and their own ugliness something of a depressing reality."

Josepina looked up at the night sky and then at Evangeline, "I will walk with you to the Duke's" She began to walk and Evangeline stepped up beside her.

"The way we are now," Josepina continued, "vampires as you like to call us, is a stagnant way. We cannot change, on the outside or the inside. You have seen that Ehvan can memorize facts, but his mind will always be that of a child. The inner maturation of his brain is related to the physical changes that happen within it. Something that cannot happen in this state. Someone whose mind was not very...developed...before, will not develop much now. They will know more facts. Learn skills. But they will not grow inside as humans."

"And you?"

"I suppose my goal was always to understand other humans and through that to understand and know myself. I never considered that it was anything unusual, but looking around me now, I see that it is a rare goal."

"I wonder what I would be like as one of you," Evangeline said offhandedly.

"An odd thing to wonder after seeing us," Josepina said, "though the fact that you actually thought to ponder this means that you would do better than most. You have almost no sixth sense ability but you have more depth than most pretty, young girls.

"Thank you. You know, I didn't think you liked me much, to be honest."

"I'm still deciding," Josepina smiled shrewdly, "However, you stood in front of a city of beings that could rip you apart and you were able to look at us and speak to us as if we were still people. I respect that. Respect is more important than like."

Evangeline let a couple minutes pass in silence before she asked the next question, "So, is it really true about the physical intimacy? I mean, is it impossible for you now?"

Josepina looked at her with that half-curious, half-knowing look and Evangeline quickly added, "I'm just wondering since there are some married couples that I have seen..."

Evangeline was doing her utmost to convince her face not to turn red. Of course she wasn't just curious out of the blue. She was in an unspoken, apparently platonic, bed-sharing arrangement with a male whom she wanted to kick in the head for the majority of each night while at the same time looking forward to each morning in his room. Every day, when she put down her book and climbed under the covers she lay stiff and anxious, wondering if he would lie down beside her, knowing that he occasionally did, but never being awake when it happened.

Josepina's lips curled into a wide, knowing smile and killed any chance Evangeline had of keeping the colour on her face normal.

"This...constant hunger, constant lust for human blood...it alters the way other physical needs get processed," Josepina said, "the emotional parts; love, friendship, hatred...though they are clouded by our hunger, they stay mostly the same. We love our children, our families. To care and be cared for. It is those emotions that keep us human inside more than anything else. But the physical, it all becomes one and the same desire. We do not want sexual contact with everyone we drink, but those for whose bodies we hunger we want to drink the most. A physical want can be expressed physically in the only way our physical needs are ever expressed; by biting and killing," Josepina stopped and looked at Evangeline, turning serious, "The more sexually attracted we are to a being, the more we want to bite them and even have them bite us. However, it's circular; because we do not hunger for each other's blood, we rarely feel a sexual desire for each other."

Josepina paused again, her eyes and mind off somewhere else suddenly. Then she pulled herself back to the present and looked at Evangeline, "You, my love, are an interesting case. Your blood no longer pulls us; as if one of our own. Yet, everything else about you is still human and you are quite lovely. We remember what human desire is. What we feel is a desire to desire in that human way. We always know what we would desire if we could. Out of mere curiosity...who turned you?"

"Eros."

"I see no bite marks."

"Oh, it's just covered by the gown," Evangeline could feel her face beginning to burn again.

"On the shoulder?"

"No, just...a bit under my neck."

Josepina's gaze ran down Evangeline's open neckline to where her dress finally began, right above the cleavage. She raised her eyebrows and simply smiled. Evangeline could feel that not only was her face burning now, so was her neck and her entire cleavage. Trying to get the attention off of herself by any means she asked, "Where is your bite mark? I don't see it either."

"Oh, I venture to guess even lower than yours."

Evangeline couldn't help laughing through her embarrassment and Joespina joined in, thankfully letting the topic finish.

They were already in the Duke's neighbourhood since Evangeline was now able to easily match everyone's regular walking gait, which for a regular human would have been a run. Josepina said goodbye, saying that she would now stop by her own house.

"Eros said you lived in the eastern end of town," Evangeline said, confused.

"I did. I relocated to that villa," Josepina pointed to a large villa, hidden in a cluster of trees, "since you come to this neighbourhood nightly it is more convenient to have a living space here."

"Oh, I'm so sorry. You shouldn't have had to relocate."

"Don't worry. In truth it has been a nice addition of variety. I kept my regular home, meaning that I may now amuse myself with tending two places of residence to perfection in order to prevent boredom and thus impending madness," Josepina smirked and with a quick goodbye turned off towards her newly acquired villa.

Chapter 42

THE PICTURE THAT CALLED TO HER

Only two paintings made it to Bambi's home. The first was the massive canvas of the man with the sword. This painting had taken up half the hallway and of course wouldn't fit in any garbage can. The art teacher told her he would only keep it in his classroom until the end of the day. Bambi thought he would just ditch it afterwards if she didn't come back for it, but instead he had cornered her and told her to get it and take it home.

So Bambi dragged it outside and was going to drag it to the dumpster, but as it so happened her mother had then arrived and not wanting to answer questions Bambi pretended it was yet another art project and her mother attached it to the roof of the car as she had done so many other times with Bambi's various other canvasses.

The second portrait that made it all the way to her room was the unfinished picture of the ragged woman. Bambi was about to chuck it in the trash like all the others when her eyes landed on something. With shaky fingers she lifted the picture to her face and stared at the tiny letters written on the canvas. She wanted to throw it away but couldn't. Slowly, she had walked back to her locker and placed it inside.

She was sitting on the floor of her room now and looking at the face of the man in the large portrait. She remembered clearly the beautiful, condescending face of the young prince. Almost nothing distinguishable remained of it in the shrivelled leftover of a human being that had been so skillfully portrayed. The only beauty that was left was that of the sword.

Bambi ran her hand over the blade on the canvas. Evangeline must have painted it. A huge pit rose to her stomach. She had felt from the first moment when she saw Evangeline in grade nine that it was fate. She recognized that massive, curly hair and the black, daydreamer eyes as those belonging to the child from the night when she and her mother had entered through the lightning.

That day, in grade nine, as soon as the teacher had announced for them to find partners for a poetry project Bambi had pounced to her feet and run across the room towards Evangeline, only to be smashed into by Ian Horvath who was also apparently pummelling towards some desired partner. He didn't even notice that he completely knocked her down and just kept going.

Once she had gotten back to her feet and regained her breath enough to look up, Val Striker was already sitting beside Evangeline.

Evangeline had become "popular" very quickly after that and Bambi began to think that fate was really just depressing coincidence. But she couldn't help watching Evangeline over the years, sometimes even going as far as to trail her home. Once she re-learned Evangeline's address she snuck out every couple of months in the middle of the night and made her way into Evangeline's backyard, wandering around and hoping for some epiphany. She had even tried to reopen the portal in Evangeline's backyard in the middle of the night, vaguely remembering how it had been done so long ago. Nothing ever happened though.

Then the night of the Halloween party when she saw the sword, Bambi knew this was it and Evangeline was the key.

"You were the key…to my memories," she said, staring at the sword and thinking of Evangeline, "thank you."

Evangeline had freed her from an illusion and had given her the opportunity to finally live life in the present.

Raffael had stolen her mother's hat after the party but Bambi didn't feel the urge to wear it anymore anyways. Suddenly she was even tired of her black wardrobe and would rack through her closet trying to find something that was at least in the grey tones. She gave up, went to her mother and asked if they could go shopping.

"Oh, do you need a new, black t-shirt? I can just pick one up on my way home from work," her mother had said without even looking up from her computer.

"No. Actually, I was thinking...white? Or maybe blue? I don't know. Do you think blue might be my colour?"

Her mother had almost had a heart attack at this statement and a simple trip to the mall had turned into a full day event of shopping, lunch and manicures. What her mother had desperately hoped was just a black phase, had finally ended. Bambi was pretty sure that her mom would even have rejoiced at a hormonal, teenage freak-out from Bambi's, as long as it wasn't accompanied by the colour black.

Bambi pushed the large canvas away with her foot and it crashed against the wall. A couple of months ago she would have been thrilled to have it.

She turned away from it and looked at the second, small picture. The woman in this portrait looked familiar also, though she couldn't quite place her finger on who it was. Then again, she had been quite young when they left and many of the people she may have remembered would probably be indistinguishable in this state.

Bambi couldn't piece together why, and how, Evangeline had drawn this woman. Only the prince and that thing that followed him around had known of the portal. Only they had been there. Or had they? Had someone else followed through? This thought terrified her and she unconsciously cradled herself in her arms, her body shaking.

After a minute she composed herself and determinedly brought her face closer to the portrait. She squinted her eyes and stared up and down the woman in it slowly. Then for the hundredth time, her eyes moved to the bottom of the frame. Right below the woman's hand, which seemed to be trying to reach out of the picture, were her mother's and her names, written in tiny, but perfectly clear, font.

Chapter 43

LATINA'S BIRTHDAY

"Don't you have a weekend? Like a Sunday when you go to midnight mass or something?" Evangeline groaned at the sound of the usual morning bell above her face. The bell stopped and she squinted her eyes open to see Eros standing above her, fully ready for training as usual.

"Alright. Take the night off tonight. There are other things I need to do around the city. I will let my mother know that training will resume tomorrow night."

Evangeline opened both eyes wide. Was he sick? Could they even get sick?

"You Okay?"

"Yes, I am fine," Eros said in a calm tone, his eyes looking somewhere above her head, "I will see you in the morning." With that he simply walked out.

Evangeline sat up on the bed staring after him. Unless she was imagining things he actually seemed gloomy today. She got up and made her way to her own room, disappointed.

Evangeline could sleep for twenty-four hours straight if allowed to, however, she hadn't actually wanted training cancelled. She was improving and it was exciting. The previous night Eros had barely managed to catch her before the finish line and had eliminated her five second head start.

By the time Evangeline went down for her first meal of the night everyone was already gone and she sat alone at the large table, slowly picking at her food. She knew that Eros and Julia checked up on each part of the city as much as possible but couldn't figure out why training had to be cancelled for that since it never had been before. Well, she supposed she could spend more time watching Ehvan and maybe try and track Josepina again - see if she could get a chat out of it.

She walked over to the weapon training centre where Ehvan was practising mace and warhammer skills today. Ehvan, as always, was excited to see her and when he found out that her training was cancelled asked if she would stay for his whole session.

Evangeline agreed, wondering why Ehvan didn't appear surprised about the cancellation. She had no time to find out before he resumed with the warhammer. Weapons' lessons were something she enjoyed watching least, especially with kids. Seeing Ehvan's child-frame fling around deadly weapons was just creepy and she was glad when it was over.

"Where's you next lesson, Ehvan?"

"It is almost time for my mid-night meal. After that I will dust and clean the empty homes in the north end. Do you want to come?" Ehvan asked with a smile.

"Nahh. I'm not allowed to help. I'll just get in the way. But thanks. You're not spending any time with Eros or your mom today?" Evangeline asked innocently. Ehvan had no verbal filter so whatever she said to him, she had to make sure could be heard as-is by either Eros or Julia. In this case, she didn't want Eros to think she was cross-examining Ehvan about his moods and whereabouts.

"With my mother only. It's Eros' birthday so he doesn't want to see anyone. I think he went in the fields."

"Oh...that's strange."

"Why?"

"People usually celebrate their birthdays," Evangeline said, "well...maybe he just doesn't like it because he isn't really getting older?"

"Actually, he hates it," Ehvan said nonchalantly, "Mother says it's because after the final battle, when he woke up changed, it was the day of his birthday. He was supposed to become twenty-five and he never did and he says that his birthday is the anniversary of his greatest failure." Suddenly Ehvan's face scrunched up, "Mother told me Eros hates it when anyone remembers his birthday. Do you know how to pretend that you don't know about it?"

"Don't worry," Evangeline put her arm around his shoulder and smiled, "I won't let on that you told me anything."

~

Perhaps Ehvan was right. Perhaps she should pretend she knew nothing, but she couldn't. It was too depressing. There had to be a better way to do this every year than hiding miserably for a day.

Evangeline ran to the kitchen and asked Samina if she could eat a little earlier. With a nod, she was served and after gobbling down her meal to Samina's almost visible delight she found some rope with Laura's silent and expeditious assistance and went out the door.

She tried to avoid the mid-meal herds at the various food gates as she made her way across town, not having gotten over the sight, sound or smell of strangled chickens being sucked dry. Finally, she reached the city wall, specifically a spot on it where a small tower rose from its top. She got the rope ready.

It was now time to find Eros. Ehvan told her he was in the fields so at least she didn't have to question random citizens or suffer through Josepina's knowing grins if she asked her.

The fields within Latina were almost bare rock surfaces running partially up the edges of the harsh, impenetrable mountains which closed off the city from the sides where the wall didn't.

On these surfaces grew grasses with roots that wrapped themselves around the round rocks and boulders. The grasses could be considered Latina's equivalent of grains and were picked at the very last moments of fall, which was now.

They picked the grasses using a specific method that Max had given her a detailed and painful explanation of just a couple nights before, while she smiled and prayed for salvation. The stalks were cut at just the right spot above the roots, right above what was called the regrowth point. From this regrowth point the grass would again grow the following spring. However, in order for it to do that, as soon as the grass was picked off a rock, the rock had to be flipped, the regrowth point and top roots resting in the shallow earth through the winter months. Apparently, the interaction with the dirt, as well as the deoxygenation of the regrowth point when squashed under the rock put it in a sort of hibernation stage until the following spring.

Although the citizens had no use for the edible grasses they kept up the yearly harvest so as not to forget how and used the grains to feed the pigs and chickens and... well, lately Evangeline, making her vegan bread from those grasses. There was also one variety of this grass which was a type of wiry fibre and this one was used to make fabrics resembling cotton, but more water-resistant. She had been told her travel shirts would come from this.

Evangeline made her way to the fields and began to sniff around, trying to locate Eros in the large expanse which was covered with citizens all picking the harvest. She knew Eros' scent like the back of her hand by now and wandering the fields easily picked it up. After following it for a minute she saw him in the distance.

Evangeline knew that Eros joined in various duties around the city, as the law was for everyone, but she had barely ever seen him do it. Harvesting the fields and flipping rocks was dirty work and just like many of the other male citizens Eros was wearing the shabbiest of pants and no shirt. It was late fall and the weather wasn't exactly sultry, but they felt little to no cold.

Evangeline was going to simply approach Eros but now she suddenly didn't know how to do it. Eros lifted himself up to stretch and the moonlight hit his exposed back and she gasped. There were not one or two bite marks on it but over a dozen. He started to turn towards her and she quickly spun and ran out of his line of vision, hiding behind some citizens. They gave her the usual stares as she smiled at them awkwardly. She was trying to figure out if it was in fact a good idea to approach Eros in the fields at all when he appeared right in front of her, making her scream out in surprise.

"Have you decided to flip rocks out of boredom today or are you attempting to stalk me?" Eros had thrown on a loose, old shirt and wiped his dirty hands on its bottom as he spoke, after which he put his hands on his hips and looked at her.

"Actually, I was looking for you. I thought I smelled your scent close by."

"How did you know I was in the fields? You couldn't have picked up my scent from the castle." Eros' expression was guarded and she was starting to doubt the merits of her idea, but thinking, *how bad can this go?* She said, "I went to visit Ehvan and he told me. I want to show you something."

"What?"

"I want to show you, not tell you," Evangeline said and grabbed his dirty hand before he could protest, pulling him out of the fields and across the city. He wasn't following willingly but he wasn't fighting either and they reached the city wall in silence.

Evangeline had tied the rope to an old cannon at the top of the wall and it hung all the way down to their level. She took the end of it and passed it to Eros, saying, "You're a crappy climber so I thought I'd help you out."

Eros could climb better than any regular human but with his large body frame he could not even climb half of what Evangeline could at this point. She was now better at climbing than anyone in the city that she had seen, excepting maybe the Mole, but she hadn't been able to test herself against him. She could scale practically flat walls, using the tiniest cracks as footholds as she sprinted upwards like a retreating thunderbolt.

Evangeline had never told anyone that she had scaled the city walls though. She didn't know if she was really supposed to, so she didn't ask, doing it only after the sun came up, knowing they would never know.

The walls, with their immense height combined with a flat surface were unscaleable for everyone else in the city. It was better that way. They had barred or destroyed any stairways up the wall and placed boulders which needed a group of citizens to lift, in front of any exits. Without seeing the outside, the citizens stopped running off madly, simply to kill themselves when the morning came. It also stopped the regular fires from entering the city and prevented any potential human from stupidly entering, though that part had obviously failed as of late.

Eros now looked at Evangeline astonished, but she just grinned.

"Come on blockhead," Evangeline yelled out as she started to scale the wall like an Olympic spider.

After a couple of seconds Evangeline heard him groan and she smiled. He was following her, scaling upwards with the aid of the rope.

By the time Eros reached the top Evangeline was waiting there, standing and staring out along the wall, half at the city and half at the wasteland beyond. Seeing Eros, she motioned for him to follow her along the wall to a tower, which they climbed until they stood inside its topmost enclosure, glassless windows lining its circular diameter. From this height, even the forest beyond the wasteland was visible and Eros looked out in all directions.

"I haven't seen what's beyond the wall in years. How often do you come up here?" He asked.

"Just every now and then," Evangeline looked at him and smiled. He was breathing in deeply, like a prisoner who has been released after years in jail.

"I was always a bit of a claustrophobic," Evangeline said, "It's not that I want to leave the city, I'm just not used to being kept inside a place by walls. Being up here I feel that I am not being kept in. I am here because I choose it. Does that make sense?"

"Hmmm. Yes," he smiled back and looked out at the forests beyond, adding tonelessly, "I am not sure if I am choosing to be here or if I am kept in."

"I know you well enough to know that you choose everything you do without delusions or excuses."

"Hmm...so why are we up here, Evangeline?"

"Because I wanted to celebrate a very special day," Evangeline said and Eros looked at her darkly. She quickly continued, "The more-or-less twenty-fifth anniversary of the survival of Latina."

"The twenty-fifth anniversary of Latina's survival? Hmm...and how would you know today would be more or less the day?"

"Oh, I just heard around town," she shrugged too nonchalantly.

Eros cleared his throat, "And is that all you heard?"

"No, I also heard that you celebrate special occasions with a dance known as the Rocciaonda, or otherwise known as the Rockwave," with that she did the little tap dance she had learned so far and Eros' lip curled up in amusement.

"I knew Betel took you on, but I thought it was just to stop you from trying to help around town. That's not bad for the limited lessons you've had. Let's see more."

"No. This isn't a display dance. This is a partner dance," Evangeline said, readying her hands for him to enter within them. She hadn't actually gotten to the point of successfully combining her moves with those of a partner but again she thought, *how bad can this go?*

Eros raised his eyebrows and didn't move and she thought he would turn around and leave. Just when she was about to put her arms back down he approached her silently and weaved his arms within hers.

The result was not very graceful and the question of *How bad can this go?* was quickly answered. Evangeline was basically tap-dancing all over Eros' feet and finally, after banging his forehead as well, Eros told her to stand still and use her arms only. This part wasn't so hard and she began to do the moves which she had learned with her arms stretched out to the sides. Eros approached again and standing in front of her let his arms intertwine within hers in waves and circles.

Evangeline looked from side to side and smiled at the effect.

"Now, move them upwards slowly," Eros said and she began to raise her arms above her head while still doing the dance. Eros moved closer in, easily keeping his arms within hers, his moves smooth and skilled. By the time Evangeline's arms were fully above her head, he was standing almost nose to nose with her, his eyes focused on hers.

Evangeline was trying to keep up the moves but her senses had been highly improved with Julia's training and at this proximity she could smell nothing but Eros and hear nothing except the quickened rhythm of his heart and the sound of his breath. Her hands seemed to still be doing something but she had no idea what.

Then, slowly, Eros moved away, his hands unwinding from hers. Moving a couple of steps away from her he said, "I am wondering if you knew before bringing me up here that bringing attention to my birthday is not good for most people's health."

"Really? It's a good thing we aren't celebrating your birthday then. It's not today, is it?" Evangeline grinned impishly, finally breathing out properly.

"I should be incensed."

"But you're not."

"How does one manage to be simultaneously irritating and charming?"

"It's a special talent I like to foster. Did you just give me half a compliment by the way?" Evangeline raised her eyebrows at Eros. He rubbed his chin, grinning, and said, "Just half."

"Hmmm, if I didn't know better I might thing that you like me."

"It's a good thing that you know better. Now, what other ceremonies have you planned for this...magnificent...occasion of Latina's well-being?"

"You know, I think it really is magnificent," Evangeline said, putting her hands on her hips in response to his sarcasm, "Latina functions better than half of the world of regular people. I don't know any other obnoxious jackass like you who could pull this off, make it work against all odds...and that's a full compliment. So, Happy Birthday."

"I thought we weren't celebrating my birthday," Eros said and although he narrowed his eyes slightly his mouth still turned up in a smile. Evangeline smiled back.

Eros sighed and stared out into the wastelands, "Maybe you're right. Maybe Latina does deserve to celebrate. You were right when you pointed out that we had little middle class before. In some ways, being this way has made us all more equal. It has actually made us see the humanity in everyone. Ironic, isn't it?"

"Hmmm. Good, " Evangeline said, "now that you are ready to celebrate in honour of this magnificent country"-she spread her arms out for a second then stretched them out towards Eros- "as well as this arrogant ass who also happens to be slightly cool on occasion, we have his favourite...a poetry reading."

Eros looked at her in shock as she picked up a book from the ground. It was the inane poetry book that he kept in his room to help him pass out.

"You're not really-" Eros began but Evangeline put up a hand to stop him and opening the book to a marked page began to recite the most tedious poems at the top of her lungs.

"Let me describe the blade...oh yes, that one blade of grass. It may take days, it may take years, and all may pass...but that one blade of grass."

"You brought me up here so I would finally give up on life and throw myself to the sun? Give me that, you little imp," Eros swung out his arm, trying to grab at Evangeline but she jumped to the side in the nick of time, reciting through her laughter, "Come now, oh prince. We are going to do an ode to Latina starting from the blade of grass all the way to the tiny stain on a random wall. It may take years and all may pass but deathly, boring details, they will last! Poetry! The wine of the soul! Come, Eros."

"I swear, when I catch you..."

Chapter 44

JUST FRIENDS

"Alright, I will admit just this one time that this was the first twenty-fifth birthday in twenty-four years that didn't completely...suck, as you would say," Eros said. He had met Evangeline in the hallway after his last meal and they were walking towards his room together.

Just as they entered his room, he asked, "Are you still frightened of sleeping alone in your room?"

Evangeline was taken aback by the question, "Oh...no. It's Okay now. So...I'll go to my room. I'm sorry. I got used to the daily tradition of you insulting me and me not taking you seriously. It's become almost, kind of fun."

"Almost, kind of?"

"Yeah, I didn't want to say it's lots of fun. Wouldn't want your head to get any bigger than it already is." Evangeline said.

"Well, no one ever complimented me on my 'funness'. You would be the first."

"What? Nooooooooo. I don't believe it. People not thinking of his highness as fun?" Eros sucked on his teeth and Evangeline laughed, "How could anyone not see you as the rainbow-coloured ray of sunshine that you are?" She laughed harder as his face became more unimpressed and then she turned, about to walk out of his room.

"You know those miniscule, pesky flies that make that annoying sound in just one of your ears just as you are about to fall asleep? That's you," Eros cleared his throat and when she turned back he was half running his hand through his hair and half scratching his head with it, a slightly abashed expression on his face. "But," Eros continued, "since you are already here, you might as well stay. I barely use the bed anyways and it's full of your half-eaten fruit by now."

Evangeline cocked her head slightly and looked in his face but he turned away and plopped down in his chair, immediately sticking his face in a book as if he were completely immersed in the topic.

Evangeline grinned and began to make her way very slowly towards him with a purposely comical, gliding gait. He didn't look up but she could see his eyes following her feet. She stopped right in front of him and stood, waiting. Finally, Eros groaned and looked up, but before he could say anything Evangeline bent down and kissed him on the cheek.

He was thrown off and she used that to her advantage, quickly getting away before he had a chance to react by potentially chucking something at her head. Taking one leap over to the bed, she jumped up on it, grabbed the nearest book, opened it up and stuck her face inside, pretending to read. Then, she lifted her face above the page, looked at Eros staring at her and grinned, "Don't worry. You can keep pretending you don't like me," and swiftly put her face down in the book again.

"Precisely like that miniscule, irritating fly," Eros said and Evangeline laughed from inside her book.

They were silent for a while, but after some time began to chit chat in the usual manner until Evangeline became sleepy. She took the books off the bed and piled them up on the cabinet, then climbed under the covers, blowing out the candles nearest her. To her surprise Eros rose from his seat and she heard him approach the bed. Then she felt the sheets move as he pulled them up and lay down underneath them, beside her.

Evangeline's eyes popped open in the darkness and she lay stiff and motionless, staring at the ceiling. This could obviously not be related to anything...sexual. So, what was he doing? He never did this. Maybe he was cold. He didn't get cold....

She stiffly turned on her side, her face away from him, not sure how to react. Positioning herself in her usual, curled up, fetal position she cleared her throat and said, "Well...good night. I mean, good sleep."

Did it feel like you could slice the tension on the bed with a knife, or was it just her? They were both motionless and silent for what seemed like an eternity to her. Although he made no other movements she didn't think it was possible for her to fall asleep and had no clue how she actually did.

~

Evangeline opened her eyes the next evening to find Eros fully dressed, sitting on the leather chair with arms loosely placed on the rests, watching her. When he saw her eyes open he snorted in his usual manner, "A new record."

"Wha...? What time is it?" Evangeline almost rolled out of the bed and onto the floor, trying to lift herself up. Eros shook his head at her.

"Long past mealtime and the time when your training should have begun. I was feeling generous today. Next time I will wake you with a bucket of water. Your food is in the kitchen. I will see you in the garden in half hour." Eros stood up and walked out of the room, her groan following him out.

"You're evil."

"I'm a vampire. Downstairs. No more than half hour."

~

The night passed as usual and Evangeline began to think that she was exaggerating things in her head.

The next morning arrived and she stayed outside as long as possible. The sun no longer hurt unless she had gotten a scratch or cut during the night, which would then simmer and burn painfully while it healed in the rays of light. Otherwise, all she ever felt after a night in the dark was a slight tingling for a couple of seconds.

She wandered the empty streets, pondering. Was she supposed to be getting the hint that she should leave his room? Or would she hurt his feelings if she did? The whole royal family's appearance was beginning to get traces of returning to the state in which she had originally seen them. It was nothing major because the regular chicken blood slowed the deterioration, but she had noticed the odd grey hairs returning and their complexions were beginning to lose their sheen.

If she moved back to her room now, would Eros think that she couldn't handle being in any way close physically because of what he was beginning to look like again? Or potentially worse, would she have to suffer through taunts of how full of herself she was to think that he was trying to get it on with her when he obviously didn't have that desire.

But Josepina said they still desired to desire and knew what they would have if they could. A part of her that couldn't be ignored wanted him to at least wish he could have her. Simultaneously she became nervous and scared. How would she actually react if he did do something? At this thought her stomach clenched in a tight knot and breathing in and out deeply she told herself that all this was stupid. If Eros was acting like nothing was out of the ordinary then she would too.

She went back, got on her night gown and made her way to his room. He was sitting in his chair and reading as usual when she opened the door and said "Hi."

However, when she started to walk towards the bed he stood up.

"Are you coming to bed? I was getting tired of waiting," Eros said nonchalantly.

Evangeline swallowed. Okay, she couldn't do this. She had no idea what was going on here.

"I'm sorry, but isn't this strange for you?" Evangeline blurted out, her arms doing random movements at her sides, not really knowing what they wanted to do with themselves, "You and me under the covers together? I'm confused. I know it's not sexual but-"

"You have been coming to my room and sleeping beside me every night but I lift the covers and the situation becomes strange?" Eros looked at her, his eyes filling with anger, "What? Is this some amusing game in your world? You're right. My lust is blood, not sex. But you think it's normal to kiss a man, climb into his bed and then insinuate that he is inappropriate because he thought it might mean something? Am I expected to feel ashamed suddenly for taking your actions to the next level?"

Evangeline's eyes were wide as she stared at his indignant face in the shadows of the candles. She was a dumb bimbo. He was right. She had done all this, but she hadn't meant for any of this to be sexual. Or had she? Hadn't she enjoyed their banter which always bordered on flirting? And she had understood for a long time now that his teeth on her skin meant more than just combat training but she had said nothing, letting him continue, enjoying the feeling of his attraction. Was it some sort of sick thrill to see if she could arouse the un-arousable? She had been playing a sick game and he had called her on it.

"Well. WHAT wench?" He had taken his lightning quick stride and was right in front of her, his face directly facing hers. Evangeline had almost forgotten that he used to call her a wench in that tone. His tone, even at its most indignant, in the last weeks had been that of someone who, slightly grudgingly, cared for her. Hearing him spit the word out at her now was like a punch to the stomach and her eyes filled up with a blur of tears, both at her own stupidity and vain selfishness, and his anger.

"What di-" Eros started and noticed her watery eyes. His anger was thrown off balance and he took a small step back, looking at her with slightly widened eyes.

Evangeline hung her head down, too embarrassed to have him stare at her face. She quickly wiped her eyes, breathed in and not looking at him said, "I'm sorry. I didn't mean to play some sort of sick game. I just...like being with you. And I feel safe when I sleep with you. I'm sorry," she repeated, "I know I acted like an idiot and then I reacted like an even bigger idiot. I just...I haven't actually ever slept with someone so...maybe I don't really know exactly how far is too far...anyways..."

She tried to get past him and get to the door without meeting his face, but all of a sudden heard him laugh aloud, "You haven't slept with anyone?" It was half a question and half an incredulous statement and she looked up at him still embarrassed, but now also offended.

"So? I have been with guys and done things, I just haven't...done it all. Sorry I haven't been around the whole kingdom like you." Evangeline pushed Eros out of the way with both her arms and pulled open the door.

Eros was still for a second, then grabbed her around the waist from behind with one arm, preventing her from leaving. Slightly hesitantly he brought his face to the back of her head and said, "I'm sorry."

"You have nothing to be sorry for," Evangeline said, pulling herself out of his grip, still not turning to look at his face.

"Stop. Please," Eros said, pulling her back, "I am sorry. I didn't expect you to be a virgin. I've seen...boys... in your life, and well, the way you always talk..."

"Well, you're the prince who's apparently been around the kingdom and back. Do you think I was going to tell you so you could laugh your ass off? Anyways, it's private...I'm going to go now, Eros. Even you have to admit I've been embarrassed enough for one day. Have a good sleep and I'm sorry for, you know, all this drama."

Eros was scratching his chin, his brows furrowed. When she tried to get out of his room yet again his arm went to the door and he pushed it closed, out of her grip. She looked at him confused. He groaned and breathing out loudly, squared his shoulders and looked into her eyes, speaking slowly, "You're going to make me admit how much I like you, aren't you?"

"Wha -?"

"Don't go," Eros said, "I enjoy our mornings together and I might even enjoy you being a pain in the ass. I almost forget about the hunger every time you exasperate me or drive me mad with your commentary. So, it was not just your doing. I like being close to you," he took another breath and let it out slowly, "I have always been the prince, Evangeline. All my acquaintances, all my lovers, were always affected by that title and the meaning it held. But I have nothing to offer you and you are still my friend. As much as I hate to admit it, that makes you the best friend I ever had...and the only woman friend."

Eros stepped closer to her and leaned his forehead against hers, "I suppose that means I have absolutely no idea how to have a woman friend. So, I also pushed. It felt good to have this closeness."

Eros lifted his forehead away from hers and ran his hand through his hair, then he put both hands on her shoulders, "I know I am what I am and that makes any kind of relationship strange and in many ways undefinable. Just stay. I won't push again. Not that it could even go anywhere," he half laughed.

Evangeline stood in the door, looking at Eros and biting her lip. She wasn't sure what to do or say. He looked at her questioningly then rubbed his hands against the sides of his legs and grinned.

He strode to the bed and quickly smoothed the sheets, watching her and grinning the entire time. Then he jumped on the bed and threw himself on top of the sheets on his usual side, arms straight out on both sides.

"Perfect. See?" Eros said and lifted the sheets on her side. He beckoned with a motion of his chin for Evangeline to come over,

"Look. There's an apple. Let us have fun and spit some seeds under the pillow as usual."

"Jackass," Evangeline laughed, then stopped and bit her lip again. Eros was looking at her silently, his face now serious and intent, "Evangeline, please. Me on top of the sheets. You underneath. Nobody pushing and no one misunderstanding."

Slowly Evangeline walked towards the bed. When she reached it, she took her half of the sheets out of his hand, but instead of climbing under them, she put them down again and smoothed them. Then she climbed on top of them like Eros and scooched over to him. Lifting his arm, she crawled into his armpit space, curling up, facing him, underneath his arm. Eros was still for a second. Then, slowly, he tightened his arm around her as she snuggled up against him. Turning his face away from her for a second he blew out the candle.

"You know, I have not slept with anyone for the last twenty-four years, which is longer than you have been alive so...that makes me as virginal as you," Eros said, then after a pause added, "Well, no. No, it doesn't."

"Shut up." Evangeline could feel him sniggering in the dark and poked him in the ribcage with an elbow. He laughed aloud.

"You said you saw other guys in my life? What things did you actually see?" Evangeline said.

"Well, lately there's been...Ian? Before that there was...well, it wouldn't be as much fun for me if you knew, would it?"

"You are such an ass. I am never letting you live down the fact that you admitted to liking me."

"My mother always did tell me that I need to learn to keep my mouth shut," Eros said. He bent the arm that was around Evangeline and put his fingers through her hair. She looked up at him and laughed.

"You should learn to listen to your mother."

"My mother also told me to keep you alive. I listened to her then and see where it got me."

Chapter 45

THE ONE THAT STAYED HUMAN

Bambi's eyes were bloodshot after a couple of days of absolutely no sleep. The woman in the portrait was plainly not her mother at any time or in any state. Yet Evangeline had written Lola clearly underneath it. It was too much of a coincidence that she would have simply come up with that name. It wasn't exactly a commonplace name in this world. It was like that woman's hand was just reaching out, as if for help, calling out to her mother and her...

Maybe it was some bullshit of Val's again, trying to get some sort of reaction out of her. But no one knew her mother's name. No one.

So, Bambi had started simultaneously avoiding and stalking Val daily, not knowing precisely why. At one point Val was talking to Ian in a crowded hallway and Ian nudged Val, pointing to Bambi who had been staring at the two of them from a couple of feet away. Val turned and looked straight at Bambi but when she took a step forwards it sent Bambi into a state of unexplainable panic and she ran for her life, away from them. Bambi knew that even she would have thought she was behaving strangely if she had seen herself.

The lack of sleep was obviously not bringing clarity of thought with it and by third period that day Bambi was too tired to even groan when Liza wouldn't stop whispering ostentatiously to her all through History.

"You are hiding something from me, Bambi. We are supposed to be best friends. I can see you need my help. Let me help you. I'm your only, *true* friend."

Bambi just put her head on her fist and stared at the teacher through blurry eyes.

~

It was as if Bambi were watching a movie, seeing herself from the outside.

Her mother was shaking as she ripped her own ragged skin with her nail and let the blood pour straight on top of Bambi's head.

"What are you doing, mamma?"

"Nothing, *cara*. Don't worry. You see nothing." Her mother said as she stared into Bambi's eyes and ran a hand in front of Bambi's face, making the world go blank as always.

Her mother took her bloodied hands and began to smear the blood all over Bambi, masking Bambi's scent with her own as the small child looked blankly at her.

"We will run now. Very fast. It will be like you are flying! Won't that be fun?" her mother said and smiled, her arm still shaking, though the skin was visibly healing to its regular, shrivelled state, the cut disappearing with each second.

Her mother lifted Bambi up to the hatch on the ceiling, which she opened and threw Bambi through. Then, she herself jumped up and out, right behind Bambi. And then they flew. With Bambi in her grip her mother ran like a blaze, up multitudes of old, hidden staircases and finally through the main level of the castle which was shrouded in darkness.

Bambi heard moans and growls coming from various directions and repeatedly tripped over fallen stones and bricks as well as pieces of broken and demolished furniture, with her mother flinging her up and over the rubble as much as possible, as she ran.

Even the darkness couldn't fully hide the dilapidated state of everything that Bambi had once known. Outside of the castle it was worse. Everything was scorched. There were no trees left. No greenery. All buildings that had once been wooden were now ash. Only random brick walls and pieces of dwelling rooms remained, with decrepit creatures wandering aimlessly or simply crouching or sitting against walls. Bambi's eye fell on what was once a child. The creature sat with her small arms cradling her stomach, moaning in agony as she rocked herself. A woman, most likely the mother, seemed confused and shook and shivered as she tried to comfort the child.

Suddenly, the shrivelled girl raised her head and her piercing eyes landed on Bambi. A growl escaped her lips and the shaky mother followed her daughter's gaze, raising her nose to smell the air. She picked up the smell of Bambi's live flesh under the smeared blood and pounced to her feet. She sprinted at a speed which did not match her haggard appearance and cut Bambi and her mother off, flinging herself directly at Bambi. Bambi's mother intercepted and caught the woman by her raggedy hair and threw her full force off to the side.

Others now noticed them though and even the blood smeared over Bambi couldn't mask her fresh humanity as she fell to the ground. The creatures were lifting their faces to sniff the air, slowly beginning to rise from their individual stupors. Her mother was panicking as the other woman kept picking herself up for repeat attacks, determined to get to Bambi at all costs and attracting more and more attention in the process.

Her mother grabbed the woman by the neck with one hand and threw her against the wall. With her other hand she grabbed the woman's hair and pulled the head back, about to snap the woman's neck. The woman looked into her mother's eyes and her gaze showed that she knew this was her last moment.

"My child. I need to feed my child," the woman groaned out.

"You can't eat MY child. She's the only human child left. The only human. The is no hope without her." Her mother was again about to snap the woman's neck when she saw others readying themselves to attack Bambi. In terror she looked at the woman in her grip and begged, "Help her. Help save the last human child. If you save her, there will be hope for the rest...for your child."

The woman looked into her mother's eyes and then at Bambi who was becoming terrified, the stupor which her mother had washed over her slowly beginning to wear off again.

"I have little strength. So much hunger...run...but promise she will come back for us. Promise she will save us."

"She will return. I promise you. I have seen it in my mind. The one that survives will save you. She will be the cure," her mother said as she let go of the woman and pouncing towards Bambi grabbed her and began to fly through the desolate city again. She turned back only once to see the creatures who had picked up on Bambi's scent and had begun to approach now hurtling after them while the woman crashed into them, trying to hold them back. In rage they all pounced on her and her animalistic shrieks of pain pierced the night as she was attacked from all sides.

Remorse filled her mother's face but she did not stop. In mid run she looked down at Bambi's confused and terrified face and staring into her eyes ran her hand across Bambi's face until it again went blank. Then she grabbed Bambi under her arms like a sack and soared through the night.

They ran nonstop for the majority of the night, hurtling over barren rubble as the dark sky thundered with an approaching storm. They ran to the point at which there would be no way to return to the shelter of the decomposing city before the sun rose. It was at this point that Lola threw them down in a little dip in the barren ground, covered them as best as she could with rubble and dirt and waited, staring ahead into nothing.

After some time two figures came up, out of the ground, a distance away. They emerged from a trapdoor which had been almost invisible beyond the rubble. Her mother did not seem surprised at all, but rather readied herself as if for an attack.

The shrivelled prince straightened himself to his full height as did the small figure beside him. The figure was that of a girl. She too was shrivelling but traces of her white cheeks and brown curls remained. She was somewhere between eight and ten years of age.

As they stood up they vaguely looked around, obviously having no expectation of anyone else being there. Bambi's mother held her breath and put her hand over the still mesmerized Bambi, whose whole body was almost completely under the rubble.

After a quick glance the girl directed the prince, placing his sword between them and putting her hands just within touching distance of his. Then she began to repeat a mesmerizing set of words over and over again, until finally after numerous repetitions they both lifted the sword, its red jewel glistening from within the blade as the two of them held onto it simultaneously.

That was when the thunder struck. It flew through the sky, aiming directly into the middle of the two of them, hitting the sword and then stopping, hovering just above the ground.

As soon as the thunder struck the sword, Bambi's mother shot up and picking Bambi up sprinted at full speed towards it. The prince and the girl spun their heads in surprise and then looked at each other. Their hands were on the sword and they could not let it go to stop Bambi's mother since they were holding on to the lightning with it. The prince seemed to decide to beat Bambi's mother with speed and spun his head back towards the lightning. He forced the sword in with determination plastered all over his face and began to slide it open into a doorway. But having to keep the sword in the hold of the much shorter arms of the girl accomplice made him clumsy and slowed him down. Just as he managed to slide open a space large enough for himself, Bambi's mother jumped over him and flinging Bambi in front of herself pushed the two of them through.

~

Bambi was now standing on a quiet street in a typical, middle-class suburb. Flower beds lined the houses and large trees bent their limbs towards the ground as the evening welcomed the moon. She saw her mother wandering the streets in a daze, bloody tears sliding down her cheeks.

Her mother's face was plump and healthy again, the human blood of this world having rejuvenated her dark beauty. A child was sitting on a porch. She played with her dolls in front of the front door, the child's mother checking up on her every now and then.

Her mother was full now, having just finished drinking some other unlucky passerby and only gazed over at the little girl as she strolled the street without any visible purpose. But, as her eyes fell on the small face they saw the long dark hair and the features so much resembling Bambi and she stopped in mid step.

The girl looked up, frightened, and stumbled up to run back into the house but Bambi's mom was in front of her before she could reach out her little arms to the door. With her eyes staring into the child's, her mother's hand moved slowly across the small face until it went blank.

Tears fell down her mother's cheeks as she ran her fingers over the little girl's face, gently caressing her cheek as she spoke, "I'm sorry, Bambi. I'm so sorry, my *cara*. I didn't mean to throw you. I never want to hurt you. That's why I keep away from you, love. I don't want to hurt you. I love you so much. I am so frightened of hurting you."

She put her arms around the child and began to rock her back and forth, whispering, "I love you so much, Bambi. I'm trying. I'm trying. The one who survives will be the cure."

As she rocked the child she burrowed her face within the little neck and suddenly taking in a deep breath she lost control. Her eyes glazed and her teeth burrowed in the veins of the neck as she drank the blood of the stupored child until the lifeless body crumpled in her arms.

She stared at the child in shock and began to choke on her own words, "No. No, Bambi. No." She dropped the small body and ran through the streets blindly.

The dream zoomed in on the face of the dead child. As the girl's face came closer and closer the features began to change and suddenly it was Cynthia's face in front of her. Cynthia opened her eyes and stared directly into Bambi's, smiling a pale smile at her.

"Evangeline is waiting. The one who survived has the cure. The blood opens the portal."

Then Bambi saw her mother's ashes slowly disperse in the morning sun, the black hat on the sidewalk beside them.

~

Bambi was screaming in the classroom. The whole class was staring at her, some people sniggering and some just dumbfounded. The teacher stood stock still.

Both her mother's tear-stained face and Cynthia's pale, deathly one were still clearly visible in her mind as the history classroom, along with Liza and everything else, came into focus. Bambi's breath was sharply coming out in spasms as she tried to put a coherent sentence together, "I... I fell...asleep."

"Had a bad dream I guess?" The teacher said and more people sniggered or called her any one of a number of names under their breath, ranging from freak to reject.

"Yes," Bambi just said, her head turning left and right in the directions of the various pet names that were being whispered by the other students.

"Seems like you did more than the usual doze-off in my class today," the teacher stated and the students laughed harder.

"I... well..." Bambi started, her thoughts still only partially coherent. The teacher was about to say something else but looked a little closer at Bambi's face and stopped. Bambi knew she didn't look particularly well. Dark circles lined her eyes and her skin, a dark olive in colour since she had disposed of her white, vampire makeup, was now approaching a ghastly blue. The teacher squinted his eyes at her, "Go to the nurse's office, Bambi. Actually…go to the front desk and get them to call your parents to pick you up. You don't look well. Can someone go with her please and make sure she gets there safely?"

Liza jumped out of her seat and seeing her, Bambi blurted out, "No! I mean, it's Okay. I'm fine."

"I don't think so, Bambi," the teacher said.

"Yes. I mean, no. I mean, I don't feel good but I'm fine enough to go to the main office. It's fine. I'm fine." Bambi grabbed her things and burst out of the classroom before Liza had time to volunteer her assistance.

~

Bambi left the school without bothering to go to the main office. Her home was about an hour walk away and she trudged slowly down the empty sidewalk, ignoring a bus as it passed by. She knew that she was still being trailed intermittently by that weird man and for a second froze in her spot, her eyes darting left and right, images of Daniel dragging her into some tinted car going through her head.

Then she realized that it wasn't actually the end of the school day. No one knew she was out. Her muscles loosened and she began to walk again, though still cautiously.

The pit in her stomach was bringing up vomit and she felt dizzy. Her mother had been human inside to the very end and she had tried to keep her daughter safe from herself to the very end. And that other mother, she was still also human inside.

Her mother had said that Bambi was the chosen one and she had done everything to save her, even, and most specifically, from herself. She believed that Bambi was meant to go back and save their world. *How can I go back there though? But how can I not? My mother sacrificed herself in order for me to do this.* Bambi's hands were around her head and she was standing still in the middle of the sidewalk now.

Why did I see Cynthia's face? Is she dead? Or is this some sign or metaphor?

It didn't matter. She had to keep her mother's promise. Bambi turned around and started walking back towards the school to find Val.

~

Lola looked on from beyond a corner as the people dressed in blue pulled the shrieking Bambi out of the machine where the dead girl that looked so much like her daughter lay. She wished Bambi hadn't seen the child, but it was over now. Bambi was safe now. They had found her. Now Lola had to do one last thing to make sure that her daughter would be safe always. That she would never know where she came from and would never find a way to return there.

Lola realized fully now that she had lied to the woman and her child the day of their escape from Terra Nova. Her sixth sense had told her that the one who survives will be the cure. Her sixth sense was wrong. Bambi would not save them. She would never go back. Lola would make sure of that. Because there was no way to stop the hunger. There was no way to ever be human again.

Lola turned her face away from the scene and walked a little ways. Then, stopping, she slowly took off the black hat which had covered her face for so long. She placed it gently on the ground and then stood, looking to the sky and the slowly rising sun.

She would not scream, she told herself as the first ray hit her body. She would not scream. No one would ever know. Most importantly, Bambi would never know.

The ashes fell to the sidewalk, landing around the hat as the sun burned through her, her body torn and decimated with each ray. She made no sound.

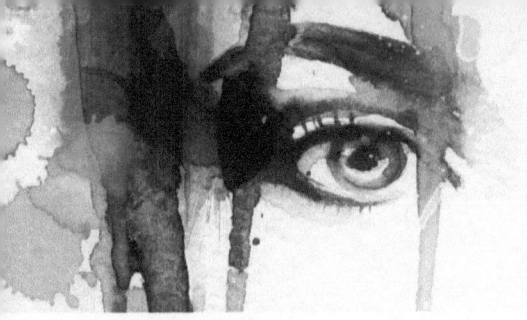

Chapter 46

STAY

Julia couldn't help herself. She began to observe Evangeline and Eros. She knew this made her the type of mother she had always despised but, she was, after all a mother and she was beginning to worry for her son.

If one heard Eros and Evangeline only from a distance, one would think from the constant insults that they had absolutely no cordial feelings towards one another. However, getting a little closer, Julia would notice a hidden smile on Eros' face and tiny, playful nudges between them.

Lately it had gotten more noticeable. If Evangeline fell during practice he would help her up and then keep his hand around her waist longer than necessary, or let his teeth run a little bit up her neck whenever he bit her during training. Not that the constant biting was appropriate behaviour to begin with.

Julia had left her old room, the one that Evangeline and Cynthia had been caged in, and moved to a more secluded corner of the castle shortly after the change. This room was much smaller, but she preferred its darkness, feeling almost cozy each morning when Ehvan came and snuggled up to her for the day.

Initially, after Ehvan turned, she had wanted to keep an eye on him. It was unpredictable how the daily hunger would affect his actions and she would rub his back and comfort him as he cried each day until the next nightly meal. Eventually they all became accustomed to surviving through the day and Ehvan calmed, even sleeping for portions of the night. However, she still kept near him, feeling more secure this way.

Julia watched Ehvan's breathing now and knew that at least for a brief moment he was asleep. She left the room and walked softly down the hall, past Eros' room. This was not the first time she had done this. Since Evangeline's turning she walked past his room regularly, always hearing Evangeline's even breathing as she slept, while Eros' breathing clearly signified that he was awake.

Eros could hear even her softest footsteps and knew if she was outside the door so Julia would walk by without stopping, pretending to take a sleepless stroll, as many of them often did. This time as Julia passed by the door, she slowed. Eros' breathing was stable and slow, matching Evangeline's. Sleep happened rarely for most after the change, and almost never for Eros. As she listened to his breathing now, she knew he was in fact asleep. She approached his door and opened it silently, just enough to look inside.

Julia swallowed hard. Eros was in bed with Evangeline, his arm around her and his face burrowed in her hair, both of them sleeping. The calm, happy look on his face was something she had not seen on him before with anyone, at least not since he was a little boy snuggled in her lap.

What was he doing? Why was he doing this to Evangeline? To himself. Julia was screaming inside her head as she closed the door silently.

She returned down the hallway nightly after that, sometimes to find them sleeping peacefully against each other and other times to hear them talking and laughing through half the day. She didn't know why she kept torturing herself in this way, but she could not stop. Now she was one hundred percent the type of mother she had always despised.

How had she not realized he was falling for Evangeline? But then again, she had never seen him fall for anyone; not any of the girls who had amused him in half the rooms of the castle and definitely not his fiancée, whom he had politely tolerated, accepting his duty to join the two families in a politically beneficial alliance. After Chiara had turned and begun to go mad Eros had even accepted his duty to care for her as if they were already married, and to stand by her till the bitter end.

He had said nothing after Chiara had to be condemned to death, but Julia had felt utter relief.

Julia had never been able to fall in love with her husband either, their connection also being political in nature. However, she had respected him. To stand by a girl whom you barely tolerated, had never respected and who now did not even have beauty or useful connections left to make her bearable, would have killed Eros on the inside over time, until he would have been the one to go mad.

Looking at Evangeline's peaceful face for the umptieth day in a row Julia sighed. Two and a half decades of watching Evangeline grow from a scraggly six-year-old meant that she always thought of her as that. She had failed to see that Evangeline was a woman now.

She supposed that Eros had also not expected to see her as a woman and must not have realized that he was falling in love until he already had.

Two and a half decades of watching this girl had also made her almost a daughter in Julia's eyes and she could not fault her for lying in Eros' arms, except that she would leave them, and then what?

She stared at Eros' face and knew that even during moments when he had been absolutely livid with Evangeline, he had been more alive in the last couple of weeks than she had seen him be for a depressingly long time. What were the chances that Evangeline could find a cure for them out there? What were the chances that she would find a way to her own home? Would she even survive outside these city walls? She was pathetic with weapons and would never be even a bearable hunter. How long would she last past her food supply?

Everyone in the city felt more alive with Evangeline around. Eros was happy. Evangeline was happy. She didn't even seem to mind their lifestyle anymore. What was the point in her leaving then?

Neither Evangeline nor Eros ever brought up her departure date, although Eros knew that Evangeline was close to being as physically ready as he could make her and the food preparations were nearing completion.

So… if Julia said nothing, no one would say anything and… Evangeline would just…stay.

~

It took Raffael a while to get them all together, even with everyone having the pay-as-you-go phones. Their group was simply too conspicuous and Bambi maintained that she still occasionally saw a tinted car in her neighbourhood, which she assumed belonged to Daniel or someone associated with him.

Eventually, they did manage to meet at the same spot in the forest where Bambi had run off on them three weeks ago. It was after 2:00 a.m. on a Tuesday night, the easiest time for the teenager portion of the group to sneak out unknowingly; adults were fully asleep due to the next day's work and assumed their kids were sleeping also.

Liza and Jack were missing from the group; Jack because he wanted nothing to do with it and Liza because no one wanted her to have anything to do with it. Bambi admitted that as far as she knew there was no magic number of participants since the first time she saw the portal open it had been done by only two people.

She had made all of them listen to absolutely everything she remembered. She said she would not do this until they were all aware of what they were getting themselves into before they proceeded.

"You were there? The first time the portal opened behind our house? And that man was your…prince? Daoud?" Raffael asked incredulously, still having a hard time believing that anything that came out of Bambi's mouth was actually plausible.

"Raffael, man, I was a non-believer like you," Mark said to Raffael's furrowed forehead, "but you gotta open your mind. You gotta let your senses guide you. Trust them."

"I thought he was just slightly dense. Now he's turned drunk hippie on us," Raffael heard Val whisper to Ian who whispered back, "Maybe those janitorial Smarties had more in them than just chocolate."

"I wouldn't say that I was ever the, uhm, supernatural type," Monica said over the sniggering, looking at Raffael, "but we all agree on what we saw and we all agree it was real. That means we believe Bambi. So, the question is, who is willing to go to what Bambi states is a very dangerous place? It's everyone's individual choice. Raffael, I am coming."

Raffael barely had time to give her a heartfelt smile before another verbal circus trapezed out of Mark again, "Of course I'm coming! This is the opportunity of a lifetime. This is what movies are made of. This is what you fucking regret for the rest of your life if you don't do" -his head shot towards Bambi- "if we all die I just want you to know that even though I was faking wanting to date you before, you look really hot in that blue shirt."

"Uhm, thank you?" Bambi's voice was mostly confused, though slightly bashful as well. Raffael guessed this was probably the first compliment she had ever received from the male species and as touching as this would have been in a teen-flick, right now he just shook his head at its inappropriate timing.

"Alright, well, I'm in. I've always been in," Ian said and Val nodded in agreement, "Yeah, I've always been in too."

"Are you sure about this?" Raffael looked around at the shadowed faces in the darkness, "I have no clue what we are doing here. Evangeline was my sister. You guys don't need to do this."

"Come on, just open the damn thing. Let's go kick some weird, half-dead ass," Val said and walked towards the huge bag, unzipping it to pull out the sword, "I hate to admit it, but I'm even starting to miss Cynthia. According to Bambi she looked dead in her dream. It would definitely be amusing to see Cynthia still trying to put on makeup and tight clothes as a walking dead."

They redid the ceremony just as it had been done before. They stood with hands almost touching, chanting unanimously after Bambi. Then, after chanting until their arms ached, they approached the sword and Bambi grabbed it. Nothing happened.

"Two people grabbed it before," Raffael said and they tried again. Bambi grabbed the sword with Raffael, with Mark and with each and every other member of the group. Then they grabbed in groups of three and even all together. The night air remained still.

Morning was nearing and Raffael was leaning against a tree, head down with no clue what to do.

"You said in your dream that Cynthia told you the blood opens the portal. Did you or Evangeline cut yourselves when you fell on the sword?" Monica suddenly asked.

"I didn't. I don't think Evangeline did, but I don't know. We fell on top of it...so maybe?" Bambi shrugged and looked around.

Raffael came towards the sword and opening his palm ran it quickly against its blade, his face flinching with pain. Raising his hand above the sword he let the blood drip on top of it then nodded at Bambi. She approached and they both took hold of the blade yet again.

That morning each one of them returned to their homes, each with a cut on the palm of one hand, the sword silently sitting in the bag and the sky just as plain as always.

One thing became clear, and Mark finally voiced what Raffael couldn't, "If blood really opened the way, then it must have been Evangeline's blood that did it."

Chapter 47

THE MOLE'S SUNRISE

Evangeline stood in shock. Eros had pinned her against a tree, her neck in his hand. She had grabbed his holding arm in both her hands and used it to leverage herself as she swung her entire lower body upwards, wrapping her legs around his arm. Then, she had twisted each leg in a different direction and heard a sudden, loud crack as Eros' arm broke and he dropped his hold on her.

"Oh...God," she stuttered.

"It's alright, Evangeline," Eros took the broken arm in his other hand and quickly manipulated the bone into its proper position. Then he stood still as it fused back together. It was obvious that he was in pain from the set look on his face but he barely flinched, instead trying to smile at her. When his arm was back to its original state he stretched out his neck and exhaled.

"The main issue with broken bones," Eros said, "is that they heal extremely quickly. If you do not set the bone in time it will fuse in an entirely wrong spot and you will need to then re-brake it. It is not an enjoyable process. However, this is fine." He extended the arm in front of himself and moved it in a couple of circles.

Evangeline breathed out in relief and then gasped, "Oh my God. I kicked your ass."

Eros' eyes widened momentarily. Then his expression returned to normal, "That is a slight exaggeration, don't you think?"

"I got out of a neck grip in less than ten seconds. I kicked your ass!"

"Yet again, let's not exaggerate, tornado head. You did get out of the grip. True. However, unless you attacked me and actually managed to put *me* in any sort of grip, I wouldn't call your actions an 'ass kicking'."

"Ahhh, the poor, little prince got a royal ass kicking," Evangeline was now doing a victory dance and singing, "We will, we will rock you." Eros looked at her with brows creased together and said, "Well, I suppose that we have finally found your weapon of choice. That sound which I believe you think is singing could kill anyone."

"I am not *that* bad," Evangeline stopped dancing and put her hands on her hips.

"Ohhhh, yes, you are," Eros sniggered, "and I suppose that body shake thing you were doing is dancing in your world? Seeing you do it in the hospital I initially assumed you had grown up to be a high-class prostitute. However, apparently your world simply has a very interesting idea of what dancing looks like. I have to say I like it. Let me see it again."

"You wish you were that lucky."

"Hmm...yes, I do."

Evangeline turned on her heel and walked towards the doors out of the courtyard, her face slightly flushed. She saw Eros grin as he stepped in behind to follow her.

"Come to the orchard after your meal," Eros said as they were about to split up with Evangeline going to the kitchen and Eros to his own feeding area, "We are collecting the last of the fall fruit. You may join and help."

"What? Are you actually allowing me to touch something? I'm not going to infuriate the entire city by stealing someone's duty?" Evangeline said, laughing.

"Well, you did kick my ass today," Eros grinned.

"Man, I'd love to come and celebrate that victory but actually, tornado head here needs another haircut," Evangeline said, "Ehvan begged to cut it again. He did a pretty good job last time so I figured I'd make him happy. For some reason he thinks cutting my hair is almost as exciting as your special-occasion-pig-meals."

~

Evangeline wolfed down her meal, with Samina and Lorenzo watching her across the table. Even without the ability to really taste human food anymore or obtain many of the ingredients from the past, Samina was constantly creating amazing flavours for Evangeline's meals. Evangeline could only imagine what masterpieces Samina had created before.

Samina was not much more expressive now than she had been the first day they met, and generally said no more than two words per day. However, whenever she could, she would sit and watch Evangeline eat the food she had prepared for her. She would observe every miniscule expression on Evangeline's face and over time Evangeline realized that she used this as her guide. Every nuance of Evangeline's facial muscle seemed to guide her in her next meal preparations.

Evangeline smiled at Samina with her mouth full. The good thing about Samina was that she didn't need to act like a lady around her. The more she stuffed her mouth, the happier Samina became.

After finishing her food Evangeline made her way up to her room and pulled out a chair. She put a large-toothed comb and large sheers on it. She decided she would change into a gown after Ehvan finished with the haircut so for now she simply threw herself down on her bed and waited for him. Ehvan had a short lesson after his meal tonight so she figured she had another half hour before he arrived.

Evangeline lay on her back with her hands folded behind her head and her eyes closed, mentally planning a route to take around the city that coming morning when she smelled something foreign. Then, she heard one, slow exhale.

Evangeline lifted up her head curiously, knowing that the smell didn't belong to anyone in the household, and when she opened her eyes she saw a flash of scrawny limbs flying at her. Shrieking she rolled at lightning speed out of the way, falling off the bed and onto the floor.

She leapt up and, using the wardrobe as a bouncing board, sprang upwards and landed on the chandelier. She heard a giggle beneath her.

"You jump well. You jump high."

"The Mole? I mean, Romeo, Sir?" Evangeline looked down and relaxed at seeing the little, scraggly man on top of her bed on all fours, "you scared me to death." She was about to leap down to the floor when she saw the look on his face. She had seen that look a number of times before she turned; it was the look of an animal about to attack.

Her body tensed again and her eyes went to the door as she spoke, "What are you doing here Sir?"

The Mole didn't answer, instead, quickly following her gaze he did a running jump and landed on top of the half-opened door.

"Oh no, no, no, little princess. You cannot leave before you give me a snack. They say I am a messy eater. Don't mind if I rip you up a little. Must get my vitamins." He was eyeing her with a wild madness on his face and Evangeline suddenly knew what Eros and Julia meant about the point of no return. The mole's face and eyes had nothing human left in them. All that was there was a predator searching for its prey. There was no thought, no feeling and no remorse. His eyes had lost all depth and if the eyes are a mirror to the soul then his soul had left.

Evangeline had little time to think, as the Mole, after calculating the room with his beady eyes, leapt from the top of the door frame. His foot pushed the door closed with a bang as he jumped and using the wardrobe as his bouncing board as well, he flew at the chandeliers and Evangeline.

Pushing herself off the chandelier Evangeline did a flip in the air, her flying speed allowing her feet to run a couple steps along the ceiling. She used the last step to push off into a second flip which turned her right side up and landed on top of the curtain rod.

As Evangeline tried to stay up perilously, the Mole screeched in outrage, "My snack! My healthy snack! Bad snack. Romeo will tear your legs off when he catches you."

Evangeline started screaming at the top of her lungs. Part of it was from sheer terror and part in hopes of attracting someone. Anyone. Unfortunately, Samina and Lorenzo did other duties for about two hours after their mid night meal, Julia and Eros were gone for their duties for God only knew how long and Ehvan wouldn't be back for at least another twenty minutes. The Mole must have known this she realized, but she screamed nevertheless.

The screaming outraged the Mole and he began to sprint and leap at her furiously, the two of them flying across each corner of the room. Every time Evangeline almost got to the door he somehow managed to cut her off and the circular chase continued. Evangeline was determined to stay out of his grasp. She was absolutely no match for Eros in straight on combat and though the Mole was a quarter of Eros' size she still had no desire to test her skills on this rabid, mad thing.

At approximately the fourth circle around, Evangeline jumped at the curtain rod and felt the wall give out. She let go, jumping out of the way as the whole thing crashed down on the ground. One of her landing posts was now gone and the Mole, swinging from the chandelier, screeched in mad glee, "Foul snack. I'll rip your limbs. No more jumping, my little vitamin. I'll drink every drop and tear you to shreds now."

Evangeline was on the ground near the chair and grabbing the scissors that she had laid out on it she stuck her arm up in the air just as the Mole leapt from the chandelier at her. She was screaming again, this time a combined terror of the Mole and the terror of the scissors actually stabbing through the Mole.

The scissors never pierced the Mole. At first Evangeline had no idea what flew at him midair and smashed him against the wall. Trying to escape the grip of his captor the Mole threw his head forwards, his teeth gnashing into the captor's shoulder with such strength that the flesh ripped off the bone. Then, Laura's face came into view as she swung around, hollering in pain. The tiny Mole was still in both her hands and she flung him full force at another wall.

It was the Mole who was screaming now. Picking up his crumpled, skinny body and flinging himself at the door he reached it just ahead of Laura's hands and disappeared into the hall.

Laura was about to follow, but then looked at Evangeline and instantaneously turning back to her usual, deathly calm she shut the door of the room and secured it with a chair only enough so that no one could surprise them with their entrance.

Evangeline was still holding the scissors, her hands trembling and her breath coming out in quick, shallow spurts when Laura spun around and leapt towards her. She began to walk in circles around Evangeline, looking her up and down, "You are not broken? Yes?"

"No, I'm fine," Evangeline was thankful but confused. She pulled herself up and Laura began to lift Evangeline's arms, shaking them out and poking at her from various angles.

"I'm fine, Laura. Really. Thank you. How are you? Are you Okay?" Evangeline was looking at the huge, grotesque hole in Laura's shoulder which was very slowly healing. The sight made her cringe and the pain must have been horrific, yet Laura didn't seem to notice it, still walking around in circles and poking at Evangeline, who physically was perfectly fine.

"My master will be unhappy if you are broken. He will not handle it well. He will go mad."

Evangeline suddenly realized why no one had worried about Laura hurting her. Laura would protect Eros in any way. She would let nothing hurt him physically or emotionally. This meant that anything and anyone she saw as important for him, she would both die and kill for. Laura had been watching Evangeline to make sure Evangeline was no danger to Eros while simultaneously making sure nothing happened to Evangeline, for Eros.

Evangeline grabbed Laura's hands in her own to stop Laura from poking and tried to look her directly in the face, though Laura's eyes were still running up and down Evangeline as if her eyeballs were having a sugar rush.

"Laura. Laura. I'm fine. I'm Okay. How are you?"

Laura did not seem to hear or register Evangeline's words and Evangeline repeated in a louder and more pronounced tone, "Laura, how are *you*? Are *you* Okay?"

Laura's eyes stopped and stared into Evangeline's. They widened and she began to look at herself confused, as if she had just remembered that there was such a person as herself.

"How are you, Laura? Are you Okay?"

"Yes," was all she said, her eyes still wide.

"Yes? Okay. Let me clean your shoulder then while we wait. Ehvan will be here soon. We can send him to inform the others of what happened." Evangeline pushed Laura gently towards the bed where she sat down and silently let Evangeline clean her shoulder while she watched her.

~

The man hunt didn't last long. The Jumping Mole may have been one of the best at jumping and evading but he could not do it for long with thousands simultaneously hunting for him.

Near the end of the night Evangeline sat on a step in a courtyard near the castle where a large dormium cage stood in the middle. In it was Romeo, the Jumping Mole, awaiting his last sunrise. There had been no trial. No discussions. The law was absolute.

She knew he had meant to kill her and as he screeched and flailed around madly she knew there was nothing left of him already. None of that made it any better. She could feel the tears silently sliding down her cheeks as she sat and waited with him, determined that as horrific as it would be to watch him die, at least he would not die all alone. He had been a man once. Long ago he had been a great man.

Eros approached, standing beside her and looking at the Mole as well, "You do not want to see this, Evangeline. It is horrible enough to hear it. You know that."

Evangeline shook her head and didn't move. She thought of Cynthia. She had been back to see her tomb regularly, bringing her night blooms from Leonardo's garden. Cynthia had loved beauty just like Leonardo's wife. The night blooms seemed fitting.

She didn't cry for Cynthia often, though she did think of her, many times in odd moments. Nostalgic thoughts. Regretful thoughts. She wished they could have been real friends before the end. That they would have had more time to enjoy the friendship they had found too late. She wished she had been there when Cynthia died. She wished Cynthia hadn't died alone.

Evangeline turned to Eros' face. There was a question she had wanted to ask him for a long time. "How did you kill her? Chiara?" She didn't mean the actual process but rather the emotional allowance to kill someone you love. He understood and smiled but his eyes didn't join, "I was happy to."

Evangeline didn't know what to say. She moved her head from side to side slowly, her eyes staring at him without comprehension.

"My mother, I'm sure has told you some about Chiara. It was irrelevant that she couldn't hold an intelligent conversation for the length of time it takes me to sneeze. The marriage was arranged. She was a perfect, political alliance. Perfectly bread. Perfect lineage...but when there's no depth in a person they don't take to the Condition well. All she did was beg for me to tell her she was still pretty." Eros laughed, staring out into the distance, "Days and nights and all she wanted was to hear that she was still slim and her gown was pretty while blood dripped down each wall of the city."

Evangeline stared at him, simultaneously feeling cold and sweaty. Eros looked at her long and deep, "The last words I said to her were 'You look beautiful' and then I thanked any God or spirit that was listening that it was all over...for her and for me."

Eros kept looking at her face with a strange intensity, then said quietly, "I have to go in. Promise me you will return directly to the castle after."

Evangeline nodded. He sighed and gently squeezed her shoulder before going, "Evangeline, this isn't your fault. You know that. You are not the cause of this."

"I know. But it's hard not to feel as though I am. Just let me be here. I want to be here for him."

"Alright, but remember your promise."

~

The Mole flailed and screeched for what was left of the night, but strangely when the first rays of sun began to hit the city he calmed, his face taking on a look of pure ecstasy. That thin sliver of sun that he had not seen for so long bringing him joy he had most likely forgotten feeling.

Perhaps this is the best way to die, Evangeline thought, mesmerized by his face. That was until the rays hit him and he began to burn. She could not compare the horror of this to anything she had ever witnessed in her life. His body seared and scorched, turning to ash with no urgency, letting him scream in unbearable pain, until finally, thankfully, there was nothing left of him.

It was only in the very last moments that he seemed to realize again who he was and focusing on Evangeline cried out, "Burn him, princess. He must burn...ahhh, how I wish I could have tasted you..."

~

Eros paced the throne hall as the Mole's screams pierced the morning. Why did he let her stay out there to see this? Why? And after what happened, how was he stupid enough to even let her be out by herself?

"Eros, she is in the sun. No one can hurt her," his mother said, standing a couple of steps away. Still pacing, Eros ran both hands through his hair, trying to relax.

"No one can attack her. For now." His mother let each word out very slowly and he stopped and looked at her.

"You know what I am saying, Eros," his mother said, "there was a moment...I thought she could stay...but we both know this is not her life. I know you think I am only thinking of Lola's prophecy and the cure, but I am not stupid Eros. I need hope so I keep it and I have done some stupid things for it...I know that. But I realize the truth, and that is that Evangeline is alive in a way we are not and in order for her to live that life, she must leave. With or without Lola's prophecy."

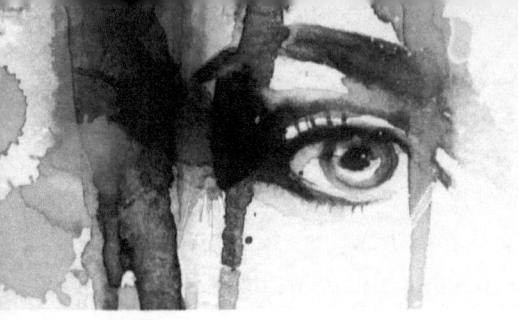

Chapter 48

EVENING ANGELS

The Evening Angel fountain was in a fairly secluded square behind the castle and Evangeline had not spent any time there during her stay in Latina. In days gone by the square had been a prestigious spot, to see and be seen by only the highest tier of society. Now it was one of the more eerie spots, its small, secluded location coupled with the dark curtained windows being not particularly welcoming. The fountain, being permanently off these days, added an even more desolate feel to the square, which the magical Evening Angel could not remove.

Evangeline walked to the fountain now, sitting down at its edge beside Eros. She had seen him pondering there for a while now through the kitchen windows.

"Eros, the Mole was one, isolated incident in many weeks and out of thousands of citizens. There are chances I am taking in here but there are also chances out there. Raffael isn't coming. You and I know that," Evangeline looked at Eros' face and laughed, "don't start trying out the nice thing now. I know the truth. I opened the portal with that sword. Now I'm on one side and the sword is on the other. If I leave, do you think I will find anything else out there? Honestly. I can stay here. I choose to stay."

Eros looked at her and interweaving one hand through her hair pressed his forehead against hers and said quietly, "You truly are my best friend. The best friend I ever had, Evangeline. And because I want to be a true friend to you, I want you to leave."

"Why-"

"You know why. We don't talk about it because we both know it, whether or not you let yourself see it. The more I want you, the more I want to bite you...kill you. The Mole was not an isolated incident. It is what happens to each one of us, one by one, until we will all be gone. Evangeline, you're right. You are the one who opens the portal. So, if you find your way home, take it. Don't look back. Don't feel guilty. Don't return to Latina."

With their foreheads pressed against each other they remained silent. Evangeline wanted to argue but her arguments failed her. She hated his truth. There had to be more than just this one truth. She kept opening her mouth slightly, trying to say something to counter his position.

"I want to save this city," It sounded stupid, but it was true.

Eros lifted his forehead away from hers and said, "There was a time...when I thought that I would have to kill my mother...As strong as I like to think I am, as much as I want to say that I live for this city, I think our human nature is to put the individual ahead of the group. I think...I would have destroyed the city, this world, rather than sacrifice the individuals I love for its better good." He looked at Evangeline with tight lips, "so if you want to save this city...you have to leave because I can't see you die and I can't take the chance that one day, I might have to kill those that I love for you."

"I'll make you a deal," Evangeline said, "I'll return to Latina when I find a cure."

Eros started to shake his head at her, but she wouldn't have it, "I've spoken with your mother. I have no real talent for sixth sense but the two of you were able to visit me through my subconscious states, like my dreams, when I was willing. I haven't been very willing since the arrival...and Cynthia. But I can do this now. I probably won't be able to speak with you. I wasn't able to before. But minimally you'll get that weird subconscious replay of my days like you used to, so you'll have some idea of where I am and what's happening."

Eros was looking at her, disbelief all over his face. Evangeline shrugged, "I'm not sure where I am in terms of forgiveness. I'm sorry. I know it's your mom. I wish I were like you...and your ability to forgive the Duke. Anyways, it's a step I guess."

"I've had decades to forgive the Duke and it's easier to do when you know you are the same. You can empathize with us, but you can't be us... Anyways, it's been...almost amusing. No one's ever told my mother off before except for me."

Eros grinned at her and Evangeline laughed, "Yeah, and now because you also stink at sixth sense I have to mentally chill with your mother."

Eros' grin lasted barely another second before he started to play with his tongue around his teeth, his hand scratching the back of his neck as if wanting to say something and yet not really. Evangeline watched him, waiting.

"Evangeline," he finally said, looking at her only briefly before turning his face slightly away, "if you do ever return I just...well...you should keep in mind that I will most likely look the way I did when you first arrived. This human appearance is slowly...well..."

"I know," Evangeline said, "I've noticed the changes, Eros. Don't worry. I will recognize you. You will still be you; a pompous jackass, no matter what you look like."

"And you a buffoon, even though you are beautiful," Eros said and Evangeline cocked her head at him and grinned, "Wow, another half compliment."

"Only half," Eros smiled then lifted his face up, his nostrils flaring slightly. Evangeline followed suit, smelling the air with him, turning in the direction of the scent, pretty sure she knew who it belonged to, but surprised she was actually approaching of her own accord.

Eros' muscles tenses and she put her hand on his shoulder and shook her head to calm him, just as she saw a small head peak out of an alley. A tall, slim frame accompanied it, as always.

"We don't want to eat her," the tall boy said, looking at Eros' ready stance, "we heard she's leaving. Sofia wanted to see her hair again."

"You've followed me every second day almost, since the last time we spoke," Evangeline said and looked down at the small girl with her hollow, wanting eyes.

"Every second day we are too busy to," the boy answered.

"Did you want to tell me something?" Evangeline asked Sofia but the small child only shook her head no, staring just as blankly as always.

"That's Okay, I have a present for you. It's...well, I'm not sure you will like it but since you like my hair..." Evangeline pulled out a short, little braid of the hair that Ehvan chopped off the day after the Mole's burning. She had long planned to give it to Sofia who she knew stalked her only to stare at her curly mass. She held her hand out towards the girl. Sofia stared down at the hair without moving.

"If you don't want it, it's Okay," Evangeline suddenly felt stupid holding a chunk of hair and the girl just staring at it, "I just thought-"

Without warning Sofia snatched the little braid out of Evangeline's hand and said, "Evening Angel."

"Oh, yes. It's the Evening Angel fountain-" Evangeline began but the boy interrupted, "No, Sofia means you." Then, he turned on his heel and holding Sofia's hand in one of his own while she clutched the chunk of hair in her other, they walked off.

"Bye?" Evangeline said after them but they didn't turn around or respond, "What's his name, anyways?" She turned to Eros.

"Natan," Eros said, still squinting his eyes after them suspiciously.

"You don't seem to like him much," Evangeline said.

"Hmm, well, it is hard to say now. He is one of the rare cases that is much better in this condition than he ever had been as a human. Let's put it that way.

"He seems to really care about his sister."

"That's not his sister. His family was notorious for trading illegal slaves. Sofia was one of them. Now Sofia is all that's left of his past. She holds the tie to his humanity and with that she is now his master...you call that karma, don't you?... However, he's right, about you," Eros looked at the fountain and then at Evangeline, "Evangeline. Evening Angel. It's true. You're just here, like this statue, not even aware that you are in the middle of everything that is nothing like you. And you just stand there and shine."

Evangeline knew she was blushing and resorting to her backup humour, she laughed, "That was a full compliment, Eros. You are losing your knack for disdain."

"Pick up a sword or start singing and I will have plenty."

"You know, on a slightly different note," Evangeline said, "Josepina said that even right after you drank my blood you still did not look fully like your old self. I was thinking the other day that it's strange. There are no depictions of you or your family. Obviously, you had famous sculptors and artists. Didn't they ever paint or sculpt the royal families? In our old castles there's always portraits of all the kings and Queens."

"The same case was in our castle. However, after the change we preferred to put those depictions away. It isn't good for one's morale to see the past and then have to look the present in the mirror."

"Oh...yeah, I guess it might be hard."

"Do you want to see?"

~

They were on the main level of the castle in far-removed, old servant's quarters. The rooms lay empty except for those which had been filled with numerous pieces of art, stacked against the walls.

Eros stood to her side holding a large candelabra while Evangeline poked through the pieces, looking at the faces depicted in each. Josepina had been correct. Evangeline had not seen Eros at his very best. Even though he had been fairly handsome after drinking her, the Eros in the portraits was more so. The jet-black hair lay in waves around his face, his olive complexion dark and glowing. His features were sharp and his eyes harshly piercing. She turned her face from the painting to the real Eros beside her, cocked her head, and squinted her eyes, "You know, you were good looking. I'll give you that. But, I like you better now."

"You have strange taste then."

"Seriously. You looked really pompous then. I mean, *really*."

"I was not *that* pompous," Eros said, looking at his own face in the painting.

"Really? You weren't?" Evangeline pulled a large portrait out from behind. In this one Eros was sitting proudly on an overly decorated horse, looking haughtily at the painter.

"Put that away. That painting is not a good one and not representative of my personality."

Evangeline laughed aloud and pulled out another portrait of Eros in ridiculously intricate garb, sitting pompously on a large, gold framed chair with a crown on his head.

"I was forced to do that pose! That's it, wench. We are leaving this room. You have had enough amusement for one day," Eros grabbed the painting from her and threw it to the side, pulling Evangeline to the door. She escaped his grip, laughing, and ran towards the very back of the room, where some frames lay covered.

"What are these? You combing your hair? Wearing an even frillier shirt?"

"Stop. Evangeline..." Eros said, all humour gone from his face.

It was too late. Evangeline had already flung aside the tarpaulin and saw the whole-family portraits beneath it. In the first one was Julia, with her golden hair streaming down below her waist in a thick braid, her face, though that of an older lady, distinguished, with thoughtful, intelligent eyes. Beside Julia stood the king. There was no denying that he was Eros' father, his face marked by the same dark, sharp features, only his body shorter and with a protruding belly. In front of them were Ehvan with his soft, golden locks, pale skin and dreamy eyes, Eros, looking around the same age as in the other most recent paintings, and a girl with black waves of hair pulled up in a loose style, her skin dark and her face hard like Eros', but her eyes dreamy like Ehvan's.

"Who..." Evangeline began, quickly realizing that the girl must have been Eros' sister. Evangeline had noted from the start that there were five thrones in the throne hall, not matching the number of family members that the royal family seemed to have. She had never asked about this. A part of her had been scared to. And now, as she stared at the face, she wasn't sure why, but the girl looked familiar.

"Helena. She didn't survive."

"You never..."

"No. We never say anything. It's too hard on my mother...and Ehvan. He blocked it. Does not even seem to remember that she ever existed. It is better that way...safer for him. There are moments, things, better not remembered. You understand."

"Yes," Evangeline said, thinking of how horrible Helena's death must have been for Ehvan to block her whole existence from his mind.

Eros came over and looked for a minute at Helena's face. Then he pulled the tarpaulin back over the painting.

"I don't mind that you saw her," he said, "but I ask you not to mention her to my mother and most especially never to Ehvan."

It was only later, when Evangeline was wandering the empty city in the cold light of the late autumn day that she looked up at one of the castle walls and the image came back to her; a girl, lying, still bleeding, on top of one of those walls. It was the image from the hospital. The image of Helena.

~

"I'm really very sorry for your loss," Raffael said into the phone, "I'm sorry for having called. I really didn't know. I just thought that perhaps my sister could talk to your daughter for support...thank you. I'm sorry...yes, bye."

Raffael hung up and sat, silently holding the phone, staring at it. He had just finished contacting the last person on his list. The fifty-fifty PNH patients. The ones Daniel wanted.

The blood opens the way. Maybe it wasn't necessarily Evangeline's blood. Maybe it was just the fifty-fifty blood; the *only* blood Daniel wanted.

Out of the eight fifty-fifty patients that had moved on to Daniel and that Monica had been able to piece some contact information for, three had died, due mainly to blood thrombosis, their families having answered the phone. Two were dead via car crashes that happened to kill the whole family, and three were completely untraceable. Raffael figured those three were dead too. This couldn't be it though. Somehow, someone had to be alive...

Chapter 49

THE FOREST AWAITS

The gravel crunched beneath Evangeline's feet and the dust flew up around her face as she walked for the fourth day and night through the barren wasteland, taking only short sleep and food breaks on the hard dirt. The forests were now within her reach and as she neared them she became more frightened, her pace slowing. The wasteland somehow still belonged to Latina. The forest was the final goodbye.

In her last days in Latina Evangeline and Eros said little to each other in his room. They didn't even bother to pretend to read. They would simply go under the covers and lay against each other silently, Eros' arm around her, both of them knowing that their time was limited.

Their relationship, something between friendship and romance, felt like an unquantifiable enigma that Evangeline could neither describe nor fully understand and so preferred to silently enjoy the last days of it rather than trying to figure them out and label them.

On one of those last days, they were lying in the spoon position and Eros, putting his arm over her, intertwined his fingers in hers. She turned her face to his and smiled. Looking at her intently, Eros let go of her hand momentarily, then took it again and placed something on her finger.

Evangeline looked at her hand and was surprised by his ring on her finger, the one with the red stone, "What..."

"Keep it. For good luck."

"It's beautiful. Are you sure?"

"Yes."

In the last nights, Evangeline had also said her goodbyes. One of those goodbyes was to Josepina. It was easy to find her now. Josepina knew that the Duke was last on Evangeline's daily wanderings' list and was always in her new house at that time. Approaching it Evangeline heard faint sounds and smelled more than Josepina inside.

Josepina apparently smelled her too as she appeared outside with half a smile, "So this is your goodbye visit."

"I prefer the 'see you later' visit."

"You will find your way home, Evangeline."

"I've counted, Josepina. I've been here over forty days. That's twenty days in my world. The doorway isn't reopening."

"You're right. But, the doorway has found you twice. So, whatever is meant to happen, you are a part of it."

Evangeline didn't want to talk about the portal or the door any more than she had to. The way she kept herself happy, the way she kept herself as Evangeline, was by keeping her thoughts in the here and now; her past life still too close for her to let herself ponder it. The fear and nostalgia were too overwhelming for her to function with them on the surface.

"By the way," she said, changing the topic, "you have visitors? I smell other people. If I'm interrupting, I can return."

"Don't worry. There is often someone at my house. I like it that way. It reminds me of the days when there were never fewer than a hundred visitors at my establishment most nights of the week."

Evangeline laughed and brushed a wild strand of hair out of her face. As she did so Josepina's eyes went to Eros' ring on her finger, "Eros...gave you that ring?" Josepina said, her eyes intent on it.

"Yes. It was a good luck gift."

"Was it?"

"Yes..." Evangeline was a little confused by Josepina's sudden intensity and tried to hold her hands down in a way that the ring would be put out of view, "I know it's a bit much but he insisted. Anyways, tell me about some of the visitors at your establishment. I need some good stories to stock up on for my trip."

"Ahh. Alright," Josepina took her eyes off Evangeline's hand and smiled, "Did you know that even Lola visited me once?"

"Lola? Bambi's mother?"

"Precisely."

They walked for some time, Josepina sharing stories of many visits from those in the highest positions who had one or two little secrets or pleasures. When it was time for the last nightly meal, Josepina stopped and looked at Evangeline, "I hope you do return, but only if there's a cure. Otherwise, live your life as it should be lived."

"I already heard this speech from Eros," Evangeline said.

"Hmm. Truly?" Josepina raised her eyebrows and Evangeline looked at her confused.

"Well," Josepina continued, "remember how you asked if I like you? Like...that's often a hard one when you've seen as many people's hearts as I have, but you have retained my respect." With that Josepina turned and left.

The Duke, as usual, was last on Evangeline's list. She waited for him until he returned from his meal, but rather than sitting at the usual outdoor table she stood by his door. When he arrived, he approached the door confused.

"You must not have time for tea on this last night."

"I have time. Of course," Evangeline smiled, "but it's getting cold outside. If you don't mind I would love to come in for tea."

The Duke didn't answer but only put a hand on her cheek and smiled.

The main table was still outside so they made themselves comfortable in a pretty sitting room where the Duke proudly lit candles all around for Evangeline to see everything. The sitting room, like everything else, had been maintained immaculately by the Duke in the feminine style, with soft colours and curves, which his wife had done the whole house and yard in.

"This is lovely," Evangeline commented as she sipped her tea, looking around herself, "Is that your wife?" She pointed to a large portrait of a slightly girly looking woman, with pouty lips and a heart-shaped face, holding a baby in her arms.

"Yes, my Lilia. She was not so much younger than me, but doesn't she look as sweet and innocent as a child? I am sure even now, she is still as beautiful."

Evangeline smiled, thinking that Lilia looked more silly than innocent. However, maybe it was the fault of the portrayal. After all, the Duke was still so enamoured by her, even after all these years, she must have been something special.

"And that is my son, Leonardo. He was not much more than one when they escaped. He should be close to twenty-six years of age now...Evangeline..." The Duke's tone turned uncertain, "if it is not too much to ask, I have something...for my son. He is a man now. This was to be his."

"Oh, of course, but-"

"I know you may not find him. But I know he's alive, and the weapon ... it always finds its true owner, Evangeline."

"I would be honoured to give your son anything you would like me to," Evangeline said and the Duke stood and left the room. He returned holding a short dagger, placed on a piece of wood.

"This is a family heirloom," the Duke said, "we pass it on to the eldest son. It was made by a master, with our family sigil engraved in the dormium blade. If you see him, please give it to him, and until then, perhaps it may serve you well. As you know, those with our...issue...don't like dormium much."

Evangeline grinned and took the beautiful dagger, touching its blade to feel that special tingle. The Duke then gave her a belt, which she put around her waist and placed the dagger within.

"For Leo junior," Evangeline smiled.

"Yes, for Leo junior," the Duke laughed lightly, then he took her hand and opening it, placed something within, "This is for you. It was to be my wife's...she loved flowers. I did not have the chance to give it to her. I would very much like you to keep it."

Evangeline looked down to find a chain in her hand with a small, lovely flower at the end, its surface melted out of a copper looking material with tiny, red stones around the outside of each petal.

"I couldn't, Leonardo."

"You can. Lilia will not mind. She had many, you see. She even took her favourites with her. She refused to run without them into the wilderness like a savage, she said. She was so gentle and distinguished."

"Oh, thank you then. Thank you for everything," Evangeline let the Duke put the chain around her neck, wondering about his wife. She said nothing though, only looked at the Duke and pondered what an odd match him and his wife seemed to have been.

As she left, she picked the last of the year's night blooms, placing them on Cynthia's tomb that morning and saying her final goodbye.

After her last day with Eros, Evangeline woke up to an extraordinary meal. It was her last meal and Samina and Lorenzo had gone all out. Evangeline could barely swallow but forced herself to eat a bit of everything, smiling at Samina who then packed the leftovers to be eaten in the first couple of days on the road. After that she would be living off the dry fruit and meat provisions that had been so painstakingly prepared by the citizens, just for her.

There was no emotional goodbye with Samina and Lorenzo, though she had seen them every single night. Lorenzo only smiled a rare smile and Samina said the rare sentence, "Eat well."

Evangeline made her way to her room to collect her travel pack and to add Samina's leftovers to it. She was already dressed in the perfectly fitted travel clothes that Josepina, along with some others, had sewn for her. The shirt was brand new, made out of that fall's harvested grass, while the leather coat and warm tunic were re-stitched from previous owners to fit Evangeline. Extra clothing and supplies were in her pack.

Julia walked beside her and regurgitated last minute instructions while Ehvan followed them wide eyed. He was more excited than sad, having been promised that he could join Eros and Julia in Evangeline's subconscious every now and then. He had talked to no end about getting to see the world beyond through Evangeline's mind, promising to research everything and help her on her journey. Evangeline was happy he did not seem to consider that there was such a thing as the possibility of Evangeline not finding a cure or not surviving.

"You have little aim with the bow and arrow and you have difficulty killing a spider so, as we discussed, you must ration your food well because the chances of you hunting anything down are slim, especially since we had nothing to practice on except terrified chickens...and we stopped that because you had nightmares when you finally managed to kill one."

Evangeline shrugged in embarrassment as they walked. It was true. After shooting down a chicken, she had had dreams of vampire chickens out to get her. After three days of this she finally broke down and told Eros, who took double the usual time to stop laughing about it.

"If you do attempt hunting, what are the rules?" Julia continued drilling her.

"A wounded animal is an enraged animal and highly dangerous," Evangeline said in a droning monotone, regurgitating the information for the hundredth time, "therefore, I shoot for small prey because I have no clue how to skin and prepare anything larger than a rabbit anyways. I learn the smell and sound of the forest when I enter it. I don't know the smell of humans but if I know the smell of the forest, I will know when something foreign appears in it. I have the fire starter but I don't light fires until I need to cook. I sleep in the trees. I travel in the trees. I am invisible unless I am certain that what I find is safe."

"It is not a joke, Evangeline," Julia said, her stern, mother tone coming out.

"I know, I know. I'm sorry. I remember everything, Julia. You have taught me everything you could."

"Ehvan, please go and make sure that the way to the gate is not too crowded," Julia turned to Ehvan, "There needs to be walking space for Evangeline. I don't want her having to shove through."

Ehvan bounced his head up and down and ran off.

"I can't believe the whole city is going to see me off. I am more nervous about that than the trip itself," Evangeline said, but Julia only responded with a "Hmm" making it obvious that she wasn't listening.

"Evangeline," Julia said as soon as Ehvan was out of hearing range, "I know that perhaps I do not have the right to ask you for favours...there may be a part of you that will never forgive me, but, Evangeline, even if you do not mean to come back to us, make Eros believe that you will. Eros needs to believe that you are in his life. Whatever happens, make him believe that you are...and not just for Eros. It is for Ehvan too. If Eros perishes, so will Ehvan."

"Julia, I do mean to come back."

"Then make Eros believe that. And I know this means little, but, I am sorry."

"Julia, it's still hard sometimes to trust you the way I initially did...but I know that I could only be so lucky to be as good as you, if I were you. And I definitely doubt that I could have gotten us in that cage...so...I can't say that I have fully forgiven you, but in some ways I am also sorry."

Julia looked at her silently for a minute, then nodded her head and looking down, took Evangeline's hand in her own, observing the ring on her finger.

"This is our family ring. Did you know?"

"I thought it might be. Do you want it back? I feel like I shouldn't have it."

"No. It was Eros' choice to give it to you. It means you have a family to come home to now."

"Thank you."

"And Evangeline, not many could outjump the Mole as you did. You are ready."

Evangeline tried to smile. She did not feel ready at all.

They had stopped in the upstairs hall and now walked the last steps to Evangeline's room. Eros was waiting for her inside and Julia left them to say their farewells, as Evangeline began to collect her things.

"You look good. Pants suit you. These were mine when I was a boy, did you know?" Eros said, looking her over.

"Seriously? I'm wearing your refurbished kid clothes?"

Eros laughed and then put his forehead against hers, just as he had done at the fountain, "Stay safe and dream lots, tornado head."

"Thanks, blockhead. I will," Evangeline said, "You must be totally full of yourself now, knowing that I'll be dreaming of you almost every night."

"Of me and my mother. Yes, I feel like a complete 'stud' as you say."

Evangeline dug inside her pocket and pulled something out.

"I have something," she said and put the tiny, scorched mint box from her mother in his hand, "this isn't pretty or, well, very expensive, but it's from my mom. It's the last thing she gave to me so it's special. It's the only thing I have from my old life. You know I'm a disaster. I'm surprised I haven't lost it yet...so maybe you could keep it for me until I come back."

Eros looked at the box and closed his hand over it. This was the only way Evangeline had of telling him that she would be back. She hoped it was enough.

He ran his cheek against hers, then put his mouth on her neck and bit lightly, smiling at her, "You're dead."

They had moved the massive boulder just enough for her to exit properly through the main gate, Julia absolutely forbidding Evangeline from scaling the wall or trudging through canal water to get out of the city like some animal. Besides, the citizens had carefully double-sealed the canal exit not long after she had crawled through it, the day after she turned. So now Evangeline would have a proper exit, even if half the city had to push boulders.

She walked down the streets slowly, Julia in front of her, Eros behind her and Ehvan beside her. It was both her farewell crew and her bodyguard crew...just in case. The citizens had left just enough walking room in the middle of the road, as they lined up on both sides of it all the way from the castle steps to the boulder. The ones that didn't fit on the street were again in the windows and on the rooftops. Just like on the first day when they had come out to see her, their silence was stunning. This time though, they waved and many smiled with their grey faces.

She saw Josepina in her wild, floral garb perched on a rooftop as if suntanning under the moon and further down was a large, square shouldered woman who looked familiar, smiling and waving. Evangeline racked her brain for a moment, realization finally clicking in, that this burly creature in a dress was Max from the smoke house whom she had always assumed to be a man with a squeaky voice. She smiled and waved to Max just as she reached the Duke, who stood close to the bouldered entrance near the front of the crowds. Evangeline smiled at him but was suddenly distracted by the small body of Sofia who squeezed out from behind him.

Sofia had taken Evangeline's little braid of hair and weaved it into her own grey one. Evangeline wanted to compliment her on her work but the effect of the blond with the ratty grey wasn't actually pleasant so all she could do was reach out and touch her part of the braid and smile at the staring face. Sofia looked at Evangeline's face and said blankly, "I used to be blond."

Evangeline ran a hand gently over the small, wrinkled face, then turned to the boulder which stood before her. Julia squeezed her hand and she walked to the boulder's edge. The last people her eyes focused on were those that had been her family. She tried not to look at Eros too long and knowing that his eyes wouldn't budge from her face, she forced hers to finally move on to Ehvan and Julia before they went back to the boulder and she squeezed through, waving goodbye to the city as she did so.

The boulder rolled closed a second after her feet hit the gravel and for a minute she stood frozen, the terror of this sudden finality washing over her. Taking a deep breath, she began to walk. After some time she turned around to see the wall stretching behind her, its height blocking almost all visibility of the city from this distance.

Then, far to the right she saw him. He stood in the tower where they had spent his birthday and secretly left the climbing rope behind. He waved at her and she waved back, standing for a minute and looking at him. Finally, she forced herself to turn in the direction of the forest, not allowing herself to turn around again, knowing she would break down if she did.

A line of trees stood in front of Evangeline now and she stared at them. Then, slowly, she reached out her hand and touched the first tree. She grabbed hold of the trunk and her body sprinted up. Standing at the very top of its canopy she said one last goodbye to Latina, then turned in the direction of the green, not ready at all to enter its expanse.

The End…or is it?

www.ingramcontent.com/pod-product-compliance
Lightning Source LLC
LaVergne TN
LVHW091527060526
838200LV00036B/513